Then Came You

Jennifer Weiner

Then Came You

SIMON &
SCHUSTER

London · New York · Sydney · Toronto

A CBS COMPANY

First published in the USA by Atria Books, 2011
A division of Simon & Schuster Inc.
First published in Great Britain by Simon & Schuster UK Ltd, 2011
A CBS Company

1 3 5 7 9 10 8 6 4 2

Simon & Schuster UK Ltd
1st Floor
222 Gray's Inn Road
London WC1X 8HB

www.simonandschuster.co.uk

Simon & Schuster Australia
Sydney

Simon & Schuster India
New Delhi

A CIP catalogue record for this book is available from the British Library

ISBN Hardback 978-0-85720-810-1
ISBN Trade Paperback 978-0-85720-811-8
ISBN Trade Paperback (Australia) 978-0-85720-825-5

Printed and bound in Great Britain by
CPI Mackays, Chatham ME5 8TD

For Phoebe Pearl

"So," said Estella, "I must be taken as I have been made. The success is not mine, the failure is not mine, but the two together make me."

–CHARLES DICKENS, GREAT EXPECTATIONS

PART ONE

~

Sweet and Sour

JULES

The man in the suit was watching me again.

It was March of my senior year in college, a clear, chilly afternoon, when I felt what was, by then, the familiar weight of a man's gaze, while I sat by myself in the food court. I looked up from my dinner, and there he was, at the end of the line for the salad place, looking at me the way he had for the past three weeks.

I sighed. The mall was one of my favorite places, and I didn't want to give it up because of some creep.

I'd found the mall my freshman year. If you walked off campus, across Nassau Street and into a kiosk in the center of town, you could buy a discounted ticket with your student ID, and the bus would take you to a fancy shopping center with a fancy name, the Princeton MarketFair. There were all of the chains: a Pottery Barn and a Restoration Hardware, and Gaps, both Baby and full-grown, a Victoria's Secret where you could buy your panties and a LensCrafters where you could pick up a pair of sunglasses, all of them in a sprawling, sterile building with marble floors and flattering, pink-tinted lights. At one end of the mall was a big, airy bookstore, with leather armchairs where you could curl up and read. At the other end was a movie theater that showed four-dollar matinees on Mondays. Between them was the food court.

Shortly after my discovery, I'd learned that only losers used public transportation. I'd found this out when I heard two of my classmates scornfully discussing a date that a girl we all knew had been on. "He took her to the movies. On the *bus*." Giggle, giggle . . . and then a quick look sideways to me, for my approval, because, tall and blond and with two juniors on the varsity crew team vying for my affection, I couldn't possibly fall into the bus-girl's category.

The truth was I liked the bus, and I liked the mall. It felt real, and Princeton's campus, with its perfect green lawns and its ivy-clad, gargoyle-ornamented, stained-glass-windowed buildings, and its students, none of whom seemed to suffer from acne or obesity or even bad-hair days, felt like a film set, too wonderful to exist. On campus, everyone walked around as if they'd never had a second of doubt, an instant of feeling like they didn't belong, carrying their expensive laptops and textbooks, dressed just right. People at the mall did not look as if they'd just stepped out of catalogs. Their clothes were sometimes stained or too tight. They walked past the shop windows yearning after things they didn't need and couldn't afford: end-of-their-rope mothers snapping at their kids, boyfriends sighing and shifting their weight from foot to foot as they lingered outside the dressing rooms at Anthropologie, teenagers texting each other from a distance of less than three feet away across the table; the fat people, the old people, the ones with walkers or oxygen tanks or wheelchairs— all of them reminded me of home. Besides, I could practically be guaranteed to never see anyone from school there—not on the bus, for sure; not at the movie theater, at least in the daytime; definitely not scarfing kung pao chicken from China Express. Maybe my classmates came here to buy things, but they never stayed long, which made the mall my secret, a place where I could be myself.

Most Mondays, when my classes ended at 2:00, I'd take the bus and I'd browse in the stores, maybe trying on shoes or a pair of jeans, and I'd see a matinee of whatever movie looked interesting, then have dinner in the food court, or at the sit-down seafood restaurant if I'd managed to pick up some extra hours at my work-study job in the admissions office. For less than twenty dollars, I could make a whole afternoon and early evening pleasantly disappear.

I looked up from my plate again. The man was holding his briefcase, standing in profile, looking like he was trying to decide what to do next. It could, I knew, go one of two ways: he'd keep staring, or he'd work up the nerve to cross the tiled floor and say something.

When I was thirteen, my father sat me down and gave me a little speech. "There's something you should know," he'd said. We were in the family room, half a flight down from the front door, a room with pine-paneled walls and mauve-colored carpet and a glass-topped coffee table on which there were a decade's worth of yearbooks, one for every year my father had been the yearbook advisor at McKinley Junior High.

"What's that?" This was in the fall; I'd been wearing my soccer uniform; shorts and shin guards and a sweatshirt I'd pulled on for the bike ride home. My dad was in his worn black recliner, a glass of ice cubes and whiskey in his hand, still dressed in the coat and tie he wore to school. My mom was in the kitchen making baked chicken—she'd dip each piece in a mixture of buttermilk and mustard, then roll it in cornflake crumbs. That chicken, along with Rice-A-Roni and a cut-up head of iceberg lettuce doused in bottled ranch dressing, was my favorite meal, and all I wanted was to take a hot shower, pull on my sweatpants and a too-big T-shirt, eat my dinner, and get to my homework. For the first time, math was actually hard for me, and I knew I'd need at least half an hour to get through the problem set we'd been assigned.

My dad ducked his head, sipped his drink, and said into the knot of his tie, "Men are going to look at you."

This wasn't news to me, and hadn't been for a while. "It's not your fault, Julia," said my father, pulling off his glasses as he spoke. "It's what men do. It's how we're wired, maybe, men and women. We're programmed to notice each other."

I'd flicked my ponytail over my shoulder. I was already five foot four inches of the eventual five foot nine I'd reach. My hair was thick and butterscotch blond, and that fall I'd graduated from a training bra to an actual B-cup, and started junior high. These events combined made me feel as if my body wasn't really me anymore, but something I lived inside; a borrowed blouse I'd snuck out of my mother's closet, something I needed to treat carefully and could, if I was lucky, one day return.

Men will look, my dad had said, watching me with a mixture of love and regret. Sometimes, he'd quote a line of Yeats, about how "only God, my dear / could love you for yourself / And not your golden hair." It made me feel strange, a little proud, a little ashamed, especially because the truth, which maybe he'd guessed, was that men were already doing more than looking: they'd hoot, they'd whistle, they'd make sucking, smooching sounds when I was alone, walking home from school, and they were in their cars. One of my classmates, Tim Sather, seemed to have decided that his mission in life was to snap my bra strap as often as he could, and Mr. Traub, the gym teacher, would wrap his arms around me, letting his jogging-suited torso press, briefly but firmly, against my back as he helped me with my volleyball serve. That summer I'd been wearing my swimsuit, a dark-blue one-piece, and running through the sprinkler with the Lurie kids, whom I'd been babysitting at the time, and I'd looked up to find Mr. Santos, who lived next door to the Luries, staring at me over the top of his fence with his mouth hanging open. A few weeks later, my older brother, Greg, had gotten in a fight at the town park's swimming pool. When my mother had fussed over his black eye and swollen cheek, demanding to know who'd started it, Greg had muttered that the boys had been saying stuff about me. My mother hadn't asked him anything else, and I'd been embarrassed, unsure of how to behave. Did I thank Greg? Did I ask him what the boys had said, if I'd done anything to provoke it? Finally, I decided to say nothing, to pretend the whole thing had never happened. That seemed like the smartest thing to do.

The worst part wasn't the boys; it was the girls, the ones who had once been my friends. *She thinks she's sooo pretty,* I'd heard Missy Henried sneer to Beth Brock one day at lunch after Matt Blum, staring at me across the cafeteria, had almost walked into a table. Like I'd asked for him to stare. I had a mirror, and I'd seen enough magazines and TV shows to know that I was what was considered good-looking, maybe even beautiful. But the beautiful girls on TV or in those glossy pages all seemed happy. They never looked lonely, like their faces, their hair, their bodies were traps keeping them apart from everyone else. I couldn't figure out why I felt guilty when boys stared, like I was lying, or offering them something I didn't really have. All I knew was that Missy and Beth and I had been Brownies together; we'd trick-or-treated every October, giggling in the costumes that had turned us into cheerleaders or witches or Pink Ladies from *Grease,* posing on Missy's front porch while her father struggled with his video camera. Now I was their enemy. Now they were on one side of a wall, and I was on the other.

"So what am I supposed to do about it?" I asked my dad. Back then, I thought he knew all the answers. Our house was full of books he'd read, biographies of presidents and scientists, thick hardcover novels with approving quotes from *The New Yorker* on their backs, different from my mother's mysteries, which were bright paperbacks with actual people on the covers and titles spelled out in foil.

He'd patted my shoulder. "Just be aware." Almost ten years later, whenever I felt a man's eyes passing over me—sometimes lightly, like water, sometimes like the high whining of a mosquito in my ear—I'd remember my father, mumbling into his tie, my father, when he was still all right. *Love you, sweetheart,* he'd said, and hugged me, the way he hardly ever did since my breasts had gotten bigger than bug bites on my chest.

In the food court, I speared a maraschino cherry on my chopstick. The man in the suit made up his mind, walking away from the salad stand, heading straight toward me. I thought he was in his late thirties, maybe his forties, with dark, curly hair and a handsome, coddled face.

I bent over my dinner, hoping he'd just keep walking, and began the time-consuming process of separating the chilies from the chunks of chicken and pineapple, wondering whether he'd work up the nerve to say something or if he was just cruising by for a closer look. When I looked up again he was standing right in front of my table for two, with nothing to eat.

"Excuse me," he said. "Do you go to Princeton?"

I nodded, unimpressed. I was wearing jeans and a sweatshirt that said *Princeton* right across the chest. No makeup, except a little lip gloss and the mascara and eyeliner I never left the dorm without, because my lashes are so sparse and fine that they're basically invisible without a swipe or two of Lash Out, and my eyes are such a pale blue-gray noncolor that they tend to blend into my forehead without liner, giving my face the look of an underbaked pie.

"You like it there?" he asked. I nodded again.

He lifted his briefcase and moved as if he was going to sit down across from me. I edged my metal-legged chair backward, preparing to tell him, politely, that I needed to finish my dinner and get going because my friends were waiting, when he asked, "Do you play any sports?"

This was a surprise. I'd been betting an either *What's your major* or *Where are you from* . . . either that or he'd ask me for help, the most common ploy. At the mall, guys would ask which movie I'd seen and if I'd liked it, or if I could help them pick out a necklace or a sweater for their sister or their mom. At the gym, guys would point at the controls for the StairMaster, feigning confusion. *Hey, do you know how to work this?* In the grocery store, they'd need my assistance picking out pasta or plums. At the gas station, they would require directions; in class, they'd want to know if I'd read the assignment, if I had plans for the weekend, if I'd read this book or heard that band. I know this makes me sound as if my life was a nonstop parade of men who were dying to talk to me, but it's just the truth. When you look a certain way—blond and tall, with D-cup boobs, with wide-set eyes and a straight nose, and full lips that are dark pink even without lipstick—men want to talk to you. Usually they ask you out, and twice in my life, once in this very mall, I'd been asked if I was a model.

"Field hockey and lacrosse," I said. I'd played both in high school, but not since.

The man sat down, uninvited. "Are you twenty-one?"

I narrowed my eyes, one hand on the strap of my backpack, wondering whether he was going to propose something illegal or seamy, like phone sex or stripping. Up close, he was older than I'd thought, older than he should have been if he was hitting on a girl my age, maybe forty-five, with a plain gold wedding band on his left hand, and I didn't want to have dinner with him, or give him my number or my e-mail address or tell him where I lived or let him buy me a drink or a frozen yogurt; I just wanted to finish my food and go back to my dorm room, avoid my boyfriend, curl up with a book, and count the days until graduation. That was when he smiled.

"I'm sorry," he said. "I'm getting ahead of myself. Jared Baker," he said, and stuck his hand across the table.

I shook it quickly. The skin of his palms felt as soft as I imagined the skin on his face would. I got to my feet, never mind that half my dinner was still sitting there. "Excuse me, but my friends are probably waiting for me." I had my tray in one hand and my backpack in the other when Jared Baker said, "How would you like to make twenty thousand dollars?"

I paused. My skin was tingling. *Illegal,* I thought. *It has to be.* "Doing what? Smuggling drugs out of Mexico?"

His smile widened so that I could see his teeth. "Egg donation."

I set my tray back on the table. "Sit," said Jared Baker, coming around the table to pull my chair out for me. He looped my backpack's straps over the chair and did everything but spread a paper napkin in my lap. It was a funny performance, like a parody of a man tending to a wife who was fragile as an egg. Or who was carrying fragile eggs. "Eat your dinner." He frowned at the plate. "Skip the spring roll, though. Saturated fats."

Looking him right in the eye, I dragged the roll through the slurry of Chinese mustard and duck sauce I'd made, and took a giant bite. His grin widened. "Moxie," he said. "That's nice. People like a girl with a sense of humor."

"Are you serious?" I asked once I'd swallowed. "Twenty thousand dollars for an egg?" I'd seen ads, of course, in the school paper, online, and on fliers posted in the student union and the library. *Families seeking egg donors. All expenses paid. Please help make our dreams come true.* But I'd never noticed the fee for the egg itself, and I'd never guessed it would be so high.

Jared Baker was friendly, but not smarmy, serious and calm as he asked me more questions: Where had I grown up? What were my SAT scores? Had I ever had an IQ test? Had anyone in my family had cancer or diabetes or mental illness? I gave him the numbers and said no to the illnesses. He pulled a notebook out of his briefcase and asked if I had siblings, how old my mother had been when I was born, and how much I'd weighed as a baby. I was careful with my answers, thinking about what he'd want to hear, what story would go best with the girl he was seeing, a tall, blond, jockish girl in a Princeton sweatshirt who was eating by herself only because her friends had finished first and were waiting for her in the bookstore.

"Ever been pregnant?" he asked, the same way he'd asked if I was a vegetarian or if heart disease ran in my family. I shook my head, ponytail swishing. I'd only had sex with three different boys, an embarrassingly low tally at my age. I was starting to think that I was one of those people who didn't like sex very much. Maybe it made me lucky. I wouldn't spend my whole life getting my heart broken, chasing after this guy or that one.

"And are you single?"

I nodded, trying not to look too excited, to give the appearance that men stopped by the food court to offer me piles of cash every Monday I went to the mall, but my mind was racing, imagining what I could do with twenty thousand dollars, a sum I hadn't imagined possessing unless I won the lottery or married very, very well. Even with the investment-banking job I was going to take after I graduated, I'd have to manage rent in New York City and start paying back my loans, so the idea of having five figures' worth of discretionary income was new to me, extraordinary, and alluring.

Jared Baker handed me a business card, a rectangle of heavy ivory paper with embossed letters on top that said PRINCETON FERTILITY CLINIC, INC. His name was underneath, with telephone numbers and an e-mail address. "Be in touch," he said. "I think you'd be an excellent candidate."

"Twenty thousand dollars," I said again.

"Minimum," he repeated. "Oh, and if you wouldn't mind telling me your name?"

"Julia Strauss," I said. "My friends call me Jules."

"Jules," he said, giving me another appraising look and shaking my hand again.

So that was how it started: in the Princeton MarketFair, over a Styrofoam plate of sweet and sour chicken and a spring roll that I never got to finish. It seemed so simple. I thought that selling an egg would be like giving blood, like checking the Organ Donation box on your driver's license, like giving away something you'd never wanted or even noticed much to begin with. And yes, at first, I was just in it for the money. It wasn't about altruism, or feminism, or any other *ism*. It was about the cash. But I wasn't going to blow it on clothes or a car or a graduation bash, on Ecstasy or a trip to Vail, or Europe, or one of the hundred frivolous things my classmates might have chosen. I was going to take that money and I was going to try to save my father . . . or, more accurately, I was going to give him one last chance to save himself.

ANNIE

I stood in the kitchen with the telephone in my hand, heart pounding, until I heard a familiar voice on the other end say hello. "Ma?"

"Annie?" she asked. I could hear the sound of the TV set blaring in the background. My mother loved her programs, especially *The View*, which was why I knew exactly where to find her Monday through Friday from eleven to noon. "Are you still coming?"

I exhaled. She'd remembered. That was good. I wasn't sure whether my mom had anything more than regular forgetfulness or something worse, like early-onset Alzheimer's, which I'd looked up a few times on the Internet, but if there was something important, something you needed my mother to remember, you had to tell her and tell her and tell her again, and even then be prepared for the possibility that it would still slip her mind.

"Nancy's here already. We're just going over my bank statement."

I imagined my sister sitting at my mother's kitchen table with her acrylic nails tapping at her calculator. "The boys and I are on our way. And I've got some good news."

"Ooh, fun," she said. "Bye-bye, now."

I switched off *The Backyardigans*, wondering when it was that my mother had started sounding more like a child than my actual children, and hurried Frank Junior, five, and Spencer, who had just turned three, upstairs to the bathroom, the only one in our three-story, five-bedroom farmhouse in Phoenixville, about forty-five miles outside Philadelphia. Frank and I had bought the farmhouse at auction five years ago. It had been a bargain, a big, sprawling place originally built in 1890, on three acres of land, with what the Realtor called "outbuildings" that had once been chicken coops and stalls for horses, along with a working outhouse that stood just off the back porch with the door now stuccoed shut.

Frank and I had grown up in the Great Northeast, in a working-class neighborhood of Philadelphia. I'd lived in a ranch house with my sister and my parents; Frank and his mother and father had a duplex a mile away. Both of us loved the idea of a big place to spread out in and raise our own family: a garden to grow vegetables and flowers, a yard for children to run in, a big country kitchen with two ovens and a six-burner stove where our families could gather and I could cook. When the farm came up for sale, we scraped together enough money for a down payment and convinced a bank that we could afford it. I had a little money I'd inherited from my grandmother, Frank had some help from his parents, and in those days, not so long ago, the banks gave out mortgages like they hand out lollipops, to pretty much anyone who asked.

We'd been so excited about what the farmhouse had—hardwood floors, wood-burning fireplaces, that big, sunny kitchen with whitewashed walls, the thicket of raspberry bushes at the edge of the yard—that we'd barely noticed the things it was lacking: working toilets, reliable appliances, closet space. We hadn't thought about the high cost of heating and maintaining such a big home, or the time it would take to mow the lawn in the summer and how much it would cost to get the driveway plowed in the winter. Frank had a job working security at the Philadelphia airport, but that wasn't a permanent thing. He was going to school to be an airplane mechanic; we'd planned on his getting raises and promotions, but of course, we had no way of knowing that the economy would crash and the airlines would end up in trouble. But now, I thought, I'd found a solution, a way to get ourselves out of the hole we'd fallen into and move up a few rungs on the ladder, the way my sister had.

"Frank Junior, you go first," I said, pointing my oldest son toward the toilet.

He frowned at me, eyebrows drawn, lower lip pouting. "Privacy," he said. Frank Junior looked just like his father, tall for his age, lean and wiry, with nut-brown skin and tightly curled hair and full lips. Spencer looked more like me: lighter skin, straighter hair, a round face and a sweet, plump belly I'd kiss every time I changed his diaper. People who saw the three of us together, without Frank, didn't always realize that I was their mom. I took a secret pleasure from that moment, when they'd look from the dark-skinned boys to the white lady taking care of them and try to figure out the deal—was I the sitter? The nanny to a famous rapper's kids? Some do-gooder who'd done an Angelina and adopted a poor black child from Africa?

I changed Spencer's diaper, made both boys wash their hands, inspected them to make sure their zippers were zipped, their buttons were buttoned, and their shoes were Velcro'd shut, then bundled their warm little-boy bodies into their coats—it was April, but chilly—and loaded them into the car. My parents were still in Somerton, the neighborhood where I'd grown up, but they'd moved to a condominium that my sister, Nancy, had helped them buy after she and her husband decided that "the house was getting to be too much for them."

I knew I should have been grateful to my big sister. She'd been right about the house. Three years ago, my father had had a heart attack—a mild one, but still—and my mother was always forgetting about things like having the furnace filters changed and the gutters cleaned and the paper delivery stopped when the two of them went on their bus trips. Still there was something that bothered me about the way Nancy had done it, as if the doctor husband and the degree from Penn State meant that she was smarter than the rest of us, that she was the one who knew best.

But that was Nancy for you, I thought, snapping the buckles of Spencer's car seat closed, then hurrying back into the house for string cheese and sippy cups, to pull my cell phone out of its charger and grab my purse. She used to be fat and bossy, and then, when she finished high school, she'd gone to work in a doctor's office that did gastric banding and gotten the procedure and become skinny and bossy. One of the doctors in the practice had fallen for her, so now she was married and bossy, with that college degree that she never once let us forget about, the first one that anyone in our family had earned. I should just be grateful, I thought, as I got behind the wheel, that she and Dr. Scott were generous, even though I could feel a bitter taste crawl up the back of my throat whenever Nancy sweetly offered my parents a loan or slapped down her platinum card to pay for their gas or their groceries.

My mom was waiting at the door, waving as if she hadn't seen us in months, when, in fact, we'd had dinner with her on Friday. She looked like a children's book drawing of a grandma, short and plump, with white hair drawn back softly in a bun, a rounded face, and pink cheeks. She wore a flounced denim skirt, a frilly white blouse, boiled-wool clogs on her feet, and a yellow-and-pink apron in a cheerful paisley pattern around her waist. Frank Junior and Spencer pelted up the concrete stairs and into her arms. "How are my handsome boys?" she crooned, hugging them, making me feel ashamed for the way I judged her. Maybe she was silly and forgetful, maybe she spent a lot of time involved in the feuds and dramas of the Real Housewives of whatever city Bravo was visiting that season, but she loved my father, she loved me and Nancy, she loved her grandsons, she loved Frank, and she even managed to love Dr. Scott, who had the good looks and personality of a dried booger.

The condo was toasty warm, smelling like baked-apple air freshener and cinnamon potpourri. It wasn't a big place to begin with, and my mom had covered every available wall and surface with framed stitched samplers, frilly doilies, cushions embroidered with inspirational sayings, scented candles, fringe-shaded lamps, and collections of commemorative snow globes, shot glasses, and thimbles from every place from Branson to Atlantic City to Disney World. On the coffee table were cut-glass dishes of nuts and foil-wrapped candies whose colors would change with the season and were currently pastels for Easter. In the bathroom, extra rolls of toilet paper were tucked underneath the skirts of dolls with old-fashioned dresses and yellow yarn hair. There was even a crocheted sock-style wrap for the air freshener can. The first time we'd visited, Frank said my parents' place looked like a Cracker Barrel had thrown up in the living room.

"I baked cookies!" she cried as Spencer inserted a whole pistachio, still in its shell, up his nose, and Frank Junior crammed a fistful of pale-pink M&M's into his mouth. Moving fast, I scooped the nut out of Spencer's nostril, gave Frank Junior a stern look, gathered up the dishes of peppermints and butterscotch candies, Hershey's Kisses and Swedish Fish, and put them out of reach.

I turned from the mantel, from which Christmas stockings hung year-round, and saw my sister standing in the kitchen door, studying me.

"Hi, Nance."

She nodded. In high school, she had our mother's rosy cheeks and fine, flyaway light-brown hair. She'd been pretty, sweet-

faced, with soft features and a body as plump as a bunch of pillows tied together. It had been hard to take her seriously when
she told me what to wear and what to do during the daytime
when, at night, I'd fall asleep while she cried over some insult,
imagined or, more often, real.

Now she was a size two with a butt and belly you could
bounce quarters off of, and she worked as a part-time book-
keeper and receptionist in Dr. Scott's office and spent most of
her time working out, buying clothes to show off her new body,
and, as she'd told Mary Sheehan, a classmate we'd bumped into
Christmas shopping at the Franklin Mills mall, "planning our
next vacation."

"That was kind of rude," I told her when we stopped at the
food court. I was having a pretzel, she was sipping bottled water.

"It's true," she'd said with a shrug of her narrow shoulders.
"She asked what I do, and I told her."

I took a bite so I wouldn't say something smart, or point out
that Nancy and Dr. Scott, who had chosen not to have children,
weren't exactly renting a yacht and cruising the Greek islands or
spending weekends in Paris. Scott's idea of a good time began
and ended with squash, so Nancy's job—quote-unquote—was
to find the resorts that were hosting some kind of medical conference and also had regulation squash courts, so that Dr. Scott
could play his game and take the whole thing as a write-off.

My sister's face was a smooth and poreless beige, and her
hair, which she had chemically straightened every three months,
hung in stiff curtains against each cheek. Her mouth was lipsticked and her eyelids shaded, and her jeans looked brand-new.
She wore a black sweater tucked into her waistband, which was
cinched with a black leather silver-buckled belt, and high-heeled
leather boots on her feet. I turned to hide my smile. She looked
like Oprah when she'd wheeled that wagon of fat across the
stage, a thin, white Oprah full of the talk-show host's confi-

dence and self-regard. I hugged her, feeling dowdy in my own jeans (unpressed) and sweater (untucked) and boots that were not leather or high-heeled but, instead, rubber-soled lace-ups lined with dingy fake fur, fine for a muddy Pennsylvania spring but not what you'd call fashionable. Once I'd been the pretty one, the thin (at least by comparison) one, the stylish one. But I'd kept on about ten pounds of baby weight after each boy and there was hardly any money for new clothes. These days, what I wore had to be practical, and I barely had time to comb my hair, let alone style it, or pay someone three hundred dollars every three months to do it for me. I looked ordinary, a woman of average height, a little rounder than she should have been, with light-brown hair usually in a ponytail and blue-green eyes usually without shadow on their lids or mascara on their lashes, a woman with a diaper bag slung over her shoulder and a plastic bag full of Cheerios in her pocket who maybe could have been pretty if she'd had a little more time.

"Mom said you had news," she said. "Are you pregnant again?" She scrunched up her nose, loading the question with just enough distaste that I could hear it, but not enough that I could call her on it. My mother lingered by the oven, watching the cookies and keeping an eye on us for signs of violence.

"No, I'm not pregnant." I tried to keep my own voice pleasant, thinking, *You're not the only one with plans. You're not the only one with dreams.* "But that's part of what I wanted to tell you, Mom."

My mother perked up. "What's going on?"

"Give me a minute." I got the boys set up in front of the TV in my mother's living room, telling myself that a half hour of something educational was a necessary evil. Normally, I tried to limit their TV time and get them out and moving in the fresh air as much as I could. *You've got to run boys like dogs,* my mother had told me when Frank Junior was just two. I'd thought it was a terrible thing to say. Once Frank Junior started walking I understood, but in my parents' condo complex there was nowhere to run. Most of the residents were older, and the tiny rectangles of deck off their kitchens were all they had. The playground was just sad, with a rusted swing set, a broken teeter-totter, and a single basketball hoop. There was a pool, but the one time we'd tried to use it, the lifeguard had yelled at the boys for running, for splashing, for cannonballing, and for improper use of the water aerobic teacher's foam noodles, all within ten minutes of our arrival. We'd never gone back.

Back in the kitchen, my mother was pouring coffee. Nancy sat at the table, which was draped in one of my mother's paisley-patterned tablecloths. In the center of the table there was a bouquet of dried roses ("Explain to me the difference between 'dried' and 'dead,' " Frank had said after noticing my mother's dried-red-pepper wreath) and ceramic salt and pepper shakers in the shape of Minnie and Mickey Mouse. Nancy had her legs crossed, one pointed toe of her leather boot turning in small, irritated-looking circles. "So what's the big announcement?" she asked.

"I'm going to be a surrogate." This was not exactly true. What was true was that, that morning, I'd gotten a phone call saying I'd been accepted into the Princeton Fertility Clinic's program. My information was now available to their clients on their website. Hopefully, soon a client would click on my profile, read the essays I'd worked so hard on and the pictures I'd cropped and retouched, and ask me to have her baby.

"Huh," said Nancy, fiddling with the zipper on her boot. My hopes of my family's being happy on my behalf were dwindling. My sister, as usual, looked bored and slightly hostile, and my mother, as usual, looked confused.

"It means," I began, before Nancy jumped in, leaning forward in her best college-graduate-sister-giving-a-speech mode, which had only gotten more obnoxious since she'd married a doctor and felt qualified to lecture about all things health-related.

"It means she's going to have a baby for a couple that can't have one."

"Or a single mother," I said, just to stick it in Nancy's face, to show her that she didn't have all the answers. "Or a gay couple."

"Oh," my mother said. "Oh, well, that's sweet."

"She's not doing it to be sweet," said Nancy. She pulled her iPhone—one of the new ones—out of her bag and started tapping at the screen with one painted fingernail, like a bird pecking for feed. "She's doing it for money."

"That's not exactly true," I said. My tone was light, but inside I was furious. Leave it to Nancy to make it sound like it was all about the fifty thousand dollars I'd be paid . . . and, also, to be right. For years I'd been trying to find a way to earn money while staying home with the boys, clicking on every "Make Hundreds of $$$ at Home" ad that popped up on the Internet, figuring out whether I could sell makeup or Amway during the ninety minutes three days a week when Frank Junior was at school and Spencer was asleep. I'd filled out an application to be a teacher's aide at Spencer's preschool, but the job paid only eight dollars an hour, which, between gas and babysitting meant I'd be losing money if I took it. "Yes, I'll be getting paid, but it's not just that. I really do want to help someone."

"That's nice." My mother had drifted toward the sink. She picked up a roll of paper towels, each sheet printed with a row of pink-and-blue marching ducks. I wondered if she was trying to figure out how to make it cuter somehow, to stitch a quick ball-fringe onto the wooden dispenser or cover it in Con-Tact paper patterned with dancing milkmaids.

"How much will they pay you?" Nancy asked, without looking up from her screen.

"Why would you want to know that?" I inquired pleasantly, which was what Ann Landers said you were supposed to do when someone asked you something rude. I'd never asked Nancy how much she earned working for her husband, answering his phone in her clipped, just-short-of-rude voice and planning their squash getaways. "It's a lot," I said when she didn't answer. "I'm working with one of the best programs on the East Coast."

"How do you know they're the best? Because their website says so?" Nancy ran her fingers through her hair curtains and tilted her head, giving me the same wide-eyed, quizzical look the morning-show newscaster used when she was asking the hiker who'd hacked his own arm off whether he shouldn't have told someone where he'd be going before he got trapped in that slot canyon.

"They have a very high success rate. Very satisfied customers."

"So how does it work?" my mother asked, joining us at the table with her coffee.

"I wait for a couple to choose me. The egg will be fertilized in the lab . . ."

"So romantic," Nancy scoffed under her breath.

". . . and then implanted. Nine months later, I'll have the baby, and give it to the parents."

A frown creased my mother's face. "Oh, honey. Won't that be hard?"

"It won't be my baby," I explained. "It'll be more like being a babysitter. Only no cleaning up." I tried to smile. My mother still looked worried. Nancy had gone back to glaring at her iPhone. "Lots of women do this," I continued. "Thousands of them. Lots of them are military wives. The insurance pays for everything to do with a birth . . ."

"Even if the soldier isn't the father?" Nancy asked.

I bit my lip. This was sort of a gray area. Frank was in the reserves, and his insurance would cover my care as long as my name was still on his policy, but Leslie at the clinic had told me it might be better not to mention to the nurses and the doctors I'd be seeing that this wasn't Frank's baby. "We've never had a problem," she explained. "There's a long history of Tricare looking the other way in cases like these, and we can recommend doctors and nurses we've worked with successfully before. They know how little men like your husband get paid for the important work they do, so they understand about how wives would want to contribute to the family income." It sounded like this was a speech Leslie had given before. Still, it made me nervous. When the baby was born, I guessed it would be white, like me; white, like most of the couples in America who hired surrogates. It wouldn't be too hard for anyone who was paying attention to figure out that Frank wasn't the father . . . but I'd worry about that when I got picked. If I got picked.

"What's your problem?" I asked my sister, tugging at the hem of my sweater, wishing I'd worn something that fit me a little better and wasn't six years old . . . which, inevitably, led to wishing that I had things that fit me better and were new.

"Girls," my mother murmured, clutching her mug like a life buoy.

"No, seriously, Nancy. If you've got a problem, you might as well tell me now." Not that I'd let her objections stop me. Nancy drove a Lexus and had that iPhone and her platinum card. She had no idea what it was like to live in a big old house, to feed and clothe two boys who seemed to never stop growing and never stop eating, to keep everything repaired and running on one paycheck that never stretched far enough. She could object, she could complain, she could be sarcastic, but unless she was prepared to give me money, nothing she could say would change my mind.

She tucked her hair behind her ears, allowing me a glimpse of the pearls in her lobes—real ones, I knew, that Dr. Scott had bought her for her birthday. "I don't know," she finally said. "It just seems unnatural."

"Like getting your stomach stapled? Because that seemed pretty unnatural to me."

Nancy jerked her head back like I'd slapped her.

"Banded," she said. "It's not stapled, it's banded."

"Girls," my mother repeated. She'd never been the one to break up our fights. Our father was the disciplinarian. He was a baker at a supermarket, a big, husky man who stood six foot three and weighed close to three hundred pounds, not many of which were fat. He baked bread, mostly; rolls, sometimes croissants, leaving the sweet stuff—what he called "the fancies"—to other bakers. The one exception he made was for our birthdays, when he'd get up extra early to bake and frost our cakes. They were beautiful, those cakes. One year I'd asked for the Little Mermaid, and my father had covered my cake in an ocean of turquoise-blue icing that peaked in tiny white-capped waves, tumbling toward a golden shore upon which a topless mermaid with tiny pink-tipped boobies lounged underneath a green gum-drop palm tree.

"It's just strange," said Nancy . . . and she sounded truly confused. I hadn't heard that tone much since she'd gotten skinny and gotten married and gotten the idea that she knew everything there was to know about everything. "I saw a TV special about these women in India. Women in America hire women there to carry their babies—mostly because they can't have kids of their own, but sometimes just because they don't want to. They don't want to gain weight or have stretch marks or be inconvenienced. It just seemed wrong. Women shouldn't use each other that way."

"Well, I'm not being used, and I won't be having a baby for someone who just doesn't want to be inconvenienced," I said, even though I wasn't completely sure if this was true. The clinic's literature said I'd be helping an infertile couple—*fertility* was, of course, right there in the place's name—but I could imagine some rich woman saying she was infertile and getting a surrogate just because she wanted to wear a bikini that summer, or didn't want to miss out on a wine tasting or a ski vacation. Or, I thought meanly, a squash trip. "I'm going to be helping someone."

There was a wooden bowl full of apples next to the salt and pepper shakers. My mother took one and started peeling it with a silver fruit knife with a mother-of-pearl handle that she'd ordered from QVC, a channel she affectionately called "the Q." *Only your mother,* Frank had said, *has pet names for her favorite stations.* "Do you think you can do that? Have a baby and then just hand it over?"

I looked past her into the living room. The boys were on the couch, their crumb-laden napkins on the coffee table. Frank Junior was holding Spencer's hand, the way he did when his little brother got scared at the movies. *My boys.* I thought about the bicycle Frank Junior wanted, a red Huffy in the window of the shop downtown that he would visit every time I took him on my errands with me. I thought about being able to sign Spencer up for sports readiness at the Little Gym, where classes cost four hundred dollars a semester. I thought about buying new winter coats and boots, instead of scouring the cardboard boxes at the church's winter swap for hand-me-downs, and not worrying if they lost a mitten or if Frank Junior tore the sleeve of a sweater that I'd been planning to pass down to his brother. "I think I'll be sad. But it won't be my baby. It'll be theirs. The intended parents." *Intended parents* was a term I'd learned from the surrogacy websites. "As long as I can remember that, I should be fine."

"And Frank?" My sister, I'd thought more than once, was like a woman on a long car trip with her finger pressed against the stereo's "search" button, scanning up and down the dial, looking not for music but for trouble. "Have you talked to him about this?"

"We've discussed it." *In my head*. In fact, this discussion was my rehearsal, my trial run for how I'd tell my husband what I'd done.

"I think it's great," my mother said.

"I think it's crazy," said Nancy.

"You're entitled to your opinion," I said stiffly, and got up from the table. But Fancy Nancy wasn't done yet.

"I know you," Nancy said. "You're tenderhearted." The way she said it—*tenderhearted*—it was like she was telling me I had bad breath, or hepatitis C. "They're going to give you that baby to hold and you won't want to let her go."

"Why do you think it'll be a girl? I only have boys." The words came out more ruefully than I'd intended. I'd always wanted a girl, and I'd hoped, privately, that Spencer would be one, and that I could dress her in all the beautiful little pink things I'd looked at when I was buying Frank Junior his tiny jeans and sweatshirts. I'd felt a little sad when they'd told me I was having another boy, because two was our limit, unless Frank won the lottery or I found a way to change his mind. I would have loved a big family, but we couldn't afford one.

"Especially if it's a girl," said Nancy. I sighed. We'd shared a bedroom until she left for college. She'd watched me dress up my Barbies in outfits I'd sewn myself and cook cakes for Roxie, the cocker spaniel next door, in my Easy-Bake Oven. If anyone in the world knew how much I would have loved having a daughter, it was Nancy.

"I'll be fine," I said, and looked at my mother. "Want to take the boys for pizza? I told them we'd do Chuck E. Cheese."

"Oh, right. Let me get my coat."

I turned to my sister. "You're welcome to join us."

Nancy rolled her eyes. "Those places make me feel like I'm going to have a seizure. And you know I don't eat wheat or dairy."

Or anything else. "Okay, then. See you soon."

I got the boys back in the car, feeling as if a thundercloud had settled in my chest. All I'd wanted was for someone to be happy for me—happy with me, straight-up happy, not happy with questions, or happy with reservations, or happy but confused, or not happy at all . . . and there was no one in my life, including my husband, who fit the bill.

BETTINA

I met my stepmother—not that I would ever dignify the bitch with that title—the spring of my senior year at Vassar. My father placed the call to my dorm room himself, instead of having his assistant call me, and then making me wait on hold until he could come to the phone. *Big news*, I thought. *Important.* "Tina," he said. "There's someone special I want you to meet."

He sent a car to take me home for the weekend. As usual, I asked Manuel to collect me at the coffee shop downtown, even though I wasn't fooling anyone—in the era of Google and Gawker, all of my classmates who cared to make the effort of typing my name into a search engine knew exactly who I was.

Manuel drove me to Bridgehampton. The two of them, my father and India, were waiting for me in the doorway of the gray shingled house, like an ad for Cadillacs or Cialis, or for one of those Internet dating services for old people. When I saw him standing there, his arm around her narrow waist, I knew. "This is India," my father said.

"The subcontinent?" I asked. India had laughed like she was reading words off a script: "Ha . . . ha . . . ha." Then my brothers arrived, Trey pulling up in the minivan he'd bought when his daughter was born, Tommy slouched in the seat beside him, like he was ashamed to be riding in such a desperately unhip vehicle. My father beamed and dispensed hugs and introductions, and we all went in for dinner.

I sat quietly, observing, in the big kitchen with its white-painted floors and blue-and-white-striped cushioned benches. My parents had bought the place when I was ten, and my mother had decorated in a nautical theme, all crisp blues and whites and windows shaped like portholes, with canvas slipcovers for the couches and sisal rugs on the floor. I wondered if India was already dreaming of the improvements she'd make, the addition she'd build, the bedrooms she'd annex for her Pilates equipment and her clothes.

Once the meal was finished and my father and India—quote-unquote—had adjourned to the living room (India in her heels and fancy jeans and the fringed tweed Chanel jacket that she'd worn to pick at a meal of hamburgers and Carvel ice-cream cake), my brothers and I excused ourselves, then snuck through the butler's pantry and out onto the back porch. Tommy pulled a pack of cigarettes out of his pocket and gave one to me and one to Trey. My classmates would have howled to see me smoking—to them, I was Bettina the straitlaced, Bettina the pure. The truth was, I only smoked with my brothers, and I only did it because it was one of the rare times they'd let me into their circle and talk to me like a person.

"Now, I ain't saying she a gold digger," Tommy sang. Trey shoved his hands into his pockets and gave a hooting laugh. I rolled my cigarette between my fingers and announced, "If any of those parts are original, then I am the queen of Romania."

"Dorothy Parker," said Tommy, tipping the bottle of beer he'd snagged from the refrigerator toward me in a toast. "Nice."

Tommy flicked his lighter and shielded the flame with his hand until my cigarette was lit. I inhaled, blew a plume of smoke into the starry night sky, and delivered my one-word assessment of our father's new ladyfriend: "Bitch."

"C'mon, Bets," said Tommy. "Maybe she's not that bad."

"Oh, she's that bad," I assured him. I knew her type. India— not that I believed for a second that India could actually be her name—had made an effort during the meal, asking Tommy about his band, Dirty Birdy, and Trey about his daughter and me about my internship appraising European paintings for Christie's. She let us know that she knew things about us, where we lived and what we liked and what our hobbies were: that Tommy played the bass and guitar, that I collected things— seashells and bottlecaps when I was little; antique compacts and cigarette cases now. She was polite; she was—or at least acted— interested. She'd laughed ("ha . . . ha . . . ha") when she'd gotten ketchup on the sleeve of her blouse, and hopped up from the table to clear the dishes. All of this should have eased my mind, but there was a hardness about her, something calculated, flinty and unkind. I could see scars behind her ears, beneath her chin. The skin of her cheeks was too taut and her breasts were too big for her frame. Her hair was dyed, her nose was done, and I sus- pected tinted lenses were responsible for the luminous indigo of her eyes. *Who are you, really,* I wondered as she rinsed and dried plates and kept up her expert, cheerful chatter. *Who are you? And what do you want with my dad?*

"I bet her name's really something like Tammy," I told my brothers. Trey just shrugged, and Tommy said, in the calm way that made me crazy, "Trying to make something of yourself isn't a crime."

"Making something of yourself is fine," I replied. "Getting a boob job, dying your hair, getting your nose done, chang- ing your name, whatever. That's all fine. I don't object. But she should make her own money, instead of going after his."

"Dad's a big boy," said Trey, thumbing his BlackBerry, probably to see if his wife had called or texted or sent pictures of the most recent adorable thing that nine-month-old Violet had done during the three minutes since he'd last checked.

"And he's lonely," said Tommy.

I exhaled. This was the truly infuriating part. If our father had serially discarded his wives, trading up for younger, hotter models, we'd have rolled our eyes and agreed that he was getting what he deserved with the world's Indias. But our mother had left him. After all her time in Manhattan, her years as a stay-at-home mom, a PTA volunteer, a fund-raiser for cancer research and the preservation of historic churches, she'd fallen under the sway of her yoga instructor, one Michael Essensen of Brick, New Jersey, who, after a six-week sojourn in Mumbai, had renamed himself Baba Mahatma and opened a yoga center and spiritual retreat five blocks from our apartment. The Baba, as my brothers and I called him, started popping up in passing in my mother's conversation: *The Baba says Americans should eat a more plant-based diet. The Baba says colonics changed his life.* A few months after she'd started taking classes, we would come home from school and find the Baba himself in the kitchen, in all his ponytailed, tattooed, yoga-panted splendor, dispensing wisdom over a pot of green tea. "Oh, hi, guys," my mother would say, blinking like she was trying to remember our names. The Baba, who had a chiseled chin and an artificial tan and flowing locks inspired by Fabio, would give us an indulgent nod, pour more tea for both of them (never offering me or my brothers a cup), and continue talking about whatever cleanse or fast or ritual he was endorsing that week. At fourteen, I'd been able to identify his spiel as incense-scented nonsense, but my mother had believed every word of it, swearing to her friends (and, eventually, to the strangers she'd corner in the schoolyard or the dentist's office or the fish counter at Russ & Daughters) that the Baba was magical, and that his ministrations had helped her survive the mood swings and hot flashes of menopause when the hormone therapy prescribed by the top doctors in Manhattan had failed.

My mother had been born Arlene Sandusky in a suburb of Detroit in 1958. She'd married my father at twenty-three, then moved to New York, where she'd had three children and become an enthusiastic baker of cookies and trimmer of Christmas trees, a woman who liked nothing better than taking on some elaborate holiday-related project—assembling and frosting a gingerbread house, or running the schoolwide Easter egg hunt. In the wake of her association with the Baba, she'd ditched her traditions and her Martha Stewart cookbooks. She'd grown her hair long and let it go gray. She'd swapped her designer suits and high heels for embroidered tunics and thick-strapped leather sandals, and traded her Bulgari perfume for a mixture of essential oils that made her smell like the backseat of a particularly malodorous taxicab, sandalwood and curry with hints of vomit. She'd gotten a belly piercing that I'd seen and a tattoo that I hadn't—I hadn't even been able to bring myself to ask *where* or *of what*—and, eventually, she began slipping the Baba tens of thousands of dollars. When my father's accountants finally started to ask questions about what the Order of New Light was and whether it was, in fact, a tax-free C corporation, she'd announced her intentions to get a divorce and follow the Baba to Taos, where he was building a retreat offering intensive yoga training, raw cuisine, and a clothing-optional sweat lodge.

I came home from school one afternoon and found luggage lined up in the hall and my mother in her bedroom, packing. "I am renouncing the meaninglessness of the material," she said, sitting on top of her Louis Vuitton suitcase to get the zipper closed. I pointed out that the meaninglessness of the material did not seem to cover the great quantity of Tory Burch tunics and Juicy Couture sweat suits that she had packed.

"Oh, Bettina," she said, in a tone that mixed scorn and, unbelievably, pity. "Don't be so rigid." She kissed me, taking me into her arms for an unwelcome and musky embrace.

"Be good to your father," she said, smoothing my hair as I tried not to wriggle away. "He's a good man, but he's just not very *evolved.*"

After that, my mother communicated by letters and postcards, while my father became Topic A in the gossip columns and, when he started dating again, prey for single ladies of a certain age. There was the magazine editor famous enough to have been skewered in a movie, played by an actress who, in my opinion, was ten years too young and significantly too pretty to be a plausible stand-in. She was followed by a real-estate mogul with a face permanently frozen into a look of startled puzzlement, then a newspaper columnist, similarly Botoxed, who'd made a career out of being bitchy on the Sunday-morning political chat shows. In that realm of gray-suited, gray-faced men, it turned out that even a not-terribly-attractive fifty-two-year-old could pass herself off as a babe if she wore pencil skirts, kept her hair dyed, and made the occasional reference to oral sex.

Even when my father was technically attached, it didn't stop other women from trying. There would be a hand that lingered on his forearm, a cheek kiss that ended up grazing his lips, a business card with a cell phone number scribbled on it, pressed into his palm at the end of a night. My father had resisted them all, the waitresses and the young divorcees and the actress-slash-models . . . which was why it made no sense that he'd fall for this hard-edged, new-nosed, fake-named "India," who was no more in her thirties than I was the winner of *America's Next Top Model.*

"Are you worried she's going to spend our inheritance?" Tommy asked, spinning the wheel of his lighter.

"It's not about the money," I said, ignoring the twinge I felt at the thought of this stranger squandering what should have been mine. I had a trust fund, worth ten million dollars, that I'd be able to access on my twenty-first birthday, which was coming in two months. My father had already told me he'd buy me an apartment after I graduated, in whatever city I ended up working. Needless to say, I had no student loans. I'd most likely get a job that offered health insurance, and I'd inherited all the clothes, shoes, furs, and jewelry that my mother hadn't sold before decamping to New Mexico. Even if my father married some grasping bitch (unlikely) and didn't sign a prenup (even more unlikely), my brothers and I would be fine. I knew, for example, that my dad had already set up a trust for Trey's daughter, Violet, and that he'd bought new amps for Dirty Birdy, which specialized in thrash-metal covers of female singer-songwriter ballads.

I ground my cigarette under my heel. "It's not the money, it's the principle of the thing. This woman just thinks she can waltz on in here and have . . ." I waved my hands out at the lawn, which rolled, lush and green, down a gentle slope to the ocean. ". . . all of this, and she didn't earn any of it."

"Well, when you think about it," Tommy said, "we didn't exactly earn any of it, either."

"We survived Mom and Dad," I reminded him. I'd given the matter of what we were and were not owed considerable thought . . . sometimes while I was walking into what passed for downtown Poughkeepsie so my roommates wouldn't see me being picked up by a driver.

"I think we need to give her a chance," said Tommy.

"Do we have a choice?" I inquired, and Trey, who'd been looking at his BlackBerry again, shook his head and said, "We do not."

I sighed. Tommy finished his cigarette. Trey put his telephone back in his pocket. "Dad knows enough to be careful."

I didn't answer. My brothers had both been away at school when my mom had left. I'd been the only one home. What happened to my dad hadn't been dramatic . . . he'd just gotten quieter and quieter, more and more pale. Prior to my mother's departure, he was rarely home before eight o'clock at night, but, after she left, he started returning at five, then four, then three in the afternoon, locking the bedroom door behind him, saying that he needed a nap. My mother had left in September. By Christmas he'd stopped sleeping. He'd take his naps, then sit up all night by the windows, not eating, not drinking, not talking. I'd ask him, over and over, if he was all right, if he wanted anything. He'd shake his head, trying for a smile, unable to manage more than a few words. I'd talked about therapists; I'd mentioned antidepressants—half the kids I knew had been on some kind of medication for something at some point in their lives. I'd called my brothers, who'd told me—brusquely, in Trey's case, kindly, in Tommy's—that Dad would be fine, that this was just something he had to get through. Easy for them to say. They weren't the ones who saw him frozen in an armchair, underneath a de Kooning on one wall and a Picasso etching on another, not noticing the art, or the sunsets over the park. They didn't see the way his pants sagged around his shrinking waistline and flapped around his diminished legs, or the silvery stubble glinting on his chin.

One dark day in February, I came home from choir practice and found every dish in the kitchen smashed and my father shin-deep in the shards of china and porcelain. My parents had had half a dozen sets of dishes, and the mess was considerable. My father stood there, blinking, a dish with a blue bunny painted in its center in his hand. When I ran to him, I could feel the jagged edges of shattered bowls and plates and coffee cups biting at my ankles, ripping at my tights. "Daddy?"

He gave me a wavering smile. "I . . . well. That felt better.

That felt pretty good." Together, we swept up the mess, filling a dozen garbage bags with the wreckage. Things improved after that. By spring, he was, as he put it, "stepping out," whistling as I attached cuff links to the starched cuffs of his shirt, taking women to the benefits and balls my mother used to dread.

I picked up my cigarette butt and slipped it in my pocket, a thief removing the evidence, while I wondered about India's strategy: whether she could get my dad to marry her, whether she was young enough to seal the deal by getting pregnant. I would watch. I would wait. I would do what I could to keep my father safe. India struck me as a formidable enemy and the money meant that the stakes were high   but I was my father's daughter, and I loved him very much.

INDIA

You've been spotting, hon?" the nurse asked.

I nodded mutely. *Spotting* was what I'd told my obstetrician on the telephone that morning, *spotting* was what I'd written on the forms in the office that afternoon, but I was actually bleeding, not spotting. After three failed in vitro attempts, I knew the difference.

"Let's take a look. Lean back, now. Deep breath." I shut my eyes as she pushed the ultrasound probe inside me. Marcus squeezed my hand, and I thought how this office was the one place, maybe one of only a few in the world, where it didn't matter what he was, that he'd sold his first business at twenty-five and started his own hedge fund at the age of thirty-one and now, twenty-six years later, had hundreds of millions of dollars and clients all over the world. Here, we were just another infertile couple, a little desperate, no longer young, flipping through limp magazines in the waiting room, hoping that we'd win the prize.

I knew, though, even before I looked at the screen, that it hadn't happened this time. It was just like the previous two rounds: a positive pregnancy test, then rejoicing, even though I knew it was too soon. A few days later, a blood test had confirmed the pregnancy but revealed a low hCG count. hCG, as I'd learned, was human chorionic growth hormone, the stuff that shows up in your blood and lets you know that the embryo's developing. The level's supposed to double every forty-eight hours. In my case, that had never happened. The hCG number would rise, then stall, and then start dropping. A week or ten days later, the bleeding would start and I'd come to this office for an ultrasound, the crooks of my arms bruised from blood draws, and the doctor would tell me what I already knew: that there was a fertilized egg that had started to grow and then stopped. There was no heartbeat. You lose. Again. *Blighted ovum,* the Internet called it, though my doctor had never used those words, or any words that sounded like they assigned blame.

"I'm sorry, hon," said the nurse. I'd seen her before, a no-nonsense lady in her fifties with short hair dyed blond and kind eyes. "Doctor will be right in."

She pulled out the probe, pressed a pad against me, and left me and Marcus alone. It was sunny outside the windows, a perfect May morning, the whole city in bloom, from the daffodils in the planters in the median on Fifth Avenue to the trees in Central Park. "Shit," I said, and shut my eyes. "Shit, shit, shit, shit, shit."

"Oh, babe," said Marcus. He leaned forward to kiss my cheek, letting me feel the warmth of his skin and smell the cedar and vetiver in his cologne. He was crying a little. Perversely, that made me feel better, like I hadn't forced him to do this. Marcus was in his late fifties, with three grown children, all of them out of the house and reasonably self-sufficient. He would have been well within his rights to tell me he was done with babies. But he hadn't. Marcus loved me. He wanted me to have everything I wanted. "We can try again next month, if Dreiser says it's all right."

Dreiser was Dr. Theodore Dreiser of Harvard and Columbia, acknowledged by *New York* magazine and everyone else who mattered as the top reproductive specialist in the city. I shook my head.

"No more."

"Listen. You don't have to make up your mind right now. We'll get some lunch, you can have a glass of wine."

I smiled. These days, the only times I drank were after doctors' visits such as these . . . or after the D and C that would follow. Then I pulled the cotton gown down over my bare knees (tanned, hairless, absolutely jiggle-free, looking better than they had when I was a teenager) and sat up. "I'm not getting any younger." This was true. I might have had the body of a woman in her twenties—I certainly worked hard enough at it—but I was forty-three years old, even if Marcus thought I was thirty-eight. "I don't think we've got any more time to waste."

Marcus, impeccable in his made-to-measure shirt and silk tie, started to answer when the door opened, revealing the doctor, slim and erect in his white coat, with a neatly trimmed salt-and-pepper beard, oversized Roman features, liquid brown eyes, and an expression of consternation. He didn't like being a loser any more than I did. It meant that *New York* magazine and the ladies who mattered, the ones who could pay for treatments even after their insurance ran out, might start sending their friends somewhere else. "Guys, I'm so sorry," he said. Marcus squeezed my hand again. I turned my face toward the wall and finally let the tears come, the ones that had been threatening since the spotting—bleeding—had started.

I was thirty-seven when I met my husband—thirty-seven as far as he was concerned; forty-two in real life, but if I looked thirty-seven and had ID to prove it, then why tell people I wasn't? Honesty has its place, and its place is not in the dating world. For the past five years, I'd run my own public-relations shop, a boutique agency with a handful of clients, a mix of reliable-but-boring businesses—a jewelry designer, a chain of magazines—who'd pay their bills on time and rarely need my help in the middle of the night, plus a handful of celebrities who were neither reliable nor boring, who'd pay a minimum of five thousand dollars a month to keep me on retainer and sometimes would require my services in the wee small hours.

Every day I went to the office dressed in one of the designer suits I'd bought secondhand at Michael's Consignment on the Upper East Side. I'd wear Manolos and Louboutins—I had two pairs of each, and rotated them every day. My jeweler client lent me necklaces and bracelets and cocktail rings; the makeup line I represented sent over a basket of freebies every month. I bartered with a dentist to get my teeth bleached and traded with a personal trainer and a dermatologist for their services, but I still paid to get my hair highlighted at Frédéric Fekkai, which was insanely costly but a necessary expense, the kind of thing you couldn't scrimp on. Everyone saw your hair every day and everyone worth knowing would know whether you were paying for those buttery chunks or trying to get the same look at a less-expensive salon or, God forbid, by doing it yourself.

I had an apartment in the right neighborhood, a one-bedroom walk-up sparsely furnished with the beautiful things I'd saved up and bought with cash: a gorgeously curvy couch upholstered in fawn-colored velvet, a queen-size bed with Frette sheets, a Turkish rug, glowing blue and gold and ruby-red, that I'd admired in a shop window for months before buying.

Instead of paintings or sculpture, I had an expandable metal pole, an extra-long version of the kind meant to hold a shower curtain, that ran the length of my small living room. The pole held the clothes I'd bought at sample sales or secondhand or saved to pay retail for. The skirts and shirts and dresses, carefully culled and curated—cotton and taffeta, crisp linens, plush velvet, luscious silk—served as a movable, changeable display, hanging just above the low shelves filled with fashion magazines that ran along the wall.

There was no TV, but there were stacks of scrapbooks that I'd worked on for years, filling the pages with photographs I'd torn from magazines or snipped from the newspaper—pictures of models and socialites attending benefits and balls, pictures of women with three names, at least one of them belonging to an inanimate object or a fruit: the Sykes sisters at charity balls, Loulou de la Falaise presiding over a gala at the Met; Audrey Hepburn at the Oscars, Jackie O. on board the yacht *Christina*, in her oversized sunglasses, with an Hermès scarf tied beneath her chin. That was all I had by way of decoration, all I wanted. The apartment wasn't a home as much as a cocoon, a place where I'd crawl in as a caterpillar and emerge lovely and transformed . . . and rich, with all the security that piles of money implied.

I met Marcus at a Starbucks on Fifty-sixth between Sixth and Seventh, across from the Parker Meridien hotel, where I was hosting a party for my jewelry designer. Hearts and Bones was the theme. The tables were draped in blood-red chiffon, and the disc jockey was a skeletal young person who went by the name of Q, who'd flown in from Los Angeles with a sobriety manager. We were serving baby back ribs and molasses-basted chicken wings, Day of the Dead sugar skulls and, for the daring, tiny quail hearts pierced with silver skewers. I was going over the details in my head, waiting in line at the coffee shop for my usual, a tall skinny latte, extra hot, no foam, when Marcus pushed through the glass doors and stopped in the middle of the store. I noticed him as he stood there, rocking back and forth, peering at the menu with his chin raised, oblivious to the disgruntled hipsters and office workers backing up behind him.

"Coffee," he said, half to himself. "I just want coffee."

I could tell, with one quick glance informed by five years' worth of reading *GQ* and *T Style,* that his suit was a two-thousand-dollar Brioni, that his shirt was made-to-measure and his shoes were hand-sewn. He was in his fifties, I figured, but fit, with the tall, broad-shouldered frame of a former football player and an easy, confident stance. He had a high forehead and features a little too small for his wide, round face, a snub nose and deep-set eyes and a rosebud of a mouth. His hair was thick, glossy black, beautifully cut, and even though he was freshly shaved, I could see bluish-black dots of stubble on his cheeks. If he kissed you, you'd know you were kissing a man, not one of these pampered, facialed metrosexuals who could tie scarves better than a Frenchwoman and talk knowledgeably about moisturizers. He had a cleft in his chin and big hands, with black hair on the knuckles and on the inch or two of wrist that I could see. No ring. My mouth went dry as I gave up my place in line and walked over to him. "Small, medium, or large?" I asked, standing close enough to give him a whiff of my perfume, Coco by Chanel, a little sultry for the office but perfect for this occasion. Spotting the Rolex on his wrist, I thanked God that I'd worn it.

He turned to me with a grateful look. "Large. Black."

"Could make a dirty joke here. Won't do it," I said.

"I appreciate your restraint. May I buy you a coffee?"

"My treat," I said, and stepped up to the barista, handing her my platinum AmEx card, the one I used for business expenses, ordering my latte and adding, "And one venti house blend for my friend."

"Name?" asked the bored girl with tattoos of hyacinths twined around her arms. She would regret them later. I'd had my own tattoo, far nicer work than hers, lasered off the small of my back here in New York three months after my arrival, at considerable pain and expense.

"Marcus," he said—half to me, half to her. "Marcus Croft."

My brain did a fast Google while the girl scribbled *Markus* on a cup. *Finance,* I thought. I'd seen his name in the papers recently—a merger? A divorce? My heart was beating too fast. This was it, the thing I'd been waiting for.

When the coffee came, I fitted the cups into a cardboard carrier while Marcus watched, impressed. He held the door for me, and together we walked out onto a sidewalk that seemed to have been freshly paved, and strolled across the street, which cleared, magically, just as we stepped off the curb. "Do you work around here?" he asked.

"Downtown," I said. "But I've got an event here tonight."

"Oh, yeah? What kind of event?"

"A cocktail party for a client. She's introducing a new line of necklaces made with semiprecious stones. Fun and functional," I recited from the press release I'd written.

He frowned, broad forehead creasing. "Is jewelry ever functional?"

I widened my eyes, feigning shock. "I'm doomed." I clutched his arm and lowered my voice to a whisper. "You won't tell anyone, will you?"

"Your secret is safe with me."

I laughed, low and throaty. My wrap dress was cut short enough to show off my legs, waxed just a few days before. My hair was freshly colored, and I was wearing one of my client's pieces, a heart-shaped chunk of amber on a lacy gold chain. I felt good, my muscles warm and loose after my morning run, a six-mile loop through Central Park. It was a day full of promise, one of those perfect New York mornings where the city looked like it had been power-washed, the sky a rich blue, the trees thick with glossy green leaves, a gentle breeze blowing. The taxicabs honking their way up Sixth Avenue glowed golden. The people on the sidewalk were fit and scrubbed and full of purpose. And here I was, alongside the kind of man I'd moved to New York City to meet, my reward after all the pain and expense I'd endured. The apple was hanging from the tree, warm and ripe in my hand. All I had to do was pluck it.

Marcus had taken my elbow as we had crossed the street. Later, I would learn that he had a car and driver, which he'd left at the corner, waiting, and that the only reason he'd been in the Starbucks in the first place, puzzling over the difference between a grande and a venti, was because one of his assistants was in the backseat on the phone to a broker in Tokyo, and the other had been sent ahead to Teterboro, making sure the catering company had arrived to provision his private jet.

"Here's my stop," I said when we'd reached the hotel's revolving glass door. I pulled his coffee out of the carrier and handed it to him, noticing how small the paper cup looked in his big hand.

"Would you like to have dinner sometime?" he asked.

"I could be convinced." I gave him my business card. He rubbed it between his fingers, reading out loud: "India Bishop, President, Bishop PR."

I nodded demurely. "That's me." I loved the name India. My mother had named me Samantha, but I was a long way from the place I'd been raised, from the girl I'd been. I'd taken the name from a book I'd read, *Mrs. Bridge*, about a married, settled midwestern lady with a name that was the most exotic thing about her. India suited me better, and so India was what I'd become.

"India," said Marcus Croft. "I'll be in touch."

Upstairs in the ballroom, waiting for the banquet manager to go over the menu one last time, I flipped open my laptop, slipped off my shoes, and typed "Marcus Croft" into my search engine. The computer spat out eleven thousand hits—the *Times*, the *Wall Street Journal*, *Forbes*, *Businessweek*, the *Robb Report*. It didn't take me long to learn that the man who'd been so nonplussed by the Starbucks offerings was the real deal, an arbitrageur who'd launched one of the world's most successful hedge funds, a man who owned pieces of everything from sports teams to fast-food chains to clothing factories in China. Married once, to his college sweetheart, the former Arlene Sandusky; divorced for five years, three children, almost grown. He was fifty-five. That was older than I thought, but I could work with it. I figured that, barring an early and lucrative divorce, we could be man and wife for twenty years, and if he was considerate and didn't linger, I'd have plenty of years to be a very merry widow.

But that was getting ahead of myself.

I dug deeper, refining my search, typing in his name along with the name of his wife. It didn't take me long to learn that the ex–Mrs. Croft had taken a lover—her yoga instructor, which was not terribly original—and taken off for an ashram in New Mexico. *All the better to replace you with, my dear,* I'd thought, clicking the link for pictures, which revealed a generic society-woman-of-a-certain-age, in an updo and a satin gown at the Met's costume ball. I was prettier than she was; thinner, younger, bigger boobs, a higher ass; the winner by technical knockout in the only categories that mattered.

My telephone rang. PRIVATE NUMBER, read the display. I put my finger on the button, readying myself, a backup quarterback who'd just been called into the big game. In that moment, I remembered going on the one vacation my grandparents and I ever took, to a cabin on Lake Winnipesaukee in New Hampshire that one of their friends had won at a church auction and had, for some reason, been unable to use. One morning my *opa* had woken me up before the sun had risen, and we'd slipped out of the cabin, leaving my grandmother still snoozing in the saggy-mattressed bed. Sitting in a wooden rowboat, one foot trailing in the shockingly cold water, holding the fishing rod my *opa* had brought up from the basement the night before we'd left, I felt at first a gentle tug, then a sharper one. The tip of my rod bent until it was almost touching the surface of the lake. I jerked back on it as hard as I could, until my *opa* stopped me. *Easy,* he said, his arms against my shoulders. *Remember. He's a fish. You're a big girl. Play him in easy, and remember: you're smarter than he is.*

You're smarter than he is, I thought, and arranged my face into a pleasant smile, crossed my legs, shook out my hair, and lifted the receiver to my ear.

JULES

I was in ninth grade when my dad had his accident. Miss Carasick, the guidance counselor, who was known, inevitably, as Miss Carsick, pulled me out of French class and hustled me down the hall into her office, which was decorated with posters from different colleges. "Your father's in the hospital," she said.

I'd been slouching in the seat across from her desk—cringing, actually. I was afraid she'd found out that Tricia Barnes and I had been hiding out in the girls' room after we'd pled menstrual cramps to get out of gym class. I hadn't seen my parents that morning, but that wasn't unusual: most days, my father left for school before I even got out of bed and my mom stayed asleep until after I was gone. "What? Why? What happened?"

Miss Carasick sat back. Her glasses shone in the glare from the fluorescent lights overhead, and I could see a sprinkling of white flakes—dandruff, or dried mousse—at her hairline. "All I know is that there's been an accident."

"What . . ." My mouth felt frozen. I wished she had caught me and Tricia; that would have been a million times better than this. "What happened?"

I remembered the way she rolled her lips over each other, her lipstick making a faint smacking sound. Later, I'd found out that my father'd had his midterm performance review the previous afternoon and gone to a bar directly after. How, at closing time, the bartender had tried to take his keys away and my father had refused. How he'd driven his little VW Rabbit through a stop sign and hit a car with a young woman behind the wheel and her three-year-old in the backseat. How both of them, mother and child, were in the hospital, both of them expected to make a full recovery, although the toddler had been touch-and-go at first. How my father had been drunk at the time of the accident, with a blood alcohol level almost double the legal limit, and how he was in the hospital and under arrest. The police, I learned later, had come by the house first thing in the morning; they'd brought my mother to see him and she'd left without leaving a note.

I thought a lot about it later: why Mrs. Carasick hadn't been kinder; whether I'd misremembered; or if she'd actually been gloating when she'd given me the news. Years later, I'd imagine looking up her address, knocking on her door, and standing there with my hair loose over my shoulders and telling her what a bitch she'd been, that I was a fourteen-year-old, a girl who had no idea that her father had had a drinking problem.

Afterward, I could see the signs—the way he'd always had a beer as soon as he walked through the door after school, the wine with dinner, the tumbler full of whiskey and ice by his hand when he'd grade papers; the way he'd go out to play poker Friday nights and, how on Saturday mornings, my mother would make me and Greg talk in whispers and walk barefoot. *Shh*, my mother would tell us, shooing us into the kitchen, away from the closed bedroom door. *Your dad's had a hard week.*

The weekend after I'd met Jared Baker of the Princeton Fertility Clinic, I made my monthly trip home. I left at four, after my last class on Friday, stopping at the Wawa, the convenience store at the edge of campus where students could buy cheap hot dogs and hoagies after a night of drinking. I filled my thermos with hot coffee and bought a ticket for the Dinky, the little train that ran from campus to Princeton Junction. At Princeton Junction I'd catch a New Jersey Transit train to Philadelphia. In Philly, I'd walk from Suburban Station to the bus terminal and buy a bottle of water and a roast pork sandwich at the Reading Terminal Market, standing in line with rough-handed construction workers and puffy-faced nurses on their way to work, and catch the Greyhound home.

When I got to Pittsburgh early the next morning, my mother was waiting for me at the station, the sounds of NPR filling the car. NPR was my father's station—my mother favored country music and AM call-in shows. All those years later, after his hospitalization, his trips through detox and rehab, his trial for driving under the influence and attempted vehicular manslaughter and the six months he'd eventually spent in jail, she still listened to his radio stations, still kept one of his coats in the closet and cooked his favorite things for dinner, as if, someday, he'd walk back through the door, the same man she'd fallen in love with.

It would never happen. My father had lived at home briefly after he'd been paroled. Then the drinking had started again. My mother had given him a version of the speech it was rumored Laura Bush once delivered to her not-yet-presidential husband— "It's me or Jack Daniel's"—and kicked him out. My father had rented a studio apartment and, once that lease ran out, he'd moved in with another woman.

My mom could have forgiven my father for what he'd done, for driving drunk, for hitting an innocent woman and child, but she couldn't forgive him for Rita Devine. It had soured my mother, who'd always been so sweet, delighted by the smallest things: a trip to the shore, a bouquet of sunflowers, a mug of mulled cider in the backyard while my brother and I raked leaves.

I dropped my backpack in the trunk, kissed my mom's cheek,

and buckled myself into the front seat. My mother drove with a light hand on the wheel, steering the car through the morning sunshine, along the familiar streets, until we merged onto the freeway that would take us from downtown to Squirrel Hill. "Classes okay?" she asked.

"Classes are fine," I told her.

"And how is Dan?"

"Dan's great." Dan and I had been a couple for four months, but sometimes I thought I didn't know him any better than I had the first night we'd hooked up. He was good-looking, well-mannered, a rower with formidable shoulders, and had a fondness for 1990s-era grunge rock . . . and that was it. "Well, you look great," said my mom and I nodded.

My mother and I have the same fair skin and pale eyes, and I know, from pictures, that her hair was once like mine. But now her skin was etched with hundreds of tiny lines, blotched and splotched with souvenirs of the summers when she used to gild herself in Johnson's Baby Oil and lie in a bikini on a beach towel in her backyard. The pink of her lips had faded to beige, her hair was a too-bright lemony color, her fingertips were permanently stained from hair dye and cigarettes, and her body was slack and soft beneath her clothes.

"I hope you're hungry. I made a chicken pot pie for dinner." She gave me a quick once-over when traffic slowed. "You look great."

"I've been running a lot. Five miles yesterday."

"Five miles. Wow. Good for you." She looked at herself ruefully. "I bet I couldn't run a mile. Not even if someone was chasing me."

"You just start slow. Run for thirty seconds, walk for two minutes. Start with twenty minutes a day . . ."

She shook her head, smiling. She'd heard this before, my prescriptions for healthy living, advice about diet and exercise, and she'd listen with a smile, then ignore whatever I'd suggested. As far as I knew, she'd never been on a date since my father had left. "I'm just not interested," she'd told me the one time I'd asked.

My father and his girlfriend lived in an apartment complex, a place called Oakwood Towers that boasted no oak trees and where the buildings topped out at three stories. The three-building complex, shaped like an H, was Section 8 housing, with a parking lot full of secondhand cars held together with Bondo and tape and baling wire, and apartments full of new immigrants and newly single men, families who'd cram eight or ten people into a one-bedroom unit, tired-eyed grandparents with babies and toddlers. My mother would drive into the parking lot, but no farther.

"See you at two?"

I nodded, leaving my backpack in the car, taking the plastic bag full of stuff I'd brought for my father. On the scraggly lawn in front of his building, two boys in corduroy pants and T-shirts kicked a soccer ball back and forth and chattered to each other in a language I didn't recognize.

I pressed the buzzer, waited until the door opened, and then walked past the empty fountain in the lobby (sometimes there was a girl in a football helmet sitting on the lip of that fountain, rocking and drooling), down a disinfectant-scented, green-carpeted hallway to apartment 211.

Rita wasn't there—she worked on weekends, a part-time job at a sporting-goods store. My dad was waiting for me at the door. He'd gained weight since his time in jail, and now his face was red, his fingers thick, his hands and cheeks swollen as he hugged me and said my name in his hoarse, raspy voice. He smelled like cigarette smoke, but nothing worse: sometimes when I'd hug him I could catch a whiff of whiskey or the strange, chemical odor I could only guess was drugs, but not today.

"Come in," he said, leading me through the cluttered living room. Coffee mugs and sections of newspaper and DVD cases sat on every table; clothes were piled on the couch and the chairs. The windows were streaked with dirt; the pillows on the sofa were squashed; the knickknack shelf where Rita kept a few framed family photographs and some china plates and crystal glasses was dusty. My dad walked to the little kitchen, where there was a frying pan on the stove and three teacups beside it, one with cut-up onions, one with green peppers, and one with grated cheese. "I'm making a Denver omelet."

"That sounds good." I watched as he scooped a spoonful of margarine from a tub and put it in the pan to melt. His hands were shaking, but this could have meant almost anything: some of the drugs he'd been prescribed had tremors as a side effect, or he could have been going through withdrawal, or he could have been high, right at that moment, for all I knew. After all the years, I'd never gotten any good at telling.

I found forks and knives in a drawer, plates in a cabinet, and two juice glasses in the dishwasher. My father was concentrating hard on the pan. He'd dumped in the onions, which were cut in large, ragged chunks. He shook his head, then picked up a spatula, the end still crusted with melted cheese. I poured us small glasses of generic orange juice—as part of his disability payments, my father got food stamps, although they weren't stamps anymore, just what looked like a regular debit card to use at the grocery store—and found paper napkins and a loaf of wheat bread for toast. I was starting to straighten up the living room when he called me in for breakfast. Feeling uncomfortable and out of place, the way I always did in his apartment, I took the seat across from him at the table. The eggs were burnt dark-brown in places, and he'd forgotten the peppers.

"It's really good," I told him.

My father sighed. "Ah, I'm no cook. That was your mother."

I didn't answer, watching as he maneuvered a bite into his

mouth. If he missed us, this was as close as he'd come to saying so. An onion fell off and got stuck in his beard. "Dad," I said quietly, pointing, and waiting until he'd used his napkin to get it out.

If you saw my father on the street, walking or sitting on the bench outside the duck pond behind his building, you wouldn't cross the street to avoid him. Maybe you'd think that he was just a regular guy enjoying the sunshine, a man with a job and a family and a house to come home to. If you looked a little closer you'd see the thumbprints smeared on his glasses, the way one of the earpieces was mended with duct tape, the way his skin was unnaturally red and his eyes filmy. If you noticed that, maybe you would pick up your pace and try to put the sight of him out of your mind. You wouldn't want to think about how many people like him there were out in the world, unsupervised, untethered, unloved. At least you'd want to believe they were untethered and unloved, that they didn't have wives, or sons, or daughters, because you certainly wouldn't want to think about that.

I put my fork down on my plate. "Hey, Dad," I said, "if I could pay for you to go to rehab, would you go?"

He didn't answer right away. I looked at him, his swollen face, his greasy hair. He used to be handsome. He used to wear suits on the first day of school, no matter how hot it was. He used to kiss my mother in the kitchen when he came home from work, grabbing her around the waist and lifting her briefly into the air as she laughed. He used to live in a house with three bedrooms and an above-ground swimming pool . . . but I stopped those thoughts before they got too far.

He pulled off his glasses and turned them over slowly. "It's not your job," he finally said. "Not your job to take care of me."

"I'm almost done with school," I said, pulling out the pages that I'd printed and passing them across the table. *Willow Crest: A Community of Care*. I'd done enough research to show that the place was conveniently located and well-regarded, with a respectable success rate. The intake counselor I'd talked with the day before said that they'd have a bed available within the next three weeks. "I've got some money to spare. Would you go?"

He scratched his nose, forehead furrowed, then poked at the pages. After he had his accident, insurance paid for detox in a hospital, then twenty-eight days in rehab in a place up in New Hampshire. He was diagnosed with depression while he was in there, and he did okay for a while once he got out, even though he'd been suspended from his job and was on disability while the school board figured out exactly what to do. Then came the trial. "Area Teacher Sentenced for Drunk Driving Accident," read the headline on page B-6 of the *Pittsburgh Post-Gazette*. My mother, who was normally a stickler about education, had let me and Greg stay home from school the day after the verdict. Greg had disappeared out the back door as soon as she'd left for work. I'd stayed in bed, not my bed but the one my parents used to share, watching game shows and talk shows and court shows, thinking it was quite possible that I would die of shame, that my mother would come home and find nothing but a girl-shaped puddle of embarrassment with, perhaps, some blond hair attached.

The school district hadn't been able to fire him, but by the time he got out of jail, his job was gone. *Downsized,* they said, claiming that it had nothing to do with what had happened. I couldn't blame them. Teachers could have a whiff of scandal in their histories—in my high school, there was a math teacher who'd left her husband for a shop instructor—but they couldn't have hit a mother and child while driving drunk, and gone to jail for the crime.

With no job, he had no benefits. With no benefits, he couldn't afford the hundreds of dollars of medications he took each month for the depression and anxiety they'd diagnosed in rehab, the conditions that I believed had started him drinking in the first place. Without medicine, he started drinking again, and ordering painkillers from Mexico and Canada on the Internet, and eventually moving on to the stuff you can buy on the street. One of the first times I'd visited, looking underneath the bathroom sink for more toilet paper, I'd found a crack pipe, an airline-size vodka bottle split in half with a glass pipe duct-taped into the seam. I'd dropped it like it had burned me . . . then I'd put it back.

I don't make excuses. I know what he's doing is illegal. I know that he's a drain on taxpayers' resources, that people who work hard at their jobs are the ones paying for his apartment and his food, for the cops who bust him and the counselors who hand him pamphlets about AA and methadone. I know that the radio talk-show shouters would hold him up as an example of everything wrong with America—how we're entitled, how we're weak, how instead of facing our troubles we lean on the crutches of chemicals. But he's my father . . . and I don't believe that it's his fault. It's not like he's lazy, some privileged rich kid trying to escape from some imaginary heartache or chasing some feel-good high. He takes drugs so that he can feel something close to normal, and I believe that normal is all he's after.

"You ready?" I asked. From his apartment complex, it's a short trip to a strip mall, with a diner and a barbershop. I walked closer to the traffic. My dad walked beside me, his gait a little unsteady, his eyes on the ground.

We went to the barbershop, where I paid for my father to get a haircut, flipping through *Sports Illustrated* while the barber made small talk, then sprinkled talc on the back of his neck. Back in the apartment, I straightened up some more while he made coffee and read the paper. At one-thirty I handed him the plastic bag, my haul for the month.

The shaking in his hands had gotten worse, I saw, as he opened the bag and rummaged inside, pulling out four paperback novels, a razor and a can of shaving cream, a jar of Kiehl's moisturizer, and three bars of Dial soap, all of which I'd scavenged from campus. It was easy: my classmates were constantly leaving their buckets of toiletries in the bathrooms, their clothes in the dryer, their bookbags and backpacks everywhere. Sometimes I would slip into the boys' bathroom and slip out with a razor and a canister of shaving cream in my bathrobe pocket, or I'd hang around the basement laundry room and wait until it was empty and I was alone with a dryer-full of men's clothing. It wasn't as if the boys at my school couldn't spare a little soap or a copy of whatever book it was fashionable to tote around that semester. Because of my job, I knew who had money and who, like me, was on work-study, and I was careful to take stuff only from the ones I knew could just buy more, in the unlikely event that they even noticed what was missing. I was, I told myself, like Robin Hood, stealing from the rich and entitled and careless, giving to my father, who needed it more than they did.

"What are you reading?" I asked him. This was a safe question, because he was always reading something.

"*Great Expectations,*" he answered. "It's spring."

"Oh, I loved that one," I said, not taking the bait, not mentioning that he'd taught that book every May. "Magwitch was my favorite." Magwitch, Pip's mysterious benefactor. Someday, I thought, I would like to be somebody's mysterious benefactor, too; giving gifts to someone who didn't know me; watching, from a distance, their delight.

I looked out the window as my father went into the back of the apartment, where I'd never been, to put the soap and shaving cream away. The kids who were playing soccer had taken their ball and gone home. Now there was a woman in a bright orange sari outside, standing behind a baby slumped in the plastic cradle of a swing. She pushed him back and forth as the chains creaked. The baby sat quietly, its brown fingers gripping the edge

of the black plastic, its face stoic, as if swinging was a punish-
ment it was sentenced to endure. When I heard the honk of my
mother's horn, I couldn't lie, even to myself, about the emotion
that flooded through me. It was relief.

Twenty thousand dollars. I thought about it as I ate pot pie, as
I dried my hair in the bathroom, where the shelves were filled
with products my mom had bought at cost at her salon. *Twenty
thousand dollars,* I thought, lying on the bed. Twenty thousand
dollars could pay for rehab. It could buy medicine. Twenty thousand dollars could save him . . . and, with that thought, I finally
fell asleep.

ANNIE

My husband and I have fights, like any other couple: about money, about whether we're spending too much time with my family and not enough with his, about whether or not to spank the boys—but we have always gotten along in the bedroom. From the first time I was close to Frank, I couldn't wait to get my hands on him, and feel his hands on me. I loved the muscles of his chest and his legs, the tightly curled hair on his chest and around his penis, the look of our hands entwined, his dark skin against my pale fingers.

That night I got the call from the clinic, saying that I'd been approved as a surrogate, I waited until the boys were sleeping. By nine o'clock they were both dead to the world, full of pizza and worn out from an afternoon of Skee-Ball and table hockey. I lit a candle, zapped the TV into silence, took Frank by the hand, and led him upstairs. In the bedroom he looked around, blinking. The bed was neatly made, the pillows plumped and smooth; the laundry and toys were stacked and folded in their baskets, and I was wearing a tight red Phillies nightshirt that ended about eight inches past my panties. I thought it made me look like a link of chorizo, but it was, I knew, his favorite.

Frank stuffed his hands into the pockets of his work pants and looked me over. "Did you get in another accident?"

"No, silly. I just missed you," I said, not wanting to bring up that I'd only ever been in one accident, and it had happened because someone had parked too close to me at the supermarket. I knelt on the bed, resting my hands on his shoulders, so close that my shirt brushed against his chest. He untied his heavy black shoes, then took me in his arms, nuzzling my neck with his stubbly cheek as I giggled and squirmed against him.

"Well, hello there," he said, brushing his palm against my stiff nipples.

"Hello," I said, and kissed him, first lightly, then more deeply, opening my mouth and feeling his tongue slip inside like it was part of me, like it belonged there. "Hello."

Frank had been a virgin when we'd started going out. I hadn't learned that until later, of course. I'd slept with my first boyfriend, Brian Blundell, when I was fourteen, and then, after Brian dumped me for my friend Laurie Zimmer, I'd slept with Brian's best friend, Fritz, although "slept with" wasn't exactly right, because we'd had sex just once on the basement stairs and I wasn't even sure it counted because I didn't think he'd actually gotten himself inside of me before he finished.

Frank had wanted to wait. He was religious—he and his family were Baptists, and he went to church every Sunday morning and to Youth Fellowship meetings on Wednesday nights, and he'd taken a pledge to stay pure until he got married. His resolve lasted until our fifth date, when we were lying together on the long backseat of his father's car, after forty-five minutes of kissing and grinding, after my bra and his shirt lay in a tangle on the floor and I was too turned on to feel self-conscious about my jiggly thighs or the stretch marks on my breasts. I'd pushed myself upright and straddled him, unzipping his jeans as he tried (not very hard) to push my hands away, and pulled his penis out of his boxer shorts, stroking it gently. Penises were so strange, in my limited experience, ugly, odd-looking, veiny things, but Frank's was smooth and brown, hot-skinned and silky, and it felt just right in my hand, like Goldilocks's bowl of porridge, or the bed she'd eventually settled on: not too hot and not too cold, not too big and not too small. I rubbed it up and down experimentally, tugging the loose skin over the cap. "Oh, Annie," he groaned. "We shouldn't . . ." Then his arms were on my shoulders, and I was on my back, one hand in my purse, groping for the condoms I'd bought that afternoon at the drugstore, just in case.

Seven years later, in our bedroom in the house we'd bought, a room with high ceilings and bare floors and no furniture besides a mattress and the Tupperware bins where we kept our clothes, it was just as thrilling, just as sweet. I knew the place on the small of his back where he liked me to brush my fingertips, and he knew to put his mouth right up against my ear so I could hear his breathing change as his hips sped up, then stuttered to a stop. His sounds, his taste, the feel of his forearms in my hands, his head tucked into the hollow between my neck and shoulders, every inch of him was so familiar and so dear.

When we were done, he fell asleep almost instantly, sprawled facedown, naked on the bed. He had a better body than any of the movie stars in *People,* a muscular back that narrowed to a slender waist, a gorgeously curved bottom. Curled against him, breathing in the scent of his sweat and skin. I let myself doze for a few minutes. Then I settled the comforter over his back and collected my panties and nightshirt from the floor. Frank was so tired these days. He'd work an eight-hour shift at the scanner, examining the X-rays of carry-ons or beckoning travelers through the metal detectors, dealing with people who screamed and cursed and even spat at him, taking out their frustration with the nightmare air travel had become on the most convenient target. After work three days a week, he'd spend three hours more in a classroom, where he was training to do airplane maintenance. Those were union jobs; the pay started at thirty dollars an hour, plus benefits and three weeks of paid vacation. We'd agreed that the time and money he spent was worth it. By the time he graduated the airlines would be hiring again, but it meant that he left the house before seven most mornings, and on nights he had classes he rarely came home before ten.

I crept into the kitchen to empty the dishwasher and surf the Internet, looking at surrogates' stories, pricing home renovations and wall-to-wall carpet and new couches, trying to figure out how to continue the process I'd started upstairs, the marital magic of not only getting Frank to agree to let me be a surrogate but also making him believe the whole thing was his idea.

I thought about it while I drove Spencer to nursery school, while I swept the floors or weeded the garden or folded a load of laundry, imagining the feeling of being someone who could give instead of someone who was taking. I would picture the look of gratitude on the new mother's face as I placed the baby in her arms. *Oh, thank you, Annie, we can never thank you enough.* It would be so different from the look I saw on our pastor's face when I was rummaging through the church swap bins for winter boots or the one I imagined the credit-card representative wearing when I called to explain that our payment would be late again.

For weeks, I'd been working on Frank, but carefully, the way I'd learned to do it. Instead of bombarding him with requests or giving speeches, I'd casually slip something into a conversation: "Did I tell you Dana Swede from Vacation Bible School had a miscarriage? It's her third, poor thing." He'd give me a look and I'd ladle another scoop of tuna casserole onto his plate and tell him I was baking Dana a pie. When the actress from his favorite TV show was on the cover of *People* magazine with her baby twin girls—they'd been carried by a surrogate in Minnesota—I snuck the magazine out of the pediatrician's office and onto our coffee table, where I could be sure he'd see it. When *Good Morn-*

ing America did a piece on military wives making extra money carrying babies, I inched the volume up. When the toilet broke and we had to call the plumber, I allowed myself one small sigh over the bill, and I permitted myself another sigh when the doorknob on the front door came off—again—in my hands, and I'd had to send Frank Junior in through the kitchen window to open the door.

That was Part One of my plan. Part Two took place in the bedroom every night that Frank didn't have class. Instead of collapsing on the couch as soon as I'd gotten the boys down and rinsed their toothpaste out of the sink and re-hung their towels, I'd put on something Frank liked—a pair of lacy panties or a tight tank top, the negligee I'd bought for our honeymoon. I'd light that candle and stay up in bed, waiting. Most nights I didn't have to wait long.

On one Tuesday morning—a week after the *Good Morning America* story—I loaded the dishwasher, turned off the TV, and said casually, without looking at him, "What do you think about it? That surrogacy thing?"

Frank Junior and Spencer were at the table, fighting over the last piece of toast. I put the orange juice back in the fridge, shut the door with my hip, then looked at my husband. His dark-blue shirt, with the TSA patch on the shoulder, was neatly pressed, his shoes were shined, and he was freshly shaved, but he already looked tired. His ID badge was in his pocket. He hated that badge, which let the angriest passengers use his name. It was always the last thing he put on and the first thing he took off. "I don't know. It's interesting."

"They pay a lot. I could look into it. What do you think?"

He looked at me closely. "You want to do that? Have a baby for someone?"

"I don't know. Maybe."

He shrugged. "I don't know. Maybe find out more about it."

"You mean it?"

"Why not?" He frowned at the boys, at Spencer in particular, who had a pink crayon in his hand and was scribbling dreamily in his coloring book. "Sit up straight, men." The two of them stiffened their backs, imitating the posture Frank had brought home from the service. I turned back to the sink. He didn't look happy. I understood why: he wanted to be the one to provide for us, to give us the things we wanted . . . and I suspected that seeing me walking around with my belly all big from another man's baby would bother him, even though there'd be no sex involved, no cheating. But it had been so long since I felt like I was doing my part, and since I didn't feel guilty pulling out my debit card at the grocery store or at Walmart.

"I'll see what I can find out," I said. My hands were cold, the way they got when I was nervous or excited, or when I was telling a lie. My heart was breaking for Frank, but I was also excited, thinking about the money and how we could spend it, imagining, for the hundredth time, the moment of placing the baby into another woman's arms, or even a man's arms, although I doubted that would happen. My cousin Michael was gay, and he and his boyfriend were two of the kindest, gentlest men I knew, but Frank felt differently, thanks to all his years in church hearing about sinful this and sinful that, and I knew not to push my luck. I imagined, too, the look on Nancy's face; the two of us walking together at the Franklin Mills mall, Nancy getting ready to pull out her platinum card as someone we knew from high school spotted us: *Oh, Annie, I heard about what you're doing and I think it's just amazing. So generous.* Maybe I'd take a few college classes, too, show Big Sister that she wasn't the only smart one in the family. Maybe I'd take all of us on vacation, my parents, too, someplace that didn't have a squash court, or maybe we'd stay on-site the next time we went to Disneyland.

I kissed Frank by the door, handing him the lunch I'd packed.

I gathered Spencer in my arms and loaded him into his stroller. He was getting too tall for it, his feet dangling almost to the ground, but he was still too little to manage the trip to the bus stop and back. I helped Frank Junior put on his backpack, then walked both boys down the hill to the bottom of our driveway, where we waited, counting the cars that drove along our quiet street until the school bus wheezed to a stop. Back at home, I put Spencer down in front of *Sesame Street* with a bowl of raisins and pretzels, a sippy cup full of apple juice, and the remote control, which, sad to say, he knew how to work better than I did.

The farmhouse had a little room off the kitchen that had once been a cold pantry. Someday, I'd planned on turning it into an office, with shelves for canned goods and cookbooks and a desk where I could look up recipes. I'd painted the walls a creamy golden-white called Buttermilk, and cut out pictures of built-in desks and refinished flea-market chairs, but that was as far as I'd gotten.

I turned on our computer and browsed around the clinic's website, which I already knew almost by heart. It was full of video links and fancy flash effects, words that came swimming up to the top of the screen like they were surfacing from the bottom of a deep pool. CARING. COMPASSIONATE. DISCREET. The word MONEY never showed up, but *money* was what I sensed. For starters, the clinic looked more like the day spas I saw in magazines than like any doctor's office I'd ever visited. There were bouquets of flowers in the exam rooms, tables draped in real sheets, not the flimsy paper that my doctor's office used. The women in the pictures were nicely dressed—no sweatpants and Phillies shirts for them. All of them were pretty, too, which I guess made sense, because, when you get right down to it, who wants to go through nine months of pregnancy and then hand the baby over to someone who looks worse than you do?

While Spence was singing along with "Elmo's World,"

I called up my application, trying to read it the way a woman looking for a surrogate would. Most of the questions had been fairly straightforward: Did I have a driver's license? Did I work outside the home? Was I married? Happily married?

That one had worried me, because the truth was, Frank and I had hit a rough patch a few years ago, the summer when Spencer was a baby and Frank had gotten furloughed for eight weeks. He got to keep his health benefits but didn't get paid for all that time. At first it had been okay. There was plenty for him to do around the house. He'd set his alarm, same as always, and from seven in the morning until dinnertime he'd be busy, patching cracks in the ceiling, painting the dining-room walls, planing a door that had never closed properly, fitting the bathroom with a new showerhead, pulling the refrigerator out from its spot against the wall and vacuuming the coils clean. He washed and waxed the car, then used Q-tips to clean the air-conditioning vents and even shampooed the carpets. In the afternoons, when Frank Junior woke up from his nap, he'd take him into the backyard and teach him how to throw a football in a spiral.

I loved having him home, and I loved that all the things that had been bothering me for months were finally being taken care of, but it wasn't paying the bills. Finally, after an unpleasant conversation with our credit-card company, Frank and I decided that I should take a job at the new Target that had opened up in Plymouth Meeting, not too far away.

I made sure Spencer, who was four months old, would drink from a bottle, then squeezed myself into a skirt and went to fill out an application. I got hired the same day I went in, and I liked Target fine. The work itself was nothing special—stocking shelves and sweeping floors, cleaning the bathrooms and telling shoppers where to find things—but I liked the people, the jokes we had, how we got to know one another's stories, sharing soda and microwave popcorn in a breakroom with red-

and-white tiled floors and scuffed-up walls and metal lockers for our things. Most of the other employees were women like me, helping out while our men were home, laid off or furloughed or looking for work, but a few of them were college kids home for the summer, and one of them was this guy—really, a boy—named Gabriel. Gabriel was working his way through Penn State. He was tall and pale and lanky, with a narrow face and glasses and long, thick brown hair that he was always flipping off his forehead or shoving behind his ears.

I figured the college kids would keep to themselves and act like the job was beneath them, rolling their eyes at the mothers asking where to find the toilet paper or the mousetraps or the wrapping paper, and it was true that most of them were like that. Cliquey. They'd sit at their own table in the breakroom, just as if we were all still in high school, and bring things like sushi from Whole Foods for dinner, with chopsticks and little packets of soy sauce, but Gabe was always polite. That was the second thing I noticed about him. The first thing was his food. Most of us had regular stuff, sandwiches or leftover casserole or lasagna, but Gabe had interesting things: a tin of oily sardines that he'd pop into his mouth one by one, a chunk of crusty bread, wedges of cheese so stinky that they made everyone wince and crack jokes about smelly feet, sticky dates in a plastic tub, a square of black-flecked brown goo that he told me was truffled pâté and that he ate on a heel of bread, with fig jam smeared on top. "My grandma's French," he said. "We always had weird stuff around the house. I'd bring friends home from school, and instead of having, you know, Oreos and milk or whatever, she'd give us herring."

"Herring's French?" I'd never had French food, except for the one time Frank and I had gone to a fondue restaurant, where for your main course you dipped bread and vegetables into bubbling melted cheese, and then dipped fruit into chocolate for dessert.

He'd shrugged. "Not especially, but my grandma loved herring. I do, too." He'd smiled then, offering me a bite of chicken marinated, he told me, in lemon peel and crushed garlic, which tasted like no chicken I'd ever had before.

Sometimes Gabe sat with the college kids and sometimes he sat with us. He carried lollipops in his pockets and would give them to kids fussing in the shopping carts after asking the moms if it was okay. "That's nice," I said, the first time I saw him do it, and he shrugged, looking a little embarrassed with his hair flopping into his eyes. "I've got two little brothers," he said. "I understand the value of candy."

Gabe always had a book in his pocket and I usually had one tucked into my purse, and at break time we'd slip into the corners to read. After I'd been there for a week, he wandered over, casually, and asked me about my book—a Nora Roberts—and told me about what he was reading, the story of a Russian rapper in New York. "But really," he said, sitting down in the molded plastic chair beside me, "it's about what it means to be an American."

"Huh." I wondered what my book was "really" about—about love, I thought, but I could have been wrong. Maybe if I'd been to college the real story of the book would reveal itself to me, like one of those Magic Eye puzzles where if you stare at it long enough a hidden picture appears. I'd never liked school: all those things like the square of the hypotenuse and the principal exports of Uruguay would, I correctly suspected, have nothing to do with my life after graduation, my life as a wife and a mother. I did all right in my English classes, and I'd always liked to read, but just for the story's sake, for the chance books gave me to visit another world, where everyone was beautiful, where the sex was always amazing, and where, when the telephone rang, it was sometimes a handsome stranger and not the heroine's mortgage company inquiring as to when they could expect that month's check.

"You can read it when I'm done," he said, offering me the book. I shook my head, smiling. "I think I'll stick with Nora." But two days later I found the book in my locker, next to the snapshots of my family that I'd taped to the inside of the door. When I tried to thank him Gabe just shrugged. "You don't have to read it," he said. "No pressure." He held up his hands like a gunfighter showing they were empty, then tucked into his lunch, which was a salad with rice and raw tuna and a dressing he'd made of soy sauce and sesame seeds. Poké salad, he'd told me, and I'd looked it up later online.

I made my way slowly through his book, which was funny in places and slow in others, with long, twisting sentences and sex scenes that were funny and gross at the same time, and I started talking more with Gabe during our breaks. He told me he'd worked at Target ever since he was sixteen. He told me about college, how he planned on taking six years to graduate, then going for a master's degree in hospitality and maybe, someday, opening a restaurant of his own. I told him about my boys, about Frank Junior in particular, how he was smart but a handful, and how his teacher had said, at the parent-teacher conference, that he was an exhausting child. "She wants us to ask his doctor about medication before he starts kindergarten," I said. Gabe's narrow face darkened.

"Don't do that," he told me, raking his fingers through his thick hair, then hitching up his pants. He was so skinny I wasn't quite sure how his jeans managed to stay up at all, and his Target pinny, the one he'd had since he was in high school, was starting to come unraveled. Threads hung all along its seams. I wondered if anyone in his house sewed, if he had a mother or sister who could fix it for him.

"Why not?" I'd already decided on my own that I didn't want Frank Junior taking pills. I'd read some articles online, on websites where mothers debated the pros and cons, and I thought that there was nothing wrong with my son except that he was a little boy with a lot of energy who hadn't learned that he didn't need to say, or shout, every thought that came into his head—but I wanted to hear Gabe's opinion.

Gabe rocked back on the heels of his high-tops and gave me a speech about the dangers of doping little kids, how the purpose of the American educational system wasn't learning but conformity.

"What do you mean?"

He paused, flipping his hair around. "Well, 'conformity' is making everyone act and think like everyone else."

I nodded, even though I knew what the word meant. He went on, talking about how the drugs were designed to make it easier for teachers, not better for the children. Then he stopped, midsentence, looking embarrassed. "But what do I know?" he asked. "Like I've got kids."

"No," I told him. "This is good." I imagined what he must have looked like when he was Frank Junior's age. Probably his mother had kept his hair cut short, but I suspected that he'd dressed about the same way he did now, in jeans and sneakers and a T-shirt, only without the Target pinny on top.

Gabe had been surprised to learn that I was only twenty-two. "I thought you were older," he said, then quickly added, "Not that you look old."

"Don't worry," I told him. The truth was I felt older than my years, like I'd been a wife and a mother forever.

Most days I drove to work, but one night Frank dropped me off, keeping the car so he could take the boys to the free concert downtown that night. At the end of my shift I went outside to wait for the bus, and Gabe, driving by in his car, spotted me.

"You need a ride?"

"Oh, no. I'm going to take the bus."

"I'll wait with you."

He parked the car and jogged through the lot, back to me.

"You don't have to do this. I'm fine."

"Don't worry about it," he told me. "I could use the fresh air." We looked at each other, both of us knowing that the air in the parking lot wasn't particularly fresh. It had been in the nineties for three days straight. The bus stop smelled like baking tar and car exhaust, and the cigarettes the workers at Target and Marshalls and the Pancake Barn around the corner would sneak out the back doors to smoke. A humid breeze lifted my hair off my neck. Thunder rumbled in the distance; heat lightning crackled in the sky. I hoped it wouldn't rain—the last time there was a storm, Frank and I had woken up to puddles in the basement and blistered paint on the ceilings, and I'd spent all morning running around the house with empty plastic containers, putting them under the leaks so the floors wouldn't be ruined, too.

"Did you ever think about going to college?" Gabe asked.

I shook my head, glad that he couldn't see me blushing in the dark. It was like asking "Did you ever think about going to the moon?" I hadn't been a great student, and, by the time high school was over, I'd been so in love that the only thing I'd wanted to be was Frank's wife. That was what the women I knew did—they got married and got jobs you didn't need a degree to have, and they worked in between children, or when their husbands couldn't, or didn't. The only reason my sister had been any different was that she'd been too fat and too unpleasant for any boy to want her.

"You should think about it," Gabe said. "You're smart. And there's online classes."

This was something I'd considered. I couldn't imagine going to college: getting dressed, driving my car to the city, sitting in a lecture hall with all those young girls and boys—but I could do things online. I did things online already: shopping, reading the news and gossip websites, playing games on Facebook, downloading coupons, and, lately, looking things up, articles Gabe had mentioned or reviews of the books he'd given me or words he'd used that I didn't know. He'd always tell me a definition, but it embarrassed him, so I'd started to just pretend that I knew what all his big words meant, and write them down so I could look them up later: *Modified. Discordant. Ethereal.*

"How do you take a class online?" I asked, and he started to tell me. He had a book, *The Wind-Up Bird Chronicle,* in one hand and was gesturing with the other, his face excited beneath the glow of the streetlamp. He pulled a piece of paper out of his pocket, a receipt from the soda and three slices of pizza he'd bought at the snack bar for lunch, and was writing down the address of Temple's website. That was when Frank pulled up to the curb. His mother had stopped by after Bible study, and he'd gotten her to stay with the kids so he could come take me home.

I don't know what he saw, or what he thought he saw. Gabe and I weren't doing anything but talking, me in old jeans and sneakers and a no-color cotton top with my pinny balled up in my purse, not touching at all . . . but I could tell from the way Frank's jaw bunched up that he must have imagined seeing something.

He didn't say a word after I climbed into the passenger's seat, but his hands were tight on the wheel and his back was perfectly straight, not even touching the seat. I remembered after the first time we'd had sex, lying with my head against his chest, breathing in the smell of his skin, feeling completely content. He'd looked at me from under his long lashes, and I thought he'd tell me that he loved me. Instead, he'd said, in a casual, almost neutral voice, "You weren't a virgin."

I'd set one hand on his chest and pushed myself up. "What?"

I asked him. "Why do you ask? Is it . . . do you think that's bad?" He'd waited a moment before answering, "It is what it is." That was all the discussion we'd ever had on the matter, but I thought I could hear what he hadn't said: that I'd had other boys while he'd been a virgin; that I'd been the one who'd unzipped his pants and I'd been the one with the condoms.

That night, with the Target parking lot getting smaller in the truck's rearview mirror and Frank's eyes fixed on the road, I knew better than to try to explain myself. Anything I said would only make me sound guilty, and I had nothing to be guilty about. I pressed my lips together, biting back the angry words I imagined: *Yes! Yes! It's exactly what you think! Probably what you've been thinking all along!*

Frank never said a word about it, not on the ride home, not that night or after. At work the next day, Gabe was friendly, like always, but I was careful not to borrow any more of his books or taste any more of his food, and to make sure that the next time I went to the bus stop, I went alone. I didn't know whether he'd meant anything more than just friendliness, whether he liked me that way. It hardly seemed possible. He was a college boy, soon to be a graduate student, and I was married and a mother of two. In my jeans and work sneakers, with my hair in a careless ponytail, with not a lick of makeup on my face, heavier than I wanted to be after the babies and years of nibbling chicken nuggets and goldfish crackers off Frank Junior's plate, I was hardly what the kids called a MILF. But maybe, I thought, remembering the way his face came alive when he was talking about a book he liked, the way his eyes lit up and his hands moved in the air. Maybe Gabe really did think of me that way. Maybe, in another world, we could have been boyfriend and girlfriend.

I got my paycheck on Tuesday, five days after Frank had seen Gabe and I waiting together at the bus stop. That night Frank said, "I think we'll be okay for the rest of the summer." I told him that that would be fine, and gave my notice over the phone the next morning. "We're sorry to lose you," my supervisor said, and sounded like she meant it . . . and that was that. Why go looking for trouble, with a little boy and a new baby at home, and a husband who loved me?

I heard the music that told me *Sesame Street* was ending, and I turned away from my computer, looking at Spencer, still cross-legged on the floor, one hand lifting pretzels into his crumb-ringed mouth, his eyes wide, gazing at the screen. The couch cushions were shiny in their centers, the curtains dingy in the sunlight, the screen of the TV set streaked with fingerprints, even though I'd Windexed it the night before. *Please, God,* I thought. *Please, let some woman pick me.* Then I got up, lifted my little boy in my arms, and carried him to the kitchen, where he could play with the pots and pans while I cleaned, and dreamed.

BETTINA

When I thought of the words *private investigator*, a certain image came to mind—a rumpled, world-weary man in a suit and a fedora, feet on a scarred wooden desk, in an office wreathed in cigarette smoke. I pictured a name in gold leaf on a frosted-glass door, a heavy glass ashtray, a man who'd identify women—*dames*—exclusively by their hair color: *The brunette. The redhead. The blonde.*

My detective was different. I'd found her by Googling Manhattan private detectives who specialized in what they called "marital matters," reading online reviews. It made me feel like I was taking a baby step out of my dutiful life—the tasteful, classic clothes, the art history degree, the job as a junior appraiser at Kohler's, an auction house that was less well known (and, its loyalists boasted, even more exclusive) than Christie's or Sotheby's. My life had been long on ease and comfort, filled with fancy vacations, many of them spent at Caribbean resorts while my father paced the beach, barking into his cell phone and looking for the best reception.

When my appointment finally arrived, I was, perhaps, more excited than I should have been, even though the private investigator's office was on the thirtieth floor of a featureless high-rise in midtown, which put my dreams of gold leaf and pebbled glass to rest. The office had a small NO SMOKING plaque by the front door and just two last names—KLEIN and SEGAL, in sans serif capital letters—beside it. The waiting room could have belonged to any dentist or doctor or therapist, with pale-brown couches and beige carpet, a glass-and-iron coffee table stacked with magazines—*Newsweek* and *Time,* along with the week's tabloids—and a water cooler that let out the occasional burble in the corner. I gave the receptionist my name, sat down on the couch, my legs, in sheer hose, crossed at the ankle, and pinched the pleats of my skirt between my thumb and forefinger, making sure each one was smooth.

Church lady! a guy in college had called me one night when I'd allowed my roommates to coax me out of the room and to a party in a neighboring dorm. It was true that I dressed far more conservatively than most of my classmates: after a lifetime in the kilts and knee socks of my Upper East Side all-girls' school, I'd never felt like myself in pants. Besides, I had narrow shoulders and tended to carry my weight in my hips and thighs, so jeans gave me the appearance of a bowling pin . . . and after seeing my mother traipsing around in belly-baring yoga pants and low-waisted double-dyed skinny jeans, I'd only wanted to cling to my skirts even more tightly. The summer before my senior year of high school, when I'd been choosing colleges, I'd actually checked to see if there was such a thing as a non-military school that had uniforms. If I could have found such a place, I would have happily attended.

"It'll be fun!" my roommate, Vanessa, had told me, slipping into her own tight low-riding jeans and the inevitable silk tank top, with a down coat on top, because it was January and freezing. I let her drag me along, in my skirt and tights, my sweater set and my loafers, even though I truly didn't see the point of parties. If I wanted to be hot and uncomfortable in the presence of drunk people yelling at one another, it would be easy enough to arrange those conditions, but why would I ever want to?

In the dorm room, I'd stood in the corner next to the stereo speakers, sneaking glances at my watch and wondering how soon I could feign a headache and get back to my room. There was a girl I recognized from my art history seminar lying on her back on one of the desks, giggling as a boy poured tequila into her navel, then bent down to slurp it out. Maybe it was supposed to be sexy, but all I could think was *germs!* and *disease!* and *belly-button lint!* At another desk, a half dozen of my classmates stood in front of a computer, watching porn. That was a big thing at Vassar: girls watching dirty movies with their boyfriends to show that they were progressive and evolved. I turned away as, onscreen, a naked man with a six-pack and tribal tattoos pulled his penis out of the woman he'd been hunched over and smacked it, over and over, into her cheeks.

I must have been making a face, because when I looked up, a guy I didn't know was staring at me.

"Can I help you?" I asked.

He pointed. "Church lady!" he hollered. His friends started laughing, and then the girl with tequila all over her belly sat up and started laughing, too. Even after the guy who'd first said it had wandered away, probably to poop into the host's rice cooker, then post a picture on Facebook, people were still saying it and laughing. Of course, Vanessa had overheard, and she'd hustled me over to the porn computer so she could show me YouTube videos of a man dressed as a woman with a sour face and a blue tweed suit and eyeglasses on a chain acting offended about everything. The guy had undoubtedly meant it as a devastating insult. I was not insulted. Given a choice between being a church lady or one of my female classmates who'd have to wake up the next morning wondering whether her nipples were now online, I'd take the church lady every time.

"Bettina Croft?"

I got to my feet. A woman was standing in the doorway of an office. Through the open door I could see bright art on the walls, and a dozen framed photographs on a side table. The woman had a friendly-looking face, brown hair in a ponytail, and a white short-sleeved T-shirt on top of a pair of loose-fitting cropped linen pants the color of raspberries. She wore flip-flops and a necklace of brightly colored glass beads as her only accessory. "Pleasure to meet you," she said, shaking my hand and leading me inside. "Now. Before we get started, one quick question, and you have to tell me the truth," she said, after I'd taken the chair across from her desk and settled my purse beside me. "Are these pajamas?" She stood, pointing at her pants. I stared.

"Excuse me?"

"I know you're not here to talk about my pants," she said. "We'll get started in a sec. It's just, I'm so distracted! I bought them—it was this ungodly hot day, and everything was at the dry cleaner's, so I was wearing a wool skirt, and I thought I was going to melt, so I just ran in and grabbed them off the rack. They're really comfortable, and I liked them so much I went on-line to buy another pair, and they were listed under 'loungewear' instead of pants, and I'm worried that I'm actually out in public in my PJs." She made a face. "If that's true, my partner will kill me. Janie's *stylish*," she said. "She finds me very frustrating."

I examined the pants, with their elastic waist and baggy fit, wondering if I should have requested Segal instead of Klein. "They look like regular pants to me." In fact, the pants looked way too casual for the office, better suited to a picnic or a trip to the beach. There was no official dress code at Kohler's, but all the women wore skirts and dresses. You could wear pants if they were part of a suit and if you paired them with heels and the right accessories, and, even then, you couldn't wear them very often before people would start to talk.

But maybe Kate Klein was working undercover, at a pre-school or someplace like that. She smelled sweet in a familiar, evocative way, and there was a dab of something golden-brown on the hem of her shirt.

"Applesauce," she said when she noticed my stare, pouring us both glasses of water from a pitcher filled with ice and sliced lemons that sat on a table against her wall, next to potted African violets. "Kids," she said, pointing toward all those framed photographs. I saw a pair of identical twin boys and an older girl with hair the same color as Kate's, maybe as young as ten or as old as fourteen. It was hard for me to guess. I didn't spend much time around children.

Kate sat down on a chenille-covered couch thick with throw pillows, with a blanket hanging over the back. "So, Ms. Croft. Tell me what I can do for you."

"My father," I began. On the subway ride over I'd thought about how to most concisely express my problem. "He's recently remarried."

Kate Klein produced a legal pad and a ballpoint pen. Her expression was focused; her posture suggested that, in spite of her casual clothes and her comfortable couch, she was listening hard. "And you'd like us to look into his new wife. Is there anything particular that concerns you?"

"Well, her name, for starters. India." I heard the scorn in my voice.

Kate lifted her eyebrows. "Maybe her parents were *Gone With the Wind* fans?"

I sipped my water and thought of my father's bride standing at the sink at the house in Bridgehampton, washing dishes like she did it all the time, and how everything about her was fake. A few weeks ago, under the guise of looking up horoscopes on the Internet, I'd asked India the year of her birth and detected—or thought I had—a brief flutter of hesitation before she came up with a date.

Kate leaned forward with her elbows on her folded knees. "You don't think your father might have done his own check? From what I've seen of him, he strikes me as a pretty savvy guy."

"In business, maybe. But this . . . my mom left him, which was difficult." I felt the familiar mixture of sorrow at my mother's departure and fury at her for leaving rise up inside me like acid indigestion, along with shame for having to say any of this out loud.

"Do they have a prenup?" Kate's head was bent, and she was writing on her legal pad.

"Yes," I said. I'd asked my father, and he'd looked at me with an uncharacteristically sharp expression. *Why do you ask?* he'd said.

Just curious, I'd told him. Later, when he and India had gone out to dinner, I'd found the document in my father's safe, behind a Rothko lithograph in his home office—the code, I knew, was Trey's birthday, then Tommy's, then mine. According to the document, in the event of a separation India would receive a million dollars for every year she was married to my father for the first five years, then two million a year up to ten years, then three million a year. If she had a baby, she'd leave the marriage with thirty million dollars, and child support up to thirty thousand dollars a month, plus school tuition at mutually agreed-upon institutions until the baby turned eighteen. That was what worried me most, even though I figured India was too old and too skinny to get her period, let alone get pregnant. A baby would make her rich, really rich, and I couldn't imagine her not wanting to grab at that chance, to have a baby, hit the jackpot, break my father's heart, and go off to find a guy her own age, whatever that age really was.

Kate nodded, asking more questions about India—her age, date of birth, her job, and where she'd come from—before clicking her pen and looking at me. "Did you bring a picture?"

I pulled a snapshot out of my purse. I'd expected the wedding to be a gaudy, overblown affair, three hundred guests and half a dozen bridesmaids, all featured in the Vows column in the Sunday *Times*, but I had to admit that India had done it nicely. They'd said their vows in front of just forty people, on a Sunday morning, in one of the St. Regis's smaller ballrooms. Afterward there'd been a cocktail party with sushi stations and dim sum, a champagne toast, and a small, dense chocolate wedding cake with pale-pink fondant icing and praline frosting underneath. In the photograph I handed to Kate, India was smiling, wearing a knee-length white silk dress, pale golden shoes, and a single apricot rosebud tucked behind her ear. "And I've got these," I said, handing Kate a folder of printouts from when India had been in the news in connection with her PR work: the statements she'd given on behalf of a client who'd drunkenly backed her Prius into an SUV, then called the other driver white trash before racing through the parking lot and off into the night ("Miss Lowry would never use such language, and we fully expect her to be exonerated," India had said); the quote she'd given while turning away a reporter at the gates of a magazine-launch party on Independence Island ("'Invitation-only,' said Independence's publicist, glam stormtrooper India Bishop").

Kate examined each piece of paper, one finger tapping gently at her chin as she looked over the picture, the clippings, the sheet I'd typed up with the words BIOGRAPHICAL DATA centered at the top, the photocopy of India's driver's license that

I'd made after sliding it out of her purse while she was in what had been my mother's dressing room, where the masseuse who came twice a week kept a folding table. Kate kicked off her flip-flops, turned to a fresh page in her notebook, and then leaned forward.

"When I start these types of investigations, I always tell my clients to be careful what they wish for," she began. "There's a few possibilities I can see. One is, we could find out that this woman is exactly who she says she is."

"She's not," I said.

"Or we find out that it's all a lie—her name, her age, where she says she's from and what she says she's done. We could learn that she's really a lesbian whose three previous husbands all died under mysterious circumstances and that she'd been stalking your father for years before she finally got her hooks into him."

I found myself nodding unconsciously. That was more like it.

"We'll build a dossier—pictures, documents, computer files, e-mails—but you should be prepared for the possibility that your father will shoot the messenger." I must have looked like I didn't understand, because she continued, "He could get mad at you, not at India."

"Maybe," I said. My fingers had gone to my pleats again. I made myself fold my hands in my lap. It was hard to imagine my father getting mad at me, if I'd be the one to save him from heartbreak, not to mention public humiliation. If India left, it would be in the papers, and people would laugh, they way they'd probably been laughing when my mother had run off with the Baba. There'd been snarky blind items on the gossip websites ("WHICH zabillionaire's better half has ditched spawn and hubby and high-tailed it to New Me-hee-co in the company of her guru, an extremely flexible *yogini* who's been helping her unblock her chakras, if you know what we mean, and we think you do?"). I would do whatever I could to spare my father that laughter . . . and, maybe, spare myself another year like the one I'd endured after my mother had left. I'd keep him safe, and keep my family's fortune intact.

"Can I ask," Kate said, running her fingers through the fringe of the blanket that hung over the back of the couch, "why you're doing this?"

I didn't answer. Of course I couldn't tell her how awful it had been after my mother took off. I'd just met her, she hadn't signed a confidentiality agreement, and I'd never told anyone what that year had been like. But before I had a chance to say anything, the door swung open and a tiny woman balanced on black leather booties shaped to look like horse's hooves came stomping into the office. She wore a green leather miniskirt, black lace leggings, and a bottle-green velvet blazer. Her hair was piled on top of her head, and her eyes were shadowed with sparkling silver powder.

"Oh, Jesus," said the hoof-footed woman, narrowing her eyes at Kate. "Did you wear your pajamas to work again?"

"They're not," Kate said, swinging her legs onto the floor and sliding her flip-flops onto her feet. "I asked."

"Whatever they are, they're about one step up from sweat-pants," said the lady, pulling a bottle of water out of her fringed leather hobo bag. A rabbit's foot, dyed green, was clipped to its strap. She held out her hand to me. "Janie Segal."

"Of the carpet Segals," said Kate. "My partner."

"Could you not tell people that?" said Janie. "Not when you're dressed as a homeless person. It doesn't reflect well on my taste."

"I'm Bettina Croft," I said, feeling a little dizzy.

Janie lifted her arched eyebrows. "Of the Marcus Crofts?"

She raised her fist. I'd seen enough TV to know to bump it lightly with my own. "Respect."

"Bettina is a client," said Kate, looking flustered.

"Cool," said Janie, getting up. "Holler if you need me. Actually, don't holler. I'm going to have a disco nap."

She trit-trotted away. The heels on her boots narrowed until the part that actually bore her weight was barely the thickness of a sewing needle. Amazing. "Janie works nights," said Kate, sliding into the rolling chair behind her desk.

"Ah," I said.

"Back to business." Kate pulled a contract out of a desk drawer, and I skimmed it, then took out my checkbook and glanced at my watch. They gave associates an hour for lunch at Kohler's, and while I was confident that my bosses would indulge me if I was ten or fifteen minutes late, I didn't like to take advantage. The only reason I'd gotten the job, I was sure, was because my mother had used Kohler's to sell some of her things before moving to the ashram: they'd handled the auction of her pearls and her cocktail rings and the little Monet, a painting of a pond with lilies washed in lemony sunlight, which my dad had given her as a tenth-anniversary gift. There'd been two hundred applicants for my entry-level job, my supervisor had told me, and that was without Kohler's even advertising anywhere, just word of mouth. I wasn't sure if her intention was to make me work harder, but that's what I'd done. Most mornings, I was the first one into the Crypt, a windowless chamber filled with reference books, jeweler's loupes, and special raking lamps where the junior appraisers did the preliminary evaluations of lots of coins or jewelry collections or paintings we might take on for auction. I didn't want anyone thinking that I was spoiled or entitled.

"Well, let's get down to it," said Kate. "We'll see what we can see. But meanwhile—and this is none of my business, but

I give all my clients this speech anyhow—you should be thinking about what you're going to do with the information."

I nodded, but of course I'd already made up my mind. I would find out the truth—that India wasn't really named India; that she wasn't really thirty-eight, that she'd probably never been to college and that maybe she'd been married before. Maybe she even had children, starter kids she'd pawned off on someone else so that she could present herself as young and fresh and untainted. I would give my father the facts, and he would, gently but firmly, send India away. Then maybe someday there'd be a knock on the door, and my mother would be there, smelling of patchouli and musk, her feet bare, her hair gray and her eyes soft and regretful. *I've made a terrible mistake,* she'd say . . . and my father would open the door and let her in.

I walked back to work, through the soft spring afternoon, and bought lunch from a cart on Forty-eighth Street. "Pretty lady," said the vendor, scooping the hot dog out of the vat of steaming water.

"Thank you," I said, feeling myself blush. I'd never learned how to take a compliment, as my mother had more than once pointed out, and I wasn't pretty. I wasn't fat, precisely, but I was flat-chested and full-hipped, fifteen or twenty pounds more than what I thought I should weigh. I had nice skin that tanned easily, and all the pieces of my face were fine on their own—my nose, not too big; my eyes, a pretty hazel—but together, they added up to something less than beauty. My best feature was my hair, thick and glossy, somewhere between red and chestnut, that hadn't been cut since I'd been in high school. From the back, at certain angles, I could look nice, but from the front, I had problems. My teeth were too big. Either that or my lips were too thin, or my gums were abnormally large, or something . . .

"Miss?" The cart guy was brandishing my dog. "Ketchup? Mustard?"

I shook my head and paid him, putting my change in my pocket and stepping into the air-conditioned, church-like hush of Kohler's marble-floored, chandelier-lit lobby. I'd done what I could—told my story, paid my retainer. Now I'd have to wait and see.

INDIA

The last man I'd loved before Marcus was a guy named Kevin. I was living in Los Angeles when I met him. I was twenty-three and had been trying to make it as an actress for four years. I had had more or less concluded that my future might hold many things, but superstardom on screens big or small was not among them.

I wasn't great, but I'd been good enough to land a manager, a man named Travis Martin. He had olive skin and bristling eyebrows and eyes so brown they were almost black. I suspected that his name was something else, something more ethnic, but I never asked. Travis tried to get me actual paying roles. He also got me bigger boobs and a slightly smaller nose.

"No offense—I think they're adorable," he'd said, eyeing my breasts the same way a housewife might consider the chickens at the market as she put dinner together in her head. "But if you want to work . . ." He didn't even bother saying the rest. I didn't have the thousands of dollars surgery would require, and I told him so. He said he'd loan me the money, and he'd take a percentage of my checks when I started working, that it was an investment that would end up paying for itself. So I'd gone into the hospital and come out with breasts the size of grapefruits, two black eyes, and a bandage over my nose that nobody in my

West Hollywood neighborhood looked at twice. The bruises had faded, and my breasts sat high and firm on my chest, but the work hadn't come. I could sing well enough; I was a decent actress, but I lacked that special something, that gloss, that glow, that propelled an infinitesimal handful of girls each year from the open calls and go-sees to bit parts to big parts to walks down the red carpet during awards season (and then, typically, to liaisons with all the wrong men and a stint or two in rehab, but that wasn't the part I cared about back then).

When I failed to land speaking roles, Travis got me work doing background, standing in or body doubling, along with jobs that were acting only insofar as they involved costumes. I worked for three years at a real-estate office's annual Oktoberfest, dressed in a dirndl and black leather boots, pouring beer and passing platters of schnitzel and bratwurst from eight o'clock at night until two in the morning. The only acting I had to do was acting like I didn't mind when the real-estate agents with gelled hair and gold chains would grab my ass or ask me to sing "Edelweiss."

It was two a.m. the third year I worked the party, and I was thinking of nothing except counting my tips (as the night went on, men had stuffed bills into my frilly garter belts), unzipping my boots, and going home for a long, hot shower, when the cops rolled in, lights blaring, paddy wagons parked outside. The story, which I learned later that night, in jail, was that a few of the girls, like me, had come from legitimate talent-management companies, while the rest were in the employ of a soon-to-be-notorious Beverly Hills madam and had discreetly made themselves available for fun and games in a vacant three-bedroom suite.

Travis showed up with bail money, and I was released after none of the men said they'd slept with me and Travis provided W-2s to show that I really did work as an actress. We collected my belongings, my wallet and my watch, and he took me to breakfast at the Griddle, apologizing as I glared at him between gulps of fresh-squeezed orange juice and a stack of syrup-soaked pancakes. "I had no idea, Samantha," he said, gazing at me earnestly and maybe hoping I wouldn't notice that he had the same sculpted hair and heavy cologne as the real-estate agents at the party . . . the men who, I'd heard from one of the girls in the holding cell, had paid to be fellated while balancing ashtrays on the girl's head so they wouldn't have to set down their hand-rolled cigars for the act.

"It's India," I reminded him. I'd had it legally changed right after my breasts healed. I took one last bite, set my crumpled paper napkin on top of my sticky plate, and pushed it away. "No offense, Travis, but I think I need another manager."

His fleshy face hardened. "Wait, wait. Let's not be hasty here. You still owe me."

"And I'll pay you," I told him. "But I can't work with you anymore."

I got Kevin's name from a friend of a friend of a girl I knew, someone who'd actually gotten cast in a network pilot. "He's a baby agent," she'd confided. I said that didn't matter. Better a baby agent than an almost pimp.

Kevin had an office in a glass-and-marble tower in Century City. He'd gone to Rice, then moved to California and worked his way up from the mailroom at one of the big talent agencies in town. He was just signing his first clients: potty-mouthed comics who barely looked old enough to have learned the curse words they spewed onstage, wannabe starlets and fresh-off-the-bus singers and geeky fanboys who just knew they were destined to be the next George Lucas or Steven Spielberg, mostly because their mothers had told them so.

Kevin wasn't tall, maybe an inch or two more than my five foot six, with narrow shoulders and delicate wrists and hands. His clothes—sharply creased jeans and a checkered blue-and-white button-down shirt, a black leather belt with a silver buckle and black leather cowboy boots—were so well kept that they looked brand-new. He was losing his light-brown hair but not making a big deal about it, not attempting a comb-over or hiding beneath a baseball cap, and there was something about him, the way he looked at you when you talked, leaning close like it would hurt him to miss a word, that made you feel special.

He was a good listener, which was important for his line of work: after four years in Los Angeles I'd figured out that performers were black holes of neediness. Actors (I included myself in this tally, but at least I had good reasons to be needy) wanted to talk mostly about themselves, and they wanted you to listen, and if Kevin was prepared to do this—quietly, politely, intensely—then he'd be a success.

"Can you take me on?" I asked. He looked at my list of credits—scanty and padded, like my breasts before I'd had the work done—then gave me a look of earnest regret and shook his head. I wasn't surprised. It was one thing to be nineteen, new in town and full of promise, but at twenty-three, if you hadn't landed so much as a line and you'd spent four years trying, your prospects and potential had diminished considerably.

"I can't offer you representation. However . . ." And he smiled, a charming grin that lit his face. "I'd love to take you to dinner."

I figured I'd date him casually, just for fun . . . a sport-fuck, as my roommate, Terri, would say, while I tried to find another agent who could get me the kind of job that meant I didn't have to waitress, or temp, or be part of crowd scenes on cop shows, or spend all day on a gurney as an extra on *ER*. But then I learned that Kevin came from money. Big old family money, Houston oil money, the kind of money that meant that the art museum in town was named after your grandfather and your father had inherited one of the most legendary privately owned art collections in the world. It didn't take long for me to abandon my dreams of stardom and decide to dream of becoming Kevin's trophy wife instead.

Kevin lived with his brother, Carlton, who worked as an art broker. The brothers hadn't used family connections to get their jobs, but they weren't above using their trust funds to go in together on a spectacular penthouse apartment in an old Art Deco apartment building on Wilshire Boulevard in Koreatown. The apartment spanned the top floor of the twelve-story building. A fountain, with mosaic mermaids cavorting on its sides, splashed in the building's tiled lobby, where a sad-eyed, soft-spoken Dominican man sat watching the security cameras. The boys' place was enormous, with soaring, mostly empty white walls, high-ceilinged rooms with elaborate crown moldings, and all the latest electronics.

Each brother had his own wing: bedroom, bathroom, office. The two of them shared the kitchen, where very little cooking went on, and the den, where the wet bar got a lot of use, where Nintendo was played and the occasional bong was fired up on the weekends. Carl liked to party—sometimes I'd be in the kitchen in the morning, making Kevin a protein smoothie, watching as the parade of the Young and the Panty-less proceeded from Carlton's bedroom to the elevator. Kevin was more ambitious than his brother, and his late nights were all work-related. He would put in a full day at the agency, trying to get his writing clients gigs on sitcoms or doing punch-up on movies in production, trying to get his actors auditions and his singers' demo tapes into the right hands. Then he'd grab a quick bite, usually a bunless burger or a bowl of turkey chili somewhere like Hugo's or the Urth Caffé, and head out to a club to hear a comic or a band, a showcase or a play, to check out new actors or support the ones he'd already signed.

After realizing what Kevin was, and what an association with him could lead to, I'd slowly tapered off on the auditions, redone my résumé, and landed an entry-level job at a public-relations firm that managed musicians and movie stars. Some nights after work I'd join Kevin, picking my way across the darkness of a tiny theater or perching on a folding chair in a high-school classroom or church basement for a performance of *Equus* or a night of Tennessee Williams monologues.

Work kept me busy, but my real job was Kevin, and my impromptu, ongoing audition for the role of Kevin's wife.

This required editing my past. I made myself a year younger, reasoning that younger was always better and it was never too early to start. I told him I'd done two years of college before making the trip to Los Angeles. I doled out parts of my true story: that my mother had given birth to me before she'd finished high school, that my grandparents had raised me, that they were now very old and in assisted living, that my mother had remarried and that she and I didn't see each other much. Kevin raised his eyebrows, pinning me with his gaze, but I'd learned his tricks by then and knew that he could feign absolute interest while mentally choosing his five favorite Celtics or deciding whether he'd have the sautéed spinach or the quinoa on his pick-a-plate at Hugo's.

He brought me home to Texas for Christmas the first year we dated. I met two more brothers, one in boarding school and one in college; a cowboy-booted father; and a brittle blond mom who worked as a decorator and did ninety minutes of step aerobics every day. Kevin's father, red-faced and beer-gutted, had grabbed my boob after one eggnog-heavy evening, but his family seemed to accept me as the kind of girl Kevin would inevitably end up with: sweet and pretty, with a job that she'd be happy to abandon after the first baby came along.

For three years I was a rich man's girlfriend, with everything that meant: weekend jaunts to Napa Valley with Carl and whatever girl he was seeing, wine tastings and afternoons lolling in hot springs; courtside seats at sporting events; fine wine, fancy food, four-star hotels.

True, being Kevin's girlfriend, with an eye on being his wife, required every bit of the physical effort I'd put into being an actress. I'd work out on the Nautilus machines at my gym, then jog through Runyon Canyon or put in five miles on the treadmill. The upkeep was both painful and, on my salary, prohibitively expensive, especially since I was still paying Travis back. But it was all necessary: the highlights, the bikini waxes, the weekly manicures and biweekly pedicures, the haircuts and the tan, the lingerie and shoes and clothing, the constant diet It was an investment, I told myself, sliding my credit card across the hair or tanning salon's counter, writing the checks. An investment in my future.

One night, three years after we'd met, Kevin came home at six o'clock, which was unusual. We weren't officially living together then, but I spent five nights of every week at his house, using my own apartment mostly as a glorified closet. I was in Kevin's kitchen, still in the bike shorts and running bra I'd worn to the gym, running a sponge dreamily over the marble countertops, imagining that all of this was mine, when he came through the door, whistling. He'd been away for five days, first at some kind of fraternity reunion back in Houston, then off to Vegas, where a client was opening for Jay Leno. We'd talked on the phone a little, but now he didn't seem happy to see me. "Oh," he said, blinking like he didn't recognize me. "Oh, hey."

I felt my hands go cold. I knew what "Oh, hey" meant. I'd heard him say it on the phone to clients he'd been ducking, in person to sweaty comedians and bad-breathed screenwriters he wasn't going to take on, or was getting ready to drop. The song he'd been whistling on his way through the door was "Hey Jealousy." This wasn't good.

To his credit, he didn't break up with me over the phone, any more than he'd pretended he'd wanted to represent me just to get into my pants. He walked right up to me, took my cold hands in his, looked me in the eye with his I'm-listening face and said, "I think we should take a break."

What followed was predictable. I asked if there was someone else. He denied it. He asked if we could still be friends. I told him to go to hell. Then I dramatically crammed all of my possessions (and a few things of his that I thought he wouldn't miss) into a half-dozen trash bags and dragged them to the elevator, then into the Corolla I'd had for years and kept parked next to Kevin's Audi. "Hold on," he said, following me into the underground parking lot and watching as I slung the bags into the trunk. "It doesn't have to be like this. Come on, Indie. We're probably going to see each other around. We should at least be friends."

I spun around on one sneakered foot, so furious it was all I could do to keep from hitting him. He'd wasted my time, the best years of my life. I would never be thinner or prettier than I was at that very moment. My face, my body, my youth—these were my commodities, and he'd wasted them . . . or, rather, I'd been dumb enough to squander them on him. "You're wrong," I said. "You're never going to see me again."

I guess I went a little crazy then, the way you can go crazy only if you're young and female and living in Los Angeles, where there's an entire world of medical professionals dedicated to making you look even better, even younger, when you could fill out a bunch of applications and have a fistful of new credit cards in less than a week. Using these new cards, not letting myself think about how I'd pay off their balances, I had my hair color switched from blond to a rich, glossy chestnut, shot through with strands of copper and gold. A little liposuction came next, because no matter how hard I'd worked, I'd never been able to rid myself of the jiggle on my inner thighs, the bit of back fat that bulged over the top of my low-riding jeans. From there, it was an easy step to Botox for my brow and fillers for my cheekbones, injections that would subtly reshape my face, turning me into a pretty stranger, and to implants a cup size bigger than the ones I'd initially picked.

I woke up in the recovery room, on a hospital bed, alone, with an IV needle stuck into the back of my hand, in a room with tiled floors and drab green walls that smelled of disinfectant. Tears trickled down my swollen cheeks. My forehead stung from the needles; my torso and thighs felt like an entire football team had been kicking them. The anesthesia had left me queasy. When it wore off I knew I'd be starving. I hadn't eaten the day of the operation, and I'd been dieting for the month before; the looser my skin, the doctors had said, the easier it would be for them to suck out the most fat.

A nurse asked how I was feeling and helped me to sit up. A while later, Dr. Perez came in to see me. He touched me gently—my jaw, my nose, my cheekbones, tapping and prodding, murmuring to himself, before pulling open my gown. I'd been bandaged, bound from my breasts to just above my knees, in the stretchy bodysuit that I would wear for the next two weeks. "No mirrors yet," he cautioned, and I smiled, even though it hurt, imagining the state my face was in. When I'd healed, I looked just the way I'd hoped: glamorous, quietly sexy, with full lips that fell naturally into a pout and a nose that seemed made to turn skyward.

I spent three months recovering. When I told my boss I was moving to New York she sighed, scratched with her capped Montblanc pen underneath the wig she'd worn since her chemo and promised me a job in the firm's Manhattan office. After eight years in New York, years of handling actors and singers and Broadway stars who wanted you to help them pretend they were straight when they were photographed at places like the Man Hole, I went out on my own.

Six years after that, I met Marcus in the coffee shop. Less than three hours later he'd called, saying that he was on his way to Japan for a few days but would be back that weekend, and would I like to have dinner?

"Ah. Japan," I said, leaning back in my chair, kicking off my shoes, and crossing my legs, squeezing them together to keep them from shaking. "I was just there last week."

"Oh yeah?" he asked.

"I think," I told him, "that it's all about the emerging markets right now."

"Are you free Saturday?"

"I'm afraid I have plans," I said. I didn't have plans, but I knew that I had to at least give the impression of being busy on a Saturday night. "But Sunday could work." This wasn't strictly adhering to the playbook, but Marcus was the real deal, and I couldn't put him off long enough for some other girl who'd been waiting for her big chance to swoop in and take what could have been mine.

He took me to Eleven Madison Park, which had just gotten four stars in the *Times,* a fact that should have made it impossible for a civilian to get a reservation. Marcus was no civilian. "Mr. Croft! Welcome!" said the man behind the podium, sounding as if Marcus was a long-lost family member who'd come, maybe bearing good news about a dead relative's will. I stood in the vestibule, my new dress snug around my body, and inhaled the scent of fresh flowers and buttery sauces, roasted meats and rich desserts, a fragrance that meant money. I could feel my body respond, my nipples tightening, my heartbeat speeding up. *Easy,* I told myself as Marcus slipped off my coat and handed it to the pretty young girl who'd materialized to whisk it away. They never hired ugly people in places like these. How they got around the civil rights laws I have no idea, but I had never seen an unattractive bartender or waitress or coat-check girl in any of the best restaurants in Manhattan. Maybe no ugly person ever applied. Maybe they all just know to stay away.

The maître d' led us to the center of the room, past a table set with a dozen oversized glass vases, each containing a single stalk of hydrangea leaning at an angle. I ran my fingers over the creamy paper on which the day's menu had been printed—minted pea soup, roast spring chicken stuffed with foie gras, baby suckling pig, a dozen other delicacies that made my mouth flood. All I'd had that day was chamomile tea and a wheatgrass shake. After Marcus's call, I'd embarked on a five-day juice fast that had left me six pounds thinner and a little wobbly . . . but six pounds was six pounds, and I needed every ounce of advantage I could get.

With my right hand, I lifted my wineglass. With my left hand, I gripped the table so that he wouldn't see me trembling. *Don't screw this up,* I told myself. *Don't lose this one, too.*

My normal dinner was broiled fish and steamed greens, but I knew that men liked to see women eat. So I'd allowed myself an ambrosial Parker House roll, soft as a cloud in my hand, with fresh, unsalted, locally sourced butter. I'd started with a salad, but one with lardons sprinkled over the lettuce and a poached egg on top, and I had that foie gras stuffed chicken, crisp-skinned and succulent, every juicy bite of it exploding in my mouth, the flavors and textures, salty, sweet, rich, dancing over my tongue.

"You're very pretty," said Marcus. I set my fork on my plate.

"You're not so bad yourself." He wore the uniform of a successful New York businessman, but his voice was midwestern, plangent and nasal, not Chicago, like I'd guessed, but Detroit. His father had owned a garage, and his mother did the books. Marcus had invented a way to heat car seats, a technology he'd patented, then sold to the automakers, becoming a million- aire by the time he was twenty-five.

"Confidentially," he said, lowering his voice to suit the word, "that wasn't my first business."

"Oh?" I didn't have to fake my interest or my smile. Marcus was easy to listen to and not bad-looking, for his age. While he was across the room, exchanging handshakes and backslaps with a tableful of businessmen, I'd slipped a handful of *gougères* into the empty zippered makeup case I kept in my purse. I was, I knew, long past the point where I had to steal bread from the basket, or crudités from the free spread at a bar, just to be sure I'd have something to eat the next day—I had money, plus a refrig- erator full of fruit and Greek yogurt and a single emergency bar of dark chocolate studded with candied orange peel—but it was a habit I couldn't break. Maybe when I was a lady who lunched, kept in the style to which I wanted to become accustomed, I could go into therapy and figure it all out.

"So what were you," I asked, leaning forward to give him the tiniest glimpse of my candlelit cleavage, with the cheese puffs warm in my lap, "before you were a seat-heating mogul?"

He grinned, looking, with his broad, round face, like a little boy who'd gotten away with something, timing the punchline he'd clearly delivered more than once. "I sold pot."

I widened my eyes and turned my mouth into a perfectly lipsticked O of amusement. "I'm shocked." I wasn't. I'd looked him up online beforehand. The pot anecdote was one he'd told before. But I knew my lines in this play.

He gave a little shrug, a charming smile. I could smell the starch of his suit, the juice from his filet on his china plate, his cologne, layered and complex. His big hands rested on the white tablecloth; his teeth gleamed in the candlelight. "It was the eighties," said Marcus. "You wouldn't remember." I remembered the eighties just fine, but I didn't say so. Instead, I bent my head over my folded napkin, soft hair brushing my cheeks. It was like a fencing match, parry and thrust, advance and retreat. Flash him a smile, then turn away, tracing a fingertip over the tines of my fork. Lick my lips, then let him hear my skirt rustle as I recrossed my legs; get him so bewitched that he wouldn't even feel the blade slide in.

I smoothed the fabric of my dress, a three-thousand-dollar Jil Sander that I'd bought at Saks that afternoon and was wearing with the tags tucked against my skin. I'd take it off as soon as I got home, sponge off any deodorant residue, run a lint brush over it, zip it back into its garment bag, and return it the next day on my lunch hour. *I'm sorry*, I'd tell the salesgirl, with a sorrowful expression on my face. *I adored it, but my husband, not so much.*

Marcus had finished his meat and was using a bit of bread to mop up the juices, turning it in circles around the plate until the porcelain was shiny. "So how about you?" he asked. "Are you a native?"

I kept my answers short, talking about how much I loved New York: my apartment, my friends, my freedom. After the waiter handed us dessert menus, I told him about the weekends I'd walk all the way to Brooklyn (never mind that I hadn't done it in eight years, and when I'd done it last it was because I didn't even have two bucks for the subway). I said that I loved the theater and the museums, and that thanks to my job I got invited to premieres and parties, special exhibits and opening nights.

"No children?" he asked.

I paused, knowing I had to be careful to sound like I didn't care one way or the other, because what if he didn't want more kids? But saying I didn't want them would make me sound cold. "I guess . . ." I began. "Well, you know. It's probably the same for lots of women. Maybe I was too busy, and I was definitely too picky." That last part, the "picky" part, was important. No man wants to feel like he's just the latest chump to buy a ticket for the merry-go-round, the last one aboard a horse that everyone else has already ridden.

"You think it's too late?" he asked. Then, "Was that a rude question? Forgive me. I haven't done this much—this dating."

I looked down again, arranging my face in an expression that was just the right combination of rueful (over the kid thing) and amused (by him). "I don't know if it's too late. I've never really tried." This was the truth—the one time I'd gotten pregnant, I had definitely not been trying. I let it out as a sigh, then raised my eyes to his. "All I know is, when I do it—if I do it—I want it to be right." I hesitated, considering whether I was saying too much, but I'd had four glasses of wine by then, Riesling with the appetizers and a syrupy Shiraz with the chicken, and booze on top of a juice fast tends to loosen one's tongue. "I want a nest egg," I said. I'd started to say *money* before remembering that people who had lots of it rarely said the word. "More than I've got now. I've got some savings . . ." Again, true. I had a decent-size investment account, a nicely diversified portfolio that hadn't taken too hard a hit in the latest downturn, but it wasn't even close to being true fuck-you money, and true fuck-you money was one thing I was sure I wanted. Money, and what it could buy; what it could do, what it could keep you safe from.

Marcus sat back in his chair, his eyes unreadable. I imagined the feeling of a fishing line, formerly taut, going slack in my grip. *Shit,* I thought. I lost him. Then, unexpectedly, he leaned across the table and took my hands.

"I like you," he announced. It had the tone of finality, like a manager saying *you're hired,* or a groom saying *I do.* I felt my body uncoil. My head was humming with relief and the wine. His hands were big and warm and strong and dry—all the things you'd hope a billionaire's hands would be. Even better, they felt no different than the hands of a man my own age, which was encouraging, because I suspected—correctly, it turned out—that his body, while well maintained, would reflect his age. Things drooped—his ass, his balls, the flabby little man-breasts that you couldn't see underneath his made-to-measure shirts with his monogram in violet thread on the cuffs.

Marcus took me to dinners and on trips that made Kevin's steakhouses and long weekends look like jokes. Together we went to the best restaurants and the fanciest hotels, spending long weekends in the George V in Paris and on islands you could only reach by private jet. We had tickets to the opera (I guzzled Red Bull in the ladies' room to keep from dozing off during the arias) and invitations to museum openings and galas. I'd take him places, too, getting us tickets to events that I thought would amuse him and establish my hot-younger-woman-about-town credentials: a rock concert in a club downtown; out for a falafel, which he ate gamely, licking tahini sauce from his fingers, tucking a paper napkin on top of his tie.

His children, when I finally met them, were what I'd expected: overbred, overprivileged trust-fund brats with big white Kennedy teeth, thin lips, and suspicious eyes. One of the boys was in a band (*of course*, I thought to myself, keeping my smile on my face as he told me about how one of their songs was blowing up YouTube), the other boy was a lawyer working for Marcus (*of course*, take two), and the girl was an associate in the *objet* department at Kohler's. I didn't like the way she looked at me, narrowly, across the dinner table, then again while I was washing up (Miss Thing, of course, hadn't bothered to clear so much as a teaspoon). I could practically read the balloon over her head, the one that said *gold digger*. Let her think it, I told myself. Let her imagine the worst. When it comes down to a battle between two women, whether it's wife versus mother-in-law or girlfriend versus daughter, the woman who wins is the one he's taking to bed.

After five dates, Marcus told me he loved me. True, he'd

been having an orgasm at the time, but it still counted. I'd wiped off my mouth on his thigh and wriggled toward the headboard until I was cradled in his arms. I would never challenge him, never argue, never behave as if I was his equal. I'd be his comfort, his cheerleader, his appreciative audience, his unconditional supporter. *Love you, too,* I whispered, kissing his cheek, smoothing his hair off his forehead, acknowledging, to my surprise, that it almost felt like it was true.

One night in June, we went to an opening at the Museum of Modern Art. At the dinner, I was seated across from the honored guest, Laurena Costovya, a Polish performance artist in her sixties who'd come to America for a retrospective of her work. For three months, young artists would re-create some of her most famous pieces—the one where a man and a woman danced a topless tango, bashing their bodies against each other until they bled; the one where a man balanced naked on stilts for ten hours at a time, his face hidden behind an executioner's black leather hood.

Stately as a statue at the head of the table, Laurena wore a kind of nun's robe made of raw white silk, with her hair, still brown, in a heavy plait over one shoulder, and no makeup except for a single slash of red on her lips. When she was in her twenties, she'd carved swastikas into her belly with a shard of glass, and done installations where she'd run face-first into pillars until she collapsed. She'd lit her long hair on fire, and stood perfectly still for hours with her partner holding a switchblade to her throat, his thumb hovering over the button that would pop the knife into her neck. Here in New York, she was performing a piece entitled *See/Be Seen,* where she'd sit at a table for eight hours at a stretch, across from whoever cared to face her. After dinner, there was a preview. I remember the appreciative murmur as she gathered her skirts and crossed the room to take her seat. I thought about how silly the whole thing was, how far from what I thought of as "art," as she took her seat, arranging the folds of her skirt. To me, art was a painting, a sculpture, a piece of music, not some senior citizen sitting behind a desk.

"Go on," said Marcus, urging me toward the empty space across from the artist. I crossed the floor, heels clicking, and sat down, my smile firmly on my face, my hair swept into an updo, my makeup professionally applied (at two hundred dollars a pop it was an unwelcome expense, but I couldn't skip it, not with photographers on hand).

Laurena regarded me. I looked back, legs crossed, hands folded in my lap. My eyes were on hers, but my mind was wandering. I was thinking about how many calories I'd consumed that day and whether the walk I'd taken at lunchtime, twenty blocks up Fifth Avenue with a circle around Bryant Park, had burned most of them off. I was wondering how soon Marcus would ask me to marry him, whether he'd ask me what kind of ring I wanted or just buy something himself, and thinking about my little apartment and whether I'd keep it, whether he'd give me the kind of allowance that would let me slip twenty-three hundred dollars to the landlord each month unnoticed, and whether there was anything besides my clothes that I'd take with me. Probably not, but I wanted to keep that apartment. It was my secret lair, my bolt-hole, my hideaway, in case I ever had to run, to go to ground. Thoughts like this were running through my head in a pleasant, lazy loop when suddenly the artist's gaze caught me and pinned me. My face flushed, and my eyes widened. I felt as if I was being X-rayed, like my skin had been stripped off, like this woman with her plain, strong-boned face knew not only everything I was thinking but everything I was, and everything I'd done to turn myself into the woman who was sitting before her, all the parts I'd manipulated, reduced or amplified, edited and changed.

Before I could stop myself, before I knew that I even intended to speak, I found myself blurting, in a husky whisper that hardly sounded like my voice, "It wasn't really a baby."

Her eyes widened almost imperceptibly. The moment seemed to spin out forever. I felt my skin prickle and my mouth go dry as I sat there, trembling, every muscle tensed, waiting for . . . what? For her to say something? To stand up and yell *liar,* or *fraud*? For her to proclaim, in the accented voice I'd heard on tapes of the performances she'd given, that she knew my real name? She couldn't speak, I reminded myself. Silence was part of her shtick—her performance, to use a nicer word, but shtick was what it was. She sat. She observed. She could see and be seen, but she would never say a word.

I sat, forcing myself to hold still until my heartbeat had slowed and my legs weren't shaking, until I was sure I had control and that no one in that well-dressed crowd had heard what I'd said. *You might see things,* I told the artist in my head. *But I go out, I walk in the world, I do, I change.* Then I gave her a smile— more of a smirk, really—and rose from the chair. With my head held high and my face composed, I crossed the enormous room, gliding over the marble floor, feeling the lights that had been set up for the taping burn against my skin. Marcus slipped his arm around my waist. "Welcome back, gorgeous," he whispered into my ear, and I felt adrenaline surge through my body. *I win,* I thought. *I win.*

A few days later, we woke up in bed together, and I put my arms around his neck and murmured, in my sleepiest, sexiest voice, "You know, we can't keep doing this. It's not a good example for your children."

"Well, then," he said, and reached across me, opening the drawer of the bedside table and pulling out the little velvet box I'd been waiting for since I'd spotted him in Starbucks: my diamond as big as the Ritz. "I know it's early days," he said, his voice curiously humble, "but I'm sure about you."

I spent three months planning a wedding—his kids, my friends, a few of his business associates and all of his assistants, who probably knew him better than any of us. Then there was the honeymoon, moving into his place, which spanned two entire stories of the San Giacomo, one of New York City's grand old apartment buildings that stood along Central Park West. It was months before I had occasion to think of the artist again, the way she'd looked at me, the mocking curl of her lips, the way her eyes had widened as she'd stared and seemed to say without speaking, *I know what you are. I know exactly what you are.*

JULES

I was in the basement of T.I., one of the eating clubs on Pros-pect Avenue, standing in a circle of three other couples with a beer in my hand, nodding while my boyfriend Dan Finnerty talked about a hockey game. Whether this was a game he'd played in or merely a game he'd seen I wasn't quite sure, and it was too far into the conversation to interrupt and ask him, so I nodded and smiled and laughed when laughter seemed required. When my telephone buzzed in my pocket, I tried not to look too eager as I grabbed for it.

"Excuse me," I shouted in the direction of Dan's face, then trotted up the stairs to the second-floor ladies' room. You could feel the bass of the stereo thumping through the floor, but it was by far the quietest place in the building.

"Hello?"

"Julia?" It was my father . . . and he sounded like he was drunk. Even in that single word I could hear the edge of his voice, the way the *I* of my name sounded mushy.

My heart sped up. "Where are you?" I asked as I imagined the possibilities. In a bar. In a bus station. In a car accident, on the side of the road, in a spill of twinkling glass, with an ambu-lance's light washing his face in red.

He didn't answer. "I wanted to tell you I'm sorry."

"It's okay, Dad."

"No, it's not." He sounded stubborn; a little boy refusing to believe it was bedtime. "It is not okay. It's not okay what I did to you guys . . . what I did to you mom. I'm so ashamed of myself." He was crying now, horrible choked-sounding sobs, and even though it wasn't the first time he'd done this, called me up apologizing and crying, I could never keep from crying myself.

"Dad."

"I'm sorry," he said, and I could hear the sound of something slamming. Was he pounding his fist against a table? Was he hitting himself? "I'm sorry. I'm sorry."

"Dad." I leaned against the wooden wall. Somewhere not far away, normal college students were enjoying a normal college night. Soon someone would suggest a game of croquet, where you chugged a beer every time you whacked your ball through the wickets. Dan would be the game's most enthusiastic participant.

"You deserve better than me."

An icy blade slid into my heart. "Dad," I said carefully. "Are you thinking about hurting yourself?"

He managed a chuckle. "More than I have already? Don't worry about me. I'm fine."

"You're going to be okay," I told him. "Just hang on. You'll go to Willow Crest. They can help you there." But I was talking to a dial tone.

I squeezed my eyes shut. Tears were rolling down my cheeks. Where was he? Was he all right? And who could I call to ask? Not my mother. She wouldn't go looking. Not the cops, because what would I say? He called me and he was crying? I sat on the toilet, cradling my face in my hands. How had it come to this?

"Jules?"

I peeked through the crack, and there was Kimmie Park, a

girl I knew slightly. She'd been one of my first-year hallmates and, this year, a coworker in the admissions office.

"Are you okay?"

"I'm fine," I said, still sitting on the toilet. Here I was, five weeks away from graduation and the bright future my degree was supposed to ensure, and I was huddled in a bathroom, crying. Maybe it was the hormones.

I'd called Jared Baker three days after I'd met him in the mall. The questionnaire, all twenty-five pages of it, had arrived in my mailbox the next day. I'd sent in the forms, and then, a week later, biked to the clinic for an interview and another lengthy survey. What was my favorite movie, my favorite food, my favorite song? I gave answers that were somewhere between the truth and what I thought would please the customers, saying Hitchcock and Jane Austen instead of *Pretty Woman* and the occasional trashy celebrity biography, writing that I loved listening to classical music, which was true only on nights I couldn't sleep.

The next week I'd undergone the most thorough physical of my life, plus an interview with a psychologist, an earnest young woman with curly brown hair and small round glasses. A middle-aged nurse with an iron-gray bob and, I eventually learned, disturbingly cold hands showed me how to give myself hormone shots, right underneath my belly button. A doctor wrote me a prescription for the needles and the medications I'd inject, drugs to maximize the number of eggs I'd produce. "You may experience some mood swings, or feel like you're having really intense PMS," he told me, but what I'd noticed was feeling weepy all the time. Alone in my room, the sounds of people shouting and laughing outside, a half-dozen different songs blaring from iPod speakers propped up against open windows, I'd pull out the one picture I kept of my father, from a trip we'd taken to the beach. I'd look at my younger self, the cutoff jean shorts and the braces, my father, strong and handsome in his jeans and alligator shirt, and just cry and cry, which wasn't like me at all. My mother was the family's designated weeper. I got angry. I made plans. Mostly, I kept myself to myself, acting the part of a normal girl, a girl who belonged here, a heedless, laughing, bright-future girl whose father had never been in the newspapers, or in rehab, or in prison.

I watched the space underneath the stall door, waiting for Kimmie's feet to move. They didn't. *I'm fine,* I told myself. *Everything's fine.* But it wasn't. It was my senior year and I was finishing four years on a campus full of people who I didn't know and who didn't know me. Not even my boyfriend knew how, on Mondays, I took the bus by myself to the mall and ate alone at the food court. Nobody knew the truth about my family; no one knew the story of my dad. Instead of real friends, I had acquaintances, interchangeable classmates I could sit with at dinner, who'd go in with me on a late-night pizza or walk with me to the clubs, people whose names I wouldn't remember a year after graduation. Now it was June. Too late for fun, and instead of fond memories, I'd be left with nothing but regrets.

Suddenly the tears were back. I buried my face in my hands, choking back sobs.

"Jules?" came Kimmie's soft voice. "Are you sure you're all right?"

I nodded, then realized she couldn't see me, and managed to croak out an answer. "Yeah," I said. "I'm fine." Peeking through the seam between the door and the wall, I could see her, standing in front of the row of mirrors. Kimmie had glossy black hair, so long it brushed at the small of her back, a sweet face with a pert nose and neat white teeth, and a figure that was notable only in the way in which it resembled that of a ten-year-old boy. She wore Keds, laced and tied in bows, and had a slightly pigeon-toed walk.

Kimmie was a biochem major, and she played violin in the orchestra. Freshman year, I'd see her in the mornings, leaving the dorm for the day, with her black violin case in her hand and, on her back, a blue backpack as pristine as the day it had arrived from the L.L. Bean store (more than once I'd wondered if she had a closet full of dozens of navy-blue backpacks and just kept rotating through them).

The two of us were friendly enough. We'd laugh as we sorted through stacks of applications, rolling our eyes at the obvious ways the high-school seniors tried to game the system. "Do you think anyone," Kimmie would ask, pinching an essay between her thumb and first finger, "actually wants to spend a summer teaching English in Bosnia?"

"I don't think I'd even want to spend a weekend there," I replied. We'd trade off taking panicky phone calls from the students or, more often, their parents, and sometimes at the end of our shift we'd walk to the student center and split a slice of cake (I'd have coffee, she'd drink tea). We weren't friends, exactly, but that winter, Kimmie had started dating one of Dan's friends, a high-fiving, barrel-chested lacrosse player named Chet who had, in the uncharitable parlance of my classmates, a touch of yellow fever. He'd dated a series of Asian girls since his arrival on campus—Vietnamese, Chinese, Japanese, Korean, conducting his own private waist-down tour of the Far East. For the past few months, I'd been seeing shy little Kimmie everywhere— sitting across the table from Chet in Firestone Library, trotting lightly up the stairs to his third-floor dorm room in Henry Hall, taking little birdie sips of her go-cup of beer in the Ivy basement, her hand with its short, unpolished nails resting lightly on Chet's brawny forearm.

I waited until I knew I couldn't avoid coming out and letting her look at me. I flushed the toilet, rubbed my eyes, slipped the elastic off my ponytail and shook my hair out around my face, hoping it would cover up some of the blotchiness. Then I stepped out of the stall.

"Hi."

She looked me over. "What's wrong?"

"I'm homesick." It was the first thing that popped into my head, and it was, of course, ridiculous—we were seniors; we'd been away from home for four years. But Kimmie simply nodded. She held something out to me—a wad of paper towels, soaked in cold water. "Put this on the back of your neck," she instructed, in her soft, lilting voice.

I did as she told me as more tears welled in my eyes. *It's the hormones,* I told myself. It had to be. Kimmie's hand was light as she patted my back once, twice, three times, like a mother burping a baby. I waited for her to ask the obvious questions, about why I was homesick and whether that was really what was making me cry like this, given all of the other, much more obvious reasons—I'd been dumped, I'd gotten a bad grade on my thesis, someone had called me ugly on the Internet, I'd found out that I was pregnant. That last one brought a bitter smile to my lips, and it was that bitterness that finally stopped the tears. I walked to the sink, splashed more cold water on my face, and finger-combed my hair. Kimmie watched all this silently, standing a polite distance away from me, the bumps of her vertebrae showing through the fabric of her T-shirt, a few freckles dotting each cheek.

"Want to go to Ivy? Chet and Dan are there."

"I don't know if I'm up for that."

"Still life with oafs," she said. I blinked, sure that I'd heard her wrong. She lifted her narrow shoulders in a shrug and gave me a surprisingly sly smile. "That's how I always think of it. Dinners there. Parties. These boys."

"You think Chet's an oaf?"

When she smiled, a dimple flashed in one of her cheeks. "He's a sweet oaf. But an oaf, yes."

"So it's not true love."

She shook her head, hair swishing. "I just wanted to have some fun before I graduated."

I was startled at how closely what she'd said echoed what I'd been thinking, about how time was short and how I should have some fun, too. "And is he? Fun?"

She smiled, shrugging again. "If you like beer. He took me to the beach once. Atlantic City." She hummed a few bars of the Bruce Springsteen song of the same name, surprising me. I'd have figured Kimmie with her violin as someone whose knowl edge of contemporary music ended at around 1890. "And to Six Flags for my birthday." This was interesting. Princeton students made trips to New York City, for parties, or off-Broadway experimental theater, or museum exhibits, but no one I knew would ever admit to visiting an amusement park, waiting in line with the teeming, sunburned, flabby masses, unless maybe they'd taken mushrooms first and gone as a joke.

Her smile widened, displaying small, even white teeth. "Chet's afraid of roller coasters."

"He is?"

She nodded. "Come on," she said, and linked her arms with me, like we were schoolgirl chums. We walked through the soft spring night across the street to Ivy, Princeton's oldest eating club, one that had always been home to the sons (and, since 1991, the daughters) of privilege, the future kings and queens of America, a club you had to go through a rush-like evaluation process called bicker to join. It was a gorgeous, blooming spring night, but I felt awful: my breasts ached so much I winced whenever my shirt touched them, and I had an acne cyst throbbing beneath the skin above my right eye, making me feel like my forehead was trying to give birth. The grand brick mansion halfway down Prospect Avenue, entering the dining room, with its wood paneling and high ceilings, the mellow gleam of lamplight on the tables brought me back to myself. I'd be done with the hormones soon enough, and besides, I was doing a good thing, a generous thing. All of this would work out: some poor infertile woman would get her baby; I'd get my money; my father would get another chance.

Dan and Chet were out back drinking. Dan pulled me close, squeezing me too hard. The first time we'd had sex, he'd fallen to his knees in front of me, his arms wrapped around my legs, his face buried between them. "God, you're hot," he'd groaned. Looking down at him, his broad, muscled chest, his penis, moist and sticky at the tip, jerking in the air like a hitchhiker's spastic thumb, a wave of something surged through me, a feeling that felt nothing like desire and a lot like nausea. I'd had to peel his hands off the backs of my thighs and run to the bathroom, where I'd bent over the sink, positive I was going to throw up, even though all I'd had that night were two glasses of Champagne. Once the urge had passed, I'd lifted my head, looking at myself in the mirror and thought, *What am I doing? I don't want to sleep with him. He's a dolt.* Of course I'd slept with him anyhow—at that point, it would have been rude not to—but as I'd felt him push his way inside me ("Tight," he'd announced, like he was paying me an enormous compliment), I'd felt sick to my stomach, disgusted with him and disgusted with myself.

We'd slept together a few times a week since then, and Dan had been polite and accommodating each time. He was, I had to admit, nothing if not well-mannered. "Can I come on your tits?" he'd ask, in the same solicitous tone as a waiter asking if I wanted fresh-ground pepper on my pasta. He'd go down on me until I was sure his tongue was numb and his jaw was aching; he'd try his best to please me, and tell me I was beautiful . . . but it never felt right, and I'd never been able to figure out why.

He just wasn't the guy for me, I'd eventually decided, and when he headed out west after graduation, I didn't think he'd miss me much.

I took a seat next to Kimmie, knowing how the evening would unfold. There'd be a game of pool, or croquet on the back lawn, with more plastic cups of beer. I could wander down to Witherspoon Street for an ice-cream cone, or go to the movies or a lecture or a concert. Eventually, most of the students would find their way back to Prospect Avenue. They would make their way from club basement to club basement, a subterranean version of the John Cheever story where a man traverses his neighborhood by way of the backyard swimming pools.

I thought I could feel Kimmie watching me as the night went on—during the croquet game, when she sat on a plastic lawn chair and clapped as Chet smacked his ball through the wickets, then later, in the basement, where we shouted toward each other over the music. Maybe she was trying to figure out why I'd been having a breakdown in the bathroom, but she didn't say anything. I made myself wait until eleven. Then I told Dan that I had an awful headache and was going home.

"Do you need anything?" Chet asked. One of his muscled arms was slung loosely over Kimmie's shoulders, and as he pulled her close, I felt a stab of something I couldn't name.

"Just some rest."

"I'll walk back with you," said Kimmie, slipping out from under Chet's grasp and looping her arm through mine again.

We crossed Witherspoon Street and passed the great gothic pile of Firestone Library, heading along a wide slate path. A sliver of moon hung above us. The sounds of an a capella group singing "Let Me Call You Sweetheart" underneath Blair Arch echoed through the night.

"We should take a picture for the website," Kimmie said, and I nodded, surprised because, again, I'd been thinking the exact same thing—how the night looked like a recruiting poster for Princeton, how there was no way you could stroll through campus on a soft spring evening like this and not believe that this was the most beautiful school ever imagined, that the students here were the luckiest, happiest ones in the world.

"You want anything? Advil? Excedrin?" She gave me a coy smile, one I'd never seen in the admissions office. "Something stronger?"

I must have looked shocked, because Kimmie laughed out loud and clapped her hands in delight. "Oh, come on, Jules. Don't look so surprised."

"I thought you were a nice girl," I blurted, which made her clap again, before asking, "So what can I get you?"

I shook my head regretfully, thinking of my appointment at the clinic the next morning. "I better not."

"You don't drink," Kimmie observed.

Surprised again, I answered, "I had a beer."

"You held it," said Kimmie. "You didn't drink it."

I didn't answer. At parties, I'd ask for a beer, because it was more conspicuous not to have something in your hands, but I never had more than a few swallows, and, other than Champagne, I never drank anything stronger. I couldn't risk it. Not after what had happened with my dad.

We paused at the doorway to my dorm, Kimmie with her hands in her pockets, and me feeling, strangely, like this was the end of a date, when there'd be the predictable grapple for a kiss, or an invitation upstairs. An odd thought surfaced: that I wouldn't have minded kissing Kimmie. In the faint glow of the lamp, with her lashes sweeping her cheeks, she looked adorable. I shook my head and told her good night, fishing my key out of my pocket and hurrying up the stairs, wondering what on earth that had been about. Spring fever, I decided. The end of college, the end of childhood, really, with real life looming ever closer—all of that could make anyone behave a little strangely.

In my dorm room, I gave myself my last shot, then carried my plastic bucket of toiletries to the bathroom. I showered, shaved my legs and armpits and bikini line, and brushed my teeth. Back in my room, I pulled on panties and an oversized T-shirt and set my alarm for seven o'clock. I didn't have a bike, but there were dozens of them, all around campus, left unlocked at the bike racks. I'd ride one of those to the clinic, do the donation, rest for a while, then pedal back in time for lunch.

I lay in bed in the darkness, warm spring air coming through my window, and for the first time I let myself think about the result of what I'd be doing in the morning. If everything went well, in nine or ten months' time there could be a baby, a baby who was half mine, at least genetically, a little boy or girl in the world whom I would never see, never know. It hadn't bothered me before. Donating an egg wasn't like having a baby and giving it up for adoption. The eggs were nothing more than possibilities. But still . . .

Rolling onto my side, I imagined walking down a New York City street five years from now and seeing a little girl who looked like me, holding her mother's hand. Or being in an airport or a theater or in line at Starbucks and catching a glimpse of a baby, a toddler, a teenager with blond hair and light eyes and wondering if, maybe, that had been my baby. Would I stare, or feel compelled to say something? Would the mother turn the baby away from me, hustling her down the street or hurrying her out of the store? Would the child know where he or she had come from, that there'd been a girl like me involved, someone who'd given away (or sold, to be honest) part of herself so that he or she could exist? Would the baby grow up and try to find me? Would she look like me? Would she struggle with addiction and never know why?

I finally managed to fall asleep. When I opened my eyes I could see the line of sunshine underneath the window shade. I slapped off my alarm before it could buzz, grabbed my bucket, opened my door, and almost walked straight into Kimmie, who was standing in the hallway, fully dressed, neatly combed, her hair in two pigtails, each tied with a bright-blue elastic. Under the stark hallway fluorescents, I could see the smattering of cinnamon-colored freckles on her cheeks, and I thought she was wearing tinted gloss on her lips, something I'd never seen her do before.

"Hey," I said. "You're up early."

She tilted her head. "I like it when it's quiet."

I nodded, knowing what she meant.

"You want to go get coffee?"

Curling my arm around my bucket, I said, "I've actually got an appointment."

"So early," Kimmie mused. "Bootie call?"

I shook my head, still startled and charmed by this new sense of humor, a raunchiness I'd never suspected when we were filing applications or sharing snacks in the student center. "No bootie for me."

"So, what?" She gave me an assessing look. "Not a class."

"No," I said. "I'm not the only senior in the world dumb enough to take a nine o'clock. It's a . . ." I struggled for a moment. "A doctor's appointment."

I expected more questions, but Kimmie just nodded. "You want company?"

"Oh, I . . ." I opened my mouth to tell her no thanks, but somehow, what came out was "That would be great."

Twenty minutes later, Kimmie and I had liberated a pair of

bicycles and were pedaling through Princeton's quiet streets, on our way to the clinic. "Are you sick?" she asked.

"I'm not sick," I said. "I'm selling my eggs."

She nodded. The wind blew her long hair back from her forehead. The bike that she'd taken had a metal carrier over the back wheels, and she'd stowed her violin and her backpack in there.

"I need the money," I continued. I wasn't sure if it was the hormones or the impending procedure, which would mark the end of my time at Princeton, but I suddenly needed to tell somebody my story.

"Loans?" Kimmie asked when we'd pulled up to a stop sign. If you needed financial aid, the university's endowment would cover your tuition, but plenty of students—me included—took out loans for living expenses, books and travel and meal plans.

"Well, yeah. And my dad's sick. I'm trying to get money to help him."

"What's wrong with your father?" Before I could say anything, she turned, flicking one pigtail over her shoulder, and said, "I'm sorry. That's none of my business. You don't have to tell me if you don't want to."

"No. It's okay. He's . . ." I paused. I'd never said this out loud before, not to a stranger. "He's an addict. I'm trying to get money so he can get into treatment."

Kimmie nodded. She'd pulled ahead of me on her bike, so I couldn't see her face. I wondered if she was shocked, or if somehow she'd guessed this about me.

Leslie, the clinic director, was waiting just behind the desk. "I'm glad you brought a friend," she said. "You might be a little sore when it's over."

Kimmie frowned at this news, her thin eyebrows drawing together. "Do you want me to come in with you?"

"No," I said. "I'll be fine." She squeezed my hand with her small one, picked up a copy of *Town & Country*, and sat with her legs crossed like she was prepared to wait for hours—all day, if that's what it took. I went to the cubicle, where I hung my jeans and T-shirt, folded my panties and socks, and changed into my gown. Ten minutes later I was on the table, a needle in my arm, chatting with the anesthesiologist about Princeton's basketball team while a doctor in a surgical mask and magnifying glasses threaded a catheter through my fallopian tubes.

"A little pinch now," the nurse murmured. "Gorgeous," said the doctor, and tilted the screen to show me the eggs, a cluster of grapes. I watched as he plucked them, two, four, six, eight, ten.

ANNIE

Now that the boys were older, if I planned it right, I could have a little time every afternoon to myself. Spencer took a nap after lunch. He'd stay down for at least an hour, more if I was lucky, longer, if he'd had school that morning, and Frank Junior could be counted on to entertain himself with Legos for a while, playing some complicated game he'd made up involving soldiers and rocket ships and Woody from *Toy Story* as either the captain or the king. One sunny Tuesday afternoon in June, with Frank at work and Spencer in his crib, and Frank Junior with his soldiers lined up on the empty living room's floor, I pulled a pound of ground beef out of the freezer, loaded the dishwasher, and wiped down the kitchen counters, which were so constantly sticky that I sometimes wondered if the tiles oozed sap. A peek at the clock showed that I still had a half hour. I could sneak into the shower, maybe even blow my hair dry. I'd seen myself in the mirror that morning and my heart had sunk as I'd pictured my sister, ironed and combed and perfectly put together.

"Mommy?"

I turned around to see Frank Junior looking at me. "Hello, little man."

"Snack?"

I cut up an apple and poured goldfish crackers into a blue plastic bowl. He pouted. "Cookie?"

"Growing foods first." I made myself a cup of tea and sat down across from him as he picked up his goldfish one at a time and sent them swimming into his mouth. Watching him, I wondered: How would my sons feel, watching my belly get bigger, watching me go off to the hospital and then come home empty-handed? Spencer wouldn't notice—Spencer didn't notice much of anything except Elmo and his big brother—but Frank Junior would have questions, and I'd have to figure out how to answer them.

"You want to go to the sprayground?"

He chewed, frowning. "Do we have to bring baby Spencer?"

"Yes, we have to bring Spencer. I can't leave him home by himself. You know why."

He nodded, reciting the words that I'd taught him. "The authorities would frown."

"Right you are. And you should be nice to Spencer. You were a baby once, too."

He smiled, showing his perfect white teeth. "Tell me the story."

"Once upon a time," I began. Frank Junior hopped out of his chair, circled the table, and hoisted himself into my lap. I snuggled him close, cupping my hand over the less scabbed of his knees, inhaling his little-boy scent, graham crackers and salt and baby shampoo. "Once upon a time you were a tiny seed in my belly. And you grew and grew and grew and grew, until you were . . ."

He joined in, smiling. He knew what came next, because I'd told this story so often. "Ripe like a plum!"

"Ripe like a plum. I went to the hospital, and out you came. You had no teeth . . ." Frank Junior leaned his head against my chest, his knees digging into my thigh, holding still for what I thought might be the first time all day. I closed my eyes, loving the feeling of his body against mine, the rapid beat of his heart. Our days for cuddling were numbered. Soon he'd be too big to sit on his mama's lap. "And you had a tiny little cloud of fuzzy black hair, and you cried . . ." I stretched my mouth wide and did my best imitation of his peeps, ". . . like you wanted to go back in."

He smiled, holding my hand, counting the fingers—one, two, three, four, five. "I liked it in there."

"You remember it?"

He nodded. "It was dark, except when you were talking. Then I could see the light." He tilted his head, regarding me seriously. "You talk a *lot*, Mama."

"Huh." I wondered whether this could possibly be true, whether he actually could remember being inside of me.

"Tell the rest," Frank prompted, twining his fingers through mine.

"Well, I bundled you up in a blue-and-pink-striped blankie, and I gave you a little snack . . ."

His mouth curved up at the corners. "Goldfishie crackers?"

"Not goldfishie crackers!" I said, making an indignant face. "You had no teeth! What kind of mommy would give crackers to a boy with no teeth?"

He nodded—this, too, was part of the story.

"And I looked at you all over," I said, my eyes filling with tears, back in the moment again, the hospital smells, the bright morning light through the windows, Frank looking so puffed-up and proud as he held the baby for the first time. "From your toes to your knees to your sweet little belly to your neck to your chin to your forehead, and I gave you a kiss and I said to your daddy, 'I guess we'll bring him home, and name him . . .'"

"Frank Junior!" With that, he was up and out of my lap, dashing toward the door for his scooter and the helmet I insisted on, for the park and the sprayground and the promise of a warm afternoon with maybe even an ice-cream sandwich on the way home. "Wake up, baby!" he hollered, his footsteps shaking the floor, and, on cue, I heard Spencer whimpering from the second floor. *So much for my shower,* I thought, but I didn't mind much as I went up the stairs and scooped Spencer's warm, sleepy, soggy-bottomed weight into my arms.

"Wet," Spencer informed me, then plugged his thumb back into his mouth. I laid him on the changing table, pulled down his miniature khakis (copies of his brother's, which were themselves copies of his dad's pants), and unfastened his soaked diaper.

"We have to start talking seriously about that potty," I said, wiping his bottom and the creases of his thighs. He nodded, the way he'd been nodding for months every time I brought up the topic of toilet training. I thought, again, of my sons as infants, as newborns. I'd loved being in the hospital: the nurses fussing around me, bringing me meals that I didn't have to prepare, on dishes I wouldn't have to wash; having someone make my bed and mop the floor and clean the bathroom every day. I didn't even mind being woken up every three hours to have my temperature and blood pressure taken. It had been so long since I'd been the center of attention that way, since people were taking care of me instead of the other way around. When Spencer had arrived, after a brief but grueling labor, and they'd handed him to me after his bath, I'd seriously considered asking the nurses to keep him for an hour or two so I could grab a nap and eat my lunch. It had horrified me then, but it comforted me now. Maybe I'd feel nothing but relief at the chance to pass a new baby into the eager arms of another woman . . . but would it really be that easy? Would I let go without a second thought, or would I hold the baby close, turning my face away, thinking, or even saying, *No! Mine! Mine!*

Spencer was staring at me. "Pants," he prompted. I fastened a fresh diaper around his waist, pulled up his khakis, and swung him down to the floor. He took off at a run, pudgy legs pumping, calling for his brother. I watched him go, telling myself that it would be easy, wondering whether it was true.

BETTINA

Kate Klein had told me not to expect to hear from her for two weeks, but I guess she was in the underpromise and overdeliver school, because a week after my visit to her office, she called and said she had some news.

"I could come on my lunch hour."

I heard her hesitate before she answered, "This might take a little longer than an hour."

I asked for a half day's worth of personal time for the next afternoon. "A doctor's appointment," I told my boss, and she let me go without even asking me what was wrong, or when I'd be finished writing up estimates for the department's latest set of acquisitions, a pair of brass vases from the Yuan Dynasty which would probably sell for a price as spectacular as they were ugly. At two o'clock the next afternoon, after a mostly sleepless night and an unproductive morning, I hurried through a steamy June afternoon to the midtown office and hit the elevator button that would carry me up to Kate's floor.

The detective met me in the waiting room wearing a black cotton skirt (slightly wrinkled, and with an elastic waistband, but a definite step above the pajama pants), black sandals, and a white cotton T-shirt.

"This way." Kate led me past her office into a conference

room, where a manila folder sat at the center of a table. India's name was typed on its tab. Looking at the folder, I tasted old pennies in my mouth, and felt a strange mixture of excitement and regret . . . except *regret* wasn't exactly the right word. *Pregret* was more like it—the sadness you could feel over something that hasn't happened yet.

There were six chairs around the table. Five of them were empty. The sixth was occupied by a guy about my age, wearing khakis and a button-down shirt and heavy-framed horn-rimmed glasses that looked like he'd swiped them off his grandpa's bedside table. I distrusted him immediately. I think glasses should be glasses, worn to improve your vision, not as a statement, or a piece of installation art on the bridge of your nose.

"This is Darren Zucker, one of our associates," Kate said.

I held out my hand. Darren got to his feet, lazily, like he had all the time in the world, and gave my hand a single limp pump. Then he sat down and flipped open the folder to display a photograph of a much younger India, with an unfortunately pouffy perm. It took me a second to realize that I was looking at a mug shot. My father's new wife had been arrested in Los Angeles in 1991 . . . and I'd bet my trust fund that my dad didn't have a clue.

I took a seat and pulled the folder toward me. "Is her name really India?"

Kate gave me a look I couldn't decipher. Darren just appeared smug, with the light glinting off his ridiculous glasses.

"It's not," he said. "But there's a lot you'll want to look at here." He flipped the folder open, and I started to read.

Two hours later I staggered out of the conference room, into the elevator, and into the coffee shop in the lobby of the building.

The manila folder was in my purse. Part of me wanted to tip it into a trash bin. Another part of me wanted to leave it somewhere obvious in my father's apartment, where he and his bride would be sure to see it. But what I mostly wanted to do was call my mother, my sensible, pre-ashram mother, and ask for her advice. This was impossible, insofar as my mother would no longer consent to speak on the telephone. "Bad energy," she said. So I wrote her letters, and sometimes she'd write back, little notes in the cursive I remembered from a hundred to-do lists and school permission slips, on paper that smelled like sage and lavender, but sometimes it took weeks to get a reply, and I didn't have weeks.

Through the plate-glass windows I could see people strolling, enjoying the warm weather after days of rain. There were women who'd swapped their heels for flip flops, nannies chatting with each other as they pushed strollers, men in suits with loosened ties, tilting their faces up toward the sun. I sat, watching, the coffee I'd purchased untouched, feeling like I'd been beamed to a different planet and was observing all of this normal from very far away.

I pulled the folder out of my bag, set it on the counter beside me, and lifted up a corner, peeking, once more, at her mug shot. India's pouffy bangs were flattened on one side of her forehead. Her eyeliner was smeared, and she looked like she'd been crying, which made me feel like crying myself. Her whole life was on these pages, her childhood in Toledo, the year she'd spent in New London, her move to Los Angeles, the addresses of every place she'd rented, first in California, then in New York. I felt a grudging respect beginning to mix with my anger and my pity. I wondered if she thought of my father like a winning lottery ticket, the pot of gold at the end of a rainbow. I wondered, too, if this was what drew him to her—the painful things she'd endured. I studied her picture, trying to piece together the subtle transformation she'd undergone, the nose narrowed, the cheekbones more prominent, trying to guess at what she'd told my father about her past and what she'd kept secret. Had she been honest with him about who she was and where she came from? Could she make him happy? Did she really love him, and was that love enough?

"Bettina?"

I turned around, and there was Darren Zucker, with his statement eyeglasses and his smarmy smile.

"You moving in?" he asked, setting down his own drink and taking a seat at the counter beside me.

"What?"

"You've been here for forty-five minutes."

I gathered up my folder and my coffee. "I was just going."

He gave a pompous little nod. "You're in shock."

"I'm fine."

"I've seen this before. You think you want answers. You think you can handle the truth." He waggled his eyebrows in what he must have believed was a Jack Nicholson impression. "You know what you need?" He answered before I could ask him, politely, to please leave me alone. "Will Ferrell."

"I believe he's married."

He smiled, causing his stupid glasses to bob up and down on his face. "Touché. I was thinking more of one of his movies. Something stupid, with fart jokes, where he takes off his clothes."

I gathered my things and walked to the door, with Darren right behind me.

"Come on," he said. "Flabby, hairy guy, running around with no pants . . . Do you have plans?"

"I do." I'd told my father to expect me for dinner that night. I figured I'd go home, we'd have a conversation, and then he'd be in charge of the next step. I'd be there if he needed me for anything: to console him, to call his lawyer, to try, even, to get my mother on the phone if he wanted to talk to her. Now the sun was setting, people were streaming down the streets on their

way home for dinner, but I wasn't sure what to do. I'd been expecting duplicity, slyness and lies, but not anything at this level.

"Movie," said Darren, following me down the sidewalk. "My
treat. Raisinets. Big bucket of popcorn."

"Thanks, but no thanks."

"If you're sure . . ." He pulled a business card out of his pocket
and handed it over. "See you soon."

"Why?" I called toward his back. "In case I need to investi-
gate another stepmother?"

He waved without turning, and I heard his voice as he de-
scended down into the subway station. "You never know!"

I walked home along Fifth Avenue, through throngs of tourists
gawking at the skyline, past the boutiques with their windows
filled with feathered hairbands, sequined purses, eye shadow,
pearl necklaces. Maybe I'd just wait for a few days more. I'd talk
to my brothers and try to reach my mom. But when I got off the
elevator, my father and India were standing in the foyer, waiting
for me, the way they'd waited in Bridgehampton. Her arm was
around his waist, his arm was around her shoulders, and both of
them were beaming.

I set my bag down on the antique ebonized table. As usual,
there was a towering floral arrangement at its center—calla lilies
and hydrangeas in shades of orange and cream. Twice a week a
florist would come and distribute flowers throughout the two
stories of the apartment, from the big arrangement in the foyer
to the roses that my mother used to have in her dressing room,
like she was an actress on opening night. The apartment had
been photographed for *Architectural Digest* and featured in *Metropolitan Home*, but I'd long since stopped seeing its grandeur,
the important art on the walls, the views of the park and the
river and the city's skyline. To me, it was just home.

"What's going on?" I asked my dad.

He turned to India, beaming. "I'll let India give you our good news."

I studied her, wondering, again, exactly what she'd had done to go from the girl in the mug shot, with a big nose and a bad perm, to the sleek creature who'd snagged my dad; how long it had taken, how much it had hurt. I was so lost in my thoughts that I barely noticed India crossing the room until her arms were around me.

"Guess what," she cried, sounding as happy as I'd ever heard her, "we're having a baby!"

PART TWO

~

Great
Expectations

INDIA

Marcus and I had gotten married in September. Our wedding was a tasteful affair that included forty guests and cost fifty thousand dollars. *No bridesmaids,* I'd said, giving him a small smile tinged with regret. *I'm too old for all of that.* This, of course, got me out of having to include Bettina in the festivities. I cringed, just imagining her coming down the aisle, pinching my bouquet between her fingertips like it was diseased, giving me the side-eye when her father said *I do.*

We honeymooned for a week in Hawaii—we would have gone even farther away, but seven days was as long as Marcus could take off from work. Six weeks later, I was still tawny, my honeymoon glow maintained and improved with a little spray tan, and Marcus would occasionally twirl the gold band on his finger, like he hadn't gotten used to it being there. We were having a quiet dinner at home, watching the leaves spinning down to the lawn in Central Park, when he pushed his veal away, half eaten.

"What?"

"Nothing." He rubbed his hand against his chest. "Just heartburn. We brought in Mexican for lunch."

I felt an icy prickle at the back of my neck, but I kept my voice calm as I asked him, "How long has it been hurting you?"

"I don't know. Since this afternoon, I guess." He stretched his arms over his head, yawning loudly. In our time together, I'd learned that Marcus seemed incapable of accomplishing a yawn, or a sneeze, or any other involuntary action at a volume less than deafening. It should have driven me crazy, but, somehow, I found it endearing. "We got any Pepcid?"

I hurried to the medicine cabinet. When I came back Marcus was rubbing at his chest with his knuckles. Fear tightened screws in my own chest. "I'm calling the doctor."

"Honey, don't. It's nothing."

Lightly, I said, "We're paying for concierge service. Might as well use it."

"It's nothing," he said again . . . but the way he moved, stiff-legged, to the living room, before lying down gingerly on the sofa, told me otherwise.

It turned out to be a constricted artery—no big deal, the doctor said, but better to deal with it sooner rather than later. Marcus went to Beth Israel that night, and his cardiologist did a cardiac catheterization the next morning. The radioactive dye he injected showed exactly where the artery was pinched. A simple fix, said the doctor, explaining how he'd thread a catheter through Marcus's chest, inflate a tiny balloon, use a laser to blast away the bits of plaque that remained, then pop in a stent. "Your husband will be good as new!" I held on tight to Marcus's hand as he lay on the stretcher the next morning, his legs pale beneath the blue-checked hospital gown, his normal smell of cologne diminished by whatever cleanser they'd used on the patch of shaved skin on his chest. "Don't worry, sweetie," he said, and kissed my cheek. I tried not to notice that his breath was stale and his cheek felt sandpapery. *Do I love him enough?* I wondered. If something went wrong, if I ended up caring for him, would I think of him fondly, or would he just be a burden, a sick old man holding me down?

Up in the hospital cafeteria, in my three-hundred-dollar jeans and a mohair sweater, light and soft, I sipped a cup of watery coffee, imagining, in spite of myself, what would happen if things went badly. I pictured Marcus's vast fortune as a pie, a pie currently split into four slices, one for each of his children plus a slice for his granddaughter, little Violet, a squat and beady-eyed creature with two crooked teeth, notable only for her ability to produce endless rivers of drool. Unconsciously, I pressed my hand against my midriff. I was over forty and had been on the Pill for more than two decades. Could I have a baby with Marcus? Was it even possible? Maybe it was time to find out.

I tossed my coffee cup and found myself thinking about my own mother. Her parents had named her Lorraine, but when she was a teenager she'd shortened it to Raine. Raine Stavros, first-generation American. Her parents had emigrated from Skiathos, Greece, and ended up running a diner in Toledo, where they gave birth to a fine-boned, tiny-waisted girl with wide brown eyes, a proud, shapely nose, and wavy dark-brown hair.

Lorraine might have become captain of the cheerleading squad and queen of the prom before going off to the college education her parents had spent years saving to pay for. Instead, she got pregnant the summer she was seventeen, and rather than having an abortion or giving up the baby, she had me, and named me Samantha. Her high-school boyfriend said he'd marry her, had even given her a ring, but he enlisted in the army three months before I was born . . . and this was during Vietnam. Not exactly an endorsement of what he thought life with a wife and a baby might be like.

Raine—even before I could talk, she'd instructed me to never, ever call her "Mom"—dropped out of high school. Three days after I was born, she drove home from the hospital, dropped me at her parents' house, and then, full of righteous indignation, pot, and possibly LSD, she'd taken off with her best friend in a secondhand VW Vanagon to see the world, or at least the parts of it the Grateful Dead were touring that summer. She never really came home.

When I was old enough to understand, my yaya wasted no time in telling me that she was not my mother, a fact I'd already gleaned by comparing her stiff, beauty-parlor-dyed curls and lined face to the ponytails and peppy smiles of my classmates' moms. "Here's your mother," Yaya would say, tapping one fingernail against a picture of a sullen Raine in a dress that looked like it was made out of canvas, with an empire-style waist that gathered beneath her breasts, then fell straight to the floor: a good look, considering that she was four months pregnant when the picture was taken.

"Where is she?" I would ask, and Yaya would give one of her sighs and dutifully pull out the atlas, running her finger across the country to land on the location of the Dead's latest show. I had more questions—*Why did she leave me?* and *When will she come back?* chief among them—but my grandmother's pinched face, her expression somewhere between sad and furious, kept my mouth shut.

My mother would come home a few times a year and she usually managed to show up around the holidays. She'd appear the day before Thanksgiving or three days after Christmas and, usually, in the week either before or after my birthday, as if she couldn't quite remember when the actual day had been. I remember sitting at the window, watching her slam a car door shut and bounce up the driveway, still looking like a teenager. There would be presents in her hands, the smell of incense in her clothes, necklaces twinkling against her cleavage, feathered earrings tangling in her hair. There would usually be a man in tow, hanging shyly behind her shoulder, or holding her hand possessively. Sometimes she'd be tan, if she'd been out west or down in Florida. Her hair was long then, dark-brown and shiny, hanging almost to her waist. Once, she'd come with her hair in a hundred narrow braids, with different-colored beads on the end of each one. I sat on her lap and ran my fingers endlessly through those braids, gathering them into bunches, then parting them like curtains.

I remember that her fingernails were always painted, usually either dark red or silver, and that her front teeth had bumpy little ridges on their bottoms. Once she showed up in cowgirl boots made of red leather, and I wanted those boots more than I'd ever wanted anything in my life. Easter Sunday, when I was six, she showed up at church in a white lace skirt that turned out to be completely see-through in the bright sunshine of the Easter egg roll that was held on the church's front lawn (my yaya, in a polyester blouse and black skirt, had hustled her wayward daughter back to the station wagon, hissing "You're not decent!").

Raine wore a silver ring on the second toe of her left foot and the Claddagh ring that my father had given her on her right hand. She had a blue unicorn galloping over a rainbow tattooed on her right hip. "Don't tell Yaya," she'd said merrily, laughing as she soaped me off in the shower, then gathered me into one of her mother's stiff, line-dried towels, rubbing my skin until I was pink. It stung, but I wouldn't have dreamed of complaining. I wanted her hands on me, even if they hurt. I had so little of her—a few snapshots I'd peeled from my grandparents' photo albums and kept in a shoebox under my bed, a handful of postcards she'd sent from around the country, a feathered roach clip that I'd found behind a couch cushion, and saved without knowing what it was. If I could have gotten that same tattoo, I would have done it. I wanted to be marked as hers; I wanted every moment I had with her to count.

One Christmas Day when I was nine, Raine had arrived, a little tipsy at eleven o'clock in the morning, with a red-and-white Santa hat askew on her head, her mouth bright with lipstick,

flashing an engagement ring with a tiny diamond and introducing me to a shy young man who she said would be my new
daddy. My grandmother's face folded tight as she yanked out the
pullout couch, muttering in Greek. The man got the couch (my
uncle Ryan's bedroom had been turned into a study), and Raine
slept where she normally did, next to me in my single bed, in
the narrow rectangle of a room that had once been hers. The
faded pink wallpaper was dotted with red and white balloons;
the closet, behind accordion-style plywood doors, still held some
of her clothing; and her stuff was still pinned to the walls: a blue
ribbon she'd won in a swim meet, a Polaroid of her and her one-
time best friend at a pick-your-own-pumpkin patch, Jerry Gar-
cia's face, emerging from a tie-dye swirl on a black velvet poster
above the bed.

She pulled me against her, whispering about how we'd
move to Los Angeles and have a tree that grew lemons in our
backyard. "You'll love California, Sammie," she said, telling me
about a road that ran along the cliffs looking over the ocean, and
a restaurant high on a bluff where you could eat fried shrimp
and watch the surfers; the bonfires that dotted the sand at night,
and how there was music, always music, everywhere you went.
I fought to keep from falling asleep, wanting to stay up all night
listening to her, wanting to hear every word.

When I woke up, she was gone. The sheets were still warm
from her body; the pillow still smelled like her hair. I gathered
it against me, telling myself that she'd come back and take me
away, to the house with the lemon tree in the backyard, to the
beach with the surfers and their bonfires. We would eat fried
shrimp and salty French fries and listen to music all night long.
I didn't see her again until I was seventeen.

In the hospital, with my husband in surgery, with a ring
worth more than my grandparents' house on my finger, I stared
out the window and thought about slicing up that pie: Trey and

Tommy, Bettina and the baby. What would be left for me? Then I pictured Marcus waking up, how I'd lean over him, backlit by the sun, looking like an angel as I whispered in his ear, *Honey, I want us to have a baby*. I was ready now. I'd be a wonderful mother, not like Raine. If I made promises, I would keep them.

"Miss?"

An older woman in a Yankees T-shirt had tapped my shoulder. When I turned, she smiled, showing teeth that could have been improved with a few visits to a dentist. I recognized her from the waiting room where we'd sat that morning, me next to Marcus and her beside her husband, who was, from the sound of it, having his hip replaced. "I just want to tell you," she said, hands clasped at her waist, "that it's lovely, the way you're taking care of your father."

JULES

Have you ever . . . you know?" Kimmie ducked her head shyly. It was ten o'clock on a hot August Saturday night in New York City, eighty degrees and still humid in spite of the darkness, but the window air-conditioning unit chugging away kept Kimmie's place deliciously cool. We'd gone to a screening of *Blade Runner* all the way downtown at the Angelika, and now we were sitting on the futon that took up most of the space in her grad-student-housing apartment, a studio on 110th Street and Riverside with a doll-size kitchen, a refrigerator the size of an orange crate, and a single window that afforded her a delightful view of the brick of the apartment building three feet away. It was a vast improvement over my place, in a no-name neighborhood in midtown, a fifth-floor walk-up that I shared with two other girls, where the single bedroom had been chopped into three prison-cell rectangles by particleboard walls that didn't make it all the way to the ceiling.

Every morning I took the subway down to Wall Street, to my job as a junior analyst at Steinman Cox, the investment and securities firm, which had recruited me with a six-figure salary and the promise of rapid advancement. One hundred thousand dollars a year had sounded like untold riches, but the money didn't go as far as I'd hoped, not when I was dealing with New York

City rent, paying off my loans, and trying to send a little something to each of my parents every month. The egg money had already gone to pay for rehab . . . and "junior analyst" turned out to be finance-speak for "slave." I worked for an analyst named Rajit, a dark-haired guy with deep-set eyes and bristling eyebrows who came to work every day in a suit and tie, with a gold chain-link bracelet on his wrist and an eye-watering amount of cologne clouding the air around him. Rajit advised clients on investments in the Eastern markets. Every day I'd spend endless hours "building a book," putting together research about the tin trade in Taipei, or automobile manufacturing in Hong Kong. Once a month I'd be traveling with my team for client presentations, not to the glamorous destinations featured on the firm's website but, usually, to the Midwest.

Kimmie's place was tiny, but it was all hers, and she'd filled it with colorful touches. There were brightly colored prints, Kandinsky and Frankenthaler, thumbtacked to the walls, an aloe plant in a dark-blue glazed pot on the windowsill, a jade elephant that she'd bought on our recent trip to Chinatown centered on the coffee table.

"Have I ever what?" I asked her. "Had sex?" I'd let Kimmie talk me into a glass of cold white wine. After the week I'd put in at Steinman Cox, a few sips were enough to get me feeling loose-limbed and a little loopy.

"No, no. Have you ever orgasmed?"

"Orgasmed?" I giggled. Kimmie looked at me sharply.

"Am I saying it wrong?"

"No. Well, I guess most people say 'had an orgasm.' And yes, I have. I figured out how to do that by myself when I was thirteen." Kimmie looked impressed. I shrugged modestly. "We didn't have cable TV." I didn't mention that I'd never had an orgasm during intercourse with any of the three guys I'd been with. I'd never been relaxed enough, and, honestly, I'd always felt a little revolted at the sight of each of them with their clothes off, with their strange, drippy protuberances and unexpected clumps of hair.

"Can you show me?"

"Can I . . ." I looked at her. She was staring at me seriously.

"I can't figure out how. It's very frustrating." She pointed at her computer, set up underneath the window on the smallest desk IKEA sold. "I went on YouTube to watch, but it didn't work. I get close, I think . . . but then . . ." She pursed her lips and blew a small, disappointed raspberry. "Nothing."

My tongue felt heavy, and my cheeks were burning. "You went on YouTube?"

"You can learn lots of things on YouTube," Kimmie said, unperturbed. "The *Times* had a story about makeup tutorials."

"Well, okay, eyeliner, that's one thing. But masturbation . . ." I shuddered, imagining what horrors Kimmie's computer had disgorged when she'd typed her keywords into Google.

"If you'd show me, then I'd know how." Her eyes were shining. "I read on a sex-positive blog that women need to take responsibility for their own orgasms."

"That's true," I said, gulping the rest of my wine. "Hey, Kimmie, you're not looking at sex-positive blogs at school, are you?"

She looked at me disdainfully. "I'm not stupid!"

"No," I said. I was getting the giggles again. "Just orgasm-challenged."

She got stiffly to her feet. "Never mind."

I felt bad. "No, no, I'm sorry. I didn't mean to hurt your feelings."

"So you'll show me?"

I picked up my glass again. In college, I knew people who'd done, or at least claimed to have done, all manner of wild sex-things. Same-sex experimentation, particularly among the members of certain eating clubs, was practically a graduation requirement. The two girls down the hall from me junior year had let it be known that they were in a polyamorous relationship with a guy who lived in the vegetarian co-op and wore skirts to his visual-arts seminars. And, I liked Kimmie. She was the best friend I'd had in a long, long time . . . and going through life, or even just the rest of her twenties, not knowing how to have an orgasm was a significant handicap. "Okay," I said. "I'll show you."

"Excellent!" She waved me off the futon, which she quickly shifted from its upright to its reclining position, then turned down the lamp and lit a vanilla-scented candle, which she set on the coffee table, next to the jade elephant.

"Romantic," I said, starting to giggle again. Kimmie ignored me.

"Where should I sit? Right here?" She lowered herself and sat cross-legged on the edge of the futon, fully dressed except for her shoes. All she needed was a pen and a notebook and she could have been attending a lecture.

"Wherever you want." I thought for a minute, then lay on my back on the futon, squeezed my eyes shut, and pulled my jeans and my panties off over my hips. If I'd been by myself, I would have just unzipped my jeans and slid my hand down the front . . . but Kimmie wouldn't be able to see anything that way. I lifted my head, squinting through the half light.

"Can you see okay?" I felt strangely out of breath, giggly and awkward and surprisingly aroused. The whole thing was so weird, by far the strangest sexual situation I'd ever been in, a world away from my grapplings with Dan Finnerty.

Kimmie nodded. I took a deep breath, stretching out my legs, positioning my hands the way I normally did, the left one pressed against my belly (for some reason, I liked the feeling of pressure there), the fingers of my right hand resting against my cleft. I took a quick peek and saw Kimmie sitting back on her heels, watching intently as I started stroking myself with my index finger. I closed my eyes, wanting to squirm away from her scrutiny, wishing I'd shaved. "It's kind of like this," I said. "But I don't know how helpful this is. Probably it's different for everyone."

I opened my eyes, enough to see her make an impatient gesture—*keep going.* I turned my head to the side, concentrating on the sensation, trying to ignore the strangeness of doing this with someone watching. Kimmie was so close that I could feel her breath on my belly. For a minute, I thought that nothing would happen, but it had been a little while, and maybe I was hornier than I thought, or maybe it was the wine, but I was already wet, the muscles in my belly and inner thighs fluttering in the anticipation of release. I wriggled around, getting comfortable, and arranged my fingers the way I normally did, my index finger tapping, lightly and rapidly, then nibbling more firmly against my clitoris. I couldn't keep from sighing, and Kimmie sighed, too, in approval, I thought, a little cooing noise.

"Ooh," she whispered. The futon shifted as she leaned closer. I could feel her breath on my belly, her long hair trailing against my thigh, and suddenly this went from being an academic exercise to the most exciting thing I'd ever done. I felt like a porn star, or the way I imagined porn stars must feel, desirable, sexy, controlling their audience even as they lost control themselves. I spread my legs slightly, strumming my finger faster. My voice was strangled as I said, "Watch . . . I'm close . . ." My back arched. My toes curled. I felt Kimmie's breath against my face, then her lips against mine, and her tongue slipped into my mouth as I came.

When I could breathe again, I opened my eyes. She was looking at me, a pleased smile on her face.

"Oh my God," I said, feeling stunned and dizzy, my nerve endings still jangling with pleasure. "What *was* that?"

"An orgasm," Kimmie answered promptly, like the excellent student she'd been all her life.

I sat up, reaching for the light down comforter Kimmie kept folded in a basket next to the futon, and pulled it up over my legs. Then I flopped back, feeling delighted, but with a new fear dimming my afterglow. Did this mean I was gay? I'd never even considered it. I'd never looked at a woman with anything resembling desire, just evaluation, and envy of specific body parts—this one's breasts, that one's legs. Besides Kimmie, I'd never even considered kissing a girl . . . but now, I found, I was very interested in kissing Kimmie again.

I rolled onto my elbow. She was still dressed, in her jeans and her button-front Henley tee shirt. "Let's see if you got it," I said, and reached out, brushing her hair behind her ears. She gave me her trickster's grin, wriggling out of her clothes. Her body, I discovered, wasn't so boyish after all . . . and when I took her in my arms and kissed her, first her forehead, then her faintly freckled nose, then her lips, it felt like I'd been waiting my whole life to end up with her in my arms.

After Kimmie fell asleep, I lay there, sated and content, at ease in my own body in a way I hadn't been since I was a little girl, wrapped in a towel and warmed by the sun after a morning bodysurfing in the ocean with my dad. Physically, I was at peace, but my mind raced, looking for labels, asking questions about what had just happened, how it would work and whether it could last. Finally, I tried to turn my thoughts to where they usually went at night: to the eggs I'd sold.

They'd warned me about this at the fertility center. The material they'd given me included the number for a counselor to call if I found myself "dwelling" on my donation, and had mentioned that some donors had benefited from talk therapy or the short-term use of antidepressants. I didn't think I needed any of that yet, but I had definitely found myself thinking about it—dwelling—more than I'd expected.

The process had gone smoothly: I'd donated my eggs in late May and deposited my check when it arrived ten days later. Six weeks after that, my father was in Willow Crest doing a twenty-eight-day inpatient stay, which would include a physical and psychological evaluation, group therapy, individual therapy, music therapy, and art therapy. He'd made me a collage full of pictures cut from magazines—girls running, girls leaping, girls laughing over their bowls of salad—and he'd smiled when I'd told him, straight-faced, that I would cherish it forever.

I knew I wouldn't be hearing from him for a while. The counselors had explained that residents weren't allowed to have cell phones or send e-mail. There was one pay phone that was made available for an hour each day, and usually there was a very long line. As my father worked through the twelve steps, they said, he would make amends to those he'd wronged, but I should be patient, should "manage my expectations." When I'd gone out to Pittsburgh to take him to Willow Crest, he'd come to the door of the apartment to meet me. I'd peered down the dark hallway and glimpsed Rita in the bedroom, but she'd shut the door before I could call "hello." His hair was clean, cut short, combed back from his forehead, and in the new shirt and jeans he wore he looked better than I'd seen him looking in years.

We had lunch together in the place's cafeteria, a loud, low-ceilinged room that reminded me of a school, with posters on the walls (covered in AA slogans, instead of warnings about Stranger Danger or invitations to the Summer Reading Program), flimsy paper napkins and square cartons of milk. The food, too, seemed intended for children: mac and cheese served on segmented plastic trays; cheap metal spoons and forks, no knives. I'd chattered about my job, turning my pig of a boss into a charming character, telling my dad about the three meals a day they had delivered and leaving out the part about how we got free food because our corporate masters didn't want us taking longer than twenty minutes for breakfast or lunch. I made much of the Friday-night happy hours, where the analysts would gather in an Irish pub around the corner from our office, a place so generic it could have been plucked from a mall in Minneapolis. In truth, these were grim affairs, marked by too many drinks and ill-advised hookups, and they rarely began before eleven p.m. because all of us worked so late.

"Proud of you," my father muttered, forking noodles into his mouth. His hands shook as he scooted his tray closer. At twelve-thirty, a counselor wearing lots of turquoise jewelry stopped by the table. "Time to say goodbye now," she announced. I tried as hard as I could not to look relieved as I walked out into the sunshine.

On the bus ride back to the Port Authority, I'd done my best to reassure myself that it would all work out. Willow Crest had the highest success rate of any place my father could have gone. Besides, he wasn't a typical addict. He was intelligent; he had people who loved him. People who needed him. Me.

Kimmie sighed in her sleep. Her face was still flushed, her hair a tousled, fragrant mess. I put my hand on her shoulder, shivery with delight. Over our first months in the city, Kimmie and I had spent all of our free time together, reading *New York* magazine and picking out a restaurant we wanted to try or a play we wanted to see. I was in charge of transportation, using subway and bus maps to figure out the fastest and most economical route, while Kimmie scoured the Internet for coupons and discounts and last-minute tickets, doing such a good job of it that one day, I joked, the performers would pay us for attending their plays, and the waiters would leave tips on our table.

All through July, we'd traded pieces of our history. Kimmie's parents, Korean immigrants who'd met in an English as a Second Language class in 1975, ran a dry-cleaning shop in Boston. They'd papered Kimmie's bedroom walls with pictures of every Asian woman who'd succeeded in any field in America. "Michelle Kwan, Sandra Oh, Julie Chen, Margaret Cho, girl in my high school who went to Harvard," Kimmie had recited as we'd walked to a bookstore in the West Village.

"Margaret Cho the comedian? Isn't she kind of X-rated?"

"They don't care. All they know is that she makes a lot of money." Kimmie and her parents and her sister had lived in an apartment above the dry-cleaning shop that was always steamy and smelled like chemicals, but she'd never worked there. Her parents had decided early on that she'd never set foot in the family business, that she and her sister, Lisa, four years younger, were meant for better things. It had just taken them a while to determine which things those would be.

"We both had skating lessons," Kimmie began, lifting one slim finger.

"How'd that work?"

She giggled, shaking her head, long black hair brushing her shoulders. "I used to ditch and go to the movies. Then—oh, let's see. Special science enrichment classes, in case I turned out to be gifted in science . . ."

"Which you are," I pointed out. Kimmie had been a Presidential Scholar and a Westinghouse Science finalist. After graduating from Princeton with highest honors, she'd enrolled at Columbia, where she planned on getting a master's degree in biochemistry before heading south to Johns Hopkins for an MD/PhD.

She shrugged off my compliment. "Not as gifted as they thought I'd be."

"What are you talking about?" I asked.

Another shrug. "They were disappointed that I wasn't more musical. That it didn't come more naturally. My mother had been a violinist. Before they came here." I knew, because she'd told me already that Lisa was a gifted cellist, a senior in high school currently deciding between Juilliard and Harvard. I knew, also, that Kimmie believed (correctly, I thought) that Lisa was their favorite, that even with a *summa* from Princeton and three more prestigious degrees to come, they still regarded Kimmie as a bit of a letdown. Nor had they been thrilled when she'd brought Chet home. He was Christian, and that was important to them, but they'd expected her to marry a Korean boy, preferably one whose parents they knew.

"What about you?" Kimmie asked me as we lay spooned against each other on her futon, with her air conditioner humming in the window.

"What about me?"

"Are your parents proud?"

I didn't answer right away. My father had been proud, of course. He'd graduated from the University of Pittsburgh, the first in his family to go to college, the first not to work in a factory or on a farm. He'd been the one to fuel my dreams of the Ivy League, describing the schools, their history, their grandeur, the brilliant, world-changing graduates they'd produced. It was the photographs of Princeton that made up my mind—a girl, her long hair in a ponytail, perched on a window seat in a dorm room that had a fireplace. I was enchanted by everything I saw—her shiny hair, the dark wood of the window seat, the many-paned window, the fire crackling away.

My grades and test scores were solid, but I knew that it was my essay that had gotten me into Princeton. "The Addict's Daughter," I'd called it, and I'd told myself that only a handful of people would ever read it, and my father wouldn't be one of them.

Parents aren't supposed to have favorites, I'd written, *and probably children shouldn't, either, but my father and I have always shared a special bond. The first thing I can remember is the two of us reading together*—Alice's Adventures in Wonderland. *I'd read a page, he'd help me sound out the hard words, and then we'd go to the kitchen to make his coffee and my hot chocolate. My father taught English to eighth-graders. He loved being a teacher, and his students loved him, and I felt lucky to have as much of his time as I did.*

When I was a freshman in high school, he was arrested for drunk driving after he ran a stop sign and smashed into a car carrying a woman and her young son. It came unexpectedly, at least from my perspective. Maybe there'd been signs, but at fourteen all I knew was that one day he was fine and the next day he was in the hospital, in detox, and then, a year later, he was in jail. One day he was a respected, beloved, award-winning teacher, and the next he was in the newspapers, a punch line, a cautionary tale, a joke.

Hospitalization and medicine and therapy gave him back some semblance of normal . . . but then he got laid off, and lost his insurance, and began to drink again, and to substitute street drugs for the prescription medication, chasing the peace the meds had given him, that feeling of returning to himself. Now my father doesn't work at all. He lives with a girlfriend, in Section 8 housing, his life a patchwork of stopgap measures and self-medication.

I'd closed the essay by explaining that I wanted to study public policy and political science, to change the laws so that nobody fell through a flawed system's cracks again. That had been a lie. I liked the idea of working in government, but the truth was that I needed money to help him—to pay for rehab, or a deposit on an apartment, or whatever training he'd need to get his teaching certificate back. That meant majoring in economics instead of English or political science; it meant taking a junior analyst's job instead of an entry-level position in an NGO or a think tank. Maybe someday, when I'd paid off my loans and my father was well again, I could do what I'd told those admissions offices I would—get a master's in public policy, do some good in the world. But until then . . . I sighed. On the futon, Kimmie snuggled against me, then kissed my cheek.

"What's wrong?" she asked.

"My dad," I said, with my eyes squeezed shut. "My job." I could still picture the Steinman Cox recruiters: the man in a beautifully tailored navy suit and a woman whose shoes I'd seen at Saks and whose dress I recognized from *Vogue.* They'd talked about opportunities and advancement, about London and Paris and Japan. Their brochures were impeccable, their website, a beautiful enticement, filled with shots of attractive young people of many races and cultures talking enthusiastically about everything they'd learned and achieved. Of course, nobody had posted a picture of an overheated office with flickering fluorescent lights, or mentioned that I'd be working in a tiny cube, in close quarters with men who were always shouting, that the walls retained the acrid smell of body odor and fish from the sushi lunches. Nobody said that eighty-hour workweeks were common, and hundred-hour weeks not unheard of when you were working on an active deal, or that your travel would take you to places like Akron and Duluth, where you'd be responsible for things as mundane as hotel and dinner reservations and making sure the Town Cars arrived on time . . . and finding the closest strip club, should your boss be the type.

Kimmie propped herself on her elbow and looked at me. "Dad. Job. Anything else?"

"My eggs," I admitted. "I wonder . . ." I began, before stopping and shaking my head.

"Wonder what?"

"I guess," I said, speaking slowly, "that I'd just feel better if I knew where they went. What had happened. If they were, you know, just sitting around on ice somewhere, or if they'd been fertilized."

She tossed her hair back over her shoulders. Her eyes were gleaming with what I'd come to recognize as mischief. "I bet I could find out."

"No," I said. "We can't." I'd signed up for an anonymous donation, where prospective parents could find out only the information I'd provided, and I'd never have to meet them, or answer their questions, or ask them any of my own. Given my family history—given, in particular, my father—it had seemed safer that way. Besides, anonymous donors got a five-thousand-dollar bonus—presumably because our eggs would be easier to place, since we wouldn't be able to judge the prospective parents and dismiss them because we didn't like their answers or their looks or the town where they lived or the car that they drove.

Kimmie flicked her hand through the air. "They're your eggs. You've got a right to know."

"They *were* my eggs. I sold them."

"Morally," she said, "it's your genetic material. You could make a case that you've got a right to know."

I shook my head. "I signed my rights away. It's none of my business anymore."

She looked at me closely. "You really believe that?"

I sat up, pulling my knees to my chest. "I don't know. Maybe there's a way I could set it up so the kid could find me. I could watch over it. Like Magwitch in *Great Expectations*," I said, thinking back to the conversation my father and I had shared the day I'd first mentioned rehab. "I could be its mysterious benefactor."

Kimmie gave me an indulgent smile. "You live in an apartment with two other girls. You reuse plastic bags. How are you going to be anyone's mysterious benefactor?"

She had a point. "Well, not now. But someday. I could send cards. Birthday cards. Everyone likes a secret admirer, right?" If I survived Steinman Cox, if I proved that I could endure the shouting and the smells and the stomach-knotting tension and the days that began before the sun came up and ended well after it went down, then someday I'd be in the position to be a mysterious benefactor. All of this would be worth something. It had to be.

I pulled her into my arms again. She giggled, then kissed my earlobe, then my neck. "You are so beautiful," she said . . . and for the first time in my life, the words didn't make me cringe or blush or feel like a fraud. For the first time in my life, I thought they could be true.

ANNIE

I spent a lot of time thinking about what to wear to the first meeting at the fertility clinic. My clothes, I knew, would make a statement. Too fancy and it would look like I was desperate— or, worse, like I didn't really need the money; too casual, and it would look like I didn't care.

I stood in front of my shallow closet, finally taking out a black dress made of a forgiving, stretchy material. It wasn't, technically, a maternity dress, but it had enough give that I could wear it through the winter if things went as planned.

I slid the black dress off its hanger and sat on the bed with a sigh.

"Just put it on. It's fine," said Nancy, who'd agreed to watch the boys while I made the trip to the clinic, sparing me the sixty dollars a sitter would have cost. When I'd asked if she was sure she'd be okay, she'd snapped, "Don't be silly. I like kids." Instead of pointing out the ample evidence to the contrary, the way she always called Spencer "Frank Junior Junior," instead of remembering his name, and declared that she and Dr. Scott were "childless by choice," I thanked her, then asked her if she could come a little early and help me figure out what to wear.

"It's not fine," I said, holding the dress up against me. It felt like I was going on a date, only instead of getting dressed up, fussing with my hair and my makeup, hoping that the man I'd be meeting would like me and find me pretty and smart and interesting, here I was, seven years after I'd gotten married, doing the same thing, only it would be a woman doing the evaluating. And women, as any woman will tell you, are much tougher on themselves and on one another than men would ever be.

I slipped the dress over my head, slid my feet into the low-heeled black pumps I wore to church, and studied myself in the mirror. I thought I looked all right. Maybe this lady, this India Croft, would think that my woven straw handbag (ten dollars at Target with my employee discount) was deliberately whimsical, and wouldn't guess that I'd picked it because it was the only purse I had that hadn't been chewed on or spat up in, survived a spilled bottle, or housed a dirty diaper.

"You look fine," Nancy repeated, and smoothed her own highlighted hair, giving herself an approving look in my mirror. My sister had arrived at the house that morning with Tupperware containers full of various organic and sprouted things. There were soy-cheese quesadillas, goji berries, a pomegranate and a protein shake, plus her very own plates and an aluminum water bottle. "You know about the toxins in plastic," she'd said, frowning at the sippy cup Spencer was sucking. I'd murmured something about replacing the boys' cups and plates soon, thinking that on my ever-evolving to-do list, that wouldn't even make the top hundred.

I went to the kitchen for my car keys and a mug of mint tea. I would have preferred coffee. I hadn't slept well the night before and was worried about getting drowsy behind the wheel. But as an expectant mother-to-be—I hoped—I knew enough not to show up with coffee on my breath.

"Be good," I told the boys, who'd been bribed with an extra half hour of *Go, Diego, Go!* "Listen to Aunt Nancy. She's the boss while Mommy's gone. Spencer, did you hear me? Do you understand? And Frank Junior, how about you?" I repeated their names, in part so they'd acknowledge my seriousness, in part to increase the chance of Nancy's remembering them.

"Just go already," Nancy ordered as I rifled through my purse. There was my wallet, a tube of lipstick, my Mapquest directions, the list of questions I'd printed out at the library, huddling in front of the printer so that nobody could see what I was doing. I knew the longer I hung around, the more likely it would be that the boys wouldn't let me leave, so I walked to the car and started driving.

Two hours later I was sitting in the Princeton Fertility Clinic. The clinic director, Leslie, trim and brisk in her suit, had walked me back to a room that must have been specially designed for just this moment, when a prospective surrogate and the woman who'd be paying the bills (*buying the baby*, I kept thinking, and trying not to think) would first set eyes on each other. The walls were the peach of melting sherbet, and there was a painting of a mother gazing tenderly at an infant in her arms. A love seat was upholstered in a light golden fabric. I gave it a quick pat, then a longer one, enjoying its softness and its lack of stains, wondering how long it would last in my house.

The coffee table was set with a china teapot, a carafe of ice water with translucent circles of lemon floating on the top. Fanned out in a circle on a plate was a ring of Mint Milanos that it was taking all my willpower to avoid. I'd been torn about dieting. On the one hand, maybe infertile women would want their surrogate to look robust and healthy, with broad shoulders and wide hips that evoked peasants in the field, squatting to give birth without missing a swing of their scythes. Then again, rich people hated fat people, maybe because they thought that being fat was the same as being lazy, or they were afraid of becoming fat themselves. I ignored the cookies and checked out the china instead. The sugarbowl and cream pitcher had a lacy blue-on-white pattern, and the spoons and the tongs resting on top of the sugar cubes were probably real silver.

"Just a few minutes," Leslie had said before closing the door, but it had already been more like fifteen. I wondered why she hadn't just left me in the waiting room, the one I'd glimpsed online and had walked through on my way back here. I could understand why the women hiring the surrogates, the infertile ones, might not want anyone else to see them, but as for me, I was just there to do a job, same as if I'd been back working at Target, and in the waiting room at least there were magazines.

Target made me think of Gabe, and thinking of Gabe made me remember the bad patch in my marriage, the part I hadn't mentioned on the forms. For distraction, I eased a single Milano out of its place and slipped it into my mouth, letting the sugary wafer dissolve on my tongue. I was trying to rearrange the circle so it wouldn't look like any of the cookies were missing. Of course, that was the moment the door swung open and Leslie and a slender, graceful, beautifully dressed woman walked inside.

I got to my feet as Leslie trilled the introductions. "Ms. Croft, this is Anne Barrow. Annie, this is India Croft."

She was Ms., and I was Annie. *So it begins,* I thought. For a moment, the two of us stared at each other. India Croft had the look I expected, a rich-lady look (*rich bitch look,* I thought, before I could stop myself), like one of the women from those *Real Housewives of New York* episodes I sometimes watched when Frank was working. I knew better than to tune in when he was home. "Bunch of silly people who think they've got problems," he'd grumble, and I couldn't deny it, or explain to him that sometimes the problems were kind of interesting, and it was at least fun to look at their clothes and their houses, and feel good that your kids weren't half as bratty as theirs.

India Croft was white, like I'd expected, with smooth, unlined skin. Her heart-shaped face narrowed to a neat little chin. Her lips were full and glossed, her nose was small, adorably tilted, her brows were perfectly shaped, and, beneath them, her eyes were wide, almost startled. That, I figured, was probably the Botox—lots of the Real Housewives had that exact same expression, like someone had just pinched their behinds. Her hair was somewhere between chestnut and copper, with all the shades in between, long and thick and shiny. She wore a pale-lavender cashmere sweater set—at least, I thought it was cashmere, but, not owning any cashmere myself, I was really just guessing—and a crisp skirt, chocolate-brown with a pattern of loops and swirls embroidered in darker-brown thread acroos it. I would have never thought to put brown and pinkish-purple together, but it was perfect. The contrast between the pastel of the sweater and the rich cocoa of the skirt, the soft cashmere and the crisp linen, was like something I'd see on a mannequin or in a magazine. Her legs were tanned and bare. She wore dark-brown cork-soled espadrilles with ribbons that wrapped around her slim calves. I could smell her perfume, something flowery and sweet, and that, of course, was perfect, too.

Standing there, my mouth full of Mint Milano mush, sweating in my long-sleeved dress, I felt big as a battleship and just as ungainly. I swallowed, ran my tongue over my teeth, and stepped forward, saying the words I'd rehearsed in the car: "It's a pleasure to meet you."

"Hello," she said. She tugged at one lilac cuff, then the other, shaking that gorgeous hair against her back, and I felt the strangest sensation of being seen . . . not seen, exactly, but recognized. It felt as if, somehow, she was able to see me standing there in my cheap dress and my not-right purse and know me, everything I was, everything I hoped for: how I wanted to redo my kitchen and build a little office, that I wanted to buy my sons new winter jackets, that I wanted, someday, to go to Paris, and go to college, to have shelves full of books I'd read and understood, to have an important job. I felt like she saw me not just as a mother or wife or person in a Target pinny who knew how to find the Lego sets and the scrubbing pads, but as myself, loving and complicated and angry sometimes.

"Anne . . . Barrow, is it?" she said, in a pleasant voice. I pegged her at forty. A pretty forty, a young-looking forty, a forty who probably watched what she ate and worked out every day, but still, forty was forty, and forty was, in my opinion, a little too late to get started with the whole baby-making thing. I wondered why she'd waited, what her story was, and if I'd ever get to hear it.

"Annie," I told her, and held out my hand.

BETTINA

After thinking it over for a few days, I'd decided to tell my brothers what Kate Klein had found out, thinking they'd be just as alarmed as I was and that one of them would know what to do.

Trey had been with Violet when I'd called—I could hear her babbling in the background—and he'd told me, in between her trips up and down the slide at the neighborhood park, that I shouldn't rain on my father's parade. "It's America. Everyone gets a second act," he said after I'd given him the most damning portion of India's dossier. Which left me with Tommy. I had just bought a ticket for his upcoming show, thinking I'd present the evidence in person, when my cell phone rang. The number on the screen was for Kate Klein's office, but Darren Zucker was the one on the line.

"How are you doing?" he asked me.

"Fine," I said.

"Busy?"

"Not really." I'd been looking at Victorian jewelry that morning, gorgeously worked, ornate pieces, necklaces and engagement rings, the kind of thing I'd want for myself—small and special, the opposite of India's ostentatious rock.

"You sound busy." Darren himself sounded vaguely insulted.

I softened my tone, reminding myself that he was a messenger, albeit a messenger in goofy glasses, and it wasn't his fault that India was a liar. A thought occurred. "Would you like to go to a concert with me?"

"What, like a date?" Now he sounded surprised.

"As friends," I said firmly. I wasn't interested in Darren, with his limp handshake and his hipster affectations. In addition, he knew exactly how much my father was worth and probably how much I was, too, and, while it wasn't as if this information was some big secret, knowing that Darren had access to specifics made me want to keep him at a distance. I didn't like him . . . but I didn't like the thought of traipsing through Hoboken by myself, either, and all of my friends had put in their time at my brother's performances.

"You got a man?" he persisted.

"None of your business."

"Taking that as a no," he said cheerfully, and, over my protests, told me he'd meet me in front of my apartment at nine o'clock Friday night.

"So what's the band called again?" he asked as we walked along a sidewalk in Hoboken.

"Dirty Birdy," I said, keeping an eye out for broken glass and dog excrement. "They were Cöld Söre for a while. With umlauts."

"But of course," Darren said.

"But then the bass player left, and they reformed, and now they're Dirty Birdy." The band was third on the bill, not scheduled to go on until midnight, which, realistically, could mean much later than that. Darren, who still seemed to be laboring under the misapprehension that this was a date, took my arm as we navigated past a puddle of what looked like vomit. It was nice having him with me, sort of like having our old golden retriever, Mittens, loping along at my side.

I looked at the doorways, then down at my iPhone. "It should be right here. The club-slash-coffee-shop is called Drip, and I checked the address before leaving my apartment." But there was no sign on the plain red door, no number, nothing to indicate that there was a business behind it.

Darren looked at my screen, then looked at the door. Then he knocked. The door swung open. Smoke and loud voices poured out into the street, and a muscled bouncer held out one tattooed mitt. "Ten dollars," he said.

Darren peeled off a twenty. "You need a sign," I told the bouncer, who looked at me like he didn't understand English. "Seriously," I said, twisting through the crush of bodies, pulling my earplugs out of my pocket and hoping against hope that there'd be something as pedestrian as a table in the place. Fat chance. There were no tables in sight, just a bar that ran the length of the room, a couch upholstered in hideous paisley sagging against one wall, and a makeshift stage up front.

"What can I get you?" Darren asked.

"Whatever," I said, trying not to sulk, or yawn. The room was hot and crowded, crammed with people who all seemed to be having more fun than I'd ever had in my life. Girls with glitter on their faces and tattoos on the smalls of their backs swigged from cans of Pabst and Coors, waving their arms in the air and swinging their hips as they spun around in tiny circles.

"Beer?" he asked. "Wine? Sloe gin fizz?"

"Vodka and tonic," I said. It had been my parents' summertime drink. In the Hamptons, they'd carried thermoses of V and Ts to the beach. I was ready for the worst, but the drink came in a clean glass, frosty on the outside, with a thick wedge of lime balanced on the rim. I took a sip, watching the girls dancing, trying to decide if they were high.

"Not bad," Darren said, as Dirty Birdy finally took the stage and launched into their cover of Tracy Chapman's "Fast Car." "Is that your brother? He's really good!"

I nodded, wondering if Darren actually enjoyed this noise, if anyone could. Tommy had a nice voice—he'd sung in choir in school—but all of his sweetness was drowned out by the volume of the pounding drums and the squealing guitars.

Forty minutes later, Tommy bounded off the stage, sweaty and smelling of beer and cigarette smoke. I introduced them, and my brother and Darren exchanged "hey, mans" and handshakes. Then I asked Darren to excuse us and walked Tommy to the bar, where I pulled Kate Klein's folder out of my purse. "It's about India," I hollered into my brother's ear. Tommy looked inside the folder for a minute, then looked over at the blonde in a ridiculously tiny T-shirt making eyes at him from the corner. After a minute, he sighed and pushed his beer at me. I pushed it right back.

"You know what, Betts?" His voice was raspy after shouting into the microphone. "This is none of our business."

I drew back as if he'd slapped me. "Of course it's our business! He's being used. This woman is taking advantage of him." My voice trailed off. Tommy patted my shoulder the way he would a puppy's head. "Let it go," he whispered in my ear. Then he lifted his head. "Hey, you and Derek want to hang out?"

I glared at him. "His name is Darren. And it is two o'clock in the morning, so no, we do not want to hang out." He shrugged. I watched him go, standing like I was frozen on the sticky floor of the bar in Hoboken—Hoboken! I'd gone all the way to Hoboken!—before pushing the folder into my bag and stomping out the door in the jeans I'd bought for the occasion. Not that they made any difference. Even my jeans were wrong—too loose, too new, too dark, the wrong cut, the wrong brand, the wrong something.

"Hey, you okay?" Darren asked, following me into the darkness, toward the train that would take us back to the city. I could feel sweat gluing my blouse to the small of my back, where I would never have a tattoo. "Not great," I'd said.

"Can I help?" he asked.

I shook my head. "Thank you for coming," I said. We rode home in silence. He escorted me up the subway stairs, bought me a bottle of water at the Korean grocery store on my corner, and walked me to my door.

"If you want to talk about it   ." He looked sweet and hopeful, even cute, if you could ignore the glasses, but all I wanted was to be alone.

"I don't," I said. He handed me the water. Then he set his hands on my shoulders. Surprised, I stumbled backward, catching my heel on the curb. I would have fallen if he hadn't been holding me . . . but, of course, if he hadn't been holding me I wouldn't have tripped in the first place. Then, just like that, his lips were on mine, warm and gentle, and he'd pulled my body against his so that we were chest to chest, hip to hip. In that instant, I wasn't hot, wasn't tired, wasn't irritated at the way the night had gone or worried about how exhausted I'd be the next day. I wanted to keep kissing him, to have him keep kissing me, even though I'd never approved of couples who kissed on the street. Then, as suddenly as he'd started, he stopped, releasing my shoulders, stepping back onto the sidewalk. "Betsy," he said.

"Don't call me that."

"Tina?"

"Family only."

"Betts?"

"Only if I get to call you Dare."

He grinned, tipped an imaginary hat, and set off in the direction of the subway, hands in his pockets, whistling.

Upstairs, I got out of my clothes and into the shower and stood there, letting the cool water wash over me. It was almost three in the morning, and I'd met with nothing but frustration as I'd tried to make my family see the absurdity of what my father and India were attempting . . . but still I fell asleep with a smile.

The following weekend I went to the one person I thought would see the gravity of the situation; I made my first trip ever to my mother's ashram. I booked a ticket to New Mexico and flew out from LaGuardia on Saturday morning. I rented a car at the airport and followed the GPS's directions through forty-five miles of blasted-looking desert interrupted by gas stations, the occasional casino, and clusters of Native Americans selling blankets by the side of the road.

The Baba had done well for himself. The parking lot was paved, the grounds of the Enlightenment Center beautifully landscaped, oases of jewel-green grass accented with fountains and manicured beds of flowers. I sat for forty-five minutes on a stone bench in the cool, tiled lobby of a little adobe building that I refused to call a yurt, listening to the tinkling of water into a basin, sipping tea that tasted like boiled twigs, and glaring at a young woman in a white linen caftan who answered the telephone in an annoyingly mellifluous voice. "Love, light, fulfillment," she would singsong. When I pulled out my iPhone she used the same dopey voice to say that electronic devices were not permitted ("They disrupt your aura").

Eventually, my mother glided in, dressed in white robes of rough linen, her familiar musky, sandalwood-and-patchouli scent filling the air. I felt my eyes burning, and I looked away, blinking, not wanting to let her see how much I still missed her, how jealous I was of the people who had their mothers there to help them through their twenties. A mother could help you choose and furnish your first apartment; she could listen to however much you chose to tell her about your love life; she could offer a loan or a sympathetic ear or even just a night when you could go back to the place you'd grown up in, sit in the kitchen while she made your favorite meal, and be a child again. All of that had been denied me, thanks to her selfishness, and to the Baba.

I clamped down on my fury as she led me to an empty yoga studio and handed me a buckwheat-filled bolster to perch on, explaining, as she arranged her own body, the importance of opening our hips. I sat cross-legged, awkward in my skirt and heels and sleeveless silk blouse (I'd taken off my jacket and left it in the car). My mother laid a woven Indian blanket over my lap, then looked me over with a tolerant and utterly infuriating smile.

"What?" I asked.

"It's just that we don't see many women dressed like you are."

I looked down at my clothing, my Ferragamo pumps, and didn't answer, thinking that she used to dress this way, too, that I was just as she'd made me, which gave her no right to judge.

My mother took my hands in hers. "What's troubling you?" Her voice, once a combination of broad midwestern and New York City lockjaw, had become as syrupy and singsongy as the girl's behind the counter had been. Her silvery-gray hair, which she'd been wearing in ridiculous Pocahontas braids before she'd left, was clipped short now, almost a buzz cut that exposed the oval shape of her skull and her elfin ears. Her pale-blue eyes looked enormous in her face. She wasn't wearing makeup, and her skin was freckled and rosy from the sun. There were no earrings in her ears, no rings on her fingers, not a single bracelet or bangle, and she was barefoot underneath her robe, her toenails unpainted, her small feet calloused and tanned.

"Dad was in the hospital. He had a blocked artery. They gave him a stent."

She sighed. "He has so much stress in his life. He needs to slow down."

Whatever. "His new wife . . . I found out some things about her. Some bad things."

She nodded again. At least she was looking at me and not at her guru, whose framed portrait beamed down from the front of the room. The Baba had grown his long hair even longer, and was sitting cross-legged, a beatific smile on his face, like a white Jimi Hendrix in a bathrobe.

"They want to have a baby."

This, finally, got her attention. She cocked her head at a quizzical angle, eyes narrowed, jaw tight. I remembered that expression from when I'd come home to tell her that another girl had stolen my bookbag at lunch, and from the time she'd been ousted as head of the annual diabetes dance (this was the year after she'd insisted that the passed appetizers be vegan). I heard her take a deep breath, inhaling through her nose, before she said, "The Buddha instructs us to welcome new life in the spirit of gladness and joy."

"Mother."

"Satya," she corrected, touching my knee beneath the blanket.

I felt my lips curl. "Satya. They're paying some woman to donate her egg. They're paying another woman to carry a baby for them. And this woman, Dad's new wife, is seriously no good."

She reached forward, placing her cool hands on mine. "Change is the only constant," she intoned. "Sorrow is like a leaf in a stream. Sit on the banks. Watch it pass."

"You may recall," I said, with some asperity, "offering me slightly different advice before the Barneys sample sale."

She smiled. Serenely. Indicating her plain robes, she said, "Suffering ends when craving ends," like this was a message of incredible profundity instead of something her guru had probably cribbed from a Starbucks cup. "I was lost to myself in New York. Now I've come home. So what about you, Bettina? What is it you crave? How can you find your way home?"

"I've got a ticket on the five-thirty flight to LaGuardia," I said. It wasn't like I could tell her that home was forever lost to me, because home was the five of us, together, the way we used to be. Nor did I mention that, hoping against hope, I'd bought a ticket for her, too.

She rose easily to her feet and walked me to another fountain, this one outdoors, a verdigris-green bowl into which water trickled from a sculpted flower. We sat there in silence, smelling sage and some flowers I didn't recognize. "Be well," she said. I knew it was a dismissal. She kissed my cheek and glided off to her chores.

It wasn't until I'd dropped off the rental car and was flying back to New York that I figured out what else I wanted: my father's safety, his happiness, an assurance that he would not get his heart broken again. These were perfectly reasonable things to desire. Trey was too wrapped up in Violet's new teeth and soiled diapers to care; Tommy was too busy chasing women who thought it was witty when a man sang a heavy-metal cover of "Sunny Came Home"; my mother had renounced the world entirely; which meant that I would have to keep my father safe. If I did that, maybe I could keep India's bony, grasping hands off our money . . . and maybe I could have a chance at the thing I most missed and most wanted: my family back.

The Monday after my trip to New Mexico, I was down in the Crypt, wearing white cotton gloves, working with a Tensor lamp and a magnifying glass and tweezers to determine the value of an antique silver locket that was part of a new lot of jewelry. "These things are precious to me," the woman who'd brought them in had said. "They were my mother's." I'd dug out a reference book, trying to determine the age of the locket and whether the chain was original to the piece, when Darren Zucker called.

"Just checking in," he said. "How was your trip?"

"Fine," I said automatically.

"I was wondering what you decided to do." His voice was high, a little nasal, the voice of a Woody Allen wannabe for whom the whole world was a joke.

"Are you billing me for this?" I asked.

"You have a suspicious and untrusting nature. But I respect that. And no, this isn't business. I was just curious. It's how I wound up in this line of work—being curious. And I was thinking you might want someone to talk to. You know, do the Franklin list."

"Pardon?"

"Ben Franklin. Draw a line down the middle of a piece of paper. List the pros and cons. We could have lunch."

I closed my book and gently replaced the necklace in its box. Darren Zucker was not my ideal confidant, but he'd been a good sport about our trip to Hoboken, and besides, I did need to eat. There were no windows in the Crypt, but when I'd arrived that morning the weather had been a beautiful day, the sky deep blue, a light breeze stirring the treetops. September in New York City always felt, to me, like the year's true beginning. It made me think of the last days of summer, loading up the station wagon in Bridgehampton for the ride back to the city. We'd stay in the Hamptons as long as we could, wringing every last minute out of August. My parents would throw a barbecue on Labor Day, inviting anyone who was left: the neighbors, our staff, their kids, the lifeguards who'd watched us swimming all summer long. We'd eat chicken and ribs, potato chips and thick slices of watermelon on paper plates. Games of tag and Marco Polo and hide and seek would form, break up, and re-form, and, as it got late, children would fall asleep all over the house, in beds, on couches, in nests of blankets and pillows on the floor.

As the night went on, the grown-ups would gather on the porch and the lawn, drinking vodka tonics or beers. On that night, instead of their usual jeans and chino shorts and tennis skirts, they'd get dressed up, the men in button-down shirts and jackets, and the women in Lilly Pulitzer skirts or sundresses that left their tanned arms and shoulders bare. Some of them still smoked back then, and I remembered looking at the lit cigarettes bobbing and darting like fireflies, music coming from a CD player plugged in on the porch, the sound of their laughter, and how I would think, *This is how I want it to be when I grow up.*

Darren and I met at the Shake Shack in Madison Square Park. Where else, I thought wearily, would a committed hipster take a girl for lunch? He'd already staked out a bench when I arrived and was waving at me, wearing his glasses, khakis, and a short-sleeved button-down shirt, checked blue-and-white, which looked like it had been swiped from some homeless man's closet. I was in my usual office wear, an A-line black cotton skirt, a plum-colored boatneck sweater with three pearl buttons at each sleeve, low-heeled shoes, and a gold necklace. "Chocolate? Vanilla?" Darren asked, holding out two cups. "The line gets crazy, so I bought one of each." He'd also gotten two cheeseburgers with everything and an order of fries.

He opened the paper sack, and we spread our lunch on our laps. Darren took a big bite of cheeseburger and sighed happily, the way a man with his mouth full of meat will, as I removed the lettuce and tomato from my own burger with my fingertips and set them aside before carefully peeling away the cheese.

"Oh, come on," he said as I took a small bite. "Don't tell me you're one of those rabbit-food girls."

I didn't bother to respond. For years, I'd read those "Make

the Most of Your Figure!" articles, the ones that told you how to dress if you were a pear or an hourglass or an inverted triangle, and I'd used all the tips they'd recommend to try to balance my narrow shoulders and flat chest with my wide hips and heavy thighs, but I wasn't sure whether any of it did much good. Nor did dieting help. I'd done the rounds with that in high school, two weeks of grapefruit and hard-boiled eggs, a stint on Weight Watchers sophomore year and another on Jenny Craig when I was a junior. When I started college I'd tried a few of my room-mate Vanessa's diet pills, but all they did was give me a perma-nent headache and make my mouth feel like it was crammed full of cotton. Each time I'd lose ten or fifteen pounds, but it never changed my essential imbalance, the way that my body looked like one woman's torso grafted onto another woman's bottom.

"I think you look fine," said Darren, eyeing me slowly, up and down. His ridiculous glasses bobbled on his cheeks as he raised his eyebrows. "Nice gams."

I yanked at my skirt. "Nice gams? What are you, Raymond Chandler?"

"I am a detective," he said, and poked a straw through the top of a waxed-paper cup, sucking down his chocolate shake with a noise that sounded like a clogged toilet finally managing a flush.

"I just like to eat things one at a time," I explained.

He looked at my lap, where I'd arrayed the burger, the bun, the cheese, the lettuce, and the tomato, each in its own place on the white waxed paper. "Is that, like, a condition?"

"Habit." I took another bite of the burger, holding it carefully with the pads of my fingertips.

He wolfed down his own lunch in half a dozen jaw-distending bites while I looked him over. He was a rangy guy with broad shoulders and thick legs, full lips and a cleft chin and a surpris-ingly dainty nose. Thick eyebrows, light eyes, pale skin, and an unlined brow that made him look boyish, like he didn't have a care in the world as he reached into a battered canvas satchel at his feet and pulled out a legal pad and a pen. "Okay," he said, writing PROS and CONS and dividing them with a line slashed down the center of the page. "I've got half an hour, but I bet we can solve this by then. Pro?"

"My father is living a lie," I began. "His wife isn't what she says she is, and he deserves to know that."

"And you're sure he doesn't know?"

I nodded, because I was positive that if my father had any idea who India really was, he would never have married her. Almost positive. If he had some kind of ridiculous knight-on-a-white-horse fantasy . . . but then I dismissed it. There was no way my father could have known what I knew about India and married her anyhow, let alone agreed to have a child with her.

"More pros?" he asked.

"Maybe if he knew the truth, they'd get divorced. Or the marriage would be annulled," I said, thinking out loud. "Maybe my mother would come to her senses." I said it—*putting it out there,* as Vanessa, who was a big fan of putting things out there, used to say—even though I knew it was unlikely.

"Is your mom still in the city?" Darren asked.

I shook my head. "She's . . ." This was painful to admit, but Darren was basically a stranger, a stranger who'd been on my payroll, which meant that he was obligated to keep my secrets. Besides, it wasn't as if we had friends in common. There was no one he could gossip to who'd be interested. "She's in New Mexico. In an ashram."

"An ashram?" he repeated. "Whoa. Did she read *Eat, Pray, Love?*"

"She said she wanted to live authentically." The last word came out more scornfully than I'd intended. I looked around to see who might have heard, but the other people in the park seemed focused on their food, or on one another.

Darren raised his eyebrows. "You don't approve?"

I shrugged, feeling foolish, nibbling at a lettuce leaf to buy time. "She sends me pictures of herself in the sweat lodge."

"Good times." He grinned. "My mom sends me articles she clips from the newspaper. Like, actually cuts them out with scissors. Recipes, mostly. Those Mark Bittman ones, with six ingredients. You think your dad still loves her? *Your* mother, not mine."

"I do," I said automatically. My parents never fought, never even disagreed until my mother took up with the Baba. Then I thought of my father and India, beaming at me as they'd told me their "wonderful news," the way he'd tucked a lock of her hair behind her ear. I couldn't remember him ever looking at my mother like that, or touching her so tenderly. My parents had been equals—at least at first. When they'd met, at the University of Michigan, my mother was the one who came from a wealthier, more established family, and she was a year ahead of him in school. Her parents had gone to college; my father's parents had not. India was different—younger, smaller, more fragile, more in need of a wealthy man's patronage. Maybe that was what he found appealing.

"And the stepmother?" Darren asked. "What's she doing that's so bad?"

"Beg pardon?"

"I mean, did she turn your bedroom into a sex dungeon?"

I smiled—it was a funny thought—and shook my head.

"Steal your boyfriend?" Darren continued. "Run over your dog?"

"She hasn't done anything to me," I admitted. I wiped my fingers on a paper napkin. "And I don't have a dog."

"Somehow," said Darren, "that does not surprise me." He'd finished the first milkshake. He lifted the second one, tilted it toward me, and started drinking almost before I'd finished shaking my head. "Do you think she makes your dad happy?"

"I think," I said, "that if she does, it's a happiness that's illusory and transient."

He frowned. "Jesus, where'd you go to school?"

"Vassar. And it won't last," I said. "A person like that, she'll get bored. She'll leave him."

"And take all his money?" Darren's voice was innocent enough, but he knew—he had to—that India couldn't leave with more than a few million of my father's dollars. Unless this folly they were embarking on came to pass. Unless they had a baby.

"It's not that," I said. I was reluctant to say what I really thought, but, again, I reminded myself that Darren was an employee, that he'd keep my confidences. "I'm worried that she'll hurt him. That she'll break his heart."

There it was, out in the open. "Is that what happened with your mother?" Darren asked.

I nodded again. He pointed to the uneaten half of my bun. "Are you going to finish that?"

"Yes," I said, "I am."

He shrugged, sucked fruitlessly at the milkshake cup, then asked, "There's no chance she really loves him?"

I started ripping my lettuce into shreds, feeling Darren's eyes on me, his careful regard. It felt good, I acknowledged, to have a boy look at me like that. "I'm not sure," I answered, wondering in what universe I was qualified to answer questions about love. I'd never really had a boyfriend. Crushes, yes, dates, yes, kissing and fondling on dormitory beds, somewhat. I'd lost my virginity the week before college ended with a boy who I was pretty sure was gay, not because I loved him, or even particularly liked him, but because I couldn't bear the thought of receiving my diploma before I'd had sex. I knew that I was a throwback. I knew that

I would have been more comfortable in an era of corsets and clear expectations, of good manners and muted voices, where men didn't hawk phlegm on the street and undress you with their eyes and use *fuck* and *shit* like *yes* and *please*.

"I don't know how much I know about love."

Darren started to sing. "I know . . . something about love. Gotta want it bad." His voice was surprisingly tuneful.

"Are you in a band?"

"I was in a girl group, actually. I sang the high parts." He shook his head sadly. "Then Curtis started up with Deena, and Effie took it hard." He hummed a few bars of "And I Am Telling You."

"That must have been difficult."

He shrugged. "It's why I have chosen the stable and well-paying life of a professional investigator, instead of pursuing my passion for doo-wop."

I folded the remnants of my lunch into the paper sack and wiped my hands again. Darren said, "You know, my folks split up, too. It turned out to be the best thing for them. FYI." He held out his hand for my trash, tossed it, then came back and picked up his pad and his pen. "If you tell him, what good comes of it?"

"Well, then he'd know. Then he could make an informed decision."

He scratched the side of his nose. "But he's already married her. That's a decision, right?"

"Not an irrevocable one. Marriages can be annulled . . ."

He shook his head. "That's mostly for soap operas. In the real world, actually, it's a lot harder than you'd think."

"He could get a divorce."

"True."

"He could sue her for fraud. He could say she's misrepresented herself." Of course, I knew that such a lawsuit would place him even more in danger of being mocked on the Internet than a mere annulment or a simple divorce would have.

"Also true." He pulled off his ridiculous glasses, massaged the bridge of his nose, then rested his head on the back of the bench, and closed his eyes.

I glared at him. "Are you going to sleep?"

"I am not. I'm enjoying the day. This weather's great. I grew up in Miami. It never cools off down there." He stretched his arms up over his head. When they came down, one of them landed around my shoulders. I pulled away, startled . . . then shrugged and settled back against him. He was strange, but funny and interesting, I'd known a lot of guys, but not many of them were interesting, and not many of those were interested in me.

"They're having a baby," I blurted. "With a surrogate."

He opened his eyes and pulled his hands back. "Now that," he said, "would change things."

"I know that." My voice was sharp. "Don't you think I know that? My father's fifty-seven. Do you think he's got any business having a baby? He'll be seventy-five years old when the kid graduates from high school. Almost eighty when it's done with college."

"And eighty-two when it gets its master's degree."

"It's wrong. It's unnatural."

"It's technology," he said, shrugging. "Remember that woman who had eight kids at once?"

I shuddered and said nothing. Darren sat up, put his glasses back on, and flipped to a fresh page of his legal pad.

"Pros? Cons?"

I didn't answer. I couldn't tell him that a baby would mean that our family was irrevocably, irretrievably broken, that there'd be no going back to the way we were. I remembered the smallest things, every happy detail. In the Hamptons, after dinner, my father would pile us into the car for a trip to Carvel. *Bring me a small dish of Thinny-Thin,* my mother would instruct from the daybed on the screened-in porch, where she spent much of the summer curled up with the tabloid magazines she'd never permit herself in the city. *No, wait, just regular vanilla. With a little hot fudge. And maybe some whipped cream. And nuts. Actually, vanilla-chocolate swirl. And see if they'll throw on some cookie crunchies. I love those cookie crunchies. Tell them it's for me.*

If Darren thought his own parents' divorce had turned out to be a good thing, there was no way he'd understand how I felt, how badly I missed my parents as a couple, the five of us together, my parents, my brothers, and me.

I looked at my watch and brushed my hands along my skirt to remove any bits of food or lint or pollen. Darren was watching me so closely that I wondered if I had ketchup or mustard on my face, or if my slip was showing. (How Vanessa had howled when I'd unpacked my slips! "You wear these?" she'd asked, pinching one between her thumb and index finger and holding it away from her body like it was going to attack her.)

"You want to get together some time for dinner?"

"Sure," I said, thinking that maybe this was the one good thing that could come out of all this mess. I liked him. It was a nice surprise.

After work, instead of going home, I took the subway to my father's office down on Wall Street, taking the elevator up to the thirty-second floor, where he and his assistants worked in glass-walled rooms that had floor-to-ceiling views of the Hudson River. When I was little the office had been smaller, and he'd just had one assistant, who kept a stash of caramel squares in her desk drawer and let me bang on an unplugged keyboard while I waited for my dad. I hadn't been to his office in years, maybe not since high school, when I'd ridden the elevator flush with triumph, clutching my college acceptance letters. Now my dad's assistants had assistants . . . but he didn't keep me waiting for nearly as long as my mother had before waving me into his office.

"To what do I owe the privilege?" he asked.

He looked good, better than I'd seen him in years, his skin flushed, his hair recently cut and neatly combed. I thought he'd lost a few pounds—since the scare with his artery, he'd been trying to stick to a low-fat diet. He was on new medication for his cholesterol, plus a bunch of vitamins that India had researched. The last time I'd been over there'd been turkey meatloaf and oven-roasted vegetables instead of the usual roast beef and mashed potatoes, but he'd been a good sport about it, and India had smiled proudly when he'd asked for fat-free yogurt for dessert. *She's good for him*, the voice in my head said, and I told it to be quiet. Just because she could make a turkey meatloaf—or, more likely, tell the chef to make one—didn't mean she wasn't going to hurt him, or that she had his best interests at heart.

I took a seat opposite my father's desk and opened my mouth to tell him: *Don't have a baby with this woman* . . . or maybe just to remind him of the good times we'd had. Dim sum brunches in Chinatown, dinners at Daniel to celebrate each of our high school graduations, heading to the Hamptons on Friday afternoons, the five of us in a helicopter, smiling with anticipation, feeling that swooping sensation in our bellies as the city fell away beneath us.

"Bettina," he said. "What's up?" As he sat there looking at me, eyes crinkled at the corners, I noticed a new picture among the familiar shots of the five of us, over the years—Trey with braces, holding a striped bass he'd hooked in Montauk; Tommy with his first guitar; me at my debut, in a white lacy dress that seemed, in retrospect, specially cut to display my bony clavicles, dancing with my father. The new picture sat in a silver frame right next to his oversize computer monitor, and my heart sank when I saw it: him and India, under a canopy of lilies and roses, saying their vows.

"What's up, hon?"

I couldn't deny it. He looked happy . . . happy in a way I hadn't seen him looking since my mother had left . . . and I couldn't do it. I couldn't be the one to tell him that his happiness was based on a lie, or to force him to trade what I wanted—my family, back the way it had been—for what he had. It was over. The odds of a reunion had been slim to begin with, and now, with Satya burbling her coffee-cup wisdom from her ashram and India determined to have a baby, they'd dwindled to none.

"Bettina?"

"Oh, nothing," I said, and tried to smile. "I was in the neighborhood having lunch with a friend, and I haven't been up here in forever. I thought I'd just say hi."

INDIA

The morning I met my surrogate for lunch, I'd woken up in an empty bed. Marcus's pillow was smooth, the covers untouched. The curtains were open, Central Park visible through the windows, the trees pale green with new leaves. Shimmery early-morning sunlight dappled the walls it had taken me three months to have painted just the right shade of coral: not too orange, not too pink. I wondered if he'd fallen asleep in his office, or the living room, and tapped out a text asking him. Then I got out of bed, pulled on my sports bra, my tank top, my two-hundred-dollar yoga pants and three-hundred-dollar sneakers and went to meet my trainer in the lobby.

Ninety agonizing minutes later, after we'd done sprints and squats and lunges, followed by push-ups and tricep dips against the benches in the park, I took a shower, wrapped my hair in a towel and myself in a robe, and sat at the vanity in my dressing room, in front of the three-way mirror I'd had installed. Because I wasn't going out that night, I did my makeup myself, smoothing on custom-blended foundation with a fresh wedge of sponge, curling my lashes, blow-drying my hair, then running a flatiron over it, performing each step as automatically as I brushed my teeth. My clothes hung in perfect order in my immense closet, which had specially designed shelves, motorized racks, and cubbies to hold everything from scarves to handbags to suitcases and hats, and padded benches where I could sit to put on my shoes. Dressed, I looked at myself in the full-length antique mirror that stood beside the door. A stranger stared back, a stranger in an eight-hundred-dollar sweater and a nine-hundred-dollar skirt and a cushion-cut diamond insured for six figures.

I remembered the first time that Marcus had taken me home, to the apartment in the San Giacomo. I'd seen the place before, in pictures, when I was conducting my initial research. It had been featured in all of the shelter magazines and photographed for the *Times*, but it took very little effort to feign complete, jaw-on-my-chest awe when the elevator doors slid open for the first time. It was enormous, of course, gorgeously decorated, every detail perfect, from the silk carpets on the floor to the crown moldings on the ceilings to the art that was mounted and hung on all the walls, and the flowers, ranging from a soaring arrangement of cherry blossoms in the entryway to the simple bouquets next to each of the guest room's beds. I walked through, admiring, taking care not to stare or let my hands linger too long on any plush or polished surface, asking questions—*Where did you find these dishes? Is that a real Degas?*—assuming, correctly, that Marcus would be amused—"tickled," as he'd say—by my interest.

The apartment went on and on, bedrooms flowing into dressing rooms which opened into bathrooms with amenities that even spas didn't have. There was a Japanese soaking tub made of cedar in Marcus's bathroom, a steam shower, coils that warmed the marble floors and the towel racks, and an intercom system that let you call down to the kitchen if you should require, for example, some cucumber slices to lay on your eyes or some mineral water to sip while you soaked. I could barely breathe as I followed Marcus on the tour, until finally we stepped out onto the terrace that wrapped around two sides of the building and overlooked the park. "So?" he asked. Maybe I was flattering myself, but I imagined that he looked a little nervous as he waited for my assessment.

"I'm sorry," I told him, poker-faced. "I just don't know how you manage in such a small space." Inside, I was whooping, dancing with glee, with the *Jeffersons* theme song playing loudly in my head. *Movin' on up.* Yes, I was.

The deluxe apartment in the sky came with staff: maids and a cook and a tall, silent, broad-chested man named Paul who introduced himself as the majordomo. His actual job, Marcus explained, was to serve as a combination butler and bodyguard. "He's got a gun?" I'd asked. "Look," Marcus said, squeezing my shoulder. "There's a lot here to protect. You can never be too careful." Paul scared me . . . but I hardly ever saw him. His quarters, along with the maid's and the cook's, were on the lower floor, where I rarely went. I stayed upstairs, where I had my dressing room, my office, a walk-in closet that was easily twice the size of my old apartment, and a butler's pantry, with its own refrigerator and sink and two-burner stove and coffeemaker.

The cook and his assistants were just for me and Marcus, and for his children, who came to dinner once a week and always wanted the same thing—grilled steaks and baked or mashed potatoes, served with some kind of green vegetable that they'd move around their plates without actually eating. When we entertained, whether it was dinner for eight or cocktails for twenty or a holiday party for two hundred of Marcus's employees, we'd hire a caterer, and a half-dozen cooks plus uniformed waitresses and bartenders would take over the kitchen, preparing all manner of delicacies, little bites and sips of things, shot glasses of sherry-topped cream of mushroom soup, spoonfuls of risotto, bacon-stuffed dates, and curried shrimp on skewers. They'd leave every dish and countertop spotless at the end of the night. I had no idea how much any of this cost. Since my marriage, I'd never seen, much less paid, a bill.

I was a rich lady with a part-time job, a job I kept just to have something to get me out of the house each day. I had the life I'd always wanted, with all the trappings and the trimmings: the personal trainer who charged two hundred dollars an hour to hold a stopwatch while I ran, the hairdresser and makeup artist, similarly paid, who would come at any hour of the day or night. I had a car and driver—I'd send a text, and ten minutes later I'd walk out the front door, and there'd be a Town Car idling by the curb. I could buy whatever I wanted—art, clothes, jewels, a car of my own to join the half dozen that Marcus kept in a garage uptown. What I was learning was that *having* felt, sometimes, less satisfying than *wanting* . . . that dreaming of all this luxury was somehow better than actually possessing it, because once you had it, it could all be taken away.

Another troubling development was that at some point, I'd actually fallen in love with my husband. I hadn't planned on that happening; had, in fact, suspected that I no longer had the capacity to love anyone at all. But there it was. I'd wake up some mornings while he was still asleep, curled on his side in the plain white T-shirt and white boxer shorts he wore to bed, and I'd be overwhelmed with a wave of tenderness so strong it made me dizzy. I wanted to protect him, to tuck myself in his pocket and go with him when he traveled, smoothing his way, cuddling up with him at night.

I loved feeling his hand on my arm, guiding me into or out of the backseat of a car. I liked his company at dinner, the nights he was home or the times we went out. I could talk to him, joke with him . . . and if he was a little in love with the sound of his own voice, if he was already starting to acquire an old man's smell, if his balls, which I tried to avoid looking at or touching, drooped against his pale, hairy thighs, well, there were worse things in the world. Marcus was reliable, one hundred percent. He remembered everything I'd ever told him about myself, every detail about my family that I'd shared. If he said he was going to be somewhere or do something, he kept his word. If I told him I wanted something, an art book or theater tickets or a baby, he would do whatever it took to see that I got it.

Dr. Dreiser had sent me to the Princeton Fertility Clinic, after I'd declined a fourth round of in vitro. He'd been the one to steer us toward donor eggs—those, plus a gestational carrier, would give us the best chance for success, addressing all my failings: my iffy eggs, my unreliable uterus. I'd gone to the clinic's website, clicked through the links, filled out the forms, sent in a check, and picked out one of their "carefully screened eggs from donors who meet our high standards of health, medical history, and intelligence." It sounded a lot like eugenics. Then again, who'd want eggs from someone who wasn't healthy, or intelligent and gorgeous? The website said nothing about the egg donors' looks, but I could fill in that blank and assume they were all beauties. Picking the egg donor was easy: I went for tall, blond, smart, and healthy, the way any man would have done. And as soon as I'd met Annie, I'd known she was the one to carry the baby. I hadn't planned on choosing someone so young, but there was something I recognized in her expression, a hopefulness and a determination to make something better of her life. She reminded me of me, when I'd been young, and her life, as best as I could tell from the forms she'd filled out and the stories she'd told me, could have been my life, if things had gone just a little bit differently.

Annie was perfect. I'd asked for a gestational surrogate who lived in Pennsylvania, the clinic's state of choice, where the laws were clear. There'd be no legal wrangling over who the baby belonged with, whose name went on the birth certificate under "parents." I'd requested a woman within a two-hour drive, in her twenties, and Annie was twenty-four and lived outside of Philadelphia, an easy commute to the city. She'd have had kids already,

I knew: the clinic insisted on it. She was married—the clinic didn't insist on that; couldn't, legally, but Leslie had mentioned that most of their surrogates were in "stable family arrangements," which, in Annie's case meant a husband who'd been in the army and still had army benefits. The two of them and their two boys weren't rich, but they weren't destitute—the money she'd earn would make a difference, but it wasn't as if they were living in poverty. From the pictures she'd shown me, I thought their farmhouse looked charming . . . and Annie, so far, was earnest and sweet and surprisingly funny sometimes.

We were meeting for lunch at the restaurant on the seventh floor of Bergdorf's, one of my favorite places, a gorgeous little jewel box of a room that felt like a secret and served delicious salads. Annie was waiting on the first floor, by the display of purses. I stood by the doors and watched her, unseen, as she shyly fingered a silk Valentino bag made of fabric flowers in shades of scarlet and plum. I felt a stab of guilt as I noticed her clothes, sneakers and leggings and a loose-fitting tunic-style top that most assuredly had not come from Bergdorf's. Why had I brought her here? Was I showing off, trying to prove who had the upper hand, letting her know that she might be carrying the baby but I was the one with the cash?

I tapped her on the shoulder. She set the bag on the glass counter and spun around, looking guilty.

"Oh, India! Hi!"

I gave her a hug. "Pretty bag."

She lowered her voice. "It costs twenty-one hundred dollars. Two thousand dollars for a purse!"

I didn't answer. The truth was, I had that very purse in my closet at home, along with its patent-leather cousin and a wallet that matched. "Are you hungry?"

"Oh, my God. Always."

We took the elevator up to the restaurant, where the maître d' whisked us to a table by the windows. Central Park spread out on one side, and we could see Fifth Avenue on the other. I ordered my usual salade niçoise, and Annie, looking embarrassed again, asked for the filet and mashed potatoes, an item that was probably on the menu just for the husbands and boyfriends who got dragged along on their wives' shopping excursions.

"Are you feeling good?" I asked her. I'd wanted a glass of wine with lunch, but it seemed cruel to order one, to drink when she couldn't, to emphasize once again that she was doing a task I'd hired her to perform.

"I feel great," she said, buttering a piece of bread (normally, I would have waved the bread basket away, but Annie had looked so happy when it arrived that I hadn't said a word, and had even made a mental note to order dessert so that she wouldn't feel uncomfortable if she wanted something). "I told you, I'm good at this." She tore off a bite of bread. "Some skill, right?"

"I'm sure you have other talents." From what I'd heard, Annie's life sounded fun and full. She was close to both her mother and her sister, and sounded genuinely content when she talked about her garden, her sons, her plans for the farmhouse. I felt good that the money she'd be getting would help her realize some of her dreams.

The waiter set our plates down with a flourish, and I watched Annie as she ate. She wasn't fat, but she was too big to fit into a sample size, which meant she was too big, period, for New York. Clearly she didn't care for fashion, because, as I'd learned in Los Angeles, even on a budget, you could have a look. Annie had no look. To her, I guessed, clothing was something that existed strictly to keep her from being naked. Her tunic was a shapeless sack in drab purple. Her no-style hair, a pretty light brown, was brushed back from her face and secured with a headband. I could tell she'd made an effort with lipstick and eyeliner and mascara, insofar as "effort" meant putting them on. The eyeliner was smudged a little, and there was a faint track of mascara underneath one eye. The first time I'd seen her, I'd guessed that she didn't paint her face between one Sunday and another. There was a small diamond ring and a slim gold band on her left ring finger, a cheap-looking watch on her right wrist, plain gold hoops in her ears, and a black leather purse that probably hadn't cost a fraction of the bag she'd been eyeing downstairs.

I wondered about her finances. She'd been so eager to agree to everything I'd suggested: the organic foods and doctor's visits and using my obstetrician, a lovely man with gentle hands who was rumored to be generous with the painkillers after a C-section and whose office was just down the block from Elizabeth Arden so you could go get waxed before your appointments. How did they manage on just her husband's salary? Were they managing? Was she more poor that I'd been led to believe?

Annie pushed her empty plate away, looking embarrassed again. "That was great. Thank you so much." She looked at me, her cheeks rosy, eyes clear. It was true, I thought, what they said about pregnant women. Annie was glowing. "Do you have time to look around a little when we're done? Did you see the china on our way in here?"

"Are you in the market?"

"For that? No. But I like the way they're set up. It's like a museum."

"Sure," I said, thinking again how much I liked her. She was friendly and nervous and eager to please; not dumb, even if she had only a high-school degree and was completely lacking in fashion sense. I wanted to show her things: the rooms that Kelly Wearstler had designed to display the store's wares, the shabby-chic cracked leather couches and how they set off the delicate Limoges china. I could take her for tea at the Pierre, where I took my assistant every December, as a holiday treat; I could even bring her to see the apartment, put up her feet and take in the view.

"How are the boys?" I asked, after I'd ordered fruit and she'd asked for apple cobbler. When she reached into her purse for her phone pictures I knew she'd have, I saw a sippy cup, the box for a Dan Zanes CD, a wallet bulging with change and receipts, and I recognized her, the way it felt like that performance artist had once recognized me, like I could see who she really was; everything she wanted, everything she dreamed of. At that moment I felt like I could be a sort of fairy godmother, not just an employer but a friend. I could make her dreams come true the way I'd wanted someone to make my own dreams come true . . . the way I'd wanted my mother to come back, to take me out of that cold and cheerless house in Toledo and take me to California, land of golden sand and lemon trees and men who'd play their guitars on the beach.

Annie looked startled when I reached across the table and squeezed her hand, but she squeezed back gamely, smiling at me. "You must be so excited," she said. "This must feel like it's taking forever."

"I can wait," I told her. I'd waited for love, I'd waited for Marcus, and I could wait until May for the arrival of the baby who would serve as living, breathing, evidence of our love; the baby who would make us complete.

JULES

A fact I have learned as I've moved further away from childhood: if the telephone rings before seven a.m., it's never good news.

In the predawn gray on a Thursday morning in October, the buzzing of my BlackBerry jolted me awake. *Rajit,* I thought, rolling over with my eyes still shut. I'd been in the office until eleven the night before, working on the common stock comparison for a footwear factory that one of our clients in Kansas was planning to acquire, and rather than bothering Kimmie, who went to bed at ten, I spent a rare night at home. Rajit had probably forgotten his passwords again (after being up all night doing cocaine, I suspected) and was calling me to get them.

I saw a Pittsburgh area code—not Rajit, then—and pressed the button that would connect the call. "Hello?"

I half expected I'd hear my father's voice, but instead, there was a stranger on the other end of the line, a woman who sounded young and unsure of herself. "Is this Julia Strauss?"

I sat up, my mouth suddenly dry and my heart beating too loudly. "Yes."

"This is Sergeant Potts with the Pittsburgh Police Department." I knew then, before she had to say another word. "Your mother gave me your contact information. I'm calling about your father. I'm afraid I have bad news."

"Is he . . ." I swallowed hard, my throat clicking. "Is he in trouble? Did he get arrested? Does he need . . ."

"We got a nine-one-one call this morning, just after five a.m. Your father's girlfriend had found him unresponsive. The paramedics made attempts to resuscitate him, but . . ."

But.

"I'm sorry to have to tell you," said Sergeant Potts, "your father is dead."

I closed my eyes, holding perfectly still, like maybe if I didn't move I could unhear what I'd just heard. Outside my door, my roommates were stirring around me, getting ready to start a normal day, Amanda plodding into the kitchen to make coffee, Wendy flushing the toilet and turning on the shower. "Ma'am?" the police officer said.

"How did it happen?"

"The investigation isn't complete," she said. "We're still talking to people. Gathering evidence."

"Were there drugs involved?"

Sergeant Potts paused.

"My dad was in rehab this summer," I said. "He was in a halfway house for six weeks after that. He was going to meetings. I thought . . ." My voice caught in my throat. I thought he'd get clean. I thought he'd be grateful. I thought my sacrifice would have meant something.

"I'm sorry for your loss," she said.

"Yeah," I told her. "Yeah, I'm sorry, too."

I left Rajit a message, telling him there'd been a death in my family and that I'd need the rest of the week off. I pulled my laptop out from under the bed, turned my back to the door, and called my mother. "Oh, honey," she said. "Oh, no." I could picture her, in her blue robe, her hair in a ponytail, coffee mug in her hand, pitying me and Greg, of course, but maybe feeling relieved, too, glad that this was over, that he wouldn't be in the newspapers again, that he wouldn't embarrass us anymore.

"Sweetheart, there's nothing more you could have done," she said. "I hope you know that."

But it hadn't mattered. Nothing I'd done had mattered. I bit back my tears. I had arrangements to make, plane tickets to book, a funeral to plan. "Do you know anything about what he'd want?" I asked.

She sighed. "Probably the veterans' cemetery. That was what he always said."

I told her I'd call her once I'd bought my ticket. She said she loved me and that she'd see me soon. Then, because I couldn't think of what else to do, I went to the bathroom to wash my face and brush my teeth. "Jules, you're gonna be late!" Amanda sang toward the door. Amanda was an actress, which meant, these days, that she was mostly a caterer.

"I think I'm sick," I said. My voice was convincingly froggy, which would spare me the trouble of telling them what had happened. I'd have to do it eventually, have to endure their sympathy and come up with some story about my father's death, but not yet. I made sure the door was locked, picked up my phone, and called Kimmie.

"Hey!" I could hear noise around her. She was in the subway station, I figured. On her way to the lab, with her backpack bouncing on her narrow shoulders, sneakers neatly laced. Something inside of me shifted, and I felt almost faint with longing. I wanted so badly for her to be with me.

"Hey!" came Kimmie's voice again, bright and almost jubilant. "Jules, is that you, or are you pocket-dialing?"

"It's me," I managed. One tear rolled down my cheek

and plopped onto my shirt, leaving a damp circle. "My father died."

"Oh," Kimmie said. "Hang on. I'll be right there."

I packed up my makeup bag, my toothbrush, my comb. From my free-standing wardrobe, I extracted a black skirt and gray blouse, an outfit that always made Rajit, wit that he was, tell me I looked like I was on my way to a funeral. Black pumps, a bra, and a few pairs of panties. I had other stuff, sweatpants and T-shirts and pajamas, at my mother's place.

My BlackBerry lay on my rumpled bedspread, blinking, probably already filling up with messages from work. I ignored it, pulling on jeans and a long-sleeved T-shirt, yanking on socks and my running shoes and shoving everything into a duffel bag.

Forty minutes later Kimmie was at the door, with a to-go cup and a cinnamon roll in wax paper. She shooed me into the kitchen, which was blessedly roommate-free, and handed me the cup. "What can I do?" she asked. "How can I help?"

"I don't know," I said. I was collapsed at the table for two wedged into what the real-estate agent had optimistically referred to as a "breakfast nook." Part of me had known this day would come . . . but, even so, I'd done very little to prepare for it. "I don't know what to do. I've never done this before."

"Drink," said Kimmie. I took a sip from the cup. The tea was hot and strong, laced with sugar. "Where's Dad now?" she asked.

"Huh?" For a second, I'd thought she was talking about her father, not mine. I tried to remember whether I knew, finally shaking my head. "I'm not sure."

"You got that police officer's number?"

I hadn't written down the number, but it showed up on my

BlackBerry. Kimmie hit "redial" and lifted the phone to her ear. "Yes," she said, in a crisp voice, one I recognized from the admissions office, when she'd take parents' phone calls. "May I speak to Sergeant Potts, please?" She waited, then said, "Hello, I'm a friend of Julia Strauss. We're on our way back to Pittsburgh, and I need to know . . ." She paused, then nodded. *Scritch-scratch* went her pen. "Mmm-hmm. Yes. I see. And how long will that take?" More writing. I closed my eyes. I didn't want to live in my head right now, which insisted on serving up a slide show of my father, cold and stiff and dead on the shag carpet of that crappy apartment . . . and of a child with my face, a child that would be half mine, a little boy or little girl I would never know. The price I'd paid. The sacrifice I'd made for nothing.

"Can you give me that number?" Kimmie was asking. "Should I have the funeral director get in touch?" I watched her, wondering, dimly, how she knew how to do all of this. Who had she buried? I'd have to ask.

She hung up the phone and set it, facedown, in the middle of the table. "They took his body to the medical examiner's office. There's going to be an autopsy, because it was . . ." She paused, looking flustered for the first time, glancing at her notes. "Because he didn't die in a hospital, I guess, so there wasn't a doctor there. That's what they have to do."

"He overdosed." My voice was flat. Kimmie got up from the table and stood behind me, one hand resting lightly on my shoulder. "I'm so sorry," she said softly.

"Can you . . ." My voice was almost inaudible. I could barely get the words out. "Will you come with me?"

She answered instantly, as if nothing else were even possible. "Of course I will," she said.

• • •

Kimmie gave me the window seat on the plane. I leaned the top of my head against the glass and stared out at the sky. All through the ride, she kept giving me things—a novel, a honey-nut granola bar, a bottle of water, tissues. I read, or tried to; I ate and drank what she gave me; I cried, wiping my eyes with my sleeve; and every once in a while I'd manage to tell her something about my dad: how he'd taken me horseback riding once after I'd seen *International Velvet* on TV, how proud he'd been when I'd gotten into Princeton. Kimmie listened quietly, nodding. "You must have loved him very much," she said. For a while, when no one was looking, she held my hand.

It was getting dark when we landed in Pittsburgh. My mother picked us up, her eyes red, her hair still frizzy, tucked into its morning ponytail. "There's soup and frozen pizza if you're hungry, and, Jules, I put the air mattress in your room, and there's fresh sheets . . ."

"We'll be fine."

"Did Greg get in touch?" my mother asked.

"He texted." My brother had, indeed, sent a message consist-ing of two words: NOT SURPRISED. For Greg, our father had died a long time ago . . . probably the night he'd stolen Greg's prized possession, a baseball signed by Reggie Jackson, and sold it. Since then Greg seemed to have decided, maybe unconsciously, that the easiest thing for him to do was to simply hate our father, to forget that, once, he'd been a good dad.

"I'm glad you've got such a good friend," my mother whis-pered after Kimmie carried our bags up the stairs, slipping qui-etly out of the room to give the two of us time together. I didn't answer, didn't even think to wonder if she suspected Kimmie was more than that.

Upstairs, Kimmie and I took turns in the shower, then had a funny little fight about which one of us should take the air mattress. Finally, I lay down on my bed and Kimmie lay down beside me, fitting her body against mine. I buried my face in the silken net of her hair, and that was how I slept.

The next morning, my mother drove us to the Hoffman Funeral Home, then sat outside waiting in her car. "I could come in," she'd offered, her voice tentative, and I told her what she expected to hear: "Don't worry. I've got it."

The office floor was thickly carpeted; the chairs were plush and padded. There was a pitcher of ice water on the sideboard, a metal urn of coffee, and a pair of cut-glass decanters, one with amber liquid, the other with something clear.

Monday morning, I told the Hoffman who was helping us, a middle-aged, round-faced man who wore a sober gray suit and a small, sympathetic smile. I told him I would bring clothes for my dad to wear, that the coffin would be closed, that my mother should get the flag that would drape the coffin, and I'd get the bullet casings from the gun salute. ("As a remembrance," Mr. Hoffman said, and I'd nodded, wondering briefly what I was supposed to do with spent shell casings. Put them in a candy dish? String them on a length of silk thread and wear them as a necklace? Offer them to Rita, who I'd have to deal with soon?)

There was a display room, where I picked out a simple coffin—it was one of the least expensive, and still more than two thousand dollars. "Now, what were you thinking in terms of a service?"

"Small," I said. "Just the family."

"And will you be writing an obituary? We can help with that if you . . ."

"No obituary."

He raised his eyebrows. "Are you sure?"

I nodded. The air in the room felt thick and unwholesome.

The newspapers had already had enough to say about my dad, after the car accident, after his trial. Maybe they'd use the official notice of his death to dredge up the old stories, and write a piece about the disgraced schoolteacher's unsavory demise. For all I knew, the shame could have been part of what killed him. My dad could have literally died of embarrassment.

Mr. Hoffman touched my arm. "Are you all right? Why don't we sit down?" Kimmie poured me a glass of water, and I gulped it gratefully.

"Now. How many copies of the death certificate will you require?"

I looked at Kimmie, who shrugged. "I don't know. What do I need them for?"

"Your father was a teacher, right?"

I nodded, not bothering to correct him, to explain that my father hadn't been a teacher for years, that for years he hadn't been anything but a junkie and a drunk.

"So he'll have a checking account, a savings account. Investments. Cars and a house in his name . . ." I let him talk, not bothering to correct him as he listed the things that a man of my father's age and station should have had. We agreed on twenty copies, I wrote him a check, shook his hand, and told him I'd see him at the cemetery.

My mother was waiting in the parking lot, with her cup of black coffee and a book on tape. "Greg called," she said. The Camry started with an unpleasant grinding sound. I wondered how long it would run and if she'd have enough money to replace it, and whether I'd be able to help. "He's not going to be able to make it."

I nodded, unsurprised. Kimmie, meanwhile, was unzipping her backpack. "You hungry?"

I shook my head. Food sounded like a rumor from a distant planet. I couldn't imagine ever being hungry again.

"Here," she said, pulling out a granola bar and passing it to me. "Eat."

I took a bite and chewed lethargically. Behind the wheel, my mother's face was pale, her eyes circled with purplish half moons. "Can we stop here, please?" Kimmie asked from the backseat when we drove past a supermarket. She trotted inside and came out with a bouquet of flowers, white daisies and pink carnations wrapped in plastic.

We dropped my mother off at her beauty parlor and drove to the apartment building where my father had lived and died. I pressed the doorbell and we stood there, waiting. A pair of women talking in Spanish came out, followed by a grim-faced teenage boy in drooping jeans and a hoodie. MOVE-IN SPECIAL, announced a sagging banner hanging from the fence along the street.

Rita Devine hurried down the hallway. "Come in, come in. My God, I can't believe it!" she said, in her thick Pittsburgh accent, the kind that would turn the home team from the Steelers into the Stillers and employed *yinz* as the plural of *you*. Her eyes darted from me to Kimmie and back again. "Yesterday there was a dead body on my bathroom floor!"

Bathroom, I thought, feeling my body register the news. The lady cop hadn't mentioned that my father had died in the bathroom. Add one more part to the inglorious sum, this tawdry bad joke of a death. Of course he'd die in the bathroom. His life had turned into a punch line; why shouldn't his death be one, too?

The apartment smelled cloyingly of air freshener and, underneath it, that strange, acrid odor I'd smelled before on my father's clothing. Standing in the entryway, I could see the living room, still a mess, filled with jumbled piles and clusters of things—folded-over newspapers with half-completed Sudoku puzzles, soda cans, coffee cups, rolls of paper towels, magnifying glasses. I picked one of them up and peered through it, watching dust motes falling through a shaft of light.

"Your dad's eyes got so bad." Rita was wringing her hands. She was a short, chunky woman with a chipmunky face and two inches of gray showing at the roots of her hair, with thick thighs and breasts that slumped against her belly. My father's ladylove, in high-waisted jeans and bright-green plastic Crocs.

"What happened?"

More hand-wringing. "Can I bring you gals some coffee?"

"We're fine," I said, the same instant that Kimmie said, "Yes, please." Five minutes later, we each had a cup of microwaved brew, and Rita was perched at the edge of a plastic-slipcovered armchair while Kimmie and I sat on the sofa facing her.

She plucked the teabag out of her mug, realized there was nowhere to put it, and dunked it back in. "You know your dad had been really sick." *Rilly* sick.

"I know my father was a drug addict." I was done with euphemisms, done with pretending. Maybe it comforted her to think that my father had a disease instead of a weakness, but it wouldn't comfort me anymore.

She pressed her fingers to her lips. "He fought so hard against it. So hard."

"Just tell me," I said. "Just tell me what happened."

"Please," said Kimmie.

The woman sighed and pressed her hands together. "He came back here when he finished with that place," she began. *That place* was probably the sober-living house. I nodded, wondering what it was like to leave a group-living home where there were schedules and counselors and mandatory AA meetings, and then come back here, with Rita, where he'd done so much drinking and drugging. Maybe I should have made other arrangements, found another place for him to go, rented an apartment . . .

Kimmie touched my forearm. I forced myself to stop thinking about it. Hindsight wouldn't fix things. He was dead now, and what I had to do was get through the funeral and clean up the mess he'd undoubtedly left behind.

"For a while he was doing okay," Rita continued. "He'd go for walks, or to the library. He'd go to the gym, pedal that sit-down bike they have. He'd have dinner waiting when I came home from work. Simple things," said Rita. "Chicken patties, or hamburgs. Spaghetti. Like that." I nodded, remembering his sad attempts at omelets when I'd come for breakfast.

"The night it happened . . ." She pulled in a long breath. "I went to bed at about ten, that's what I do, because I work, you know, I need to be up real early." I nodded. "At two or so I heard him up, rustling around . . ." She gulped. "And then when I got up, I found him there, on the bathroom floor. His head . . . his head was . . ." More gulping followed, and a single spastic gesture with her hand. I'd find out later what she hadn't been able to tell me, from the police photographs and the autopsy report, that my dad had died with his head in the toilet and a crack pipe in his hand. It was a detail, in all honesty, that I could have gone to my own death without knowing.

I kept my eyes on my lap, the throbbing pressure of tears filling my head. It was what I'd expected, but still, hearing it like this, out loud, in this tacky little apartment, made it real. *Rill.* Kimmie took my hand. I wondered what she made of all this, how far away it was from her own life, her own diligent, hard-working parents. All I wanted was to get out of this place, to breathe the fresh air, to get back on the plane that would take me home and have all of this be someone else's problem, someone else's mess.

"I'm so sorry, Julia." My name sounded strange in her mouth. I hadn't been Julia since high school. But my father had called me Julia, and Julia was what I'd been when he'd discussed me with this woman. "He tried so hard. He fought it. He really did."

I got up before she could continue. "Thank you," I said. What did I mean by that? *Thank you for taking him in? Thank you for letting him stay? Thank you for giving him a place to die, so he didn't have to do it on the street?* "The funeral's Monday morning, in the veterans' cemetery," I said. "You're welcome to come."

When she hugged me, I could feel her soft body against mine, and I smelled her scent of stale coffee and cigarettes almost overcoming that strange chemical odor that I thought was probably *eau de* crack. When she pulled away she was crying, and talking fast, words tumbling over one another, her accent growing ever thicker. "I would have done anything for him. You don't know what it's been like. What I went through. All those years. I had a house when all this started." She gestured at the sad little room, the cheap furniture, the piles of crap that my fingers itched to scoop into a trash bag. "A house that was paid for, a car, a 401(k), my savings, my retirement account . . ."

He'd smoked it all, I thought to myself. Smoked it all up. Now she was practically yelling, her hands balled into fists on the hips of her jeans, an indignant fireplug in green clown shoes. "I did the best I could. The very best I could."

"I believe you." I was so tired. I'd never been so exhausted in my life. All I wanted to do was be in a bed somewhere, shoes kicked off, covers pulled up to my chin. "I know you tried to help him, and it must have been very hard." She closed her mouth, her face sagging. "Thank you," I said, and managed to sound like I meant it.

• • •

Kimmie walked me away from the apartment building, through the fence, past the banner flapping in the wind, across the street to a park, where we sat under a tree whose leaves were tipped with gold. Fall was here. Winter was coming. I shut my eyes, imagining my life in New York City—the job I despised, the apartment that was still almost more than I could afford, the shower stall so small that the plastic shower curtain stuck to my skin if I didn't position myself perfectly, the dirt and grit and noise. I considered the men on the subways who'd use a crowded car as an excuse to cop a quick handful of ass, and Rajit, who'd once thrown a cup of coffee at me when it was too cold. ("Keep a change of clothes," one of his former junior analysts had told me, opening the bottom drawer of her desk to show me a skirt and top, still in dry cleaner's plastic, that she'd learned to stow there after he'd thrown a salad, with blue cheese dressing, at her.)

I drove us back to my mother's salon. "How was it?" my mom asked, hugging me, and I told her it went fine, knowing that she didn't want to hear the details. Kimmie and I caught a bus home, to the neighborhood of neat little ranch houses where I'd grown up. I flipped on the television set, heated soup, buttered toast, found juice glasses, plates, and napkins, moving around like my body was made of cotton. Once, my first year at Princeton, someone had posted a picture of me, taken when I wasn't looking, online, on a website that rated the looks of all the women in our class. I'd been furious and ashamed. My roommates hadn't sympathized. "Jesus," one of them had said when she thought I was sleeping, "it's not like he said she was ugly. Or fat. It's a compliment." Indeed, my inbox had pinged steadily for a week, with guys e-mailing to introduce themselves and ask if I wanted to get together for a cup of coffee or a movie or lunch. I hadn't been able to explain how it made me feel invaded and diminished, like there was this thing out in the world, this thing with my name and my face and a great stupid hank of blond hair, this thing that looked like me but wasn't.

Sitting at my mother's kitchen table, surrounded by everything I remembered—the square in front of the sink where the linoleum had worn thin, the placemats my father had bought for me and Greg at the children's museum, the postcard of Barcelona that had been taped on the refrigerator for years—I felt that same sensation, of being there and not there, of not really being myself. I watched Kimmie. She had pulled her hair into a high ponytail, spooned her soup, and chattered to me about New York—a restaurant that made what was supposed to be the best fried chicken in the world; a musical, all in Spanish, where they gave student discounts on Wednesday nights. We washed the dishes, then I took a shower, letting the water flow over me, telling myself what to do next. *Pick up the soap. Wash your legs. Under your arms. Now the shampoo.*

Kimmie was waiting in the bedroom, in her men's boxer shorts and ribbed sleeveless undershirt, curled up on the bed. "Do you need anything?" she asked me.

"I'll be fine," I said, and lay beside her in the darkness, perfectly still, thinking about who I was: a college graduate, a junior analyst, an egg donor, a woman without a father. "He used to braid my hair," I whispered, unsure of whether I was talking to myself or to Kimmie; unsure whether she was even awake. But oh, I remembered it, every detail: sitting on the floor in front of his recliner in my favorite loose flannel pajamas, his brown lace-up shoes on either side of me, his hand moving the comb against my scalp, his calm voice asking, *What color ponytail holders? One braid or two?*

A noise came out of me, something between a moan and

a sob, a sound I'd never made before, could not imagine making. It wasn't loud, and I quickly buried my face in the pillow, but Kimmie must have heard me. She pressed her body tightly against mine. I pulled her head close to me and buried my face between her neck and her shoulder, pressing against the softness of her skin.

ANNIE

Before I left Target for the last time, Gabe gave me a reading list. Most of the books I found at the library and started but didn't finish, but there was one that held my attention. It was called *Never Let Me Go*. It was set in England, at a boarding school, and it started off slowly, the way so many of Gabe's books seemed to begin. At first I thought that it would be about rich kids in the countryside, their fads and cliques and crushes, and two girls falling for the same boy. But gradually, the book shed its disguise and showed its true self to me, and it wasn't a kids-in-school book at all. It was a horror story. The students at the boarding school weren't real people; they were clones who had been bred so they could donate their organs. When they "completed"—when they made all the donations they could— they would die.

Once I realized this, I thought the book would turn into a thriller, where the girl, Kathy H., and the boy, Tommy, would try to run away and be together. The clones looked exactly like regular people; there was nothing that distinguished them from anyone else. But that didn't happen. The two of them simply accepted what they were, what they'd been made for, their destiny. They never tried to fight it, never tried to run. I finished the book feeling sorrow mixed with recognition, thinking, *That's Frank. That's me.*

Frank and I met at George Washington High School in Somerton in Northeast Philadelphia, the winter of our junior year. We'd been in the same schools since seventh grade, but we weren't in the same crowd. I played flute in the school band and took the academic-track classes—not the honors courses, for the college-bound smarties like Nancy, but the classes for the kids for whom community college or an associate's degree was at least a possibility.

Frank was on the vocational track, for the kids who were going to work as auto mechanics or licensed practical nurses, delivering the mail or reading the meters or mopping the floors. I knew his name, in the way that all of us in our class of just over two hundred knew one another's names, but I didn't know much about him. I'd noticed him because there weren't that many black kids in our high school, and because he was so cute, with green eyes and close-cropped hair and his skin, medium brown and perfectly smooth, and his lips.

One winter day I'd been sitting in the cafeteria at my usual table with my friends, picking at the shredded cheese on my salad (I was dieting, the way I had through most of high school), when Frank walked over to our table. My girlfriends stared. Most of the shop boys, black and white, wore jeans that hung off their butts, exposing as much of their boxers as they could get away with, and heavy workboots and T-shirts advertising some band or another. Frank had the boots but was dressed in khakis and a button-down shirt, neatly pressed, the sleeves rolled up to show his corded forearms. As he came close, I could smell soap and motor oil (he'd been working in the school's garages that morning), and the good, clean scent of his skin.

"Hi there, Annie," he said. His eyelashes were long and curly, the kind a girl would spend forever torturing herself with an eyelash curler clamped against her lids to achieve. I remember exactly what I was wearing: a red jersey Henley T-shirt with three buttons at the collar and my favorite pair of jeans, the size-ten Calvin Kleins, a silver locket on a heart that my father had given me for my sweet sixteen. My hair was long, in ringlets that I crafted each morning with a curling iron, and I wore big hoop earrings, studded with fake diamonds, that swung almost to my shoulders and made me look like J.Lo, my fashion icon at the time. "Want to go to the Sweethearts Dance with me?" Frank asked.

"Sure," I said. "Sure, yeah, I'd like that."

My girlfriends started giggling. I blushed, admiring him for the way he'd asked, for approaching me in public instead of with a phone call, for risking embarrassment. I also couldn't quite believe that he knew who I was, that I wasn't just one of the faceless girls who moved through the same hallways and classrooms but might as well have inhabited a different world. But I also had the strangest sense that I knew him . . . that, somehow, my entire time in high school, maybe even my entire life, had been leading up to this conversation.

"I'll pick you up at six," he told me. He was very calm, looking at me steadily, ignoring my friends. "We can go to dinner first, if that's okay."

"Sure," I said again. "I live on Crestview."

"I know." He walked off, and my girlfriends fell on me, scooping me up like a quarterback in a huddle.

"Oh my God! Frank Barrow!" I smiled, feeling flushed, almost feverish. I still couldn't quite figure out how he knew me. The next week revealed nothing. Frank smiled when he saw me in the hallways. At lunch, he'd make a point of coming over and saying "hello." But that was all. I should have been frantic with nerves, part of me wondering if he'd asked me out as some kind of joke or dare. (In the movies I loved, the ones I'd watch every time they came on cable, *10 Things I Hate About You* and *Never Been Kissed*, things like that happened, there were pranks and jokes and misunderstandings, but the boy and the girl always wound up together, the way they were meant to be.)

My friends were useless when it came to figuring out what was behind Frank Barrow's interest, but full of suggestions about what I should wear. I had the dress I'd bought for homecoming, but I wanted something new for Frank. So I used eighty dollars of my babysitting money to buy a simple sleeveless dress in periwinkle blue, with a deep V-neck and a skirt that swished around my ankles and had braided gold metal buckles at the shoulders, an inexpensive knockoff of the Badgley Mischka gown Kate Winslet had worn to the Oscars that year. I borrowed a pair of gold strappy sandals from Nancy and paid another twenty dollars to go to the beauty school and have my hair curled, then arranged in an updo, with a little rhinestone butterfly clipped over my right ear.

Frank wore a dark-blue suit with a light-blue tie almost the exact same shade as my dress. He held my arm as he walked me to his car, which was his father's Buick, very old but very clean (I learned later he'd washed and waxed and vacuumed it for the occasion). It wasn't until he was backing out of my driveway, one arm over my seat, that I realized I didn't know where we were going. Before homecoming that fall, my date and I and three other couples had gone to the Chart House in Center City, which was, as the name implied, right on the water (the Delaware, which wasn't one of the world's prettiest rivers, but when you lived in Philadelphia, you took what you could get). The tables there were set with an array of silverware that most of us found bewildering, and the cheapest entrée, pasta with roasted seasonal vegetables, cost fourteen dollars.

"Burgers okay?" asked Frank.

"Sure!" My voice was too loud. I worried that it sounded like

I was disappointed and trying to hide it, but the truth was, I'd left the Chart House with a stomachache, brought on, I figured, by sitting up perfectly straight terrified that I was going to spill salad dressing or step on the hem of my dress or do something that would reveal to the grown-ups eating their meals at the tables around us that none of us had any business being there.

Frank drove to McDonald's on Broad Street. "Wait here," he said, hopping out of the car. Five minutes later, he came back with a steaming, fragrant bag, already spotted with grease from the fries. My stomach growled, and, instead of being mortified, I laughed—I hadn't eaten in days so I could look good in my gown.

Frank didn't say much, but it wasn't an uncomfortable silence, as he drove to Fairmount Park, then up the steep, twisting road called South George's Hill. He parked right behind the Mann Center, an outdoor concert hall that was dark and quiet that night. This was a noted makeout spot where more than a few of my dates had ended. At that hour it was too cold and dark for the runners and cyclists to be out, and too soon for the couples. The sun was just setting, the sky fading from pale blue to indigo, and the city was spread out like a gorgeous quilt of light beneath us. We sat in the car with the windows cracked open and the heater on and a wool blanket Frank had pulled out of the trunk over our laps, eating Big Macs and fries and sipping vanilla shakes.

Sitting with him, I felt none of the nerves I'd felt with other boys, none of the awkwardness of wondering whether I looked right or sounded right or was saying the right things. Frank hadn't offered me any liquor, nor had he made a dive toward my mouth or my bra hooks. He asked me questions and listened, respectfully, while I answered. We were talking about Dana Hightower, who'd allegedly transferred to a magnet school in Center City but who had really, my girlfriends and I suspected, been sent away to have a baby, when I blurted, "Why'd you ask me to the dance?"

He lowered his lashes. I remember how perfect he looked, his white shirt crisp, his cheeks freshly shaven, how he smelled like soap and a citrusy aftershave. I remember the song on the radio was called "Angel of Mine," and feeling once more that sense, undeniable, overwhelming, that this had all been arranged beforehand, that he and I were meant to be, that we were going to be, and that I didn't even have much say in the matter. "Why?" he asked. "You don't want to go?"

"No, it's not that, it's that . . . I didn't even think you knew me. Knew who I was. We never talked, and I . . ." I shut my mouth and folded my hands in my lap. I'd taken off my shoes and was sitting sideways, my legs curled underneath me. There was a bit of ketchup on my finger, and I licked it off, tasting the sweetness.

Frank looked at me, and there was no trace of teasing in his voice or on his face. "I've had my eye on you for a long time."

"But why?"

Smiling, he touched one of my cheeks with his fingertips. "You're always smiling."

"Not always," I said, thinking about the fights I'd had with Nancy.

"When I see you, you're smiling, and laughing, and there's always people around you, you know?"

Now I was blushing, and I imagined that maybe he was, too, although his skin didn't show it the way mine did.

"You always have people." He sounded wistful. I could tell that this was hard for Frank—that he knew what he meant to say, what he liked about me, but was having trouble finding the words. "And remember that one time in gym class?"

I shook my head, embarrassed that I didn't know what he was talking about.

"What I said about Ms. Hicks."

"Oh, right!" Ms. Hicks had taught phys ed since the 1970s. Some years, she'd show up in September a skinny one hundred and twenty pounds, and other years she'd come for Back to School Night closer to two hundred. That year, we'd been lined up to play volleyball and Ms. Hicks, bulging in her blue polyester gym shorts, had been explaining the rules, when Frank, standing behind me, had whispered, "I think she's been eating 'cause the Eagles had such a bad preseason."

I'd laughed out loud, then turned around, not even sure who had spoken. Frank was staring at me soberly. "I'm serious," he said, without even a hint of a smile. "The year we went to the Super Bowl? Thinnest she's ever been."

I'd been laughing when Ms. Hicks hurled a volleyball at me, hollering at me to get my head in the game. Later, I'd learned why laughter and people were so important to Frank. His mother had gotten pregnant for the first time at forty-two, after more than two decades of marriage, after she'd given up on the possibility of children and had mostly given up on her marriage as well. She'd loved Frank, but his arrival had been a disruption. Corrinne Barrow wasn't good with disruptions. Nor was she much of a laugher. She believed in God, and thrice-weekly church attendance; she worked as a medical secretary from seven a.m. to four p.m. each day; she cooked meals for the poor and visited the sick and devoted the hours she wasn't doing those things to peering through her blinds at the neighbors across the street, who had four kids and innumerable grandchildren and made more noise at one meal than Corrinne and her husband and son did in an entire year. Frank had pegged me right—I did like people, and laughter, music, and stories. I traveled in a crowd, and I loved to have parties, to fill my house with friends, to cook, even if it was just pizza or cookies, to have everyone together, safe and full and happy.

In the car, Frank took my hand and pulled me so close that I could feel his eyelashes on my cheek. "Okay?" he asked. "Okay," I answered as he slowly brought his lips to mine. I remember thinking that this was a guy I could love, really love, in a way I hadn't loved the other boys I'd dated, that he was steady and grown-up in a way that they weren't. I also knew that parts of Frank would always be a mystery, that there would always be more going on in his head than he'd be able to express with his words.

Almost without discussion, we'd become a couple that night, and, again, almost without discussion, we'd gotten engaged, then married, and we'd slipped into a life that was more or less the same as the life my parents had. By the time we went to that dance, he'd already been in touch with the army recruiter. He enlisted in the spring of his senior year and was off to basic training the week after we graduated. We got married when he came home after his eight weeks in Fort Benning, with new muscles and a new tattoo. Then he went off to Afghanistan, and I got pregnant the first time he came home on leave. His father died, and we named Spencer after him. Together, we cleared out the garage, where Frank's dad kept most of his things, and slept some nights. I'd been the one to find his cardboard box full of copies of *Barely Legal,* and I'd thrown them away without saying a word to Frank.

None of this was surprising. In our world, you finished high school and got married, and if you were a girl it was a big point of pride if you didn't get pregnant before either of those other events. I hadn't ever thought about college, or traveling, or waiting to start my own family, or having anything that you could call a career as opposed to just a job. I lived my life like a meal that had been set in front of me, never asking if there were other choices or even if I was hungry.

But then, after Spencer came along, and I knew he'd be

my last baby, without ever planning on it, I started seeing, and wanting, other things. A picture of a home office in a magazine, a description of Paris in a book, a restaurant review in the *Philadelphia Inquirer* of a place I knew we could never afford to go—these things, and a hundred more like them, would start a voice whispering in my head. *I want, I want, I want,* the voice would say. It wanted a new couch; it wanted a vacation somewhere other than Disney World or the Jersey Shore; it wanted to read the books Gabe gave me and not have to look up a word or two every page, sometimes every paragraph. When I asked the voice how on earth I could ever hope to get any of these things, the voice answered, *Simple. Money.*

I'd never known anyone who'd been a surrogate. A wife carrying someone else's baby, bringing in more money than her husband would earn in a year and a half, walking around with a belly full of someone else's child . . . that was nothing Frank and I had seen from our parents or cousins or neighbors, nothing that was even a possibility when we were kids. I should have known it would never sit right with Frank, old-fashioned as he was. What happened to us should not have come as a surprise.

At first, it all seemed easy. I got pregnant on the first attempt, in August. There were plenty of things I didn't know how to do: drive a stick shift, swim underwater, use the microwave for anything other than baking potatoes and popping popcorn. But I knew how to be pregnant. After two boys, I'd even say I was good at it.

I started showing right away, the same way I had with Spencer. Certain things bothered me—the smell of gasoline, the sound of the spoon squishing through the mayonnaise when I made tuna salad. In the afternoons I found myself napping, sometimes on the floor next to Spencer's crib, conked out on the carpet like I'd been clubbed in the head. At five o'clock I'd sit both boys in front of the TV and scramble to make sure the table was set and the meatloaf or manicotti or chicken-rice bake or whatever I was making was in the oven, that the boys had their hands and faces washed, that their rooms were picked up and their lunchboxes packed by the time Frank came home, so he wouldn't see how exhausted I was. When I was by myself, my hand resting lightly on my belly, I still felt that surge of excitement and accomplishment. *I am doing something important,* I would think. I was bringing a new life into the world, giving a family this incredible gift (never mind that it was a gift they were buying) . . . what could be better, more noble, than that?

"How's Frank handling everything?" my sister asked me when we were at our parents' house for dinner one night.

"Frank is fine," I said, even though I knew it wasn't even close to being true. Frank, who was at that moment seated in front of the television set, watching the Eagles, was barely looking at me, not at my face and certainly not at my body as it started to change. That night, on the way home, with both boys sleeping in their car seats, I'd ventured a question. "Are you okay? With . . ." Frank hadn't taken his eyes off the road.

"I guess I have to be, don't I?"

"It's just a few more months," I said softly. He didn't answer, but I felt the car speed up, as if by mashing his foot on the gas pedal he could hasten the baby's arrival.

As the fall went on, he rarely asked how I was feeling, the way he had with both of the boys. Then, he'd been tender and considerate, opening bottles of seltzer so they'd go flat, the way I liked it, before pouring me a glass, sweeping and mopping the floors so that I wouldn't have to bend. On nights when we were both home, I would prop my feet in his lap and he'd rub them with lotion, massaging them. Whenever we went out with the boys, he'd always double-check to make sure the diaper bag was packed. Now when he was home he'd sit in his recliner, eyes on the television, jaw set . . . and, more then once, running errands or at the library, I'd reached into the diaper bag and found that I was missing wipes or diapers or an extra pair of size 3T pants. Frank seemed to have decided that the bag, once his responsibility, was now my job, along with everything else around the house.

I tried to talk to him, but every time I asked if there was something wrong, he denied it. "What could be wrong?" he'd ask with a tight smile. That smile scared me, which meant that I never tried to ask follow-up questions, to point out the things I'd noticed, the way his eyes slid away from my belly, the way he hardly ever touched me anymore. The first time we'd tried to make love after the test had come back positive, everything had been fine at first—his mouth nuzzling the skin beneath my ear, my hands roaming over the deliciously taut muscles of his shoulders and his back. When he'd rolled on top of me I'd been wet and more than ready, pushing my hips up hard to meet him . . . but there'd been nothing there.

"Sorry," he'd muttered, rolling onto his side so that I couldn't see him. "Guess I had too much to drink." Except he hadn't had anything more than a single beer before dinner, and dinner had been five hours ago. I touched his shoulder, then the tattoo on his arm. "Is anything bothering you?"

"I'm fine." His voice was loud.

I pulled up my panties and pajama bottoms. "It happens," I said to the ceiling. At least I'd heard that it happened. It had never happened to Frank before, and I knew what was wrong, even if he didn't want to say anything: it was the baby. He was worried about this baby in a way he'd never worried about his own. We'd made love right up until the ninth month with the boys, only stopping because I'd gotten too tired to do anything in bed except sleep, but now that I was carrying someone else's baby, Frank couldn't . . . or wouldn't. I was never sure, because I couldn't get him to talk about it, and there was no one I could ask.

The real trouble started when I was thirteen weeks along. I was in the living room with the boys, the three of us putting together a giant puzzle of the White House on the floor—I'd bought it for a quarter at a tag sale—when I heard a crash from the kitchen, and Frank cursing. I ran in to find him throwing a loaf of bread at the wall. "Goddamn stupid crap!"

"What's wrong?" I looked at the plate on the table and saw the ragged remnants of half of a sandwich. He'd tried to fold the bread in half, only instead of folding, it had crumbled.

I crouched down to pick up the mess. "It's organic." It was true, the bread India wanted me eating, made without additives or preservatives, was considerably harder to fold than the Wonder bread I normally brought.

"It's crap," he said again, and kicked the wall on his way out. I winced, hoping the boys hadn't heard.

It took me a while to realize that it hadn't been a coincidence, Frank losing his temper the day after we'd done our bills. We paid them the same way we always did, in the living room after the boys were asleep, Frank in a chair with the stack of mail, me on the couch with the checkbook, only for once things had gone smoothly, thanks to the money from the clinic I'd deposited in our account, the first installment of the fifty thousand dollars I'd eventually get. We paid off the balance on one of our credit cards, and another two thousand dollars on a second card, instead of just the minimums the way we normally did, and we hadn't had to decide whether to be a few days' late with one of the utilities. For once, there was enough to go around, with money left over at the end, and I'd been stupid enough to smile about it, to say, "Wow, this is great," without realizing how my comment would hurt him.

"Couples fight when the woman gets pregnant," India said

via Skype the day after our fight. It was funny, listening to her talk like she was some kind of expert on marriage after less than two years as a wife. Since the insemination, I'd gone to New York twice, arranging for my mother to pick up the boys after school. India and I also chatted by Skype every few days on the brand-new laptop she had insisted on buying me.

At first I'd been worried that it would feel like India was checking up on me, but gradually we'd started to feel . . . not exactly like friends, but more like coworkers who were friendly, who could share a meal and gossip about their lives.

"Men have mood swings and cravings," she told me. "I saw a thing about it on the *Today* show."

"How about you?" I asked. I'd told her about the argument, leaving out the particulars—the broken plate, the cursing—and now I was eager to steer the talk toward safer ground. "Are you having any cravings?" That was, of course, a joke: even on the computer screen that only showed her from the neck up, I could see she was skinny as ever, her skin smooth, her eyebrows and makeup all perfect.

"Nope," she'd said. "I'm very horny, though." My mouth must have fallen open because she'd laughed. "Don't look so shocked," she'd said. "I'm not that old." This was true—she wasn't that old, but her husband was. I'd met him after my first doctor's appointment in the city. "Look at me," he'd said, escorting us down the sidewalk, "taking two beautiful ladies to lunch." We'd gone to a French restaurant near the doctor's office, a place with white tablecloths and a long, skinny loaf of bread in a paper bag in the center of the table, along with a crock of unsalted butter. Marcus, who I knew was a very big deal, had been friendly, asking questions about my house and my boys and if I followed the Phillies, but he'd been distracted when the food came, tapping at his BlackBerry, and excused himself after downing his steak frites (I'd ordered the same thing; India had sea bass *en papillote*).

He was nice-enough-looking for a man his age, with thick hair and big white teeth. I could feel the energy of the room change when we arrived, and I noticed people looking at him, the hostess's respectful manner as she took his coat. Marcus was polite to her, and interested in me in the same way, but most of his attention he reserved for his wife. He clearly adored India, but I couldn't imagine him having sex. I couldn't even picture him without a suit and tie. That must have shown on my face, because India started to laugh.

"Oh, look at you!" she said, her cheeks turning pink. "You're making me feel like a dirty old lady!"

I turned down the volume on the computer, angling the screen so it faced away from the bedroom, where Frank was still asleep.

"I'm just jealous," I confessed.

"So you guys aren't, um, active?"

I didn't want to say, but my face must have given her an answer. "Men get weird about it," she said. "Get him drunk! Buy some scented candles! Wear something fitted! I just saw the most gorgeous cashmere sweaters in these scrumptious colors . . ."

I nodded politely. India lowered her voice. "Do you think the baby's listening?"

"I don't think the baby has ears." Honestly, I wasn't sure what the baby had and didn't have. With Frank Junior and Spencer I'd signed up for e-mail updates telling me what the fetus was doing or growing at that very moment. I'd been tuned in to every change in my body, every flutter and kick, but now, with two boys to care for and a husband who wasn't inclined to help, plus the knowledge that this baby wasn't mine to keep, I wasn't paying the same kind of attention.

"So what's the problem?" India asked.

"Everything's fine. We're going at it night and day. Right on top of Mount Laundry, while the boys are kicking a soccer ball at the bedroom door."

India sighed. "I feel bad."

"Oh, no," I said, worried, again, that she thought I was hitting her up for more money. "It's no big deal!"

"I'd be happy to hire a cleaning lady . . ."

"I don't work," I said. "I can clean."

"But you're tired."

"I'm fine," I said firmly. My mother had hated housework, heaving epic sighs every time she fetched the vacuum out of the closet or the bucket out from underneath the sink, but I'd always liked it. There were few things I found more peaceful than carrying a basket full of warm, clean clothes into the empty TV room and folding them while I watched one of my shows.

"You're so cute," India had said fondly when I'd told her how I liked doing the laundry, and I'd smiled, but in the back of my mind I was thinking of another book, *The Handmaid's Tale*, a novel Gabe had recommended after I'd asked him, half teasing, if all the books he read were by men. The book was set in the future, where fertile women were given to powerful men and their old wives to have babies for them. I remembered the way the old commander's wife had hated Offred, the handmaid, the one who was supposed to bear her children, and I wondered sometimes whether, behind all the smiles and the friendliness and the gift cards for Whole Foods, India secretly hated me, too.

Then it was Christmas. We were hosting Frank's mother, Corrinne, and my parents, plus Nancy and Dr. Scott. On Christmas Day, I tried to take our usual picture in front of the tree. Frank Junior and Spencer looked adorable in their suits and bow ties. I looked pregnant in my black velvet dress. Frank, standing behind me, with one hand on each of the boys' shoulders, looked glum. Beyond glum. He looked miserable. "Smile!"

I called, running back and forth from the tripod to the fire-place, where the boys kept trying to turn around to see if Santa had refilled their stockings between shots. Frank never smiled. His eyes were hooded, his lips pressed tightly together, like he was trying to keep himself from shouting. I knew, before I even looked at the shots, that none of them were keepers.

I put a roast in the oven in the morning and slid my side dishes in to heat at noon. By two o'clock, I'd just finished setting the table when the doorbell rang. My parents came inside with their arms full of presents, my father gruff and bulky, my mother giggly and flushed. "Hi, honey," she said, and hugged me.

"Come in, Mom," I said. "Let me take your coat." She'd dressed in the plaid pants she insisted on wearing each Christmas even though she'd gained a good twenty pounds since she'd bought them, and the zipper would race down her belly, reveal-ing a beige triangle of girdle, if she made any sudden movements. On top, she wore a green sweater with an appliquéd Santa ho-ho-ho-ing across her chest. A tiny brass bell jingled from the top of Santa's cap. Red-and-green-striped socks peeked out of the tops of her shoes. She was carrying an aluminum commuter mug that read JINGLE BELLS and did not smell like it contained coffee.

"So!" my mother said, clapping her hands and following me into the kitchen as Frank ushered his mom through the door and into the living room. "How's the baby?"

"Fine," I said, hanging her coat as the doorbell rang again. "Oh, it's Nancy!" said my mother, like this was the best news in the world.

"Where can I put these?" Nancy demanded, brandishing a pair of raw sweet potatoes like they were grenades.

I put the sweet potatoes and her Brussels sprouts on the counter while Dr. Scott joined Frank on the couch.

Back in the kitchen, my mother was standing over the sink, washing the two teaspoons and the single coffee mug I hadn't cleaned yet, and Nancy was poking suspiciously at my micro-wave.

"You look great," I said, admiring my sister's belted ivory wool sweater dress and high-heeled caramel-colored leather boots.

"Thanks," she said. "Anne Klein." Nancy had a new habit of telling you either who'd designed her outfit or how much it cost. She looked me up and down, clearly struggling to find something nice to say about my dress, the black one she'd seen a million times, and my black ballet slippers. I thought about saying "Target" or "Payless" but figured she wouldn't get the joke.

"Boys, why don't you go upstairs and play?" I suggested. For Christmas, Santa had bought them a Wii that I'd put on layaway, and we'd set it up in the bedroom that would be a playroom someday. Frank Junior went thundering up the stairs to claim the first round, while Spencer hung on to my skirt, blinking shyly at his aunt and trying to sneak his thumb into his mouth.

I slid my lasagna out of the oven, tossed lettuce and croutons into a bowl, and put Nancy's sweet potatoes into the microwave, looking at the clock and knowing that Frank expected dinner on the table at four o'clock sharp.

"Roast beef, mashed potatoes, sweet potatoes, green beans . . . Frank!" I called. "I could use a hand in here!"

Frank didn't answer. Nancy, frowning, not missing a thing, pulled serving platters out of the cabinet as I put on the oven mitts, crouched down clumsily, and started pulling dishes and platters and roasting pans out of the oven and hurrying food to the table, which I'd set with an ironed white tablecloth and bunches of pine cones that the boys and I had gathered the day before.

My father carved the meat. My mother poured the wine. Nancy pulled out a serving spoon to scoop mashed potatoes. She did it like she was lifting weights or pulling something unpleasant out of the ground, fast and joylessly. Frank helped his mother to the table, then bent his head.

"Let us pray," said Corrinne. My dad, who'd already started filling his plate, set the spoon down with a clang and a guilty look. I bowed my head, then lifted it, looking sharply at both of my boys until they, too, had dropped their eyes. "Be present at our table, Lord, at Christmas and all times adored. Thy creatures bless and grant that we may feast in paradise with Thee." She paused, then said, "Help us to do Your bidding, O Lord, to be Your obedient servants, to know Your will and never presume to replace it with our own."

"A-men!" my father said, and snagged the crispy end of the roast beef off the platter before anyone else could get a crack at it.

Corrinne kept her head bent piously, her hands folded in her lap, before she raised her head and looked at me. "I've been praying for you, Annie."

Puzzled and unsure of the polite response, I just said, "Thank you." I glanced at Frank, hoping for guidance or, at least, sympathy, but he was focused on spooning green bean casserole onto his plate.

"I should tell you," Corrinne continued, "that I have concerns about what you're doing. I've discussed it with Pastor."

Anger curled in my belly and began a slow crawl up my throat. "I appreciate your concern, but I'm fine. Really."

"But you're not," Corrinne said. "I know you think I'm a busybody, but if you saw someone getting ready to jump off a building, you'd try to talk them out of it. That would be your duty."

"I'm not sure what you're talking about," I lied.

"You have sinned," she said, as matter-of-factly as if she was telling me I'd brushed my teeth that morning. "You have presumed to know the will of God. But it's never too late to turn away from wickedness."

I felt my face get hot. "All I'm trying to do is help my family. How does that mean I've presumed to know the will of God?"

"God decides who He blesses with children," said Corrinne. "All of this science, all these interventions, fly in the face of God's plan."

"That's exactly what I think," said Nancy. My jaw fell open. I made myself shut it, and looked down at Spencer, who was grimly pushing peas underneath his mashed potatoes. "Used to be, if you were infertile, you'd be an aunt or get a dog or whatever. Now, everyone just thinks they can control everything. Make it just the way they want it."

"Amen," said Corrinne. I looked at Frank again, waiting for a lifeboat that clearly wasn't coming. I narrowed my eyes at my sister, who stared back at me expressionless; my sister with her Botox shots and her banded stomach, lecturing me about how it was wrong to use technology to improve things.

"All I know," I said, trying not to let them hear my voice shake, "is that I'm making the best decisions I can, for my family."

"Has anyone tried the lasagna?" my mother chirped from her end of the table. Corrinne finally shut her mouth. My face was burning as I turned to my right in time to see Frank Junior shoving a forkful of stuffing in his mouth. He grimaced, than spat his mouthful into his napkin.

"It's not from the red box," he complained.

"Grammy made this from scratch, which is much better."

"No, it's not better." He frowned. "It's yucky."

"Frank Junior," said Frank, raising his voice, and Frank Junior, hearing the implied promise of a spanking, meekly took a bite. I looked at my husband again, hoping against hope that he'd tell everyone that he supported what I was doing; that he approved; that he was grateful. But, after glaring at his son, Frank just kept eating, and, eventually, my mother started chatting with Corrinne about canning tomatoes, and Scott started talking football with anyone who'd listen, and we made it through the meal.

There were presents under the tree for the boys, new shirts and sneakers from my parents, and a book apiece from Nancy and Scott. Spencer was delighted—honestly, Spencer would have been delighted with an empty box and a bow—but Frank Junior rolled his eyes. "More boring books," he said under his breath. Frank snatched him up so fast that he didn't have time to scream. He hustled him out the door and around the back of the house, but we could all hear Frank Junior squealing and the sound of his daddy's hand making contact with his backside; once, twice, three times. I couldn't keep from wincing. "Spare the rod," Frank's mother intoned, and my father yawned, then looked at me and said, "Come on, Annie, it's not the end of the world. You girls went to bed with warm bottoms a few times, and you're both just fine."

I struggled to my feet. "You know what?" My voice was pleasant, even, not too loud. "I'm not feeling well. I think I'll lie down for a minute." Ignoring the murmurs of concerns, my mother's offer to make me a cup of tea and Nancy telling everyone that it was probably heartburn, I hurried up the stairs, collapsed on my bed, and started to cry. I was doing a good thing, I told myself. This was money for the four of us, money that I was working to earn, putting my body through the strains and risks of another pregnancy, so why couldn't any of them see it? Why didn't any of them appreciate the sacrifices I was making for Frank, for our boys, for our family? I'd done the best I could, made what I thought was a good decision, and what had I gotten but a husband who wouldn't look at me or talk to me, a sister who thought I was no better than a prostitute, and a mother-in-law who thought I was immoral?

I rolled over, flipped open my laptop, and, before I could

think about what I was doing, connected to Skype and clicked on India's number.

Not home, I thought, but India picked up after the first ring. "Hi, Annie! Merry Christmas! How are you doing?"

"I'm fine," I said . . . but I must not have looked fine, because India's eyes narrowed.

"Oh my God. What is it? What's wrong? Did something happen? Is the baby okay?"

"No, no," I said, wiping my cheeks and cursing myself for scaring her. "The baby's fine, everything's all right, it's just . . ." What could I tell her? That I'd gotten in a fight with my mother-in-law? That my husband hadn't stood up for me? "I don't know," I finally said. "Maybe it's just the holidays."

"You're overwhelmed." India's voice was kind. "And you must be exhausted. The weather's been so terrible, and with two little boys . . . I don't know how you're managing."

"I'm okay." I was already regretting the call. What had I been thinking? That she'd fix things? That she'd know what to do? How could she give me any advice, how could she help, if I couldn't even tell her what was wrong?

"I've got an idea. You and I should go somewhere warm for a few days."

I shook my head. "I couldn't leave. I've got so much to do, and Spencer and Frank Junior . . ."

"I can find them a sitter. Or maybe your parents . . . ?"

I nodded, almost in spite of myself. More than once my mother had offered to host both boys for a few nights over the holidays, but I'd been so intent on proving I could handle everything—the boys, the pregnancy, my sullen husband—that I'd refused.

"They're in Philadelphia, right? How about this? Text me if they can do it, and I'll meet you at their house at noon. You should pack for three days." She smiled. "And bring a swimsuit."

"Oh, no, really. I couldn't."

"I'm not taking no for an answer. I'll see you tomorrow."

"Where will we go?" I managed to ask.

"That," said India, "is for me to know and you to find out."

I hid in the bedroom, listening for the slamming doors and the car engines starting, until I was sure everyone was gone. Then I came downstairs to find Frank—big surprise—in front of the TV. "I'm going away for a few days," I announced—not asking him, but, for the first time in my marriage, telling him. He nodded wordlessly, not even asking where I was going or with whom, before I went back to the kitchen to start on the dishes and he went back to the game. "Don't go to bed angry," the self-help books all said, but that night I fell asleep furious . . . and, as for Frank, for all I knew he'd never come to bed at all.

The next morning, I packed two suitcases, loaded the diaper bag and drove to Philadelphia. India was waiting for me, sitting in the backseat of a Town Car that was idling at the curb in front of my parents' condo. I got the boys out of the backseat, glad they were still neat, in jeans and miniature matching plaid shirts, that their noses were wiped and their shoes were tied. "Frank Junior, Spencer, this is Mrs. Croft." Both boys held out their hands, like their father and I had taught them. Then Spencer picked up the diaper bag and Frank started pulling the suitcase, and we led the way up the steps to my parents' door.

"Oh my God, look at them," said India, with her hands clasped at her chest. "They are the cutest things I've ever seen in my life."

I thanked her, grateful that someone appreciated the work I was doing. The boys hugged my mother, then sat on the couch, with Frank Junior spreading out the old Candy Land board on the coffee table. Aware of India watching me, I knelt down and looked at both of them. "Mommy's going away for a few days, and you get to stay with Grammy and Grampy. I want you both to be good boys. Listen to Grammy and do as you're told. Frank Junior, you take care of your brother." Frank nodded. Spencer hugged me, pressing his warm cheek against mine.

"Mommy, don't go."

My throat tightened. I'd never left him for longer than an afternoon before. "Mommy always comes back. Remember?"

He nodded gravely. "Always comes back."

"Don't worry," said Frank Junior. "I'll take care of him."

I kissed them both, hugged my mother, then got in the back of India's car. It took me until we were on the highway to realize that she was staring at me like I'd just turned wine into water, or started levitating.

"What?"

"You're so good with them." She sounded wistful. "How'd you learn to be such a good mother?"

I felt myself flush with pleasure. "Oh, I have my moments."

"Do you yell?"

I thought for a minute, then shook my head. I got impatient, got bored sometimes, and often wished I could have more privacy, more time to myself, more sleep . . . but I honestly enjoyed my boys' company, and I wasn't much of a yeller at anyone, let alone my sons.

"And you don't spank them . . ." Her voice trailed off as I shook my head again. She laughed. "Not that I'm planning on spanking this baby! It's just that you're so patient."

"You'll learn," I told her. "You'll see. When it's your own baby, you'll be surprised at how it all just falls into place." Meanwhile, I was almost falling asleep. The car had the smoothest ride I'd ever felt, and the backseat felt soft as a bed. India still looked concerned, rolling the strap of her handbag between her fingertips.

"I guess there's classes I can take."

I stifled a yawn. "You don't need classes. You'll be a natural." I could tell that she was worrying, but I couldn't keep my eyes open. I dozed the whole way to the airport, glad that we were flying out of a different terminal from the one where Frank worked, and I ended up sleeping for the entire trip down to West Palm Beach.

Another car met us at the airport, the uniformed driver waiting by baggage claim, holding a sign that read CROFT. "Have you ladies stayed at the Breakers before?" he asked.

"I have, my friend hasn't," said India.

"Well, ma'am, you're in for a real treat." He drove us through the gates of a building that looked like the largest, grandest country club in the world. India spoke to the uniformed woman behind the desk, who handed her two keys and two bottles of water. A bellman took our luggage, and India led me to the elevator.

My room—a suite, really—was beautiful, with pale-green carpet and a canopied bed, a deep tub and separate shower in the bathroom, a balcony with a view over a linked complex of swimming pools and, beyond it, the golden sand of the beach. I took off my shoes and lay down on the bed, my cheek against the pillow, which was deliciously crisp and cool. *Maybe for a few minutes,* I thought, and closed my eyes again. When I opened them again it was nine o'clock the next morning, and there were two notes that had been slipped under the door; one from housekeeping, apologizing for not being able to give me turn-down service the night before, the other from India. *Call me when you're up, Sleepyhead!*

"I'm so sorry," I told her twenty minutes later. At her instructions, I'd put on my swimsuit, then a cover-up, one of Frank's button-down shirts. We were having breakfast by the pool: eggs

Benedict, fresh-squeezed orange juice, a basket of muffins and croissants. I'd looked at the prices, then shut my menu fast and tried to tell myself that maybe the prices were in Monopoly money, or some kind of currency used only in this hotel that had no relationship to actual dollars and cents. Waiters in white shirts and green pants or skirts hovered, waiting to swoop in the instant we needed something: more water, more coffee, more tiny bottles of honey and jam for the croissants.

"Please. I feel terrible that I had no idea how exhausted you were!" She looked at me earnestly from under the deep brim of a straw sunhat tied with a jaunty pink ribbon that matched her dress. "You have to take care of yourself."

"I'm sure the baby's fine," I said.

She waved one freshly manicured hand. "I don't care about the baby. I mean, I do care about the baby, of course I care about the baby, but I care about you more right now." She gave me her dazzling smile. "You're not just the Tupperware, you know."

"I know," I muttered, feeling guilty for ever having doubted her, for comparing her to the scrawny, ancient, resentful wife in some book that I'd read.

"So here's the plan," she said. "You're getting a prenatal massage at two . . ."

"Oh, India, really, I'm fine."

She continued as if I hadn't spoken. "And then a facial and a mani-pedi, and I've got a car taking us to Joe's Stone Crab at seven—it's a little bit of a drive, but it's supposed to be the place down here, and we're not leaving until we eat some Key lime pie."

"That sounds amazing," I told her . . . and then, feeling shy, I said, "but first, can I go for a swim?"

She indicated the ocean like she'd grown it herself. "Go on."

I floated in the warm, salty water, the skirt of my maternity suit flapping out around me as the waves lifted me up and lowered me down. I wondered how the boys were doing, how

Frank was managing without me . . . then I decided that everyone would be fine; that I was here, and I should try to enjoy it.

I rinsed off in my room, then went down to the spa, where
I half dozed through a blissful afternoon of being tended to,
four hours where all I had to do was lift my arms or close my
eyes or tell the masseuse how much pressure I liked. All I had to
wear for dinner was my plain old black dress again, but when I
got back to my room there were shopping bags arranged on the
bed, clothes peeking out of pink and pale-blue tissue: a sundress
made of pale yellow linen, a skirt, and a few scoop-necked jersey
tops, the same kind of flip-flops India had worn, all with the
price tags cut so that I couldn't see how much they'd cost.

I let the crisp fabric of the sundress fall over my shoulders
and hips and smoothed lotion from the hotel's little bottle on
my skin, then took the elevator down to where India was waiting for me in the lobby. There was another car outside that took
us to South Beach. The restaurant was big and crowded, full
of groups that all seemed to be celebrating something. Over
dinner—caesar salad, warm rolls, crab legs for both of us—India
told me her story—how she, too, had grown up without much;
how she'd gone to Los Angeles to try to be an actress, how she'd
moved to New York City to work in public relations, how she'd
met Marcus in a Starbucks, of all places. "What was that like?"
I asked. What I really wanted to ask was, how had she found
the confidence to go to a city all the way on the other side of
the country, to get herself the kind of job I hadn't even known
existed, to turn herself into the kind of person Marcus wanted?
She was so much smarter than I was, so much more clever, and I
listened closely as she explained how she'd figured out what pub-
licists were and what they did; how she'd made connections and
networked with the right people to get an internship, then a job.

At the end of the meal, over decaf coffee and a slice of that
tart, rich Key lime pie, India bent her head, suddenly shy. "I

bought you something," she said. "Merry Christmas." She handed me a little velvet box. Inside was a necklace, a gorgeous green stone suspended on a shimmering length of silver chain. "Emerald," she said. "It's the baby's birthstone. I wanted you to have something so you can always feel close to her. Or him." She smiled—she and Marcus had decided not to learn the baby's gender, but we were both secretly convinced that I was carrying a girl.

My throat tightened. No one had ever given me jewelry, except for my engagement ring, and of course I had nothing for her except the card and the homemade raspberry jam I'd sent to her apartment before Christmas. "Oh, India. It's beautiful, but it's way too much."

"No," she said. Her eyes were shining. "No, it is not too much. What you're doing for Marcus and me, there's nothing we could ever pay you to thank you enough."

We hugged, and I told myself to stop being so critical, to just enjoy the night, the sweet taste of fresh crab, which I'd never had before, and how lovely it was to slip deeply into those cool, crisp sheets in an immaculate room and sleep in as late as I wanted, to wander on the beach for hours, the sand warm and firm against my bare feet.

"Now listen," she said, as we drove back to the airport. "If you start feeling overwhelmed or tired like that again, you call me, no matter what. I'm finding you a cleaning lady, and don't even try to talk me out of it. It's ridiculous that you're scrubbing floors."

"Lots of people do," I pointed out.

"Lots of people don't have a choice. But you do. So no arguments."

"Thank you," I said, for possibly the hundredth time in the last two days. The words were completely inadequate, but what else could I say? That she'd changed my life? That, looking at her, I was starting to think about how things could have gone differently for me, and what might still be possible? That it was exhilarating and terrifying at the same time?

"Travel safe," she said, hugging me . . . and in that moment I believed that if everything had been equal, if we'd met in school or working some job or pushing our new babies on swings in the playground, that India Croft and I could actually have been friends.

I made the trip in reverse: car to the West Palm Beach airport, plane to Philadelphia, car back to my parents' house to pick up the boys. "They were angels," said my mother, but she looked hollow-eyed, like she couldn't wait to go back to her couch and catch up with her TV friends. My house hadn't been trashed—there were no piles of dirty dishes or dirty laundry, no chair that had been flung through the television set—but Frank hadn't done much cleaning. Things appeared to be exactly as I'd left them after Christmas dinner, the platters still in the drainboard next to the sink, the pine cones still in the middle of the dining-room table. Frank helped me bring the suitcases inside. Then he stayed out of my way, not offering to help as I fed the boys dinner and got us unpacked.

Finally, at eight o'clock, with the boys washed and brushed and tucked into their beds, I stood at the doorway of the family room. Frank was once again planted in front of the television set, watching some comedy with a cackling laugh track. I planted myself in front of the screen and stood there until he clicked it into silence.

"Nice necklace," he said—the first words he'd spoken other than a muttered "hello" when I'd arrived.

I felt myself blushing, but I didn't back down. "India gave it to me. It's the baby's birthstone. So I can remember her."

"Must be nice," he said sarcastically. "A friend who can give you presents like that."

I felt like throwing something at him, but I didn't want to wake up the boys. "I don't care about jewelry! For God's sake, Frank, all I wanted to do was get us out of this mess, get us a little extra money . . ."

"Well, you did it. Good for you."

"Frank," I said. My voice cracked. "What do you want me to do? I can't undo this," I said, running my hand over my belly, so he'd know what I was talking about.

"I don't know." He bit off each word, and I realized that he wasn't just angry, the way I'd seen him a few times over the years, when the bill collectors would call, or the time he'd been passed over for a promotion. He was way past angry. He was furious . . . and it scared me.

He got to his feet. "I've been thinking maybe I'll go stay with my mom for a while."

"You do that." The words were out of my mouth before I could think about them, but it only took me a moment to realize that this was the right choice, maybe the only choice. Angry as he was, I didn't want to be around him, and I didn't want the boys around him, either.

"This was a mistake," he said, walking past me without sparing me a glance. Questions swirled in my head: Would he come back? Would he see the boys? Was this a separation? Did he want to get divorced? But I didn't ask any of them. I just stood there, frozen, unbelieving, as he climbed up the stairs, packed a bag, climbed into the car, and drove off into the dark.

INDIA

It started out a day like any other chilly, gray-sky April morning. I woke up feeling Marcus's lips on my forehead, hearing the soft clink as he set down a cup of tea beside me. "How is the mother-to-be?" he asked, and I smiled. Neither of us was trying to pretend that the situation was anything other than what it was, but Marcus still treated me like I was expecting. We had the ultrasound pictures stuck to our refrigerator with a magnet; we sent Annie downloadable recordings of our voices reading the baby stories and singing lullabies, and kept a calender marked with red Xs through each day before the baby's arrival hanging on my dressing room door.

Once Marcus was showered and dressed and off to work, I padded to my dressing room and pulled on the workout clothes I'd laid out the night before—tights and running pants, a long-sleeved Under Armour shirt with a fleece jacket on top of it.

My trainer met me in the lobby, and we jogged across the street, across the wide sidewalk through the gap in the stone gate and into the park for the usual ninety minutes of torture. Back at home, my breakfast was waiting for me on a tray: a white china plate covered with almonds, dried apricots, a peeled, cored apple cut into slices so thin they were translucent, and a hard-boiled egg. I looked longingly at Marcus's soaking tub before skinning off my sweaty clothes. It wasn't as if my shower was Spartan: the water assaulted me from a half-dozen nozzles and there was a marble ledge, specially designed so I'd have a place to prop up my foot while I shaved my legs. Some couples had his-and-hers sinks. Marcus and I had his-and-hers bathrooms. "It's the secret of a happy marriage," I'd told Annie. "That, and Viagra." The truth was, Marcus liked to visit me in my bathroom, knocking on the door in his bathrobe. Sometimes he'd slip into the shower with me, getting his hands slick with soap and running them over my body, and sometimes this would lead to sex, but, more often, he'd just pull up the chair from my vanity and sit by the shower, talking about nothing and everything, his children, his colleagues, the next trip we'd take. At first I'd been shy about letting him see me backstage—he didn't need to know that I used concealer or plucked my eyebrows—but, after a while, I found that I genuinely enjoyed his company, and I looked forward to those mornings more than any other part of the day.

By ten o'clock I was out the door, dressed, hair blown straight, makeup applied. In my office, I sipped a latte and returned calls and e-mails for an hour and a half, revising a press release announcing my jewelry company's new line of charm bracelets ("The perfect gift for Mother's Day!"), calling to confirm receipt for the invitations we'd sent for a cocktail party in honor of a bridal magazine's new editor, their fourth in three years. I was taking my assistant Daphne to lunch at Michael's. Then I'd head to the salon for a bikini wax and a facial. On Friday, Marcus and I were flying to the Bahamas for the fiftieth birthday of one of Marcus's partners' wives—a first wife. Seeing one of those was sort of like glimpsing a rare bird or monkey, a member of an endangered species, upright and uncaged and walking among us.

Daphne and I were halfway through our salads, and I was listening to her tell me about her latest boyfriend's new job—something to do with corporate branding and search-engine optimization—when my phone trilled from inside my bag. I bent down to look at the number. When I saw that it was Marcus's office, I picked up fast, pressing the phone against my ear and bending my head close to the table. Marcus and I e-mailed. The only times he'd call me during the workday was when it was an emergency.

"Hello?"

"Mrs. Croft?" Kelly, one of Marcus's executive assistants, was on the line, and she sounded as rattled as I'd ever heard her.

I was on my feet before I knew it. Daphne stared at me. *What's wrong?* she mouthed. I hurried through the restaurant without answering, not even sparing a glance at Barbara Walters at the table by the window, and stood on the sidewalk as Kelly gave me the details. *Chest pain . . . called the doctor . . . Beth Israel . . . intensive care.* "Does his cardiologist know? Is it the same blocked artery?"

"I'm so sorry, Mrs. Croft, but I told you everything they told me."

"I'll be right there," I told her. I ran out the door and into the first cab I saw, snapping out the hospital's address, hardly able to breathe.

What would I do without him? I thought, as the cab made its way downtown. How would I live? How would I pay the bills, how would I manage the staff? I had no idea how any of it worked. I hadn't wanted to learn. I'd been superstitious, thinking that too many questions would be asking for trouble. I'd turn myself into Bluebeard's wife. If I went poking around, I'd find . . . what? A row of my beheaded predecessors rotting in the basement? Documents showing that Marcus was secretly broke? And what was I doing, thinking this way at a time like this? Marcus. My husband. The man I'd come to love, with all my heart, in spite of myself.

Through the windows, I saw a man with a plastic bag over

his hand holding a little dog's leash, a boy and a girl walking side by side, one earbud of the iPod she carried in each of their ears. I pulled my telephone out of the purse and called Trey at the office and Tommy on his cell phone and Bettina at Kohler's, saying that I didn't know what was happening, but that I'd been told it was urgent; that I was on my way to the hospital and that they should probably join me.

"I'll leave right now," said Trey.

"Be there as soon as I can," said Tommy.

Bettina hadn't said anything before she'd hung up. I knew she was thinking that this was, somehow, my fault, even though I'd been the one to call the doctor that first time, and I'd been the one to monitor his diet, to make sure he took his medication, to buy a treadmill and hire a trainer, to tell him, every night, how much I loved him.

The cab dropped me off by the emergency room. I ran through the automated doors. "Marcus Croft," I said to the receptionist. My chest was as tight as if someone was squeezing it, the skin of my forearms pebbled with goose bumps. The receptionist pecked at her computer, then gave me directions: elevator to the C wing, down the second hallway, left and then another left, check in at the blue desk, and I hurried away, not feeling the floor underneath me or seeing the faces of the people I passed.

When the elevator doors slid open, there were three nurses gathered around a desk, talking quietly. A blue light flashed in the hall, and an orderly pushed an empty stretcher. "Marcus Croft," I said. All of them looked up, guiltily, like schoolgirls caught passing notes, and I knew, in that instant, what had happened.

"Oh, God." My knees felt like they'd melted, and I would have fallen if I hadn't managed to grab the edge of the desk.

"Where is he?" My voice was loud and high and frantic. I

could see my reflection in the pane of glass behind the desk, skin pale, hair disheveled, eyes unrecognizable.

"I'm so sorry," said the nurse. She was short, round-faced, copper-skinned, wearing white clogs and pale-pink scrubs. I knew exactly how I must have looked to her: too pretty, too thin, too young. I might as well have been wearing a tiara that spelled out the words TROPHY WIFE in flashing neon bulbs above my head.

There was a waiting area up there, a few benches, a few people, the inevitable television bolted to the ceiling, blasting talk-show noise into the hallway. That hospital smell of chicken-noodle soup and industrial cleansers, of blood and rubbing alcohol, filled the air. A mother sat with a toddler in one corner, a little girl she bounced on her knee. *I'll remember this,* I thought, trying to catch my breath. *I will remember all of this forever.*

"Do you want to see him?" asked the nurse.

I did not. I wanted to hold in my memory the way he'd looked the first time I'd seen him in the Starbucks: healthy and fit, splendidly dressed, completely in control of the world around him, confounded by the coffee. Still, I nodded and let the nurse lead me down a hallway and into the tile-floored room where my husband had died.

Marcus lay on a bed, on top of dirtied sheets, alongside a single inside-out rubber glove. There were stickers pasted to his gray-furred chest, wires hooked up to box on a wheeled stand, an IV plugged into his arm. The room smelled like shit. His eyes were closed, his hair sticking up on the back of his head, and his face seemed to have somehow collapsed, giving him the look of a much older man.

"We need to get him cleaned up before the children see him." My voice came out just right: clear and cultured, a voice used to being obeyed.

"Of course," said the nurse. She went to the corner and picked up a phone. I reached out, smoothing my husband's hair and realizing that what I'd suspected was undeniably true. He had been the love of my life. Every night, I'd fallen asleep with his arms around me and his face nestled in my neck. Every morning he'd brought me tea and kissed me. *You're my favorite person in the world*, he would say. *What will become of me?* I wondered again, touching his forehead, feeling his skin, already cool and waxy, underneath my palm.

"What do I do now?" I asked.

The nurse looked at me, not unkindly. She had a ring on her left hand. I wondered if she had children, where she lived, what her life was like, if she was happy, if she was loved. "There'll be a social worker coming along soon. She can talk to you about arrangements. Do you know what his wishes were?"

I almost laughed. His wishes were that we'd live together for years and years, that we'd travel, go to parties, go to dinners, go dancing. He wanted to buy a house in Vail and take his kids skiing. He wanted to sleep in on the rare Sunday morning he didn't have to work, and then be woken up with a blow job. "I'm a simple man," he'd always say when I was done.

"We're having a baby." My voice was faint. My hand was still on Marcus's hair. *He's sleeping,* I told myself, even though it didn't look like that at all. His features had already started to change, to become somehow cruder. The nurse looked at me, surprised, first at my face, then at my belly.

"Oh, not me. A surrogate. She's—we're—due in May."

The nurse looked like she didn't know what to say to that. I sympathized. *Congratulations? I'm sorry?* Nothing was right.

There was a sink against the wall, a container of hand soap bolted beside it. In the bathroom, I found paper towels and, in a cabinet along the wall, a kidney-shaped plastic pan. I filled the pan with soap and warm water. Someone had sliced through his shirt and pants, and they lay like a discarded wrapper against him. "Can you help me?" I asked.

"Oh, ma'am, we can take care of that."

"Please," I said, and found that I was crying. "Please."

She helped me shift his body, pulling off the clothes, throwing them away. I wiped off the backs of his legs and pulled the sticky plastic pads off his chest, found a brush in my purse and brushed his hair. "You're going to be a wonderful mother," said the nurse, helping me cover him with a clean sheet. She stepped into the hallway, murmuring briefly with one of her compatriots from the desk. Then the kids filed in, Tommy pale and sick-looking, Trey with his wife beside him, Bettina weeping, thin lips trembling over her buck teeth.

"We should call Mom," she said. "Mom should be here." They huddled together, and none of them noticed when I slipped out the door.

I left my contact information at the desk. If the nurse there seemed surprised to see me go, she kept it off her face. Maybe she was used to all kinds of strange behavior from the recently bereaved; maybe she was just glad that I wasn't screaming or tearing at my clothes or threatening to sue someone.

Outside, it was still daytime. The sun was still shining; I could hear music coming from a passing car's open windows and construction workers shouting as they gutted the building across the street. I texted Manuel and sat on a bench until the big black car glided to the curb. He held the door, and I slid into the backseat. "Mr. Croft died." It was the first time I'd said it. I imagined it would be the first of many.

He gave a small sigh, and crossed himself. "Ma'am, I'm sorry. He was a good man." I wondered about that. I knew Marcus was generous to all of his employees. He gave raises and holiday bonuses and paid vacations. I also knew he expected his people to work as hard as he did, to be available whenever he needed them, at five in the morning or in the middle of the night, or on Christmas or on weekends. I didn't know whether Manuel had a family, whether he'd resented Marcus, or liked him, or felt protective toward him, or jealous of him, or absolutely nothing at all.

"Home?" he asked, and I nodded, wondering how much longer it would be my home. The decorator had finished the nursery the week before. *Nice,* Marcus had said—a single-word assessment of a room that had cost more than thirty thousand dollars to put together, six thousand for the antique rocking horse alone. *It's crazy,* I'd said . . . but I'd loved it, and Marcus insisted that I buy it.

As we drove, I felt a bleakness settle through my body. Probably I wouldn't even be able to stay in the apartment—it would, I guessed, give Bettina and Tommy and Trey a great deal of pleasure to make me leave. *Just until the will is probated,* they'd say. *Just until we get things sorted out.* The sorting out would take months, maybe years. There'd be lawyers, hearings, court dates, newspaper stories, unflattering pictures, all my history, my secrets exposed. It was paranoid, I knew—Marcus and I were legally married; this was legally my home . . . but I couldn't shake the feeling, swelling into certainty with each passing block, that his children had never liked me and that they'd do whatever they could to harm me now that their father was dead.

I hurried past the doorman with my head down, hair obscuring my face, and was grateful to find the elevator empty. Upstairs, I took off my high heels and set them neatly by the door. Then I sat on the couch, cross-legged, my head hanging down, my eyes squeezed shut. I didn't open them until I heard the front door slam. I raised my head and saw Bettina glaring at me. Anger had reddened her cheeks and darkened her eyes. Her hair stood out around her head in ropy tangles. Her lips curled back from her gleaming teeth. In her fury, she almost looked beautiful.

"Did he find out about you? Is that what happened? He found out the truth and had a heart attack?"

"He was at a business lunch," I said slowly, repeating what I'd been told, before her words could register. *Found out about you.* For the second time that day I started to shiver. Bettina pulled a folder out of her purse and threw it in my lap. Papers and photographs spilled out onto the carpet . . . and there was my old face, staring up at me from the floor.

"Did you tell him?" Bettina asked. Every drop of culture, of private schooling and summers in the Hamptons, was gone from her voice. She sounded as common as my own mother as she shrieked. "Did he know you'd been arrested? Did he know that you were still married when you married him?"

My body sagged against the couch. Blood thundered in my ears, and when I found my voice it was a raspy whisper.

"What are you talking about? I was . . . we got . . ." *Divorced,* I wanted to say, but Bettina started talking first.

"I hired a detective. I knew you were a liar the first time I saw you. I just didn't know how bad it was."

I managed to straighten the pile of pages into a stack. My hands were steady under Bettina's glare, and my eyes were dry. "Your father didn't know about any of that. All he knew was that I loved him."

"Some love," said Bettina. "How could he have loved you? He didn't know what you were." She smiled at me, a horrible, humorless grin. "You thought you'd waltz in here and fuck him to death and get everything. Well, you were wrong, Samantha. You're not getting shit. I'm going to tell everyone." She crossed the room in three swift steps and snatched the folder out of my hand. "Everyone. I'm going to ruin you."

The door slammed shut. I was alone.

I sat for a minute, shaking, numb, breathless, forcing myself to think. What could she do to me? And what would it matter? I'd lost my love. I hadn't lost my home yet, but that would be coming soon. And there'd be a baby. A baby and no Marcus. In that moment, I was eighteen again, eighteen and trapped and terrified, with no resources, no family, eighteen and barefoot on the black-and-white tiled floor of my first husband's apartment, shaking so hard that the plus sign on the pregnancy test between my fingers was a blur, and the only words I could think were *I can't, I can't, I can't.*

In the dressing room, I flipped through the hangers until I found the jeans I wanted, a pair left over from my pre-Marcus life, dark-rinsed, worn through at the knee. I put on one of his T-shirts—freshly washed and folded, of course, but I imagined it still retained the ghost of his scent, his cologne and his skin—and a soft gray wool cardigan on top. *He is gone,* I told myself. He'll never come through the door again, never kiss me in bed, never pull out a chair for me at dinner, never pull my head into his lap while we're watching TV. He'll never see our baby. *I can't,* I thought, with the frantic desperation I'd felt as a teenager, all those years ago. *I can't.*

Our luggage was kept in specially built shelves along one of the closet's shorter walls. I took a duffel bag, a simple thing made of coffee-colored leather. It took me ten minutes to fill it up with jeans and T-shirts, underwear and bras, a set of workout clothes, a pair of sneakers, a toothbrush, and a comb.

In the media room, I sat at Marcus's desk, flipped open my laptop, and logged onto the travel site I used. There, I bought a direct flight from Philadelphia to Puerto Vallarta, leaving the next morning. A ticket from Newark to Los Angeles, leaving an hour later. From Boston to the Bahamas. From LaGuardia to Vancouver. From Hartford to Paris. My fingers flew. The telephone trilled. Fraud protection. My friends at American Express were concerned about suspicious charges. I assured them that the card was in my possession, that all of the charges were legitimate. "Is there anything else I can help you with today?" the pleasant-voiced customer service representative asked, and I told her, nicely, that I was all set.

I bought myself three more tickets—Frankfurt, London, and Lexington, Kentucky. Then I picked up my bag, hailed a cab, and slid into the backseat. "Newark airport," I said, and started to run.

PART THREE

~

Then Came You

BETTINA

I don't understand," I said, for what felt like the sixteenth time that morning. I was sitting at a table in a conference room in my father's office with Jeff, my father's lawyer, at my side and my father's baby, with her wrinkled rosebud of a face, in a car seat on the floor beside me. I could have left it—*her*, I reminded myself, *her*—at home, with the doula, but I wanted her with me as a kind of visual punctuation, a reminder to the assembled attorneys of what had happened, and the situation I was in.

On the other side of the table was Leslie Stalling, director of the Princeton Fertility Clinic, who'd brought a lawyer of her own. There was an urn of coffee, a platter of pastries, and a bowl of fruit on a table against one wall, but no one had touched any of it. Both lawyers had briefcases at their sides and legal pads in their laps, and both had set digital tape recorders out on the table. Instead of a tape recorder or a notebook, Leslie, a fit middle-aged woman with bright blond hair, a strand of pearls, and a well-cut taupe suit, had a box of tissues in her lap. She wasn't crying, but she looked like she might start at any moment.

"I'm so sorry," she said to me. "In all the years of operating the clinic, we've never had a situation like this."

"I get that." How could I not? She'd said that line, or some variation of it, at least a dozen times: *In all my years of running the clinic, in all my years of working with infertile women, in all my years on the planet I've never seen a situation like this.*

I believed her. Who could have even imagined a situation like this one? My father, the biological father of the baby, was dead. My stepmother, the legal mother (technically, she would become the mother as soon as she signed the baby's birth certificate), had disappeared without bothering even to make an appearance at her beloved's funeral or to return for her child's birth. Which meant that, according to a document the two of them had signed that I'd never known about, I was, now that I'd consented, the guardian of my newborn half-sibling. I would be responsible for raising it. Her. Whatever. It was astonishing. One day I'd been a regular twenty-four-year-old, living in my first apartment, working at my first job, waking up, getting dressed, swiping my card through the subway turnstile, standing on a train with the swaying, iPodded worker bees, thinking about whether the guy I'd been spending all my weekends with was my boyfriend if I'd only kissed him once . . . then the phone rings and there's someone I'd never met on the other end of the line, saying that I was a mother.

It had taken me a while to realize that India was actually gone. The first clue came two days after my father's death, when the funeral home called to tell me that no one had brought them clothes for him to wear in his coffin. "Have you heard from his wife?" I'd asked, and the receptionist said that, regrettably, they had been unable to reach her. I took the subway to their apartment. "Hey, Ricky," I said to the day doorman, a man I'd known since I'd learned to walk in the lobby. "Have you seen Mrs. Croft around?" It still cut to call her Mrs. Croft—that was, after all, my mother's name—but it was better than "my stepmother" or "Dad's new sidepiece."

"Not since the day your father passed," he said.

I filed that away and took the elevator upstairs. The apartment was as spotless as always. The chef was wiping down the counters in the kitchen; one maid was dusting in the living room and the other was ironing sheets in the laundry room. But there was no sign of India.

In my father's dressing room, I picked out a navy-blue suit and a red-and-gold tie, then added a white button-down shirt with his initials monogrammed at the cuff; boxer shorts and an undershirt; socks and a pair of glossy black loafers, and zipped everything into a garment bag. I had already found the picture I wanted, a shot of the five of us when Trey and Tommy and I were little and my mother was still around, posing in front of the Grand Canyon. I would tuck it in the pocket of his suit jacket, so it would be with him, wherever he was going.

I tried to find India. I called and called, leaving voice mails, sending e-mails, pestering her assistant right up until the morning of the service, at which point it was too obvious to ignore: she was gone. The minister didn't mention it, delivering a pleasant and generic eulogy that mentioned my father's loved ones without naming them. I sat in the front row of the church, against the hard-backed pew. Where had she gone? What was she planning? And what would happen if she didn't come back before the baby was born?

After the service—small, just for the family—everyone came back to the apartment. Someone, probably Paul, had arranged for food and a waitstaff, strangers in white shirts and black pants or skirts discretely moving through the room holding platters or picking up empty plates and glasses. I stood by the front door, next to a girl who'd been hired to hang coats on the rolling wire coat racks my mother had bought for occasions like these—well, not like this exactly, but any time we hosted more than a few dozen people—accepting condolences and answering questions. *No, we haven't seen her. No, we've been unable to reach her. No, I have no idea where she went.*

After enduring an hour of this, I'd gotten Tommy to take my place. Telling myself that I wasn't snooping but investigating, I slipped into their bedroom and, then, to India's dressing room. India had kept the dove-gray walls and the ivory carpets and crown moldings, but she'd reupholstered my mother's zebra-print chair in pink toile and had replaced the antique gold-framed mirror with something high-tech and fancy, circled by pink-tinted bulbs. *The better to see your Botox in,* I thought, which was a little unfair because before she'd espoused the principles of spirituality and a vegan diet, my mom had shot her share of fillers.

I trailed my finger along the sleeves of India's blouses, the tweeds and cottons of her skirts, the silk and wool of her sweaters. I considered the sequined and beaded evening gowns, each in its own zippered plastic bag. It would be impossible to figure out whether anything was missing. She could have packed for a long weekend or a week away or a three-week cruise that would take her from Alaska to the tropics, and I'd never be able to tell from the contents of her closet. There was simply too much stuff. Her laptop, which I found in the media room, was what told the story.

At first I'd tried to open her inbox, but it was locked and password protected, and, after it rejected MARCUS as a password, I'd quit trying. But her Internet browser opened with a single click, and she hadn't erased her history.

"Oh my God." I hurried back into the living room, dodging a few well-meaning aunts and cousins and my father's assistants weeping in the corner, and found Darren, who was eating cocktail shrimp and staring out the window, down at the park.

He perked up when he saw me. "Hey, Bettina."

"I need to show you something," I told him, and took his hand and led him to the media room, where I'd left her laptop open.

"She bought tickets to Mexico . . . and Los Angeles . . . and the Bahamas . . . and Vancouver . . . and Paris . . . and Kentucky. All the flights left four days ago."

He cut and pasted the information and e-mailed it to himself. "I can call the airlines, ask if she made the flights."

"So we'll know where she went."

"But not where she is. I mean, say she went to Topeka. She could have bought a ticket in the airport from there to Los Angeles. Or Paris. Or Cancun. She could be . . ."

". . . anywhere by now," I said. The house phone rang. A minute later, the housekeeper, looking apologetic, was at my side.

"Missy Bettina? Sorry to interrupt, but this lady's been calling for Mrs. Croft. She says it's important."

I lifted the phone to my ear. "Yes?"

That was when I first spoke to Leslie Stalling of the Princeton Fertility Clinic. She apologized for bothering me during such a difficult time. She told me she was sorry to be adding to my worry and stress. Then she said it was imperative that she get in touch with India Croft.

"You and me both, sister," I said. Leslie Stalling sucked in her breath. "I'm sorry," I said. "We haven't seen or heard from her in days, and now I'm here at my father's house, and I think . . . it's kind of unbelievable, really, but it's looking like she left town."

"Oh, dear," Leslie Stallings said. "That's what I was afraid of." She paused, a little three-second break to serve as a transition between life as I'd known it, ending forever, and life with a baby beginning. Then she'd told me about the arrangements my father and India had made.

Three weeks later, Rory was born.

I'd met Annie, the surrogate, in the hospital in Pennsylvania, and was shocked that she was so young. Annie was exactly my age, although that was where the similarities ended. Annie wore a wedding ring, but when I arrived there was no husband or kids in the hospital room, just a skinny woman with a sour look on her face standing beside the bed. "I'll give you two some privacy," she'd said, and shut the door harder than she had to, leaving me and Annie alone.

"My sister," said Annie. Her light-brown hair was pulled back from her face in a ponytail, and her voice got higher and higher as she asked me questions. "You haven't heard from India?" she'd asked, looking so hopeful that I felt sick when I shook my head *no.* The baby was in her arms, wrapped in a pink-and-blue blanket with a knitted cap pulled down over her forehead. I'd come, as Leslie had instructed, with a diaper bag packed with wipes and diapers, bottles of formula, and a brand-new car seat. "Are you going to be all right?" Annie had asked.

"I'll be fine," I said firmly, with much more confidence than I felt. At least I'd been around a baby somewhat recently, my niece, Violet, but the truth was that because my brother and sister-in-law had been so determined to chronicle every moment of their great adventure, setting up a Flickr account and a Facebook page, blogging about the pregnancy and the labor and, God help us all, live-Tweeting the birth, I'd ended up ignoring as much of her infancy as I could, because paying attention meant, according to Tommy, being bombarded with close-up shots of my sister-in-law's nipples. ("Can't I just sign up to see the baby pictures?" I'd asked, and Tommy had shaken his head and said, "Slippery slope, man.")

"She's a sweetheart," said Annie, and turned her face toward the window. I could hear her sniffling. It made me feel wretched. She hadn't done anything except what she'd been paid to do, and I couldn't imagine how she was feeling, thinking she'd been making a baby for a happily married trophy wife and instead handing it over to the trophy wife's twenty-four-year-old stepdaughter, who'd never had so much as a pet goldfish and who killed every plant she'd ever owned (although I hoped no one had told her that part). I put the car seat down and put one hand awkwardly on her forearm, the one that didn't have an IV needle stuck in it.

"I'm sorry," I told her. "This was all a bit of a shock, but I've got plenty of resources. I've hired a doula, and India left all kinds of things for the baby."

This, at least, was true. Even I had to admit that the nursery was exquisite, with a crib and an antique rocker and a rug with a pattern of flowers around its border. The dresser and the closet were both loaded with everything a very fashionable baby could possibly need. There were clothes in sizes newborn, zero to three months, and three to six months. India had arranged for a diaper service and had bought about a thousand scented aloe vera baby wipes and a wipe warmer. The white wicker toy chest was filled with stuffed animals, lambs and bears and kittens, and the bookcase was filled with fairy tales, books by Maurice Sendak, Sandra Boynton, and Dr. Seuss. There were two business cards stuck to the refrigerator, one from a pediatrician and one from a doula, both of whom, it turned out, were on standby, just waiting to be notified about the baby's arrival. The doula turned out to be a kind of hippie-fied, glorified baby nurse, a woman from Park Slope with a wild tangle of curls and a calm, earthmother presence who'd been hired to be on duty for the first twelve weeks of the baby's life. The pediatrician was the woman three blocks away who'd taken care of me and my brothers when we were little.

Standing in front of the refrigerator, looking at the shopping list written out in India's neat hand: greens and lean meats, ground turkey and fish and fresh fruit—I thought about how I'd told India I would ruin her. I didn't know what she'd done versus what she'd paid other people to do to get ready for Rory's arrival, but she'd done a lot, and, certainly, her preparations didn't hint that she'd planned on bolting, or that she was using the baby as a prop, or a means to an end. But she'd left . . . and no matter how pretty the nursery's flowered curtains, how cunning the crib bumpers and the embroidered pillow reading *dream time* that hung from a pink-and-green ribbon on the door, no matter that she'd arranged for a doctor and a doula, the fact was, she was gone, and I was stuck.

There were a million things for me to do and read and buy and figure out. I'd need more formula . . . and baby food . . . and a high chair, and one of those crazy little vibrating bouncy seats that had always made Violet look like she was being electrocuted. I'd also have to find other babies for Rory to be friends with. There was, I knew, at least one woman in my dad's building with a smallish-looking baby. We'd exchanged hellos in the elevator a few times, and while it was true that I hadn't noticed whether her baby was a boy or a girl, I would make a point of asking the next time I saw them.

Annie wiped her eyes while I signed the papers. "You know how to work the car seat?" she asked. "Are you sure you'll be okay?" I told her I'd be fine with the car seat and that I was positive I'd be fine. I was almost out the door with the baby in my arms when she said, "Oh! My milk!"

"Pardon?"

She pointed to a scary-looking machine next to her bed. Clear tubes ran into funnel-shaped suction cups that were screwed into bottles with ounce markings on their sides. "I was going to overnight India my breast milk for the first month. Should I still do that?"

"That would be very nice." The baby was getting heavy. I shifted her from my left arm to my right. Her head flopped back alarmingly, and I adjusted it fast, hoping Annie hadn't seen. "Do I pay you by the bottle, or how does it work?"

She shook her head. "You don't have to pay me anything. India set it all up. I've got a FedEx account. They'll stop by in the morning with the dry-ice packs and the boxes, and you should have it every day by noon." She reached onto the bedside table, where she had two of the little bottles, each one full and labeled with a strip of tape indicating, I supposed, the time she'd pumped it. "Here. This will get you started."

What do you say to a woman who's just handed you four ounces of her breast milk? One of the bottles was still warm. I shifted the baby again, trying not to cringe as I put the milk into the diaper bag. "Thank you. We'll be in touch."

"Send pictures," she said. I could tell that she was getting ready to cry again, so I quickly set the baby into the car seat, fumbled the buckles shut, and hurried to the exit, where Manuel was waiting.

That had been seven days ago, and the baby seemed to be doing well, so far. If she sensed that she was at the center of a storm, being cared for by people who were not her biological parents, she gave no indication. "She's good-natured," Tia the doula told me, pointing out that Rory cried only when she was hungry or wanted to be held or rocked. That might have been true . . . but if it was, she was hungry or lonely for most of the time she was awake. Worse, she wasn't cute. To my eyes, not only did she not resemble anyone in my family, but she didn't look like she was completely through being formed. Her eyebrows were so faint they were almost invisible. She had stubby lashes, mottled pink skin, and an unfortunate case of acne . . . but she was filling out a bit, losing some of her scrawniness and starting to look a little more like the plump pink babies I'd grown familiar with from diaper commercials.

I gave her car seat another gentle push with my toe, then glared across the conference table. "Why didn't they tell me I'd be the baby's guardian? When did they decide?" Leslie pulled a fresh tissue from the box and pressed it underneath her right eye.

"They made their decision months ago. I don't know why

they didn't tell you. We certainly urge our clients to be as forthcoming as possible about the arrangements they've put in place."

"Our guess," said her lawyer, stepping in smoothly, "is that they would have let you know after the baby was born. Maybe they would have made you its godmother, and at that point they would have initiated a discussion about the responsibilities involved if something were to happen to them."

"It would have been nice," I said, "if someone had, you know, talked to me." I sounded bratty, exactly the way Leslie and her lawyer were probably expecting I would: a poor little rich girl who'd had everything she'd ever needed, a petulant princess who didn't want to be bothered with the lab-engineered competition.

"I should let you know that you won't have any concerns financially," said Jeff, flipping through a sheaf of documents he'd pulled from his briefcase. "Your father had a very generous life insurance policy, with specific bequests set aside for you, your brothers, your niece, and this, um, new addition." He went through the specifics of what the baby would be entitled to once the will was probated, which I wrote down without really hearing. I was still stunned, sitting there in a skirt and heels and the green sweater I'd worn because it had been the first thing I'd grabbed, and bare legs, only one of which it appeared I'd remembered to shave.

From underneath the table, the baby gave a little squeak. I rocked her again, bending down to brush the top of her head with my fingertips. "Who was the egg donor?"

Leslie and her lawyer exchanged a glance "That's confidential," said the lawyer.

"I'm the guardian," I shot back. "Don't I have a right to know what I'm dealing with? Genetically speaking?"

Another glance. I exhaled loudly, letting Leslie and her lawyer know that I was getting sick of their making eyes at each other. Finally Leslie said, "India and your father chose our anonymous donation option. They never met their donor. All they had was her profile."

"Well, I'd like to meet her." I wasn't sure that this was true. What I did know was that I wanted everything I could get out of the clinic, every apology, every bit of discomfort and hard work. God knew they'd made my life hard enough.

"I suppose . . ." Leslie began, "we could contact the donor, maybe give her some sense of the, um, change in arrangements. She could agree to let us give you her contact information, but it would be entirely up to her."

"Why don't you do that." I paused for a moment, gathering myself. "There's no chance . . ." I said, and snuck a guilty look down into the car seat, worried, irrationally, that the baby would overhear me and take offense. "There's no chance that this custody arrangement was a mistake? They wanted me, not my brother?"

Without any hesitation both lawyers, plus Leslie, shook their heads. "We're here for you," said Leslie, managing to sound sincere. "Whatever support we can provide, in any capacity. We can be a resource, if you need a nanny, or any other kind of help . . ."

I shook my head and got to my feet, lifting the handle of the car seat and struggling to get my purse over my shoulder. "We'll be fine," I said, and then, with the car seat banging against my leg and the cup of coffee I'd poured myself in my free hand, I walked out the door and into my father's office, and set the baby's seat down on the floor. Someone had been cleaning. There were cardboard boxes on the mostly empty shelves, filled with photographs, the tin cup with the picture of the Eiffel Tower that I'd bought him from my junior-year trip to Paris, the finger paintings that Violet had done. I sat on top of the empty desk. His chair was gone, and I'm sure the place had been vacuumed and dusted since his death, but I imagined, sitting at his desk with my coffee beside me, looking out over the city, that I could still smell him, could feel his presence, here in the place where he'd spent so many intensely focused hours. "Now what?" I asked. No answer came. I missed my father terribly, felt his absence like a stitch in my side, a pain that never left me. In the car seat, Rory was sleeping, her chin slumped on her chest, a ribbon of drool securing her Petit Bateau sweater to her cheek, the slightly scaly surface of the bald spot on the back of her head exposed. A wave of pity rose inside me. Poor thing, I thought. Poor little thing with no parents to love her, and she's not even pretty.

"It's you and me, kid," I said. Rory, of course, didn't answer.

I took the elevator down to the ground floor. Manuel was waiting at the curb. I hefted the car seat inside, sighing with relief when I set it down. The baby barely weighed ten pounds, and the seat couldn't weigh much more, but carrying it felt like having a lead bowling ball shackled to my wrist. It took me a minute to loop the seat belt through the back of the car seat and click it shut. As soon as we started moving, Rory's eyes opened and she smacked her lips together, a move that I'd already figured out was a prelude to crying. I found the bottle of breast milk, shook it, uncapped it, and plugged it into her mouth. My phone rang, and I pulled it out of my purse, still hoping that maybe it was my mother, who'd come to her senses and was calling to say she'd come home.

It wasn't my mother. It was Annie.

"Sorry to bother you," she said as Rory batted the bottle out of her mouth. "I just wanted to see how you were doing."

"We're fine," I said. As if to disprove me, Rory started to wail. I popped the bottle between her lips again, but Rory turned her head. The nipple stabbed her in the cheek. Milk leaked out, pooling in the crease of her neck. I tried to wipe it away with my sleeve as the bottle fell out of the car seat and onto the floor, just out of my reach.

"Did the milk come this morning?"

"I'm not sure. We had an appointment. I got a box yesterday . . ."

Rory was turning an alarming shade of purple. Her mouth was open, but no sound was coming out, even though she was shaking with what I guessed was indignation. Was this normal? As soon as I got off the phone I could go online to the websites I'd bookmarked, look up *crying* and *shaking* and *purple* and see what the experts had to say. "Can you hold on for just a moment?"

I put the phone down on top of the baby, bent, grabbed the bottle, and popped it back in her mouth. This time, she started sucking. I exhaled, realizing that I was sweating. I wiped my forehead against my shoulder and used one hand to keep the bottle in the baby's mouth and the other to bring the phone back to my ear. "Okay. I'm back. Sorry about that."

Annie sounded faintly amused. "Listen. I know you've got a baby nurse, but I'd be happy to come up and help out for a few days. It would save a lot on the cost of shipping my milk."

Honestly, I did not care about how much the milk-shipping was costing. God knows I'd never see the bill. But the idea of another set of hands, hands belonging to the woman who'd carried Rory for nine months and might, theoretically, have some idea of what she wanted when she started shaking and turning purple, sounded wonderful. "How soon can you be here?" I asked.

"Tonight?" she asked.

"Perfect," I said, and hung up before she could change her mind.

Tia met me in the lobby, where she wrinkled her nose and diagnosed the problem. "I think she pooped."

"Ah." Upstairs, the mess was startling, both in color and in quantity. I stood by the nursery door, trying not to cringe, as Tia wiped off Rory's legs and bottom, applied diaper cream, fastened a fresh diaper in place, and put the baby into a fresh outfit. Her formerly peony-pink pants were a yellow-brown ruin; even the car seat had gotten splattered. Tia whisked everything away and, somehow, I ended up in the rocking chair, with the baby in my arms. When she fell asleep I sat there, too terrified to move, until Tia came back and eased the baby into the wicker bassinet.

Five hours later, Annie arrived. For someone who'd just given birth, she looked remarkably normal, in khaki cargo pants and a T-shirt and sneakers, with a wheeled suitcase in one hand, a cooler balanced on top of it, and her breast pump packed in a carrying case and slung over her shoulder. By then I was feeling foolish. Annie had caught me at a bad moment, but I was managing just fine. Now I knew that *silent scream* and *turning purple* and *not hungry* meant pooping, and I was sorry to have wasted her time. But as soon as Annie took Rory out of my arms and cradled the baby against her, I changed my mind. Everything she did, the way she held the baby, jiggling her gently up and down, the way she patted her bottom in a way that even I found soothing; the way she knew, instinctively, to support Rory's neck, made her look like an expert, and made me feel like the rankest of amateurs.

She gave me a sympathetic smile. "Why don't you take a break?" I looked down at myself. I was still in the same green top and blue skirt I'd worn to the meeting on Wall Street that morning, and I hadn't showered before I'd put them on. I went to my bedroom and shucked off my clothing. *I'll take a shower,* I told myself. *I'll call Darren, see if he's tracked India down. I'll call Tommy, ask if he wants to come visit, and Trey* . . . and then, before I knew it, I was facedown on my bed. When I opened my eyes again it was ten o'clock at night.

I scrambled into the shower, then into a pair of sweatpants one of my brothers had left behind and an old T-shirt of my father's. Annie was on the living-room couch, the baby asleep in her arms, the television tuned to an episode of *Real Housewives*. She turned around, looking guilty, and turned the TV off when she saw me.

"Tia's having her dinner. I nursed her," she said.

"Rory, not Tia, right?"

Annie looked too worried to smile at my attempt at a joke. "I hope that's okay. I probably should have asked you first . . ."

"No, no, it's fine."

". . . but you were sleeping, and it just seemed silly to pump it and then feed it to her, so I just . . ."

"Really, it's okay."

"She's an angel," said Annie, gazing fondly at the baby. I looked to see if Rory had undergone some sort of transformation during my nap, but she was the same, wrinkly and red and bald and disagreeable-looking, even in a very sweet white-and-pink one-piece outfit with a matching hat. "Here." Annie lifted the baby, holding her out to me. Before I could think about it, I shook my head. I braced myself for rolled eyes or laughter, or, worse, disgust, but Annie just said, "I remember when I had Frank Junior. I felt like I was babysitting. I think I spent the entire first year of his life waiting for his real parents to come get him."

At her mention of her son, I realized I had no idea what she'd done with her children. "They're staying with my parents," she told me. "My folks know what's going on, and I'm fine to stay for a few days."

I took a seat on the couch beside her. "Did you always know you wanted kids?"

Annie looked thoughtful. "I guess I always knew I'd have them. But that's not exactly the same thing, is it?" I shook my head as she continued. "That was just what everyone I knew did. My mother, my aunts, my cousins . . . everyone had babies, and most of them ended up raising a baby or two that wasn't even their own." She looked at me. "Did you always know you wanted to go to college?"

I considered before answering. "I guess it's the same thing. It's what everyone I knew did."

She nodded. "It's not so bad, though, is it? I mean, you had fun in college, right?"

Because it was late, because I was still foggy from my nap, because, in the past weeks, my life had changed so radically that I barely recognized it anymore, I told her the truth. "Not so much. Not really. I'm not even sure I know how to have fun."

Annie looked at me, startled. "Really? Huh. I always thought . . . I mean, if you had money . . ." Her voice trailed off.

"Money can't buy you social skills. Or friends."

"True." She sat quietly, maybe thinking that, in some respects, she was richer than I'd ever be. Rory started to stir, stretching and waving her fists in the air. "Want to hold her?" Annie asked. She handed over the baby, and this time, I took her. Rory opened her tiny, toothless mouth and yawned before settling herself against me. "Cute," I said, and meant it. It wasn't great, but maybe it was a start.

JULES

Once you're done with school, summer doesn't mean what it used to. Every day was a workday, and the only way the seasons mattered was whether it was light when I left for the office and when I came home, and what I'd wear from Kimmie's apartment to the subway. Once I was at work, time and weather disappeared. The office seemed to generate its own climate, hot and humid, the air thick with stress and gray with unhappiness. In an effort to recognize summer as summer, Kimmie and I would try to eat outdoors once every week. We'd take turns picking the spot: bistros with sidewalk seating, pocket parks, museum courtyards, restaurants with backyard gardens where we could sit and imagine we were someplace other than New York.

This week, we'd grabbed street food and were dining on the benches outside the Metropolitan Museum of Art. It was hazy and warm, the sky a washed-out white, the trees thick with glossy green leaves, a Friday afternoon, which meant that Rajit was probably halfway to the Hamptons already, and I wouldn't be missed as long as I stayed late enough to finish my research (today's enthralling topic—a sneaker factory in Paraguay). People had kicked off their shoes and rolled up their sleeves and pants legs (and, in the cases of some of the girls, their shirts) in an effort to make the most of the sunshine.

I bought a plate of halal chicken and rice. Kimmie had a container of fruit salad, a big bottle of water, and a black-and-white cookie. We spread napkins over our laps, traded plastic silverware, and split the cookie so that we each got black and white.

"We should go to the beach," I said. "I'll bet Florida's cheap right now."

"I bet Florida's hot."

"No hotter than this," I said.

Kimmie speared a bite of kiwi and held it out to me. I looked around to make sure no one was looking, then ate the kiwi off her fork. "JetBlue's got good deals." She held out a chunk of pineapple. I looked around again and, when I noticed a trio of guys in ties staring at us, pulled away. Her sigh was so soft I almost didn't hear it.

Since that first night—the night we played show and tell, as I called it—we'd spent almost every night together. I still paid rent on my apartment, and my roommates thought I had a serious boyfriend. I wasn't in a hurry to disabuse them. It was none of their business. Kimmie and I woke up together, snuggled on her futon, and made tea in her tiny kitchen. We showered together, hip to hip in her narrow tub, washing each other's hair under the spray. She'd sleep in my T-shirts, which fell to her thighs, and we wore beaded bracelets we'd picked up at the Brooklyn Flea, but we didn't hold hands in public, let alone kiss. When we'd visited her parents for Christmas, they put us in Kimmie's room, which had a single bed, and spread blankets and a sleeping bag on the floor for me. We'd spooned in the bed, whispering and giggling as Kimmie's mother rattled around in the kitchen, preparing lasagna, the most American dish she knew.

When we were together, at dinner, at the movies, or strolling through a store or a street fair, we looked like best friends.

I wasn't sure what I was—if I was gay, if I'd always been attracted to women and had never managed to figure it out. All I knew for sure was that I was in love with Kimmie. With her, I felt safe in a way I hadn't in years, maybe not ever, and certainly not since my father's accident. She was so small, so fragile, with her little bird bones. I could span both of her wrists with one of my hands, could buy clothing for her at Gap Kids, but she was stronger than she looked; smart, and fierce. When she got a cold, I bought her Theraflu and Gatorade and chicken soup from the deli. When I lost my wallet, she called my credit-card company and figured out how to get the DMV to FedEx me a replacement license overnight.

On the bench Kimmie ate the pineapple herself, then pressed her lips together. I wanted to pull the elastic out of her hair, to bury my hands in its cool silk. If she were a boy I wouldn't have thought twice. I used to rub my palm against the smooth skin on the back of Dan's neck after he got his hair cut. I'd sit on his lap in his eating club's common room and carry on conversations as if he were an anthropomorphized chair. I wasn't wild about public displays of affection, but I wasn't averse to a little hand-holding, an arm around a waist or over my shoulders, a kiss hello or goodbye. Kimmie and I didn't do any of that. We couldn't, without people labeling and judging . . . and even in a city as big as Manhattan, where there were plenty of gay men and women, I wasn't comfortable with the idea of publicly declaring that I was one of them. Given my long hair, my high heels, the skirts and blouses and makeup I wore to work, people gave me the benefit of the doubt. They gave it to Kimmie, too, I figured, if they stopped to think of her as sexual at all. With her clothes on, she still looked more like a little boy than a woman. With her clothes off . . . I gave a little shiver, thinking of it.

"You know I love you," I said. My voice was low.

She touched my cheek. I felt myself tense. Women touch

each other this way, I told myself. They do it all the time. But, out of the corner of my eye, I saw, or thought I saw, that the guys in ties were staring. They'd been joined by a construction worker in workboots and khaki pants white with drywall dust. He was holding a falafel folded in his hand, and he was definitely looking at us, staring like we were a porno movie that had just started playing, one that he could hardly wait to rewatch alone, in private.

I pulled away, faster than I'd meant to. Kimmie got to her feet. I stood up, reaching for her, wanting to touch her hair or her hand, barely managing to make contact with one bare shoulder.

"I'm sorry," I said.

She nodded, sighing. "Sure you are. Sorry, sorry, sorry. Is this what it's going to be like, our whole life? Always hiding, always afraid someone's going to see?"

I lowered my voice. "We're not hiding. We're just not, you know, taking out a billboard."

"So are we just going to lie to everyone, about what we are? Tell everyone that we're friends?"

Her cheeks were flushed. I wanted so badly to hold her . . . and I couldn't. I couldn't do it. It was as if I were paralyzed, frozen with shame. Back at work, after the funeral, when people had asked what had happened with my father, I'd said, *heart attack,* and told myself that it was the truth. His heart had stopped. True, it had stopped after he'd done an unknown quantity of street drugs. But that was nobody's business but mine.

I tried that line with Kimmie, hoping it would soothe her. "Look. You know I love you. But what we do, what we are to each other . . ."

"So we hide." Her voice was flat. She bent and, with staccato jerks of her arms, began picking up our trash.

"So . . . I'll see you tonight? At home?" Had I ever called her place "home" before? I didn't know. But it felt like home. I could picture every part of it: the glass Coke bottle with a single gerbera daisy on the windowsill next to her futon; the two-burner stove that Kimmie wiped down every time after we'd cooked something, the yellow teapot and the cups from Chinatown that she kept on a shelf we'd hammered into the wall.

Kimmie picked up her backpack and slung it over her shoulders. She paused, and it felt like my heart stopped beating before she gave a curt nod and walked away.

I watched her go. The three guys with ties walked down the sidewalk, laughing. A cloud blew across the sun. The construction worker balled up his trash, tossed it in the bin, then came and sat beside me.

"Fight with your girlfriend?"

I turned, bracing myself for the leer, the salacious smile, but saw, instead, mild blue eyes that held nothing but sympathy. For a second, I wondered whether all the people I'd been afraid of, the ones I'd thought would judge me—my coworkers, my former classmates, my horrible boss—had someone in their lives, a cousin or a sister or a daughter, who was gay. Or maybe I was too optimistic. Maybe he'd just meant "girlfriend" in the most innocent way, a friend who was a girl.

"I'm not as brave as she is," I said, in a low voice.

He nodded. Then he hitched up his sagging pants and walked off, another New Yorker, just minding his own business. I went back to the office and sat behind my computer, ignoring the deadline on the latest pitch book, ignoring Rajit, who called on speakerphone from the Jitney to the Hamptons and berated me for mistakes actual and imagined. At night, I plodded home, bought a take-out salad, then sat at the half-size table in the kitchen, poking at it, afraid to call Kimmie or go to her apartment, the place where I belonged.

"What's up with you?" Amanda asked.

"Bad day at work." There was vodka in the freezer, grapefruit juice in the fridge. I mixed myself a drink, glugged it down like medicine, then lay on my bed for the first time in weeks, wondering what I was supposed to do now.

I'd just closed my eyes when Amanda knocked on my door. "You're blowing up," she said, holding out the BlackBerry I'd left in the kitchen. Hoping it might be Kimmie, I lifted the receiver to my ear. "Hello?"

The voice was crisp, and it took me a minute to recognize it. "Julie? It's Leslie Stalling from the Princeton Fertility Clinic."

"Yes?"

"Well," Leslie began. She gave a nervous chuckle. "I can't say I've ever had a conversation quite like this before. Let me start at the beginning. Your egg was used by a couple in New York City."

My heart sped up. Hadn't part of me always known it would happen this way, that I'd end up in the same city as the baby?

"The biological father died."

"What?" I sat frozen as Leslie explained the rest of it—father dead, intended mother missing, twentysomething half sister left in charge. "She asked for your information," Leslie concluded. "We can't give that out, of course, but . . ."

"What's her name?"

Leslie told me—name, address, email, phone numbers. Which left me with only one more question. "The baby?"

Her voice warmed. "She's gorgeous. A beautiful little girl."

Bettina Croft was waiting for me in the lobby of her apartment building on Central Park West. She shook my hand, led me to the elevator, and pressed the button for "Penthouse." "We'll talk upstairs," she said. The elevator whizzed upward, giving me time to study her. She was about my age, in a scoop-necked black linen dress and black patent-leather slides: all of it simple and, I guessed, all expensive, too. Her only jewelry was a diamond circle pin at her collar. Her thick auburn hair was pushed back from her face by a black velvet headband, the way I bet she'd been wearing it since sixth grade. She was prettier than she'd looked in the picture I'd Googled on the way over. Her lips were thin, her chin a shade pointy, her teeth too big for her mouth. But her eyebrows were elegantly arched, her eyes wide and expressive beneath them, and she had beautiful skin, cream tinged with pink at her cheeks.

The elevator chimed. The doors slid open, and we stepped into a foyer, then into a living room as airy and high-ceilinged as a basketball court. Multicolored rugs glowed on the hardwood floors and important art hung on the walls. Vases and bowls full of fresh-cut, beautifully arranged flowers ornamented every corner and there was something astonishing to see everywhere I turned. I walked to the windows, past a glass vase filled with flowering cherry blossoms and a framed Picasso hanging on the wall like it didn't know it wasn't in a museum. Looking out over the twinkling lights and the treetops of Central Park, I wished that Kimmie was with me. She'd appreciate this apartment, she'd notice things I didn't, she'd hold my hand while we talked about it on her futon—how many bedrooms did we think it had, and how many people worked to clean it, and how much did it cost to live in a place like this.

"So what can I do for you?" I asked.

Bettina sat on a long, curving couch upholstered in a shimmery fabric somewhere between silver and beige, and studied me, as frankly as Jared Baker had long ago in the mall. "Figures. You're exactly the type India would go for."

"What do you mean?"

Bettina flipped one hand in my direction. "Tall. Blond. Gorgeous. Smart." Somehow, she managed to make all of those words sound like insults. "What'd you play, field hockey? And you were in Cap, I bet."

"I played field hockey and lacrosse, but only in high school. And I wasn't in Cap."

She lifted her plucked eyebrows. "You got hosed at bicker?"

This was insider lingo. "Cap" was Cap and Gown, one of the most selective eating clubs. Bicker was like rush, and getting hosed was Princeton parlance for getting rejected. "I wasn't in a club. Did you go to Princeton?"

She shook her head, adjusting her headband. "My dad did. And my uncles, and my oldest brother. But I spent enough time around the campus to know what it's like. Why weren't you in an eating club?"

"Because I couldn't afford it." Her thin eyebrows arched even higher. I wondered why she was surprised. Did she imagine that girls like her, in apartments like this, were the ones selling their eggs?

"I was hoping you could tell me about yourself." She reached into the purse she'd kept slung over her shoulder and pulled out a notebook and a pen. "Any health issues in your family? Do you happen to know your blood type?"

I knew it from the tests the clinic had done . . . which meant that Bettina probably knew it, too. "O negative," I said, wondering when she'd get around to asking me what she really wanted to know. I was still struggling to make sense of what I'd learned—that her father, the baby's father, was dead, and that his wife, the baby's mother, was gone.

"And your family history? Cancer? Diabetes? Heart disease?"

My unease was solidifying into anger. "The clinic can tell you about that," I said, sitting back in my chair and crossing my arms against my chest.

"Mental illness? Substance abuse?" She sat back, skinny legs crossed, staring at me.

"Google?" I answered back.

"If anyone in your family had an issue with substance abuse," she said sweetly, "I think that's something you might have mentioned before donating an egg."

She was right, of course. She was right, and I'd been wrong. "I needed the money," I said, dropping my eyes and wishing, once more, for Kimmie.

"For what?"

"For my dad." My eyes were stinging. "To get him into rehab. Which didn't work, as I'm sure you already know."

"You shouldn't have lied."

"I didn't lie. Nobody at the clinic ever asked."

"Well, don't you think it was something you should have mentioned?" Her voice was getting louder. I got to my feet.

"Did you bring me up here just to insult me? Because I could have just stayed at work and had my boss do that."

She surprised me by changing the subject. "Where do you work?"

"Steinman Cox. I'm a junior analyst."

"That sounds interesting."

"Yeah," I said sourly. "It's spectacular."

She sighed, finally looking her age. "I'm sorry I was provoking you," she said. "This whole thing's just very new."

"So why did you want to meet me? Because it sounds like you know all the important stuff already."

"I just wanted to see you in person. To meet you, before I asked."

"Asked what?"

She shifted on the couch, recrossing her legs. "This is probably going to sound crazy," she said, "but I want to know if you want to be . . . involved, somehow."

I blinked at her. "Involved?"

"Like . . . oh, I don't know. An aunt, or a friend of the family." She looked at me, her eyes wide, an expression that was almost pleading on her face. "My dad's gone . . ." She paused, then cleared her throat. "My dad's gone, and my stepmother took off, and good riddance, as far as I'm concerned, but this baby's got me as a parent, and I don't know what I'm doing. So I thought . . ."

"You want people," I said, remembering my conversation with Kimmie; my dream of being a mysterious benefactor.

"A village," Bettina agreed. "You know, 'it takes a village'? So I thought . . . I mean, it's probably crazy. You agreed to sell an egg, it's not like you wanted to be a mother."

I interrupted. "Can I see her?"

"She's sleeping," said Bettina. I thought this was a refusal until she added, "Take your shoes off and come with me."

I did, then followed her as she led me down a hall and eased open a paneled door with a tiny embroidered pillow on a pink silk ribbon that read *dream time* hanging from the cut-glass doorknob. "Her name is Rory," said Bettina, and eased the door open.

The nursery was lovely, all cream and pale pink and celery green. A white-noise machine broadcast the sound of waves and seagulls from one corner; a humidifier purred in another. Bettina tiptoed over the carpet to a crib in the center of the room . . . and there, in the center, with a pink blanket pulled up to her chin, lay the baby. She was sleeping on her back, her head turned to the side, arms stretched above her head like she was signaling a touchdown.

"Oh," I sighed. She had a few wisps of blond hair, eyebrows like gold, and a dimple in the cheek that I could see. The same dimple I had; the one I'd inherited from my father.

INDIA

The thing about bad decisions is that they don't feel like bad decisions when you're making them. They feel like the obvious choice, the of-course-that-makes-sense move. They feel, somehow, inevitable.

After I left the apartment, I took a cab to Newark Airport, went to the United kiosk, and printed out my ticket for Paris. I endured the pat-down at security, walked to the gate, and spent an hour browsing in the duty-free shop, long enough for the security cameras to get some good shots of me. Then, bending over my purse, exclaiming as though I'd left something—my wallet! my passport!—at home, I walked briskly back down the hallway, out of the airport, into the gray afternoon. It wasn't like it was my baby, I told myself as I walked. Not really. True, it was Marcus's sperm, but Marcus's sperm had also made Tommy and Trey and Bettina, and it wasn't like I was close with any of them. *Not mine, not mine, not mine,* I thought, climbing on board a bus.

The bus took me into Manhattan to the Port Authority, which was noisy and crowded, smelling of fast food and urine and bus exhaust. Buses were pulling in from Dallas and Kansas City, from Topeka and Toledo, from Pittsburgh and Tallahassee and all points in between. Fresh-faced girls with bags over their shoulders and their best boots on their feet were stepping into the terminal, getting their first look at New York City, planning how they'd conquer it without thinking for an instant that they'd fail; that, someday, they might find themselves forty-three years old, with a stranger's face and all of their bright plans in ruin.

Marcus kept cash at home, five thousand dollars in a box in the safe. I'd helped myself to all of it and zipped it into the various pockets of my wallet and purse. Another bus took me to Philadelphia, and a train brought me to that city's airport, where I picked up a ticket at the US Air counter and caught a late flight to Puerto Vallarta. When we landed, I bought a bus ticket for thirty pesos to Sayulita, a forty-five minute ride away. Sayulita, according to the Internet, was a little fishing village now famous for its surfing and its yoga, a place where you could still find a cheap place to stay, eat fresh fruit and hand-made tortillas, and sip *batidas* by the beach. It looked pretty in the pictures that my handheld pulled up. Pretty, and a good place to hide. My rudimentary Spanish, a lot of gesturing, and a fistful of pesos got me a *casita* for a month—one room, with a kitchenette in the corner and mosquito netting around the bed. There was a toilet inside and a shower, with half-height wooden walls, attached to the side of the house, underneath an orange tree. *Lemon trees in the backyard,* I heard my mother say. I could remember the feel of her hand in my hair, the warmth of her body in bed next to me. *When the sun goes down you can watch the surfers.*

I lay my bag down on the bed. I was back to where I'd started. Take away the banana and the banyan trees, the sound of the waves, the tortilla truck that made its way up the cobblestones every morning, edging past the street dogs and the chickens, and I could have been back in West Hollywood, eighteen and broke, with no idea of what to do next.

I'd bought a few things at a market near the airport: a cotton wrap, a bathing suit, big sunglasses, a canvas tote bag that said VISIT MEXICO in curvy red letters, and a wide-brimmed straw hat. In my cottage, I put my clothes on the wire hangers some other visitor had left behind, set my toiletries on the little table underneath a painting of the Virgin of Guadalupe next to the sink, pulled on the swimsuit, wrapped the pareo around my waist, slid a pair of two-dollar rubber flip-flops on my feet, looped my tote bag over my shoulder, and walked into town.

In a market that opened onto the street I bought a net bag and filled it with eggs, cheese, tortillas, mangos, an avocado, a sun-warmed tomato that felt ripe and heavy in my hand, bottled water, and sunscreen. I walked home slowly, doing a lap around the village square. There was a church in one corner, a stained-glass Madonna with downcast eyes in its window. Across the way was a yoga studio, and sitting on benches, or on the curb-stones that divided the street from the green, were the men that I knew I'd find, the ones with shabby clothes and sly expressions who lived in any resort town by the sea, the men who'd find the tourists what they wanted. *Missy, hey, missy, you want smoke? Pretty lady, you want to party?*

There were three *farmacias* that I passed on my rounds. I went inside to the smallest one. An ancient man, brown and gnarled as a walnut, stood behind the counter, sadly polishing his glasses. I put my hands against my temples, then laid them on my heart. *"Dolor. Muy malo. No . . ."* Shit. What was Spanish for *sleep*? *"No dormir. Ayúdame."* At first, he pulled a bottle of some over-the-counter remedy off the shelf and held it out to me, a question on his face. I shook my head, then opened my wallet, letting him see the credit cards, the fat stack of pesos. *"Más fuerte. El dolor, muy malo.* I lost . . ." I made my arms into a cradle, rocking an invisible infant. The man looked up at me, then held up one stubby finger. *"Un momento, señora."* Then he shuffled behind the counter and came back with an unmarked brown prescription bottle, into which he solemnly tapped thirty pills from a white envelope in his hand. "For the sleeping," he said. "Very strong, so *cuidado*." I nodded, paid him, and slipped the bottle into my pocket. Now I had what I needed: sunshine, sand and waves, food and water, a bed to sleep in, a town where no one would know me, and something to still the voice in my head that shrilled and mewled like a petulant teenager's: *I can't. I can't. I can't.*

I'd wake up in the morning with the sunrise. The way the roosters crowed in the cobbled streets, it was hard to sleep later than that. I'd fry an egg, slide it onto a tortilla, add a few slices of avocado and tomato, a sprinkle of salt, and take it onto my porch to eat. I'd wash the pan and my plate, pull on my swim-suit, take my tote bag, my sunscreen, and the towel that I'd hung on a tree branch to dry, and walk to the beach, a wide curve of golden sand that sloped gently toward the water. There, I'd rent a lounge chair for five pesos a day. There were bars where the beach joined the sidewalk, places that sold beer and bottled water and hand-patted tortillas filled with whatever you wanted for lunch. I'd leave my bag on the chair, slip my key, on a length of twine, around my wrist, and swim out into the clear green water. Sometimes I'd swim out even farther, until the people on the beach were no bigger than colored dots. More often, I'd flip onto my back and lie there, borne up by the gentle waves, staring into the sun.

As the weeks unspooled, I got to know people's faces, if not their names: the surfing instructors who'd paddle their long-boards past me; the young woman with the gold incisor who worked at the café where I'd order my juice or enchiladas; the man, missing most of the fingers on his left hand, who rented the beach chairs; the little girl with glossy black pigtails who followed him with a tiny rake to smooth the sand. My own hair started growing in, dark at the roots, with a few springy strands of gray. I kept it braided, tucked up underneath my hat, and I wore sunglasses that covered my face from my eyebrows to my cheeks.

One day my after-lunch ramble took me to a hotel lobby. There were a few decent-size hotels in Sayulita, inexpensive places that catered to kids from Europe on their gap year, backpackers and free spirits and families who'd decided that barebones quarters with shared bathrooms was a fair exchange for the gorgeous beaches, the fresh fruit, the quaint streets with their little shops and the men who'd sit in the square at night, playing sad love songs on their guitars. The hotels had computers, usually an elderly desktop perched on top of a folding table in the lobby, where you could rent time online.

I'd ditched my iPhone in the ladies' room at the airport in Philadelphia, sliding it into a trash can without a second look, even though I'd felt a momentary pang about the leather cover, monogrammed, soft as butter. Now I brushed my salt-water-stiffened hair off my cheeks and thumped the keys on a wheezing, overheating Dell, logging into my e-mail for the first time since I'd left, opening a screen so I could Google my name.

There it was. First, a column in the *Post* about how I'd missed the funeral. Then, three days later, the story I knew someone would find eventually. It was in the *Daily News*, illustrated with my mug shot, from when I was twenty-three, and another picture of me as a teenager, at a party, in a *Flashdance*-style sweatshirt, ripped at the shoulder. "Runaway Bride Was Bigamist."

"Here we go," I muttered, and clicked on the link. *India Bishop, the new wife-turned-widow of recently deceased financier Marcus Croft, who raised eyebrows across the city after she was a no-show at her husband's funeral on Friday, changed her name when she moved to Hollywood as a teenager. No surprise: it's a move many young aspiring actresses make. But when Bishop filled out the paperwork that would legally turn her from Samantha Marie Stavros to India Bishop, she never mentioned that she'd been married as a teenager, and that she'd never obtained a divorce. Bishop, 43 (not the 38 she's been claiming), a public-relations executive, was wed in 1985 to David Carter, a substitute drama teacher at New London High School in New London, Connecticut, who was more than fifteen years' Bishop's senior at the time. "It was a major scandal," said Andrea LeBlanc, a classmate of Bishop's. "We all figured she was pregnant, but, if she was, she wasn't showing by graduation . . . and, by August, she was gone."*

Bishop left New London and moved to Hollywood, where she worked odd jobs and was eventually arrested in a round-up of women who were working as waitresses at a party and charged with prostitution (she was eventually released, and the charges were dropped). Two years later, she was hired at JMS Public Relations under her new name.

I gripped the edges of the table, my stomach clenching, thinking that if there was any consolation to be found, it was that Marcus had died before he'd found out the truth—that I'd filed papers, but David, it seemed, had never signed them and, even decades after the fact, I had still been married to David Carter when Marcus and I had said our vows. I forced my eyes back to the screen, scanning to the bottom to read the story's final line. *Reached in his New London home, David Carter declined to comment.*

I bent my head, imagining the story being zapped around the city, landing with a cheery little chirp in the inboxes of everyone I knew. I pictured Bettina's smirk. Then I forced myself to look at my inbox. There were dozens of e-mails from Annie—the last one, under "subject," read PLEASE CALL ME! I'M WORRIED! Another few dozen from Leslie at the clinic, saying basically the same thing. Bettina had written: *Where Are You?* More spam, more reporters; a note from my saleslady at Saks, who, apparently unaware of the changes in my life, wrote to say that the new Jimmy Choo open-toed leather lace-up booties had arrived and were available in dark brown and black, and she would hold a pair in both colors until she heard from me. Finally there was one more e-mail from Bettina. Nothing in the subject line, just a picture of a baby with dark eyes and a jaunty pink beret over her head. "It's a girl," she'd written. Nothing more.

I logged out, picked up my bag, and walked into the sunshine. *Hey, lady, hey, lady,* the men on the square crooned. Back at my *casita,* I shucked off my swimsuit and stood under the water from the outdoor shower until it went from tepid to cold. I didn't bother drying off. I lay naked underneath the single sheet, with mosquitoes whining against the netting, until the sun went down, and slept until almost noon the next day . . . and when I woke up, I knew where to go, and what to do when I got there.

BETTINA

By July, things had calmed down enough that I felt able to leave the apartment for a while. Annie was staying two days and one night each week, Tia was on duty every night Monday through Friday, and Jules, who I thought I'd never see again after our uncomfortable introduction, had surprised me by calling the week after we'd met and volunteering to babysit. "I don't know much about kids," she said, looking as terrified as I must have been the first time I gave her Rory to hold.

"It's not hard," I'd said. She'd handled the baby like she was made of glass, exclaiming over her every sigh and coo. The first Sunday I'd stayed with her. The second time I'd left her with bottles of breast milk and my cell-phone number and gotten on the subway to spend an evening with Darren for the first time since Rory's arrival. Unbeknownst to him, I had an agenda: I wanted to get drunk, and then, as my old roommate would have put it, I wanted to get laid. I wanted to behave like a regular twenty-four-year-old, a woman with no vision past her own eyelashes, no plans beyond the next day, and no responsibilities beyond her own job.

Darren lived in Chelsea, in a building with an elevator but no doorman and disconcertingly narrow hallways. His apartment had, as I could have predicted, a flat-screen TV as its main piece of furniture, but other than that, it was surprisingly un-repulsive. There was an indigo-and-orange vintage poster for Orangina on the kitchen wall and a big leather couch in the living/dining room. There was no space for a kitchen table, but Darren had lined up three wood-and-metal stools in front of the narrow breakfast bar. When I arrived, he was unpacking a bag full of Chinese take-out boxes. There was fried rice and egg rolls, chicken lo mein and spicy prawns. I filled my plate, and we sat together on the couch.

"So?" asked Darren. "How's motherhood?" He was barefoot in his chinos, wearing a T-shirt advertising some band I'd never heard of, and his horrible glasses. He needed a haircut . . . but, to me, he'd never looked cuter.

"It's interesting," I said carefully. I understood the problem, the situation I was in. When Darren and I had started spend-ing time together, I was single and unencumbered. Now I had a baby. The fact that the baby was not technically mine did not, in the end, matter much. I was a woman with a child, and that did not make me more desirable than I'd been when we'd met.

"Any word from India?" he asked.

I shook my head. The truth was, I wasn't looking for my disappearing stepmother too hard. With Annie and Jules and Tia in and out of the apartment, with the baby doing baby-like things that are probably boring to everyone in the world except for the people to whom the baby belongs—*She smiled! She almost rolled over! She's holding up her head!*—I felt interested, engaged, needed in a way I didn't think I'd never been needed in my life, and if, sometimes, I was so tired it was all I could do to keep from dozing off in the tub, if I missed my colleagues at Kohler's, if I missed my freedom, it seemed a reasonable trade-off for a life I liked much better than the one I'd had. I had a tribe, a crew, friends in Annie and Tia and Jules. The baby, too, had grown on me. I'd even started posting cute pictures on my Facebook page.

"So what do you think will happen?" Darren asked.

"I don't know." In truth, I thought that what would happen had happened already: Rory had been born, I'd brought her home, and now I would raise her. But, for Darren's sake, I was willing to play along with the idea that things could still change. "I could put her up for adoption. I could sell her on eBay. Billionaire's baby. I bet I could get a nice price."

"I don't think," Darren said, "that eBay's allowed to traffic in actual people."

I looked at him hopefully. "Craigslist?"

He shook his head. I pushed a single sesame noodle around the edge of my plate, where it had already completed half a dozen laps, like it was training for a noodle marathon. Since my father's death, I'd lost eleven pounds. I was a grown-up, I told myself to shake off the memories of my dad. I was a grown woman with a college degree and a job I could return to, a baby I was caring for, maybe even a boyfriend, and so what if my life wasn't perfect? Whose life was? Lots of people missed their parents, plenty of people had it worse. Jules had told me only the barest contours of her story, and that was plenty for me to be horrified. Still, I couldn't keep from imagining it: my dad, walking through my bedroom door the way he had when I was little and had bad dreams. He'd bring me a glass of water, escort me to and from the bathroom, then sit with me, watching over me, my canopied bed creaking under his weight, until I fell asleep again.

"I can't figure out why they picked me," I said. "Why me, and not Trey and Marissa?" They had a baby, they had baby stuff, they had a nanny already, not to mention an apartment that was big enough to accommodate another. My father had bought them the place as a wedding gift.

"Maybe your father thought they had their hands full," Darren offered. I nodded, wondering if that was it, or if maybe he thought that a new baby wouldn't be as well loved as Trey and

Marissa's own daughter. "Or maybe India was the one who picked you."

I winced. "Doubt it. We didn't get along."

He used his chopsticks to help himself to more prawns. "Yes, I sensed that when you came to have her investigated."

My cheeks flushed. "I wasn't wrong about India."

"You weren't wrong about her past," Darren said. "I just wonder if maybe she'd changed. Anyhow," he said hastily as I opened my mouth to tell him that, clearly, India hadn't changed a bit, that she was a user and a gold digger who'd killed my father and abandoned her child and more or less ruined my life. "Is the food okay? You're not eating."

I popped a snow pea in my mouth. "It's fine."

"If you want my opinion, I think India made the right choice with you."

"You think I'm the maternal type?" That, at least, would explain why he'd never done more than kiss me.

"I think," he said, "they probably wanted the baby to have all the advantages that you guys had. Which means . . ."

"Money," I concluded.

"Not just money. Living in New York City. Being exposed to things. Art, theater . . ."

"The homeless guy I saw pooping in a trash can in the subway station this morning . . ."

"No kidding," said Darren. "Your subway station has one of those guys, too?"

I looked around his kitchen. There was a coffee machine, a stainless-steel blender, a gallon-size container of protein powder beside it, and a toaster oven in the corner, but no liquor. I needed liquor. Booze was part of my plan. I wanted to be a party girl, laughing, half naked, letting a stranger slurp tequila out of my belly button without thinking about germs or disease. I wanted to be naked, skin to skin, with this boy I liked. "Do you have anything to drink?"

He swung open the refrigerator. "We've got water, light beer, orange juice . . ." He gave the plastic container a swish, then held it up to the light, squinting, before opening the top to take a sniff. "Maybe not orange juice."

"I mean, drink drink." I slid off my stool and started going through his cabinets. The first one held only three dinner-size plates, two cereal bowls, two glasses, and two mismatched coffee mugs. The second featured an assortment of canned soups and pasta. I held one up. "Beefaroni?"

"Don't knock it," he said.

The third cupboard yielded a bottle of whiskey. I took one of his two glasses, pried a few cubes out of an ancient, ice-crusted metal tray I found in the freezer, poured myself a shot, and gulped it down.

My eyes watered, and I felt my face turn red. "Whoa." I filled my glass again as Darren watched, frowning.

I sipped my second drink, and took off my shoes, and pulled my hair out of its headband, shaking it free. "Are you worried about me?"

"Should I be?"

I gave my hair another shake and downed my second shot. The mouth of the whiskey bottle clanked against the lip of the glass as I poured a refill. Darren put his hand over mine.

"Hey. Seriously. Easy there."

I shook him off, put the glass to my mouth and knocked it back. My head was fuzzy, but it wasn't an unpleasant sensation, and my chest and belly felt warm. Darren was watching me from the sofa. Even in his dorky glasses, he looked delicious, all broad shoulders and solid thighs, with his face slightly sunburned from an afternoon playing Frisbee in the park and his hair flopping over his eyebrows. Without planning, without thinking, I crossed the room, straddled his legs, and kissed him. He made a noise like "mmph," his hands stiff at his sides and his lips motionless against mine. For a second, I was certain that I'd misread the signs, that he'd push me away, gently but firmly, and tell me our single kiss had been an act of kindness rather than a romantic overture, and that, while he'd always be my friend and would occasionally be my employee, he just didn't think of me that way.

Then he slid one hand around the back of my neck, pulling me closer. He stood, lifting me in his arms, cradling me, and I closed my eyes, feeling warm and drunk and, for an instant, dizzy with guilt. Why should I be enjoying this, enjoying anything, with my own father barely cold in his grave, with a baby at home, needing my care? But as Darren held me against his chest, I felt comforted and safe.

"Do you need to make a Franklin list?" I asked, pulling off his glasses and tossing them, harder than perhaps was technically necessary, onto the coffee table.

"Huh?"

"Pros and cons. Run the numbers."

"Pipe down, nugget," he said. He carried me into his bedroom and tossed me on the bed, which was made up with a dark-blue bedspread and a pair of pillows in striped blue-and-white pillowcases. I bounced, and giggled convincingly, like I'd been doing it all my life. Then he was lying on top of me, his chest crushing my breasts, his hips pressing against mine. The air rushed out of my body and, with it, my grief, and for the next little while I forgot everything that had happened, and all of my responsibilities, and everything but the feeling of the two of us together.

• • •

When it was over, I leaned over and kissed the narrow bridge of his nose. "That was something," I said.

"Uh." He was lying on his side, naked, sweating, adorable. His hair was messy, and his face, without those terrible glasses, looked younger and softer and altogether lovable. *My boyfriend,* I thought, and it was all I could do not to hold myself, to jump out of the bed and go singing into the streets. Lying beside him, still slightly tipsy, the world felt reordered, and the tasks ahead of me felt manageable. Maybe I could convince Annie to stay long-term. I could even invite her husband and her sons. There was room for them all. I could help her husband find a job. Maybe Jules would find child care so enjoyable that she'd end up being like an aunt to Rory, coming over once or twice a week. We'd be a tribe, a team, a village . . . us and our men.

I poked Darren's freckled shoulder until I was sure I had his attention. "Do you like kids?" I asked.

He opened his eyes and peered at me. "For dinner?"

"Ha." I rummaged under the covers until I located my panties. I'd need new panties, if someone was going to be seeing them on a regular basis. I'd have to add it to the list. "Get all the jokes out of your system now. Because if you're going to be a father . . ."

Now both his eyes were open. "What?"

"Well, a stepfather. A step-boyfriend-father." The whiskey had made me merry, like one of those laughing girls I'd always watched with my mouth pressed in a disapproving line. Who knew it was this easy, to find a new personality in a bottle?

"Wait. Wait." He was blinking at me, holding the sheets to his chest. "Slow down for a minute here."

I perched on the bed in my underpants, legs tucked underneath me and tilted coquettishly to the side.

"Look," he said, sitting up and holding me by the shoulders.

"I like you, Tina. I like you a lot. But . . . I mean, the thing is . . ."

I jumped off the bed before he could say any more, before he could elucidate the reasons he didn't want me. I scooped up whatever clothes I saw on the floor, feeling dizzy as I bent over, and hurried into the bathroom. *Wrong,* I thought. I'd been right about India, but I'd been wrong about him.

A second later, he was banging on the door. "Hey, Bettina. Can we talk about this?"

I decided that we couldn't . . . because, really, what was there to say? "I need to go." I combed my fingers through my hair, washed my hands and face, rinsed my mouth with water, and opened the door, pushing past him to where I'd left my shoes. Darren had pulled on his boxer shorts. His hair stood up in spikes, and his face still had that tender look without his glasses. He touched my cheek, then my hair. "Stay with me."

Are you my boyfriend? I wanted to ask . . . but the words reminded me of a book I'd read when I was little. *Are you my mother?* The mess of my life came crashing down, leaving me breathless. My father was dead, my mother was gone, and I was responsible for a baby who wasn't mine. It seemed, in that moment, more than I could bear, more than anyone should have to. I pressed my lips against his shoulder. "I need to go." I kissed his cheek, then the corner of his mouth, thinking that he wouldn't try to keep me, so I was surprised when he took my shoulders and held me motionless in front of him.

"Hey. Listen." He paused, scratching at the top of his head. "I don't know if I like babies. I've never really thought about it. I wasn't expecting to have to think about it for a while, you know?"

I nodded. I knew.

"But, the thing is, I like you. I like you a lot." My heart was rising, rising. I wanted to jump in the air, or into his arms again.

"It's like, if I found out you had, I don't know, herpes or something."

My heart stopped rising. My mouth fell open. "Are you actually equating my half sister with a venereal disease?" I asked.

Darren picked up his glasses off the coffee table, put them on, and looked at me defiantly. "You know what I mean."

"I'm not sure I do."

"It's like . . ." He scratched at his head some more, thinking. "A preexisting condition," he finally said. "I'll deal with it. Whatever it is." He opened his arms. "Now come to papa."

And, almost in spite of myself, I went.

INDIA

When I was seventeen, my junior year of high school, my grandfather had a stroke that left him paralyzed on his left side.

My yaya tried to find the right kind of facility, a place with round-the-clock nurses and physical therapy, and aides who could help lift my grandfather from his bed to his wheelchair, then from the chair to the toilet or the shower. But insurance only paid for six months at a place like that. When the time was up, my grandfather came home, where he'd fly into rages, face red, spittle in the corners of his lips, glaring at my grandmother in frustration, or in tears. *Why can't, why can't,* was the phrase he'd repeat over and over, as she'd tell him, in Greek and in English, *Vassily, calm down!* He couldn't be left alone: unattended, he'd throw things, start fires when he turned on the stove and then forgot about it.

For six weeks we managed. In the mornings, we'd work together to get him to the bathroom, shaved and dressed and into his chair. My grandmother would stay with him while I was at school. I turned down my starring role in the drama club's fall musical so I could come home as soon as school ended. I'd sit with him, watching television or reading out loud while she ran errands or napped. We'd eat dinner early, perform the bathroom routine again, and then watch TV until it was time to get him in bed. We kept this up until the morning my grandfather fell on top of my grandmother while I was at school. After an hour, she managed to work herself out from underneath him (my grandfather was almost six feet tall and weighed more than two hundred pounds) and inch her way across the kitchen floor to the phone. The ambulance she called took them both to the hospital. She'd cracked three of her ribs and he'd broken a hip.

"I don't want to do this," Yaya said, wincing as she spoke and pressing her hand against her taped-up ribs. "But I have no choice." She put the house up for sale, moved the two of them into an assisted-living complex where no one under fifty-five was allowed, and gave me the last address she had for my mother, on Alden Lane in New London, Connecticut. *Sure,* Raine had said, when Yaya had called her. *Sure, Sammie can come. Absolutely. It's time we were together.* But I'd been listening on the extension, and my mother had not sounded enthusiastic. I could hear noises in the background—kids fighting, a television blaring, a man yelling something I couldn't make out. She'd gotten married years ago, to a man named Phil, and they had two daughters, ages seven and five. She had never ended up in California—New London was about as far away from there as you could get.

I left Toledo in October with five hundred dollars, a suitcase full of clothes, a pair of boots and a pair of sneakers, and a winter coat that I'd outgrown (I hadn't wanted to bother Yaya and ask for another one). In spite of all the indications, I was hopeful. I hadn't seen my mother in years, but I remembered her as young and beautiful, always laughing, with a light in her eyes, so different from my dour, exhausted grandmother.

But the woman who opened the door after my ten-hour bus ride was different. I blinked, thinking maybe I'd gotten the address wrong, looking at the woman's hard-worn face and faded eyes, her hair dyed a brassy, straw-like blonde, and her body still thin, but soft as overripe fruit.

"Sammie?" Her voice was hoarse. There was a cigarette burning between her fingers, and I could see that her teeth were stained. I wondered if she still had the unicorn tattooed on her hip, if she remembered telling me she'd take me to California, and if she ever felt bad that she hadn't.

Her husband wasn't there. Phil was, I learned, a long-distance trucker who made cross-country runs that kept him on the road ten days out of every two weeks. Raine worked, part-time, as a cashier at a supermarket. "This is going to be just fine," she said, ushering me into the house, which smelled like bacon grease and cigarette smoke, showing me the pullout couch where I'd sleep and the closet where I could keep my things. It probably did seem like a good deal to her: a built-in, live-in babysitter for her daughters from the moment I came home from school. Usually, she'd barely bother to say hello to me as I got off the bus before racing out the door, into her car, and, I eventually learned, off to one of the Indian casinos just a few miles up the highway.

The girls—Emmie and Sophie—were sweet enough, with big brown eyes and curly brown hair. I'd babysat some, back in Toledo, and I liked kids all right. I'd walk them home from their elementary school, help them hang up their backpacks, and fix them a snack. We'd play games: Veterinarian, where we'd treat Sophie's ailing teddy bears; Doctor, where I'd pretend that my leg hurt and the girls, giggling, would decide that the only remedy was an immediate amputation. We'd play Sorry and Candy Land and Chutes and Ladders, and then, at five o'clock, watch *Sesame Street*. At six, I'd fix them dinners of macaroni and cheese or hot dogs and sweet pickles. I'd give them their baths and put them to bed before starting on my own homework. It wasn't perfect, and Raine was not what I'd expected or hoped for, but

I could get through it until I finished high school and figured out my next move.

The first time my stepfather crawled into bed with me he said it was a mistake. He explained this to me over breakfast the next morning, clutching his coffee cup, looking straight into my eyes. "Sometimes, when I'm coming in late, your mom makes up that pullout bed for me. When I saw the bed made up, that's what I thought. I didn't even notice you there." He smiled. His teeth were worse than Raine's had gotten. "Skinny little thing like you."

Phil was a lean, bald man with crinkles in the corners of his muddy brown eyes. He smelled like the tobacco he chewed, and when he came home after ten days away, he pushed his daughters away like they were pigs swarming at a trough. *Run upstairs now. Let Daddy talk to your big sister,* he'd say, with his eyes moving over me, like I was another cheap piece of furniture filling his living room, something he'd bought and paid for.

The second time he slapped his hand over my mouth and ripped off my panties before I kneed him in the stomach and wriggled away. Standing on the edge of the bed, panting, my nose running, and my knee bruised from the metal bar on the side of the bed, I'd yelled at him, loud enough that there was no way my mother could not have heard: *If you touch me again, you fucking bastard, I swear to God I'll cut it off.* He'd rolled off me and staggered away, clutching himself. Raine never came to my rescue. She never came at all.

The next morning, my mother, holding her cigarettes in one hand and her lighter in the other, sat me down at the breakfast table and mumbled, "I don't think this is going to work."

I sat there, hardly believing what I was hearing. I'd told her what had happened, but she didn't believe me . . . or, worse, maybe she did believe me, and she was taking his side anyhow.

"Phil's got a bad temper, but I know he didn't mean any-thing."

My voice sounded like it was coming from outer space. "He put his hand down my underpants. I'm pretty sure he knew what that meant."

Raine winced, then lit a cigarette. "He got confused," she said weakly. Then she glared at me. "And it's not like he asked for another kid. A teenager, for God's sake. He's got his hands full, you know."

"So where am I supposed to go?"

She didn't answer. I got to my feet, picked up my bookbag, then pulled my suitcase out of the closet and started to fill it with the few things I'd brought with me from Ohio. *Stop me,* I thought. *Tell me you love me, tell me to stay.* She didn't. Instead, she gave me the keys to her car, an ancient Tercel. "Maybe you can stay with some friends for a while. Like a sleepover." I didn't tell her that sleepovers were for little girls; that I hadn't been at New London High School long enough to make any friends, and I couldn't go back to Toledo. How could I tell people that my own mother hadn't wanted me, that, between the two of us, she'd chosen Phil?

I spent three nights at the Days Inn and then, realizing that I couldn't pay for a fourth night, I started sleeping in Raine's car, which I parked in the far reaches of the high school's lot. I'd catch a few fitful hours of rest each night curled under piles of clothing in the backseat, praying that no one would find me. Salvation arrived just before Thanksgiving, in my theater class.

I'd signed up for theater because I'd loved it back home, where my voice and my looks had gotten me plum parts in every musical. In New London, the teacher was Mrs. Rusk, a sixty-year-old battle-axe with dyed red hair and the requisite com-plement of oversized gestures and affectations, but she'd taken medical leave in late October after her breast cancer came back. She left, bidding us a teary farewell and quoting King Lear's speech to his daughters, on a Friday. On Monday morning, after Raine had kicked me out, I took my seat in the school's theater and sat, transfixed, as a man stepped out of the wings and onto the stage, then beckoned for us to join him.

"Might as well get comfortable up here," he said. "Names?" We went around a circle, saying our names, listening as he repeated them.

David Carter was in his thirties, still good-looking enough that the girls would check him out when he stood onstage to deliver a monologue, or ran lines with us, playing Romeo to our Juliet, Stanley to our Blanche.

He'd gone to New London High, then NYU. He'd been the understudy for the Phantom, and acted in an off-Broadway revival of *A Streetcar Named Desire.* He kept a coffeepot plugged in on his desk—against school rules, probably, but a theater instructor, an actor, could get away with certain eccentricities. In the mornings, he'd pour me a cup—half scalding black coffee, half cream—and I'd hold it gratefully, letting the mug warm my skin. I wasn't sure if he knew that I hadn't had breakfast and, most days, I hadn't had dinner, either, but those cups of milky coffee were the first of many kindnesses.

Being homeless as a teenager wasn't as hard as it probably was for adults who didn't have access to a high school. I'd get to school early, ostensibly to use the gym, and I'd shower in the locker room and brush my teeth at the sink. I could wash my clothes at the Laundromat. I was probably eligible for free lunches, had Raine taken the time to apply, but there was always food around the school, if you knew where to look for it: leftover birthday cake in the teachers' lounge, bags of pretzels that the anorexics-in-training would toss, still mostly full, into the trash bins in the girls' rooms. I'd pocket apples and bananas and jars of peanut butter at the grocery store, and slip string cheese and packages of crackers and gum into my pockets at the gas station.

The tricky part was finding a safe place to spend the nights. I'd rotate my spots, moving from the parking lot at the high school to the one behind the public library to the one at the Y. Twice, in the middle of the night, once at the high school and once at the end of a dirt road, the cops had pulled up, shining their lights through the Tercel's windows. It had been a different cop each time, but I'd told them both the same story: that I'd had a fight with my mother.

"Go on home," said the officer who'd found me the last time. "Whatever they did to you, no matter how mad they are, your folks wouldn't want you sleeping out here alone. It's not safe."

In November, I came to class one day to find a winter coat, brand-new, pink nylon with a pale-pink lining, hanging from the back of my chair. "I bought it for my sister, but she didn't like it. On sale, so it can't go back. Can you use it?" David asked. Later, I learned that he didn't have a sister. He'd seen me shivering in the parking lot wearing both of my sweaters at once, and had guessed, correctly, that I didn't have a coat.

It took him weeks to earn my trust, weeks of treats and compliments: a waxed paper bag of doughnuts waiting on my chair, a coupon for buy-one-get-one-free pizza from the shop in town tucked into my *Ten Monologues* book, a sweater that he told me he'd shrunk in the wash. Later, he said that getting me to talk was like coaxing a feral cat in from the cold. *Little Cat*, he called me, and he told me that he'd loved me the first time he'd seen me, all legs and big eyes, "and those tights you had, remember them? The ones with the hole in the knee."

He never touched me for all that time, except for a light hand on my wrist or the small of my back when he was directing a scene . . . but, the way he looked at me, I knew there were possibilities. I had just turned eighteen, had only had a few boyfriends, and was still learning my own power, the way boys would follow me with their eyes, the things I could get them to do. Now I was starting to wonder whether a man might be the answer to my problems.

One night at the end of November, when it was getting dark by four-thirty p.m. and the nights were getting cold, I walked to David's classroom and leaned against the door. I wore a thin white blouse, my ripped black tights, a black Spandex skirt that ended at the tops of my thighs, the Doc Martens I'd convinced Yaya to buy me the year before. He looked at me and his face lit up, and I knew that the thing I wanted—a warm place to sleep, an actual bed—was mine for the taking.

So I stood in the classroom doorway, each rib visible underneath my skin and my nipples poking out against my shirt, and I let him take me to his place, an apartment that took up the whole second floor of an old Victorian downtown. There, I let him give me half a glass of tart red wine and then, by the flickering light of a half-dozen candles, I undressed myself while he stared up at me from his bed and lay on top of him and kissed him until he groaned and rolled on top of me, taking me in his arms. Three weeks after the first time we'd slept together, he resigned from the school. No big deal, he told me; he had a little family money. The next day we drove to a justice of the peace after school on the Friday afternoon before Christmas, and became man and wife.

I finished school, at David's insistence, and it wasn't half the scandal you might imagine. For a week I was the subject of scrutiny and jokes—my history teacher, I remember, took great delight in addressing me as Mrs. Carter, and the girls all wanted to see my ring—a tiny solitaire on a band of gold—but there were two girls who were pregnant in my class, plus a boy widely suspected of being gay, and it wasn't long before people lost interest in the oddity of a married woman attending high school, especially once it was clear that I wasn't pregnant.

Another teacher was hired; and David got a job at a small theater in Hartford, as part of the company, and teaching drama to little kids on Saturday. After classes I'd walk to our apartment, stopping at the grocery store with the list David had given me in the morning to pick up whatever he needed for dinner, and the money he'd given me to buy it. Upstairs, I'd lock the door behind me and pour a glass of wine—an adult pleasure that I'd quickly adopted—and settle on the green velvet couch with my homework, or one of the novels or plays from David's shelves. The nights he didn't have shows, he'd be home by five-thirty. "My child bride," he'd say, gathering me into his arms. I'd pour him his own wine, and sometimes we'd go right to bed and make love, but, more often, he'd go to the kitchen to cook. I'd perch on the counter and watch him chop onions, sauté garlic, swirl a melting knob of butter into the pan. "I've got to fatten you up," he would say. He'd scoop pasta into my bowl, grating drifts of Parmesan on top, and keep jars of olives and wedges of cheese around for me to nibble at.

We'd eat, then read together or listen to music from David's collection of classical and opera albums. On Saturday afternoons, we'd go to the library, filling bags with books and compact discs. On Monday nights, when the theater was dark, we'd go out to dinner and then to a movie, and on Sunday mornings we'd buy the *New York Times*, take our clothes to the Laundromat, buy doughnuts and coffee, and sit in the molded plastic chairs attached to the wall, reading the paper, snacking, then folding our fresh, dried sheets and pillowcases together. Maybe it was an oddly sedate life for a teenager—most of my peers back in Toledo, I knew, were spending their Saturdays at parties in fields or parks or in houses where the parents weren't home, and

I could only assume that my classmates in New London were doing the same things—but, after all those years with my exhausted, emotionless grandparents, after being rejected by my mother and spending all those cold nights in my car, our routines and traditions were comforting.

The hardest part was seeing Raine around town. I glimpsed her once at the supermarket, a different one from the one where she worked. She looked tired and frail in her winter coat, snapping as Sophie and Emma tried to sneak a box of Lucky Charms into the shopping cart, and I'd hidden behind a stand-up display of Entenmann's cookies until they passed. Once, coming back from the Laundromat with a basket of clean clothes, I saw her and Phil and the girls on their way into church. That time there'd been nowhere to hide. The girls hadn't seen me, but Raine did, and she looked at me like I was a babysitter whose name she couldn't quite remember, a sitter she'd used once and never intended to hire again.

I graduated in June. David didn't attend the ceremony, but he was there, waiting for me outside the high school in his car, which was an immaculately kept baby-blue 1957 Chevrolet Bel Air convertible that he'd inherited from his father and kept in a garage, dressed in a custom-made zippered canvas cover. We went home. He made pasta. We made love, which, while not the rapture the movies and novels had taught me to expect, was at least pleasant enough. In September I planned to start taking classes at UConn. I would study theater and art history, like David had. In August, I found out I was pregnant.

To this day, I can remember the feeling of it, the sundress I'd been wearing, the taste of milk and Cheerios still in my mouth. I can feel the black-and-white tiles of the bathroom floor cool under my feet, and I can see the claw-footed tub with the rust stain around the drain in front of me, the pregnancy test, with its pink plus sign, jiggling up and down in my shaking hand.

We'd been using condoms . . . except a few times, when David would slip inside me for a few strokes without one. *This is the end,* I thought. *The end of everything.* Marriage was one thing, but if I had a baby, I'd be stuck in New London for the rest of my life. Even though I had no particular ambition, no idea of where else I'd want to go, what else I'd want to do, I knew I couldn't stay there forever. David had been an escape hatch, not a lifetime plan, and a baby wasn't part of my plan at all.

I waited until he went to work the next day to make the appointment at the Planned Parenthood in New Haven, an hour's drive away. I took money out of the bank—and, I'm ashamed to say, out of his wallet. I drove the Tercel my mother had given me to the clinic, and, when it was over, I bought a bottle of Advil and a bottle of water and just kept driving west. As the miles slid by, the year that I'd endured—my grandfather's stroke, my trip from Toledo to New London, my brief time with Raine, then the car, then David, had all started to feel like it had happened to someone else. Someone else had slept in the cramped backseat of the car; someone else had gotten married in front of a justice of the peace with bad breath and a wandering eye; someone else had gotten that abortion and woken up alone, a curly-haired, kind-eyed nurse handing her a sanitary pad and asking whether there was anyone waiting to take her home.

In Los Angeles, I bought a driver's license with a fake name and a birthday that made me twenty-one. Eventually, I lived so long as that girl, India Bishop, that I almost forgot I'd ever been anyone else; a girl whose mother hadn't wanted her, a girl who'd stolen food and slept in a car, a girl who'd left a husband behind.

My plane landed in LaGuardia just as night was falling. I bought a new cell phone and spent the night in a hotel. In the morning I cabbed it to Grand Central and bought a ticket for the train that would take me to New London for the first time since I'd left David, all those years ago. The trip was only a few hours, through the soupy, humid August air. Kids had opened a fire hydrant on the corner and it was dribbling water into the gutter. In the park in the center of town, teenage girls in bikinis lay on towels, and mothers with babies pushed strollers back and forth in the shade.

David's apartment was an easy walk from the station. The front door to the old Victorian, long since divided into one- and two-bedroom flats, was supposed to be locked, but it hadn't been when I'd known him, and it wasn't now. The stairs had been stripped of the green carpet I remembered, and now the wood of the walls had a mellow gleam. The banister had been refinished, and the walls were painted a pretty cream color, and the ceramic Virgin was where I remembered her, in the little nook at the top of the stairs.

I knocked at the door, and he swung it open and looked at me for a minute, staring blankly. I had to remind myself that I had a different face now. He might not even recognize me. David looked older, heavier, tired around the eyes. His hair—what was left of it—was white, and he wore glasses, which were new, and a white cotton button-down shirt, untucked, and worn corduroy pants. There was a gold wedding band, the one we'd bought together or its twin, on his left hand, and, as I stood in the hallway that smelled like soup, listening to an air conditioner whine and someone's TV play the nightly news, he smiled at me. His face lit up and he looked handsome again; handsome and as young as he'd been when we were together. "Well," he said. "Look who's here."

It was cool inside. That was the first thing I noticed as David took my Mexico tote bag and set it by the door. "Can I get you anything to drink? I've got a nice Scotch," he said, gesturing toward a bar cart made of wrought iron and mirrored panels. I looked around, remembering: the Turkish rugs he'd layered over the hardwood floors, the colorful abstract paintings on the walls, the green velvet couch, the art books and novels and old vinyl albums lined alphabetically on handmade shelves that stretched from the floor to the top of the twelve-foot ceiling, with a rolling wooden ladder in the corner. I thought back to when I was eighteen and thought this was the most beautiful place I'd ever been. We'd made love, and I'd waited until he'd fallen asleep, then crept out of his bed and ate everything in his refrigerator, including an entire jar of strawberry jam.

"Just some water, please."

He handed me a jelly glass filled from a filter-pitcher. I sat down on the couch and cupped the cool glass in my hands, letting him look me over. "What," he asked me pleasantly, "did you do to yourself?"

I managed a little laugh. "It's been a while, you know."

"You were so beautiful," David said. "Why would you want to change?"

I shrugged.

"Sammie." He reached out and touched my hair.

"I got married again." The words came out in a croak. "In New York. An older man."

He had moved to stand behind me. I couldn't see his face, but I imagined that he was smiling. "Sounds like you've got a type."

"You know," I said, without turning, without looking at him, "we never got divorced."

His hand moved slowly in my hair. "I got the papers you sent, and I know I should have signed them. I knew you weren't coming back. But I never did. I just kept hoping . . ." His hand was on my shoulder now. "Are you happy?" he asked.

Eyes closed, I whispered, "For a while, I was."

"Did you ever think of me?"

"Sometimes." It was true. In Los Angeles, when I was broke

and lonely, getting rejected at auditions a dozen times a week, I'd think of David, who had always been unfailingly kind. I'd remember the coat he'd given me, the mugs of milky coffee, his mouth warm against the back of my neck. *Little Cat, Little Cat.*

"My husband and I . . . we were supposed to have a baby. With a surrogate." He came to sit beside me on the couch. His eyebrows drew together as he studied me. I met his gaze, telling myself I wasn't the girl he'd known, the girl he'd saved, the cat who'd crept out of his bed and out of his house one summer morning with all the cash in his wallet, the girl who'd sold her engagement ring at a West Hollywood pawnshop and tried to think of that brief, early marriage as the first of many skins she'd shed, the first of many selves she'd outgrow.

"About that divorce," I said.

He sighed, nodding. "I figured someday you'd be back for that."

"I should have done it a while ago." The truth was, I'd hoped that sending him the papers would be enough, that he'd sign them and file them and it would all be over without my having to do a thing.

"Does it mean," he asked, "that you're not really married to the other guy?"

"That's a little unclear. He's dead now."

"Oh." He looked sympathetic, and I felt stabbed through with remorse. He wasn't a bad guy, and he'd never done anything except try to help me. I had treated him poorly, and being young and mistreated myself wasn't much of an excuse.

The papers I'd sent David, my petition for divorce, were in a drawer in the kitchen, still in the envelope I'd used to mail them. I felt my heart stutter, looking at my teenage handwriting, big and loopy, young and hopeful. I'd called a lawyer from the train that morning. In David's apartment I called her again, and she said she'd meet us in her office in an hour. The rules, as she explained them when we arrived, were clear: I'd filed papers, but David had never signed them, which made me guilty of bigamy. "We can file for leniency," she told us, and David had nodded. "I'll do whatever I can to make this right." My mind wandered while they talked. I wondered what would happen: if my marriage hadn't been legal, then maybe Marcus couldn't have left me anything. Maybe not even the baby was mine. I wondered, too, why David had never remarried, whether there'd been a string of teenage girls in the years since we'd parted or if maybe he was still in love with me.

Less than an hour, the lawyer had said, but by the time everything was signed and notarized it was closer to two, and then we were back out on the sticky sidewalk, underneath a low gray sky. The first hard thing was done. I was divorced. I'd made it over the hurdle. But worse was coming.

"Is my mother . . ."

He shook his head and took my hands. "I saw her obituary in the paper, maybe six or seven years ago."

"Oh." I tried to remember something good about her, the way she'd looked when she was young, how she'd smiled at me like I was the best thing she'd ever seen, the stories she'd whispered in my ear, curled up next to me in the bed that had once been hers. I knew better than to even ask about my half sisters. They'd been little girls when I'd lived here, and I didn't think I'd ever told David their names.

He walked me to the bus stop and gave me an awkward hug. "I wish you well," he said. "I always did." I nodded, knowing I didn't deserve his good wishes, knowing I couldn't answer him without crying.

The bus pulled out of the station at six o'clock. By nine, I was back in the city. By nine-forty-five, I was walking up the five flights of stairs to my old single-girl apartment. I took off my shoes and lay on top of the narrow bed, fully dressed, without turning on the lights. Tears slid down my cheeks and pooled in my ears. Tomorrow I'd get up, get dressed, leave the last vestiges of my girlhood behind, go back to the grand apartment, and be a mother.

JULES

I'd tried calling Kimmie the night after Bettina had made her proposition, but her cell phone just rang and rang. The e-mails I sent over the next ten days went unanswered, which I knew because I was checking my BlackBerry approximately every five minutes, prompting Rajit to deliver a barrage of snide remarks about the charming new tic I'd developed.

"Did your boyfriend forget to call?" he smirked, thumbs in his suspenders, monogrammed cuffs flapping.

"My girlfriend," I said coolly. It was out of my mouth before I'd known I was going to say it. Rajit's mouth hung open for a gratifying instant.

"Oh, my," he said, almost to himself. "Well. That'll give me something to think about this weekend." Normally I would have ignored him, but today I straightened myself to my full height, which was at least three inches more than Rajit's.

"You're disgusting," I said pleasantly. "I just want you to know that. You're a horrible human being, and I'll bet your parents would be ashamed if they knew how you treated people." Then I turned off my computer, shouldered my bag, and, head held high, walked out the door to a smattering of applause and a single wolf-whistle.

It was seven o'clock, still light, but getting cooler. I wondered how long it had been since I'd left the office before the sun set. Most of my colleagues wouldn't make it home for hours. I took the subway uptown and dashed up the stairs two at a home, stationing myself in front of Kimmie's building's front door. I had a key, but it didn't seem right to use it. After about twenty minutes I saw her round the corner in her black tank top, with her backpack bouncing on her narrow shoulders and her hair tucked up into a twist. I ran to meet her.

"Hey."

She looked up, then quickly looked down and kept on walking. "Hi," she said, so quietly that I almost didn't hear it.

I caught up so that I was walking alongside her. I'd lost my father. I'd probably torpedoed my job. I didn't have any real friends in the city, just colleagues and acquaintances, same as it had been in college. I'd been so lonely, lonely for years until I'd met her. I couldn't bear the thought of being that lonely again.

So I did the only thing I could think of. I grabbed her by her upper arms, and spun her around, and kissed her.

Her backpack slipped off her shoulders. My bag fell onto the sidewalk. Somebody hooted, and someone else yelled, "Get you some!" but I didn't care. Her lips were stiff underneath mine, but they softened as I held her.

Then she pushed me away. "What was that about?"

"I don't want to lose you," I said. "I couldn't stand that. I'm sorry I'm so . . . so slow about these things, but I just . . . I really . . ." I blurted out the only thing I could think of at that moment. "There's a baby. From my egg. The baby's half sister got in touch with me. They're here, in New York."

Kimmie bent down, picking up her backpack, brushing it off before slipping it back on. Then she smiled, showing me her tiny, even teeth. "You're making a spectacle," she said. She squeezed my hand. "What's the baby's name?"

"Rory." I walked close enough to her that our hips bumped as we made our way back toward her apartment, holding her hand, toward the tiny metal-walled elevator, the hallway that smelled like air freshener and chicken soup. The evening would unfold in its ordered, wonderful familiarity. We'd cook something, noodles and stir-fry or meatloaf and mashed potatoes. We'd spoon ice cream into mugs and snuggle on the couch, watching the shows we'd taped, and I would tell her about Bettina's call, about the grand apartment, about the baby. In bed with her, I'd feel safe in a way I'd once been at the dining-room table with my father, working on my homework, knowing that he was there to help. I smiled, wondering what I'd done to deserve her, to deserve such happiness.

ANNIE

My train got into Philadelphia just after eleven o'clock in the morning. It was noisy in the echoing station, where the floors were made of marble and the ceilings soared thirty feet high. The air that August morning was still and sticky, smelling like hot pretzels from a stand set up in front of the information board. I stepped off the staircase, and there was Frank, standing next to one of the curved wooden benches, waiting for me. Instead of his work clothes, he wore a clean pair of khakis and a short-sleeved jersey shirt, with sneakers, instead of heavy workboots, on his feet. PHILADELPHIA AVIATION ACADEMY, read the logo on his shirt.

I walked toward him slowly, wondering what it meant that he was here. Normally Nancy picked me up, with the boys in the car, and took me home. The house would be clean, the bed I'd shared with Frank would be neatly made, but there would be no sign of him. We'd agreed, in a terse conversation, to keep things as normal as possible. Frank would spend time with the boys during the daytime, when he wasn't working, and he'd stay for dinner, if he was home. Then he'd slip out once they were sleeping and go to his parents' house for the night.

We hadn't told the boys anything, because there didn't seem to be much to say: we were in limbo, separated but still technically living together, married but leading separate lives. For the time being, I'd told Frank Junior and Spencer that the baby I'd had in my tummy was in New York with her parents, and that I was helping to take care of her while she was still little. They had accepted this without question or comment. I suspected that Frank Junior thought that because the baby was a girl, she would naturally require more care than he had.

Frank stood up when he saw me. "Hi," he said shyly, looking me over as I approached him. I set my duffel bag by my feet and sat down on the bench, and he sat beside me. "You look pretty."

I touched my hair, wondering how I really looked to him. I hadn't gained much weight with the pregnancy—being too upset to eat for much of the third trimester had helped with that—and I was only a few pounds away from being back to where I'd been when this whole thing had started.

"Were the boys good for you?"

He grinned. "Spencer used the potty all day."

"He did?" I was delighted. He used the potty for me, but I usually put him in a pull-up before I left for the city, and I'd assumed that's what Frank was doing, too.

"How is the baby?" Frank asked.

"She's beautiful. An angel." I felt my throat thicken, a hint of the sadness that came over me when I nursed and held the baby that wasn't really mine, that there were no daughters in my future.

"Rory," he said. "I like that name."

"Me, too."

"So," he said, and settled his hands on his legs. "You like New York?"

"It's fine. I miss the boys when I'm away. But the money will help." Bettina had insisted on paying me a thousand dollars for the day and night I was up there, much too much money, I told her, but she wasn't taking no for an answer.

"I miss them, too. At night." He pressed his lips together like he wanted to suck the words back into his mouth. Then, he said, "I miss us being a family. I miss you."

I didn't answer. I'd done the hardest work of my life, the thing none of the clone-girls in that story I'd read had done. I had broken free from my destiny. I had taken myself to the city, found money and a place to live. I could stay—Bettina hadn't come right out and said it, but I knew if I offered to work as a nanny, she'd hire me, and I could bring the boys to New York and find a place for us there. I could have people like I'd had back in high school, people to talk to, to eat with. The whole world lay open before me . . . and now Frank probably wanted me to turn away from it, to come home and be what I was before.

"You weren't wrong to be upset with me," said Frank. Startled, I turned to look at him. His eyes were narrowed, his body stiff. "I wasn't being the husband you deserved."

This was unexpected. "Maybe I was wrong, too," I said.

Frank shook his head. "You were trying to help us. And if I hadn't been so stubborn about letting you work . . ." He dropped his voice until I could hardly hear him over the drone of the crowd, the noise of people coming and going. "I guess maybe you were lonely."

I nodded, almost unconsciously. Frank kept talking. "We can sell the house, move to Philly. Spencer's starting nursery school in the fall, so you'll have some time. You can go to college, if you want."

I felt a pressure inside of me building, a sob or a shout, I wasn't sure yet. "You love that farm. It's all you ever wanted."

"I want you more. And I got a new job," he said.

"With the airlines?"

"Nah. Teaching." He took my hand. "I did so well in my classes they asked me to stay on. I'm still part-time at the airport, but it's good money. Good benefits, too." He paused, like he was steeling himself. "I looked it up online. Community college has classes online, or in Center City."

I looked down at our fingers entwined. I'd thought about giving him back my engagement ring—it had cost almost two thousand dollars and was by far the most expensive thing outside of his truck that Frank had ever bought—but I hadn't taken it off yet. I wondered if I would have made different choices, if I could have gone back in time, knowing what I knew now. Part of me thought I would have undone the surrogacy in an instant, wiped the slate clean, done anything to keep my marriage intact. Another part of me thought that I'd done just the right thing, that the pain of leaving him was the cost of a new and better life.

"Come home," said Frank, his grip on my hand tightening. "Stay with us."

I sat there, not answering. Rory was getting bigger, filling out, holding her head up with her clear eyes open, taking in the world. I could send breast milk by FedEx and visit the baby on the weekends. I could start taking the classes I'd planned on—an English course, and one on computer programming— but I could do them at home, online, instead of in New York. I could give my boys the world of the city, the museums and the plays and the galleries and the musicals—but keep my house, and my husband. I could have a bigger life, like Nancy, like what I'd come to want in the last few years, only I could have it with Frank. It almost seemed like too much to hope for, but I smiled at him, then reached for his cheek, pulling him close.

BETTINA

One Wednesday morning in early August, when I was interviewing the third nanny of the morning, the telephone rang. "Someone's here to see you," said Ricky, our doorman.

"Send her up," I said, looking at my watch. If it was the fourth applicant, she was twenty minutes early, and if it was the first girl, the one who was supposed to have been here at nine, she was two hours late.

"She says she'd rather meet you in the lobby," said Ricky. "It's your . . . it's Mrs. Croft."

"Excuse me," I said to the applicant currently perched on the couch. I'd already decided not to hire her. True, her French accent was lovely, and her references were solid, but anyone who'd show up for a job interview wearing jeans with the words HOT STUFF spelled out in sequins across the back pockets was not someone I would be employing to care for a child.

I stuck my head into the nursery to make sure the baby was asleep. Then I tucked the baby monitor into my pocket, told the chef and the maids where I was going, then pressed the button for the lobby.

India was waiting for me behind the doorman's desk. "Hello," I said, having rejected *Well, look who's here* on the way down. She was casually dressed and she was tan, which infuriated me. I imagined her lying on a beach somewhere while I'd been handling the details of her husband's funeral and her baby's birth. "Did you have a nice vacation?"

She didn't take the bait. "I had some thinking to do."

I stood there, waiting, looking her over. If she was wearing makeup, I couldn't tell. Her hair was pulled into a ponytail, and her roots were badly in need of a touch-up. I saw an inch or two of drab dark brown at her scalp before her hair made the transition to glorious caramel bronze, and there were wiry silver hairs threaded through the brown. She wore jeans—probably they were the six-hundred-dollar kind they sold at Saks, but they were still jeans—and a plain short-sleeved T-shirt. No earrings, no jewelry at all, except for her wedding ring.

"I loved your father," she said.

"Which is why you didn't bother showing up for his funeral."

India flinched. "I have a hard time with . . . well. I was having a hard time with all of it."

"Oh, really? Because I thought it was a total picnic. Do you have any idea what I've been dealing with? Any idea at all?" I was shouting, I realized, and Ricky was staring, although he was trying not to, and so was my neighbor Mrs. Schneider, collecting her mail, with her little Yorkie riding in her purse. I took India's arm—it was, possibly, the first time I'd touched her since a brief, obligatory hug at her wedding—and dragged her back toward the service entrance. There was no way I was letting her come upstairs.

"I'm sorry," she said. She'd followed me willingly enough, and now she met my gaze steadily, not fidgeting or flinching. I wondered if she was on heavy-duty antidepressants, or if she'd spent the last few months sitting on a beach, hanging out in a sweat lodge, doing yoga. Maybe she'd met up with my mother in New Mexico, sampled some of the Baba's offerings. That thought made me even angrier.

"You're sorry. That's great. That's a big consolation. I got a call from your fertility clinic because your surrogate was freaking out. She hadn't heard from you, nobody knew where you were, and, in case you were confused, having a baby is not like ordering a pizza, then deciding you'd rather have Chinese. You can't just decide you don't want it."

"I know." No ducking, no tears, no excuses . . . just that same strange, narcotized steadiness. "I didn't do the right thing. But I'm back now, and I won't run away again."

"I don't believe you. Why should I believe you?"

She didn't answer me. Instead, she asked, "Have you met Annie?"

"I have. She's been staying here. Helping with the baby."

This, finally, caused a crack in India's placid exterior. She blinked rapidly. "What?"

"We didn't know where you were. I had people looking, but we didn't know if you'd turn up in time, and even if you did, we didn't know if you'd want to be a mother. Annie's been staying here, and Jules—she's the egg donor—and her girlfriend, Kimmie—they've been babysitting."

Now India was blinking even faster. "What? I don't understand. You met the egg donor? How could that be?"

"I needed all the help I could get. Annie and Jules have been great. They wanted to help me," I said, letting her fill in the blank of *and you didn't* all by herself.

"Listen," she said. This time she put her hand on my arm. "I know what you're thinking."

"You have no idea what I'm thinking."

"You're thinking," she continued, "that I'm going to be a terrible mother."

"I don't even think you planned on being a mother at all. I think you just wanted a baby to make sure you'd inherit my father's money. I think that's about the worst reason for having a baby in the world. I think you're a bigamist, and I think . . ."

"*I* think," she said, interrupting me, "that you have no clue what my life was like."

"You mean before or after you were arrested? Or before you married my father without bothering to get divorced?"

She almost smiled. "It wasn't that I didn't bother to get divorced. I served David with papers. He never signed them. And by then, I'd changed my name . . ." Her voice trailed off. "You're not entirely wrong. Money did have something to do with it. But mostly . . ."

She paused. I waited.

"Mostly," she said, "I wanted your father and me to be a family. To have something that was ours. I think that's why I couldn't handle the funeral. Why I left . . ." Now her voice was cracking. She looked away, wiping her eyes with the back of her hand. "I couldn't stand to think that the baby would be mine, not ours."

"And you'd be stuck with it," I added.

"That was part of it," she answered. "But I figured out a lot of things while I was gone." She smiled. "And I got divorced."

"You know, you probably weren't even legally married to my father. Which means you probably can't inherit."

She shrugged, but didn't answer. "I don't care about the money. I don't expect you to believe me, but it's true," she said. "I came back for my baby."

"You're right. I don't believe you. And, by the way, it's not your baby, and she has a name. Rory."

She lifted her chin. "She's not yours. I'm the mother."

"You don't think," I said, "that if I went to a judge and told him what you did, and told him what you were, that they'd give me custody?"

Instead of answering, India asked, "Do you want a baby?"

"Interesting that you'd care about that now, after you and my father decided to give me custody if something happened."

Another faint smile flitted across her face. "Your dad always thought that you were the responsible one."

That hurt, imagining my dad discussing me with his new wife; knowing I'd never hear him compliment me again. "I am responsible. And I'll be responsible." I gave her a hard look. "You should go." I flicked my hand toward the doors, in case she'd forgotten where they were. "Go rent an apartment. Or move into a hotel. Wait for the will to be probated. You might not get it all, but I'm sure you'll get something, and you can move to Majorca or wherever you want to go to catch your next rich husband. I can handle this."

"I'm sure you can. That's why your dad and I picked you. But it isn't fair."

She had to be kidding me. "None of this is fair!" I blurted.

"It isn't fair," she continued, as if I hadn't spoken, "that you won't get to enjoy your twenties. That you'll be stuck taking care of a baby who isn't yours. When your father and I chose you as the guardian, we had no idea . . ." Her voice was trembling, but she made herself finish. "We had no idea this would happen. We only picked someone because the clinic said we had to, and we thought if anything happened, it wouldn't be for years and years. It was never our intention for you to have a baby to deal with at this point in your life." She wiped her eyes. "That's why I left my first husband. I was pregnant, and I didn't want to be stuck. But you probably know about that already."

I shook my head. My inquiry into India's affairs had revealed that she'd been raised by her grandparents, rejected by her mother, and married at eighteen, but not why she'd left her first husband. If she'd been pregnant and had an abortion, maybe that was why she wanted this baby—Rory—so badly. Not because she wanted to lock down my father and her inheritance, but to make up for the baby she hadn't had when she was young.

I smoothed my hair again, buying time, thinking that India and I actually had more in common than I'd been willing to acknowledge. We both had mothers who'd let us down. We'd both gotten stuck with too much responsibility too soon. Of course, I'd gone to Vassar and she'd gone to a justice of the peace to marry her high-school drama teacher, but still. Minor details.

"I know you don't have any reason to trust me, and I know you don't like me." She was crying in earnest now, tears streaming down her tanned cheeks, not even bothering to try to wipe them. "But I loved your dad, and I swear to you . . ." She rested her hand against her heart. "I'll do the best job I can."

It would have been the easiest thing to say, *Okay, fine, you take it from here,* to tell Annie and Jules that the plans had changed, to tell Darren that my life had magically untangled itself, that I could be, again, just a regular girl, unencumbered, my nights and weekends free. Surprisingly, the thought made me sad. I liked the baby, the apartment full of women, even Annie's little boys, the one time they'd come for the weekend. I liked feeling needed . . . and admired a little, too. *No, that's not her baby. It's her half sister. Her father died before she was born, and now she's raising her. Isn't she amazing?* More than that, I felt like I was on my way to building the thing I'd been missing after my mother left: a family of my own.

"So what do you say?" India asked. She looked at me hopefully. "Do you think you could give me a chance?"

"I think," I said. "I think maybe the more hands, the better. I think I've got a good plan in place. But I think you can help."

Her smile vanished. "Help? What do you mean? I'm going to be the mother."

"I think that this baby is going to have a lot of mothers."

A line between her eyes deepened as she frowned.

"Come upstairs," I said, walking back into the lobby, giving Ricky a wave and punching the button for the elevator.

She stood behind me silently as we ascended and, without a word, followed me into the apartment, then down the hall. Rory was just starting to wake up, kicking her legs, curling and uncurling her fingers and her toes as she wriggled around. India froze in her tracks about three feet from the crib, making a noise like she'd been hit. "Oh," she said. Her mouth was open, and I wondered what she was thinking of: my father, or the baby she hadn't had. "Can I . . ."

"Fine."

She reached into the crib and gently lifted Rory into her arms. "Hi, baby," she whispered. "Hi, little baby. I came back for you."

"Watch her head," I said pointlessly. India had Rory's head tucked into the crook of her elbow, and she was doing Annie's little bouncing move, like she'd been born knowing it, born with that baby in her arms. I sighed, feeling the strangest mix of sorrow and relief, and I worried, for a minute, that maybe I'd start crying, too. But I had a future, my whole life ahead of me, babies of my own, if I wanted them.

She looked at me, eyes brimming, above Rory's head. Her bald spot was gone, and in its place was a thick tuft of glossy dark hair, the same hair as my brothers, and my dad. "Thank you," she whispered.

I could have said something snotty, like *Whatever*, or *It wasn't like you had a choice.* But she seemed at once so broken and so happy, standing in the room she'd decorated with the baby in her arms . . . and so all I said was "You're welcome."

2017

I waited by the doorway outside the primary school with the rest of the first-grade moms and sitters and the single stay-at-home dad, making small talk until the bell rang and the six-year-olds, all pleated skirts and scabby knees and oversized backpacks, came racing out into the sunshine.

"Rory! Over here!" She squinted, then her face broke into a smile as she ran toward me. Her dark-brown hair had come out of its ponytail and hung in ringlets around her cheeks, and her elfin face wore its usual merry expression. It always surprised me, how I felt when I saw her, how I loved her more than I'd thought it was possible to love anyone.

She pulled up right at my side, out of breath, and shoved a folded piece of paper into my hand. "We have to do a family tree."

I took the paper, examining it.

"See. Look." Rory snatched back the assignment, pointing at the lines that were connected to the tree trunk. "You have to put your mother and your father and your grandmother and grand-father and brothers and sisters if you've got them." She paused for a breath. "Do you know Sophie has *two* brothers and *two* sisters?" Her tone suggested that she could barely imagine such riches.

"I do know that." I also knew that Sophie's parents had conceived both sets of twins with the help of donor insemination and all four children had been carried by two different surrogates at the same time. Maybe Rory's tale wouldn't be the only strange one in the class.

My daughter slipped her hand into mine, and we started the routines of our walk home. "Candy treat?" she asked as we passed the drugstore, and I said, "Okay."

We went through the drugstore's automatic doors—when she'd been little, Rory had loved to hop back and forth over the threshold, determining just how far inside she'd have to be to get the doors to work—and selected a bag of M&M's. Rory counted each coin carefully before sliding it across the counter, then skipped home along the sidewalk, singing to herself, with the candy rattling in her pocket. Upstairs, in the apartment that Marcus had left me, along with more money than I could ever hope to spend, Rory sat at the kitchen table, sorting the M&M's by color, lining them up in rows, then eating them one at a time, first brown, then yellow, then red, then blue, and then, finally, the green ones. She practiced her recorder for ten minutes, then looked at the schedule taped to the stainless-steel refrigerator. Wednesday was her recorder lesson; on Fridays, she had tumbling. On Sunday afternoons, Jules and Kimmie came over to spend the afternoon and take her out for dinner (these days, she favored sushi). Jules and Kimmie were married now. They'd had a sunset ceremony on a beach in Martha's Vineyard and were talking about having a baby of their own. Kimmie was doing research for a pharmacology company, and Jules had left the world of finance, gone back to school for a journalism degree, and gotten what she laughingly called the last job as an investigative reporter at the last magazine left in New York.

On Mondays and Wednesdays, Bettina came over after work for dinner, and once a month she hosted Rory at her apartment downtown. She'd gone back to work at Kohler's and was still dating Darren, and, while I didn't think the two of us would ever be best friends, we enjoyed each other's company well enough when Rory brought us together.

Once a month, Rory and I made the trip to Phoenixville, where Rory would spend the weekend with Annie and Frank and Frank Junior and Spencer, who doted on her, introducing her as their sister and treating her like a doll. Like Jules, Annie had gone back to school. In another year she'd have her bachelor's degree, and then she'd apply for teaching jobs in the same school system her boys attended.

Sometimes I worried it was confusing—all these people, all these different places, different expectations, different rules—but Rory seemed to manage it all with aplomb. She was a natural negotiator, knowing, intuitively, how to get along and play well with others. In that—in so many ways, in little gestures, in the shape of her feet and her fingers, in the way she'd press her lips together, humming while she thought—she reminded me of her father.

"Homework," I said, and she ran to her room. The nursery had been all pale pink and green when she'd been a baby, before her true nature had revealed itself. Rory wasn't a pink-bedroom girl, although, like all her peers, she'd undergone a brief but fervent infatuation with the Disney princesses. Now her space was outfitted with an oversize desk that held footlong plastic bins in which Rory stored her Legos, her snap circuit kit, the collection of old cell phones and calculators she'd taken apart, and plastic bins full of laboriously printed and drawn plans labeled EXPERIMINTS AND INVENSHUNS.

We still lived in the apartment in the San Giacomo, but I'd sold the bottom floor, which meant we'd been reduced—quote-unquote—to just four bedrooms: one for me, one for Rory, and two guest suites with their own bathrooms for whoever came to stay, Bettina and Darren, Annie and Frank and their boys. I'd given a lot of the art away to museums and let go of most of the staff, although I still had someone to clean, and to cook when I entertained. I'd gone back to work part-time, and I volunteered at Rory's school, organizing fund-raising events and the annual Book and Bake Sale, raising money for the new library and the class trips to Portugal and Spain that Rory would take as an eighth-grader. I'd even made two friends, other mothers with kids in Rory's class, one married, one single. I'd thought about dating, but hadn't yet. Secretly, I suspected that that part of my life was over. I'd had my big love, and now, at forty-eight (although my friends told me I didn't look a day over forty), I had memories, friends, a weird kind of family, and a daughter I loved with all my heart . . . and, surely, there were worse things than that.

Rory came dashing back into the room in her favorite sparkly T-shirt (white, long-sleeved, with a sequined heart on the chest) and a pair of navy-blue Columbia sweatpants that Kimmie had given her. We sat in the kitchen, the room where Rory and I spent most of our time together. I'd moved one of the Persian rugs from the apartment I'd sold into one of the kitchen's corners and bought a round table and four chairs, and moved my laptop from the desk in the dressing room onto the kitchen counter. Rory would do her homework at one end of the table; I'd sit, with my laptop, at the opposite end, where I would look up recipes or send out notices about fund-raisers and committee meetings, and e-mail pictures to Annie.

Rory smoothed the page on the table. She'd written her name in big capital letters in the center of the tree trunk.

"You know the story, right?"

She gave a theatrical sigh—I wasn't sure who she'd picked that up from—and then began. "Once upon a time there was a mommy with no baby, and she wanted a baby more than anything else in the world."

"Right you are." This was a bit of revisionist history, but Annie was the one who'd come up with this story, the mythology of Rory's essential beginnings, and I'd never tried to change it.

"So the mommy and the daddy found a lady to give them a seed that would become a baby, and that lady was Jules. Then the seed got planted in another lady, and that lady was my tummy mommy, and that lady was Annie." She peered at her paper. "Where do I put 'tummy mommy'?"

"Hmm. Why don't we write her right next to the tree trunk." I tapped the paper. Rory frowned. She believed in rules and could be inflexible when it came to doing things the right way, but she let me help her write "Annie" just above her own name. I wondered again why the teachers had made this assignment, why they'd sent the kids home with a family tree with spaces for mother and father but no room for alternate configurations, when, in addition to the twins-by-surrogate, at least two kids in Rory's class had two mommies, one had two daddies, and one little girl in the second grade had parents who'd divorced their spouses and married each other, which surely made for some awkward parent-teacher conferences.

"And then my daddy died and went to heaven, where he watches over me every day."

I nodded, swallowing hard, pointing at the spot for "father." Annie, the most religious of us, had told Rory about Marcus, and about heaven, and I hadn't quarreled.

"And then I was born and the mommy was sooo happy to have me, and when I got my name everyone came to give me gifts, like in the story of the princess in Sleeping Beauty. Only people, not fairies." She waited for my nod. "Bettina gave me grace. Jules gave me . . ." She chewed at her lower lip. "What's the fancy word for smart?"

"Intelligence?"

"Right. And Annie made me happy and smiley and friendly, and you are my mom, and you give me the gift of love, and that," she concluded, her voice rising in triumph, "that is why you named me Aurora."

"Right," I said, and gathered her into my arms. Bettina had been the one who'd named her, maybe knowing, or maybe just hoping, that all of us would be there for this child, like the good fairies who'd gathered around Sleeping Beauty's crib to give her the best gifts they had. Someday, I'd tell her that, the whole story, how I'd left after her father had died and how her sister had been the one to name her. I gave her a kiss. For a moment, she resisted—she was growing up, "not a baby," as she reminded me all the time, and she was getting too old to want to snuggle the way she used to—but at least once a day she'd let me hold her. "And we all love you . . ."

". . . very, very much." Her voice was muffled, her face tucked into my shoulder. When she popped out, her eyes were bright, and she was smiling, exposing the space where she'd lost her first tooth the week before. "TV now?"

"TV," I said, and watched her go, running off, barefoot in her sweatpants, because Rory was a girl who never walked when she could run. She had her father's broad face and round cheeks, her sister Bettina's thick hair, Jules's fierce intellect and unwavering sense of right and wrong, and Annie's sweetness and generosity. She had the best of all of us, and, as for me, I had a life that was happier than I could have imagined.

ACKNOWLEDGMENTS

My thanks to my brilliant agent, Joanna Pulcini, and my unflappable editor, Greer Hendricks, for ten years of support, camaraderie, and fun.

I'm grateful to Joanna's assistant, Katherine Hennes, Greer's assistant, Sarah Cantin, and my assistant, the smart, funny, and eternally cheerful Meghan Burnett.

Carolyn Reidy, queen of Simon & Schuster, and Judith Curr, the publisher of Atria Books, are the best advocates and supporters that any writer could wish for. My thanks also to everyone on the Atria team: Chris Lloreda, Lisa Sciambra, Natalie White, Craig Dean, Lisa Keim, Hilary Tisman, Jeanne Lee, and Anna Dorfman, who gave *Then Came You* such a beautiful cover. Copyeditor Nancy Inglis keeps me honest (and grammatical).

Across the pond, I am grateful for the efforts of Suzanne Baboneau, Ian Chapman, Jessica Leeke, and Nigel Stoneman at Simon & Schuster UK.

Jessica Bartolo at Greater Talent Network makes my speaking engagements a joy. Marcy Engelman, Dana Gidney Fetaya, and Emily Gambir do an amazing job of telling the world about my books, whether the world wants to hear or not, and getting me in magazines and on talk shows, whether I belong there or not.

This is the first year I've balanced novel-writing with show-running, so I'm grateful to the writers and the stars of ABC Family's *State of Georgia* for their patience with a TV newbie. Thanks to Jeff Greenstein, who dreamed up *Georgia* with me, to Kirk Rudell, Hayes Jackson, Greg Schaffer, Regina Hicks, Annabel Oakes, Frank Pines, T. J. Johnson, Eric Buchman, and Melissa Oren for making me laugh every day, and to Loretta Devine, Majandra Delfino, and Raven-Symoné for bringing my words to life.

On the home front, my writing life wouldn't be possible without the love and support of my friends and family. I'm grateful to Terri Gottlieb, who watches my daughters while I write, and to Lucy Jane and Phoebe Pearl for sharing me with my imaginary friends.

Most of all, thanks to everyone who reads my books, and my tweets, and my Facebook feed. None of this would be possible without you.